CAVEBOY DAVE

NOT SO FABOO

by Aaron Reynolds

illustrated by Phil McAndrew

VIKING

VIKING

An imprint of Penguin Random House LLC

375 Hudson Street

New York, New York 10014

First published in the United States of America by Viking,
an imprint of Penguin Random House LLC, 2018

LIBRARY OF CONGRESS CATALOGING-IN-PUBLICATION DATA IS AVAILABLE

ISBN 9780147516596 (paperback)

ISBN 9780451475480 (hardcover)

Manufactured in China

1   3   5   7   9   10   8   6   4   2

To Gail Fleming, a super faboo leader
who practically invented creativity! —A. R.

For my Granny, Susan McAndrew, who loves to read
more than anyone else I've ever known. —P. M.

CAVEBOY DAVE

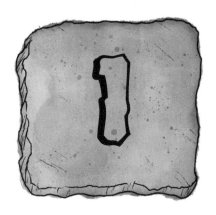

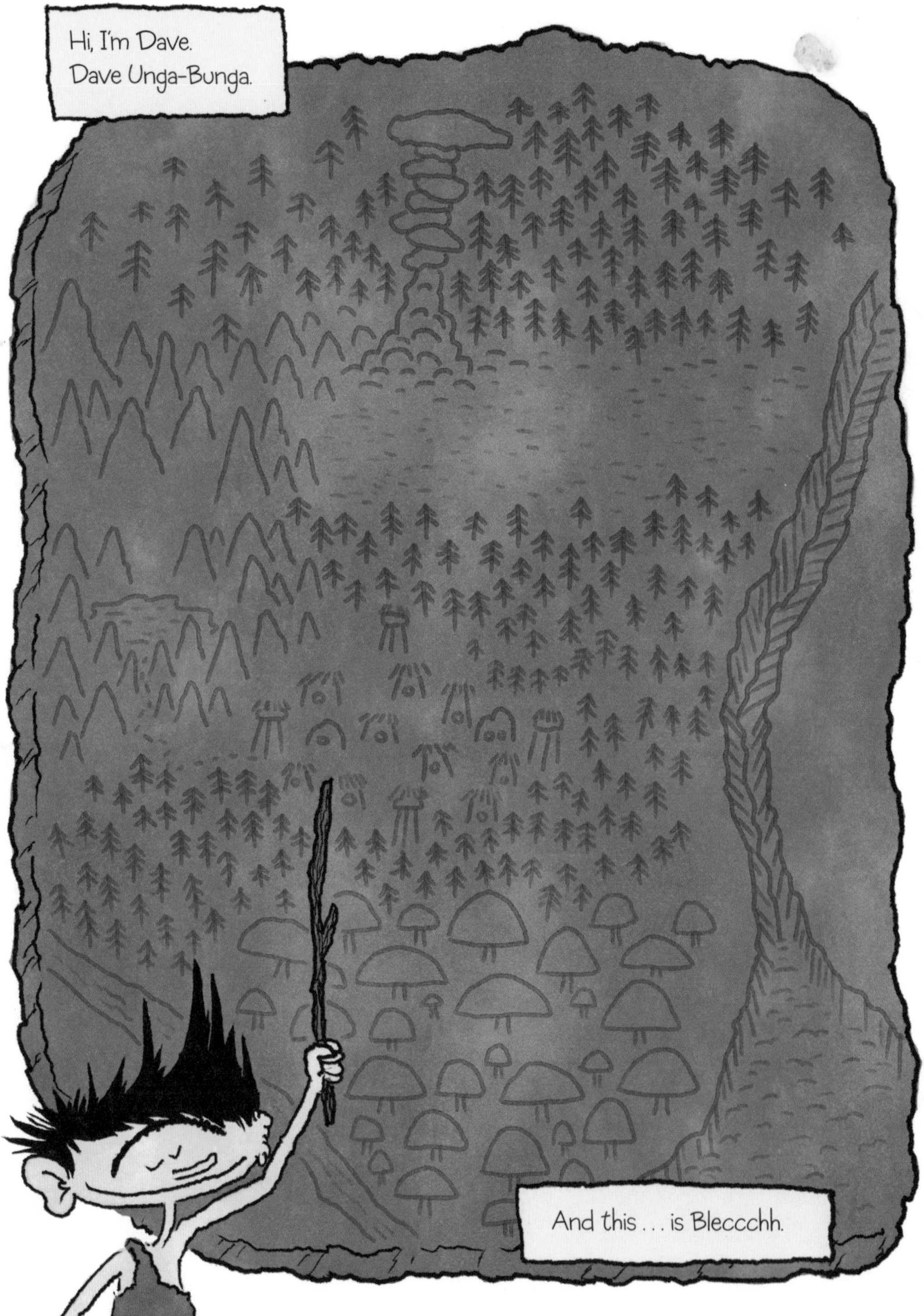
Hi, I'm Dave.
Dave Unga-Bunga.
And this . . . is Bleccchh.

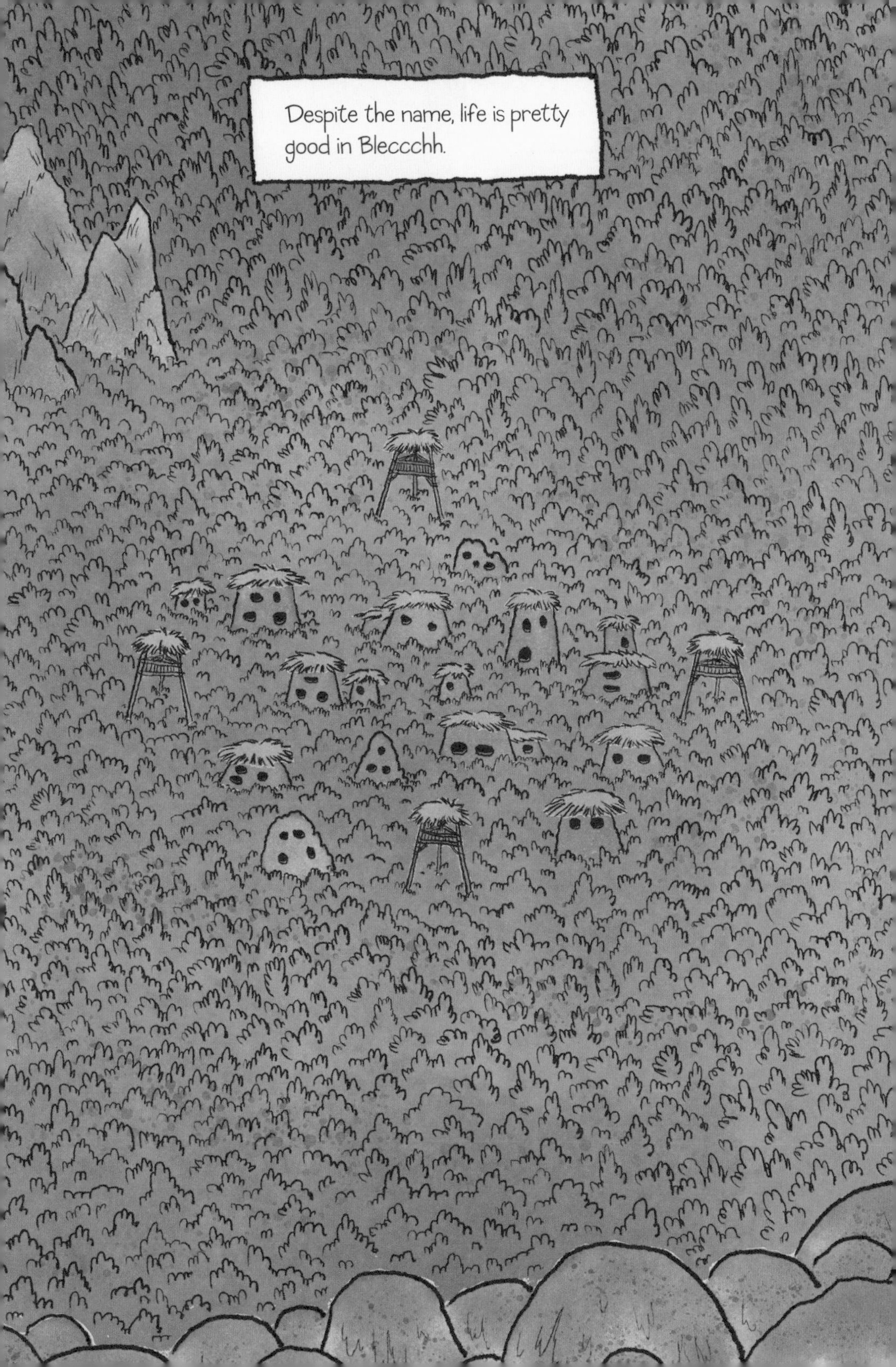
Despite the name, life is pretty good in Bleccchh.

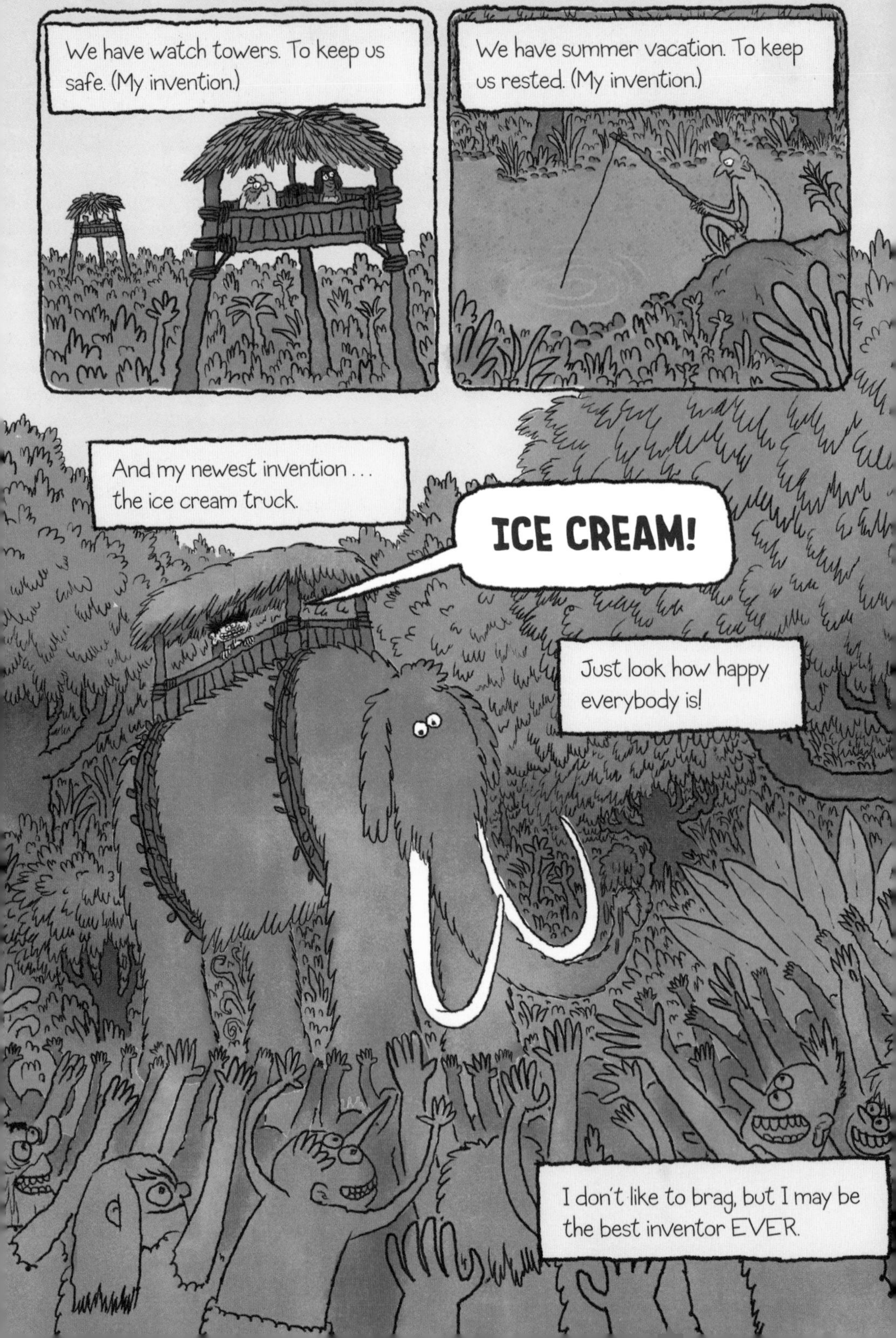
We have watch towers. To keep us safe. (My invention.)
We have summer vacation. To keep us rested. (My invention.)
And my newest invention . . . the ice cream truck.
ICE CREAM!
Just look how happy everybody is!
I don't like to brag, but I may be the best inventor EVER.

BIG D, YOU ARE THE **WORST** INVENTOR EVER!

Then again, maybe not.

WHEN ARE YOU GOING TO INVENT ANOTHER FLAVOR BESIDES **"DIRT"**?

Leave it to Rockie to keep me on my toes.

LIKE WHAT?

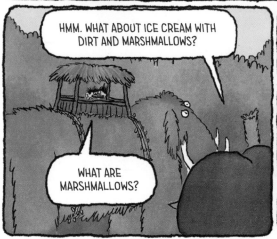

HMM. WHAT ABOUT ICE CREAM WITH DIRT AND MARSHMALLOWS?

WHAT ARE MARSHMALLOWS?

NO IDEA, D. YOU'RE THE INVENTOR! **INVENT THEM!**

YEAH, LET ME JUST ADD THAT TO MY TO-DO LIST.

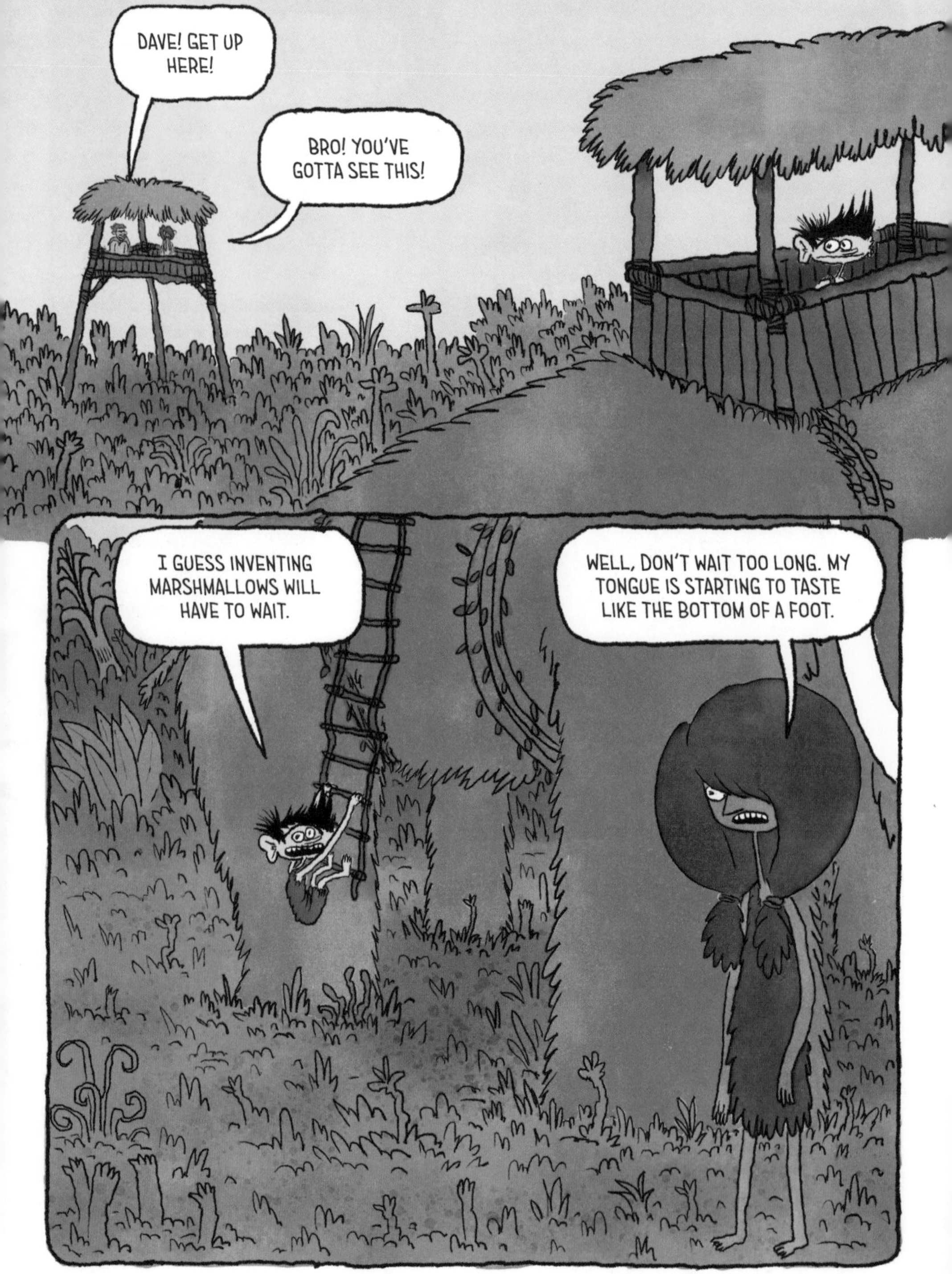
DAVE! GET UP HERE!
BRO! YOU'VE GOTTA SEE THIS!
I GUESS INVENTING MARSHMALLOWS WILL HAVE TO WAIT.
WELL, DON'T WAIT TOO LONG. MY TONGUE IS STARTING TO TASTE LIKE THE BOTTOM OF A FOOT.

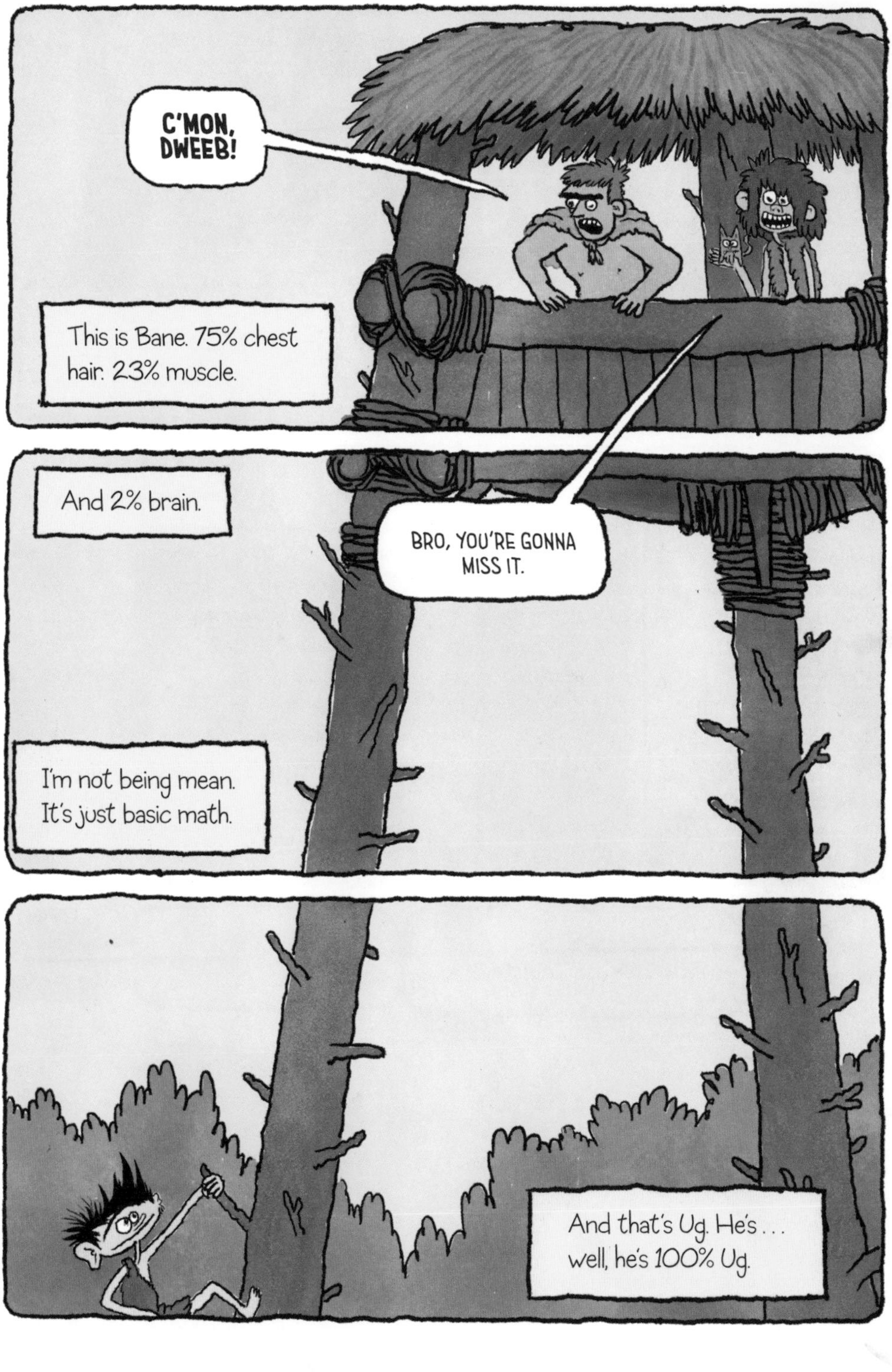
C'MON, DWEEB!
This is Bane. 75% chest hair. 23% muscle.
And 2% brain.
BRO, YOU'RE GONNA MISS IT.
I'm not being mean. It's just basic math.
And that's Ug. He's . . . well, he's 100% Ug.

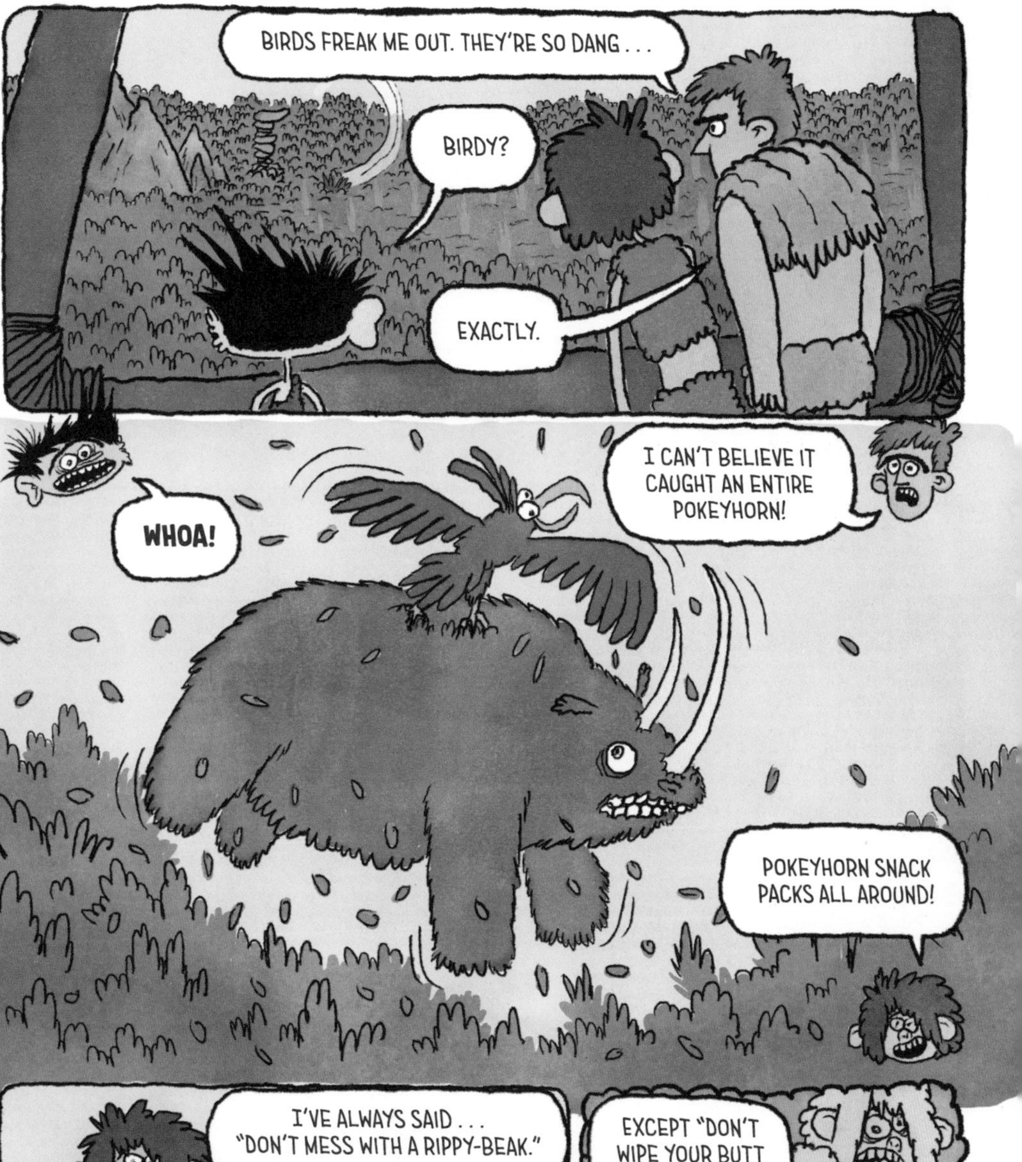
BIRDS FREAK ME OUT. THEY'RE SO DANG . . .
BIRDY?
EXACTLY.
WHOA!
I CAN'T BELIEVE IT CAUGHT AN ENTIRE POKEYHORN!
POKEYHORN SNACK PACKS ALL AROUND!
I'VE ALWAYS SAID . . . "DON'T MESS WITH A RIPPY-BEAK."
NO TRUER WORDS WERE EVER SPOKEN.
EXCEPT "DON'T WIPE YOUR BUTT WITH A CACTUS."
THOSE THINGS WILL MESS YOU UP.

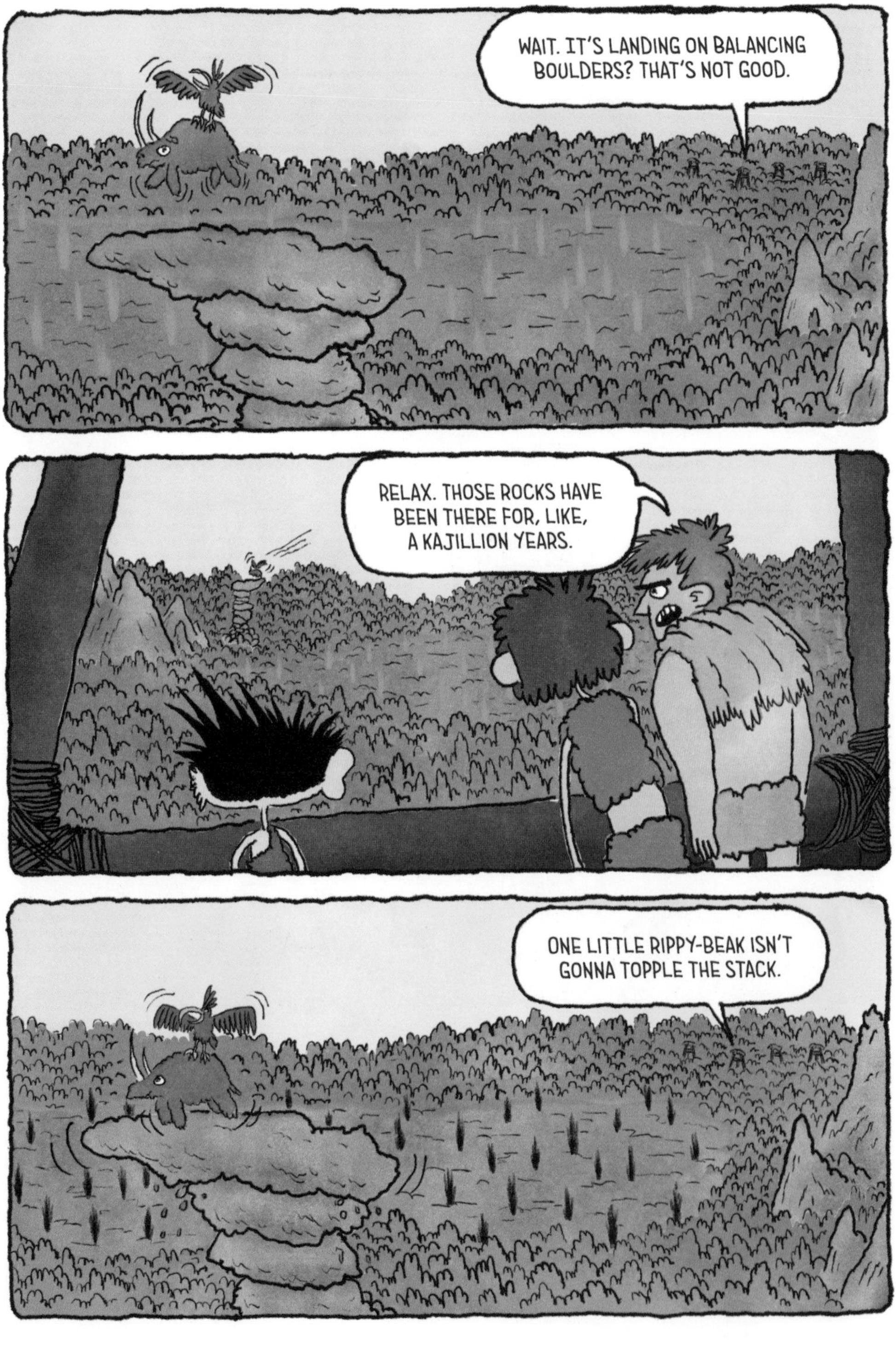
WAIT. IT'S LANDING ON BALANCING BOULDERS? THAT'S NOT GOOD.
RELAX. THOSE ROCKS HAVE BEEN THERE FOR, LIKE, A KAJILLION YEARS.
ONE LITTLE RIPPY-BEAK ISN'T GONNA TOPPLE THE STACK.

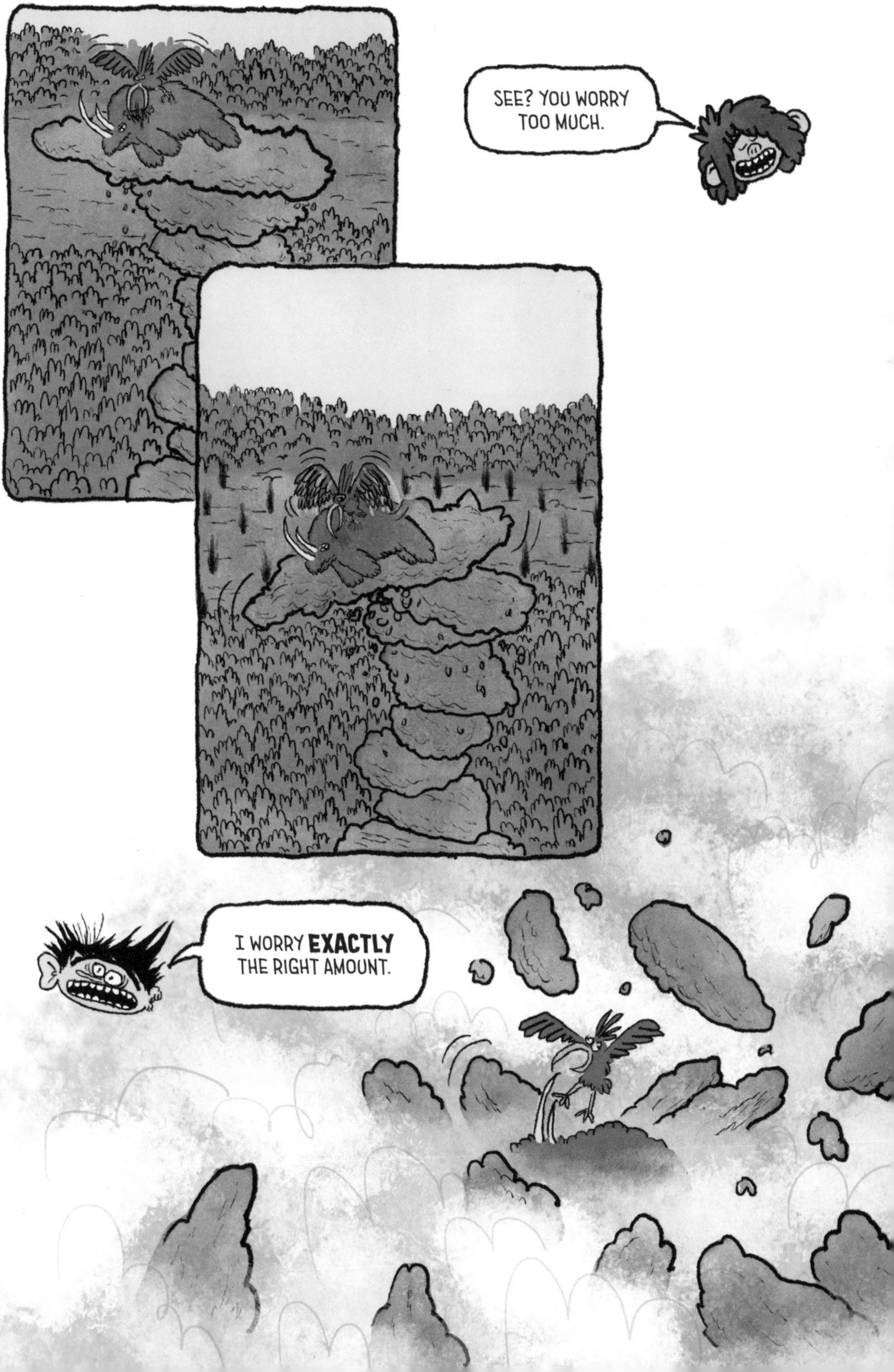
SEE? YOU WORRY
TOO MUCH.
I WORRY **EXACTLY**
THE RIGHT AMOUNT.

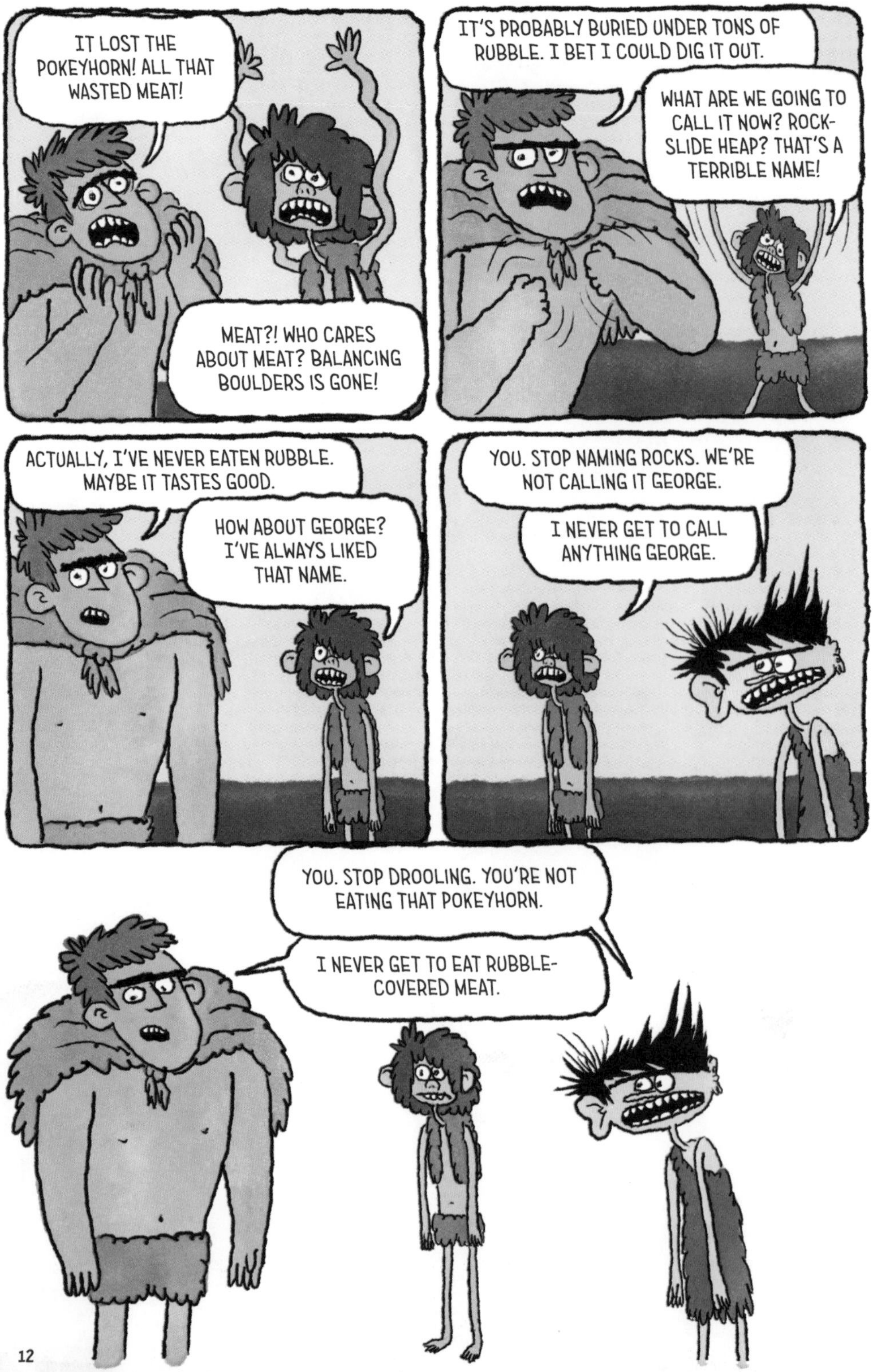
IT LOST THE POKEYHORN! ALL THAT WASTED MEAT!
MEAT?! WHO CARES ABOUT MEAT? BALANCING BOULDERS IS GONE!
IT'S PROBABLY BURIED UNDER TONS OF RUBBLE. I BET I COULD DIG IT OUT.
WHAT ARE WE GOING TO CALL IT NOW? ROCK-SLIDE HEAP? THAT'S A TERRIBLE NAME!
ACTUALLY, I'VE NEVER EATEN RUBBLE. MAYBE IT TASTES GOOD.
HOW ABOUT GEORGE? I'VE ALWAYS LIKED THAT NAME.
YOU. STOP NAMING ROCKS. WE'RE NOT CALLING IT GEORGE.
I NEVER GET TO CALL ANYTHING GEORGE.
YOU. STOP DROOLING. YOU'RE NOT EATING THAT POKEYHORN.
I NEVER GET TO EAT RUBBLE-COVERED MEAT.

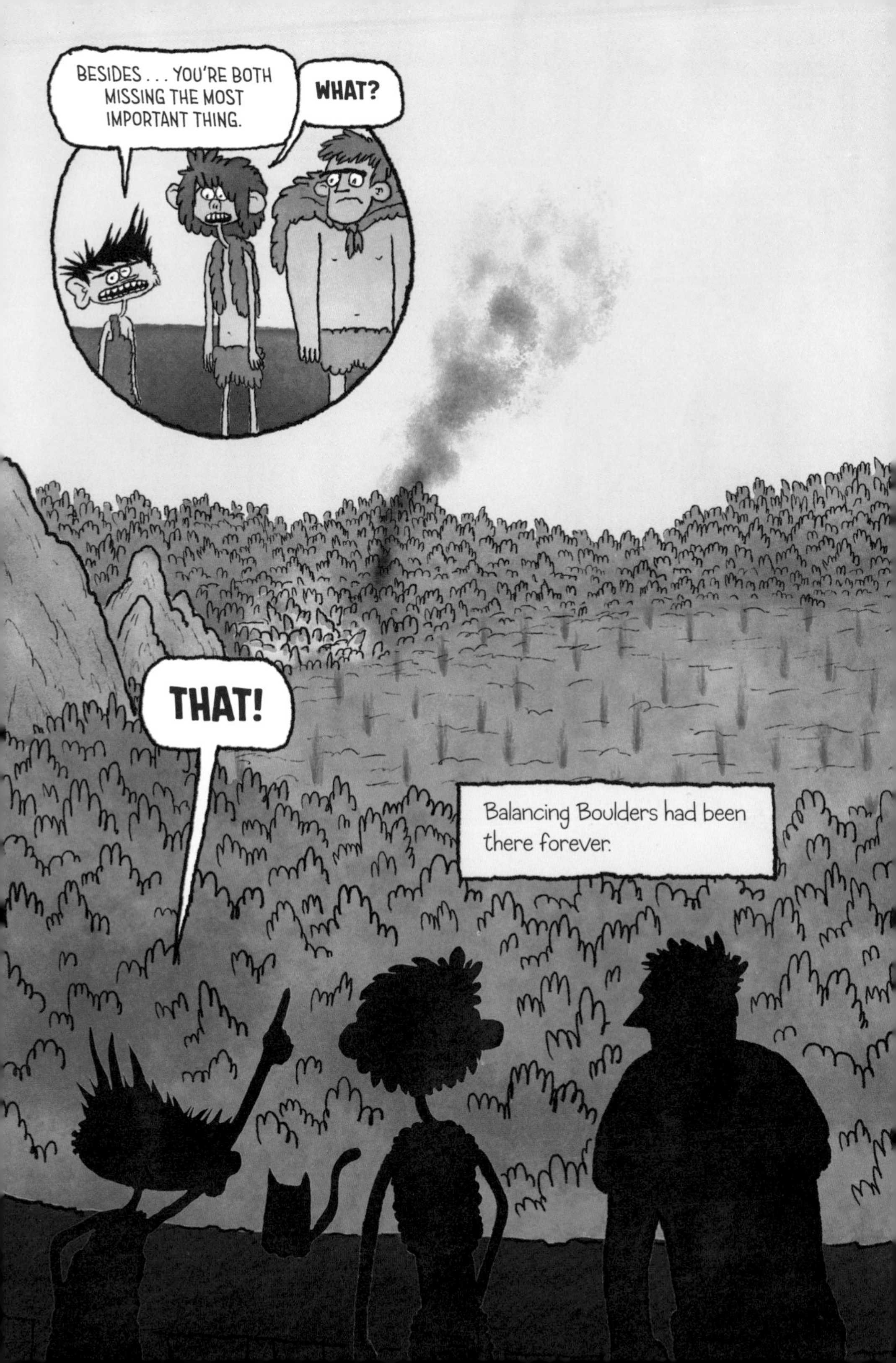
BESIDES . . . YOU'RE BOTH MISSING THE MOST IMPORTANT THING.
WHAT?
THAT!
Balancing Boulders had been there forever.

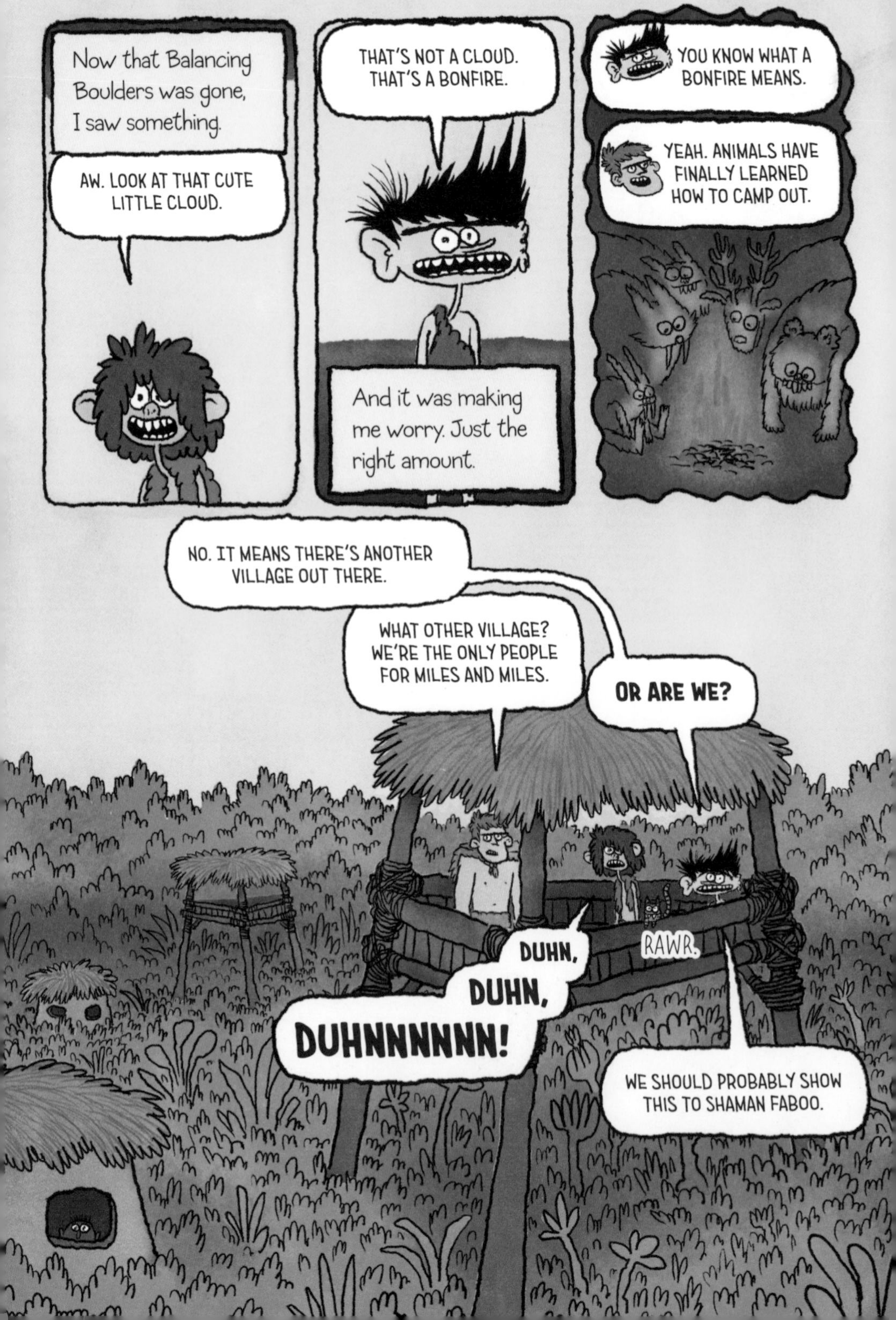

Now that Balancing Boulders was gone, I saw something.
AW. LOOK AT THAT CUTE LITTLE CLOUD.
THAT'S NOT A CLOUD. THAT'S A BONFIRE.
And it was making me worry. Just the right amount.
YOU KNOW WHAT A BONFIRE MEANS.
YEAH. ANIMALS HAVE FINALLY LEARNED HOW TO CAMP OUT.
NO. IT MEANS THERE'S ANOTHER VILLAGE OUT THERE.
WHAT OTHER VILLAGE? WE'RE THE ONLY PEOPLE FOR MILES AND MILES.
OR ARE WE?
DUHN,
DUHN,
DUHNNNNNN!
RAWR.
WE SHOULD PROBABLY SHOW THIS TO SHAMAN FABOO.

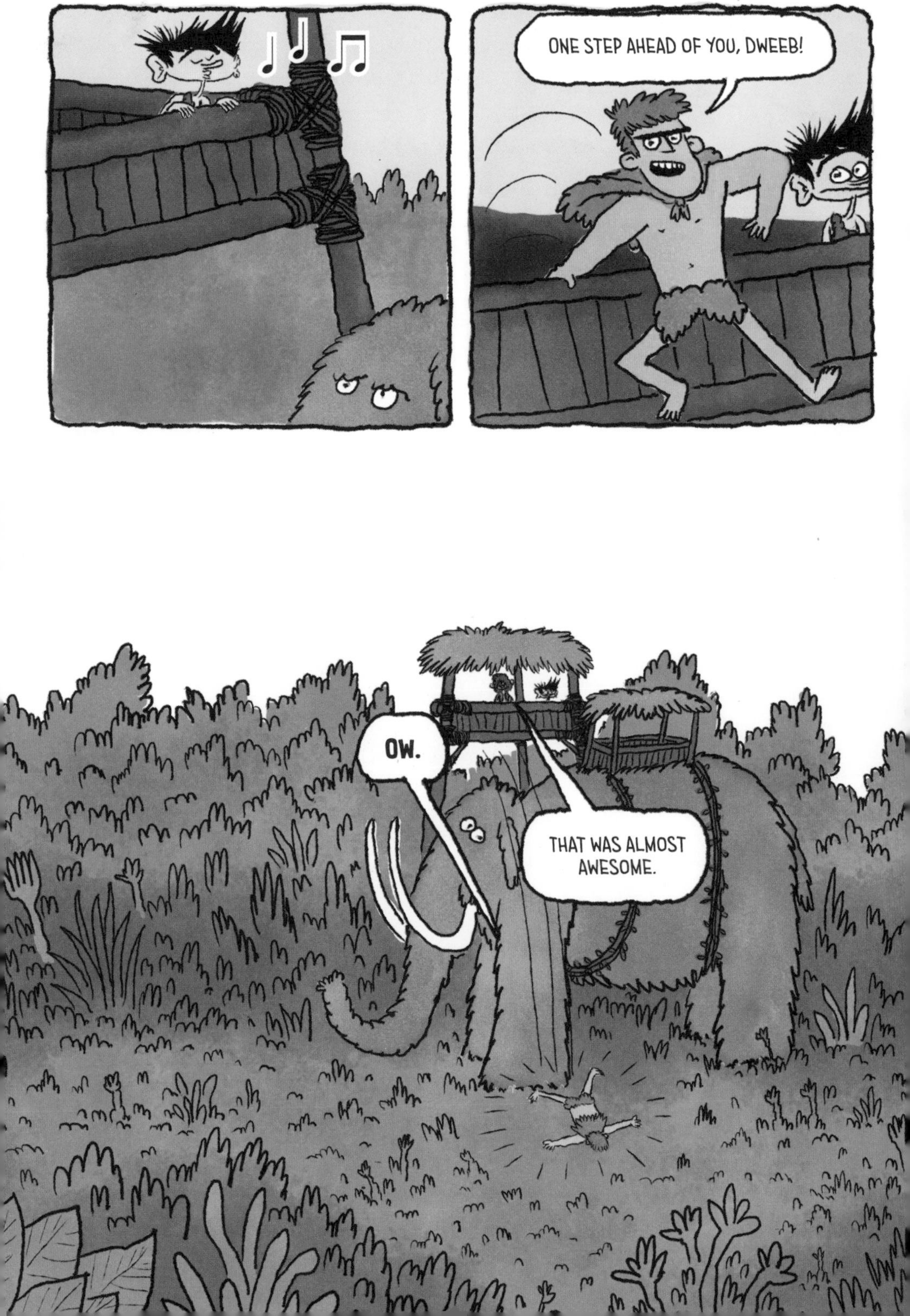
ONE STEP AHEAD OF YOU, DWEEB!
OW.
THAT WAS ALMOST AWESOME.

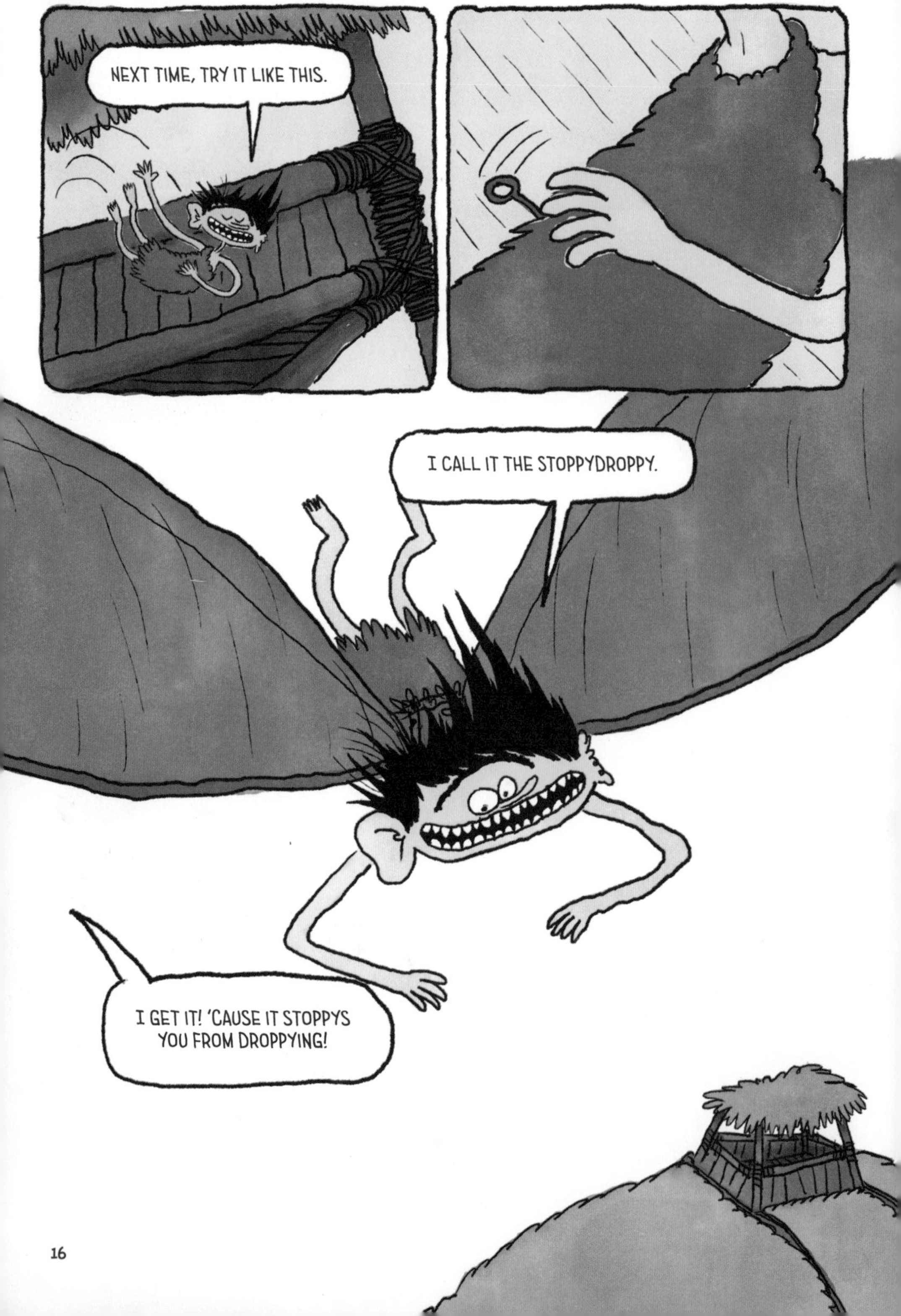
NEXT TIME, TRY IT LIKE THIS.
I CALL IT THE STOPPYDROPPY.
I GET IT! 'CAUSE IT STOPPYS YOU FROM DROPPYING!

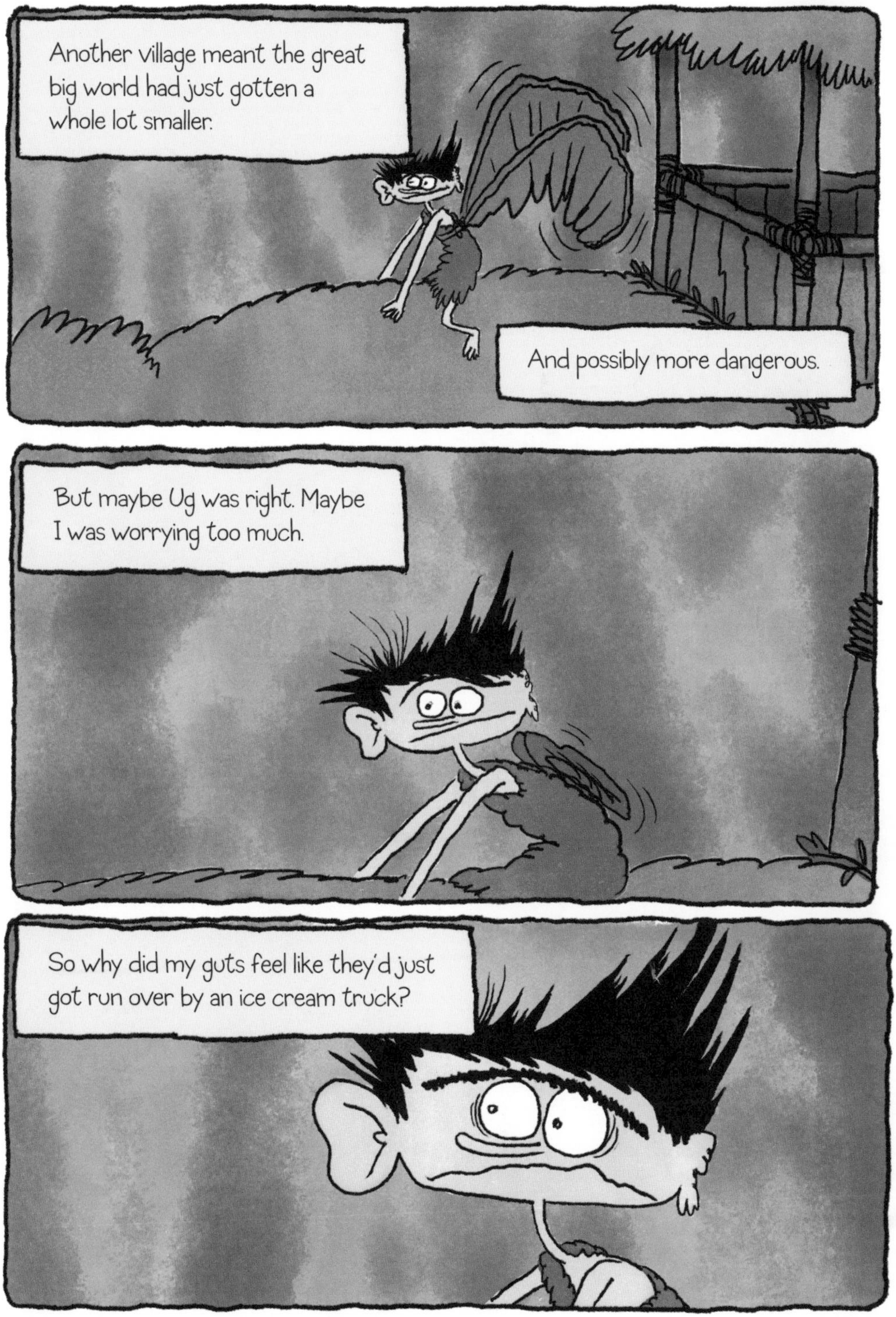
Another village meant the great big world had just gotten a whole lot smaller.
And possibly more dangerous.
But maybe Ug was right. Maybe I was worrying too much.
So why did my guts feel like they'd just got run over by an ice cream truck?

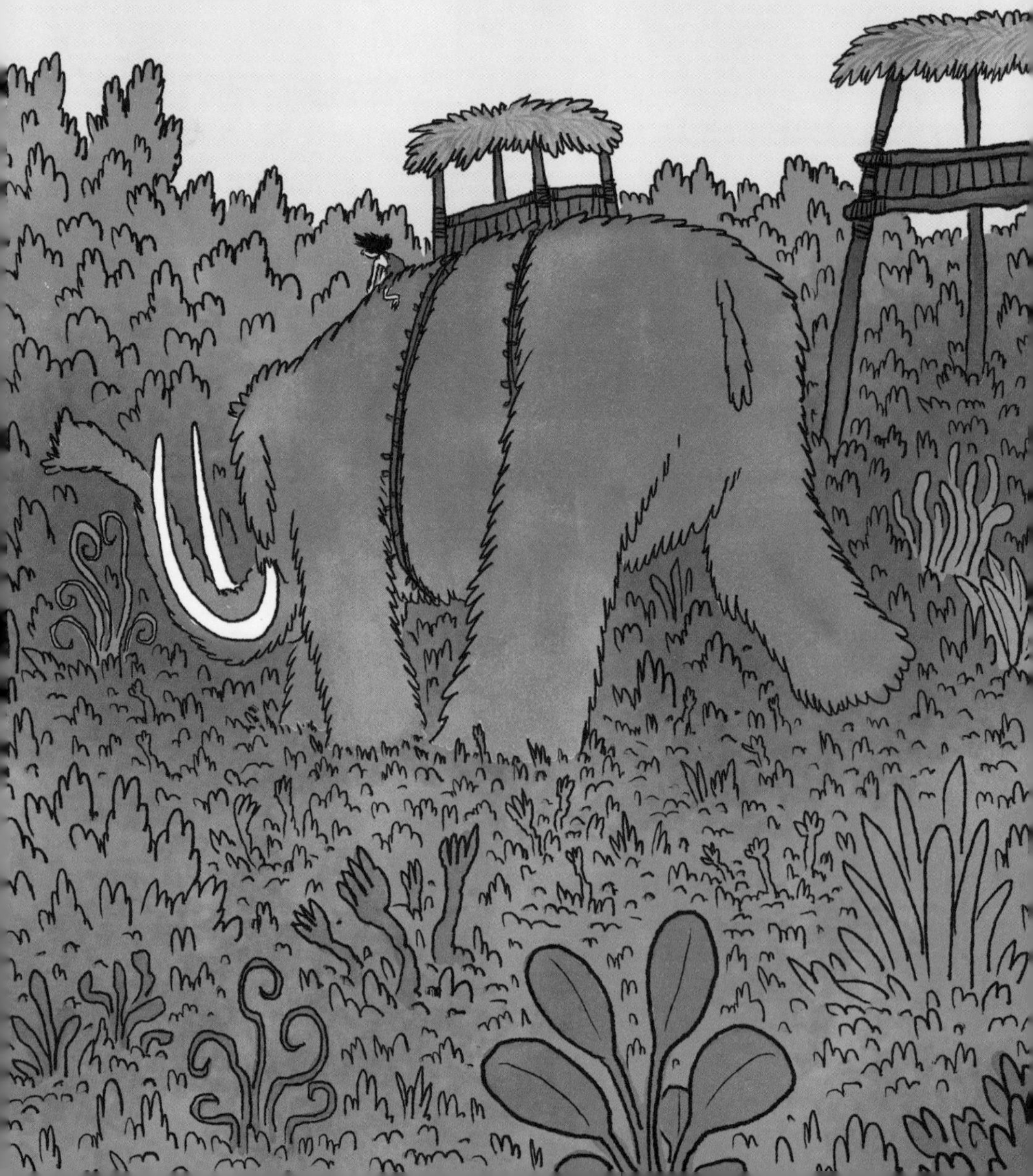

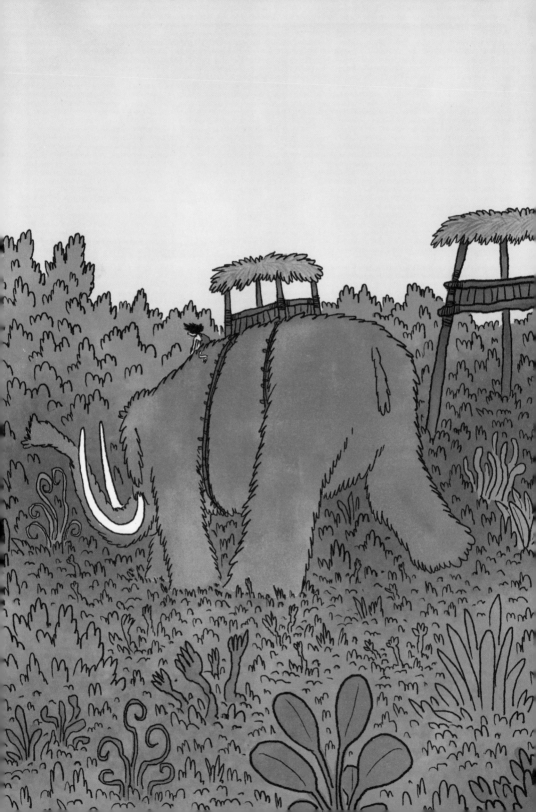

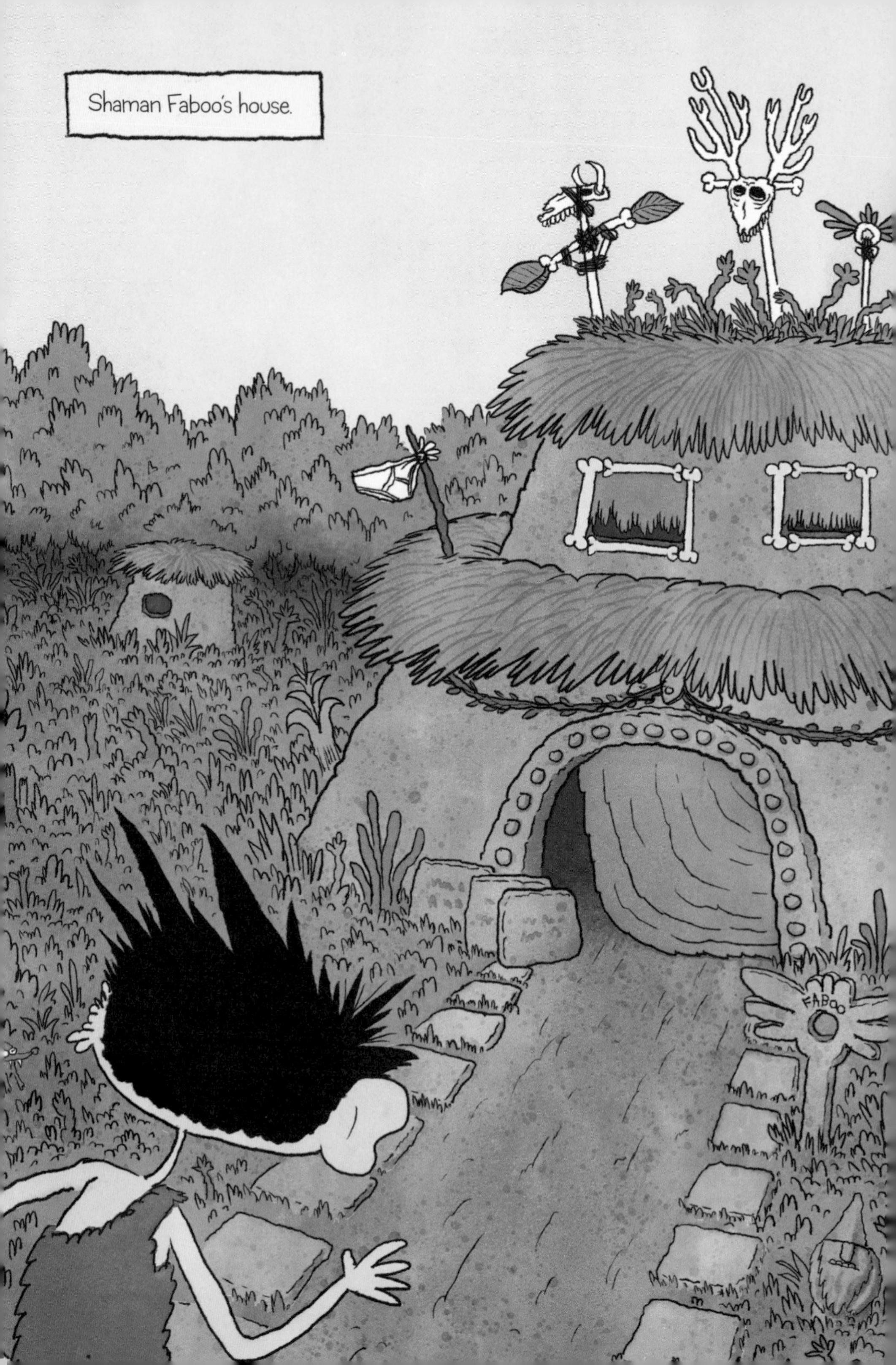
Shaman Faboo's house.
FABOO

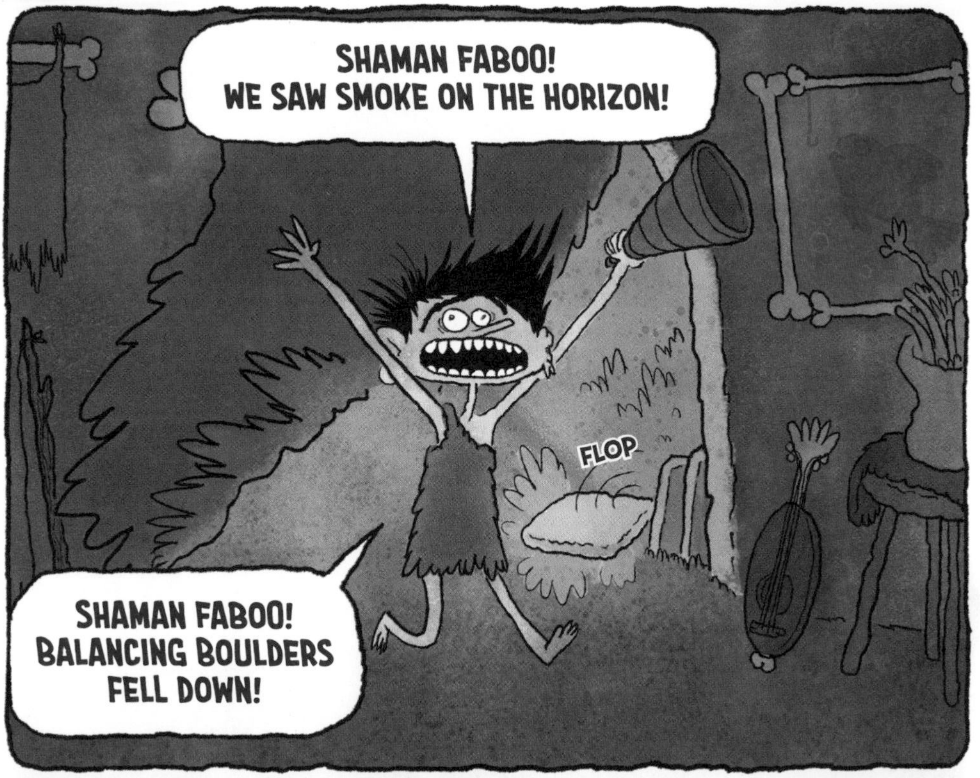
SHAMAN FABOO!
WE SAW SMOKE ON THE HORIZON!
FLOP
SHAMAN FABOO!
BALANCING BOULDERS
FELL DOWN!

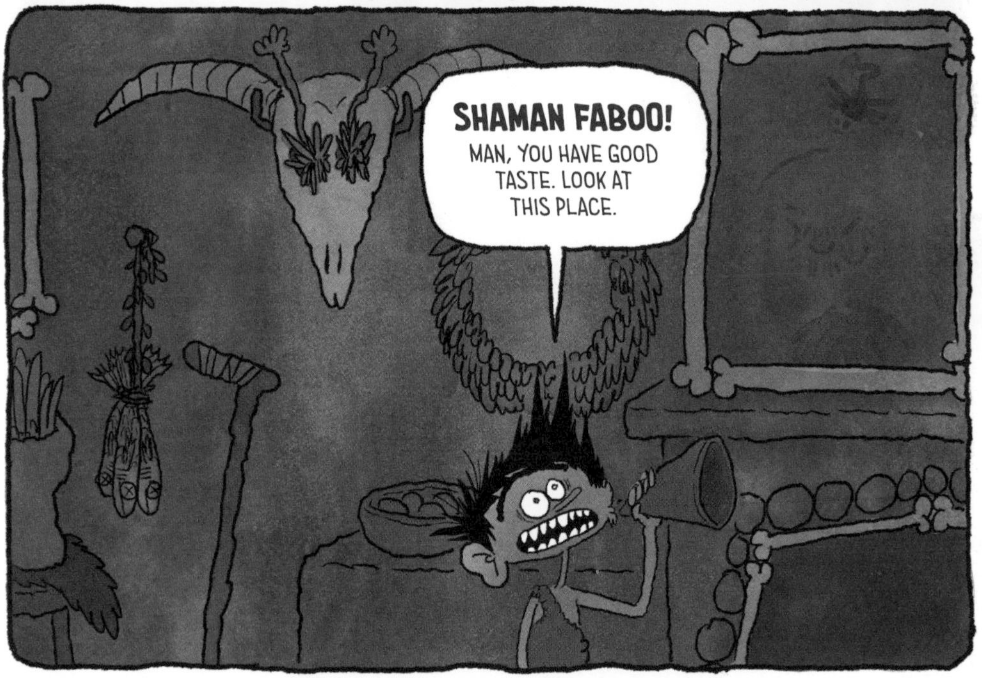
SHAMAN FABOO!
MAN, YOU HAVE GOOD
TASTE. LOOK AT
THIS PLACE.

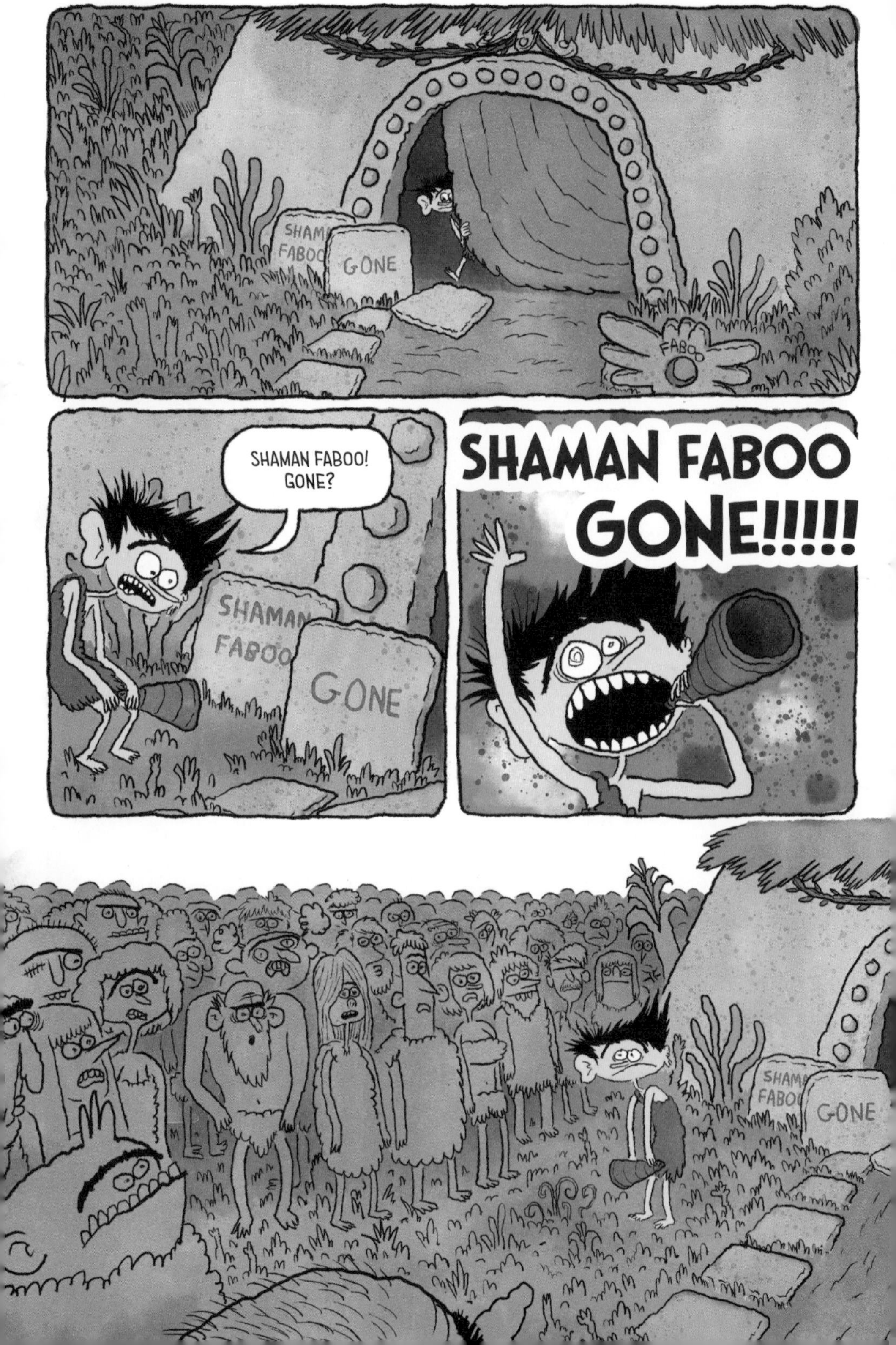
SHAMAN FABOO
GONE
FABOO
SHAMAN FABOO! GONE?
SHAMAN FABOO
GONE
SHAMAN FABOO GONE!!!!!
SHAMAN FABOO
GONE

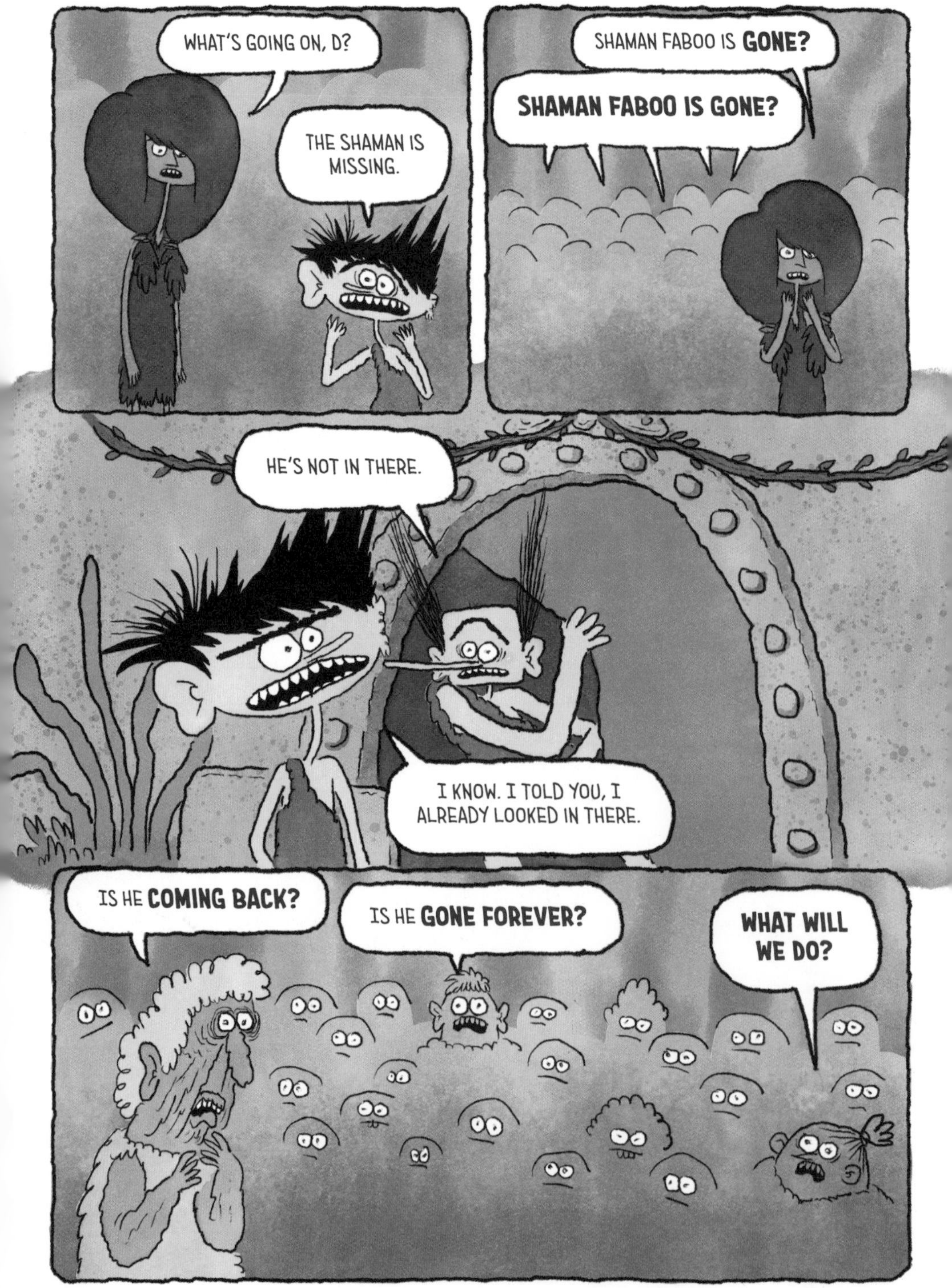
WHAT'S GOING ON, D?
THE SHAMAN IS MISSING.
SHAMAN FABOO IS **GONE?**
SHAMAN FABOO IS GONE?
HE'S NOT IN THERE.
I KNOW. I TOLD YOU, I ALREADY LOOKED IN THERE.
IS HE **COMING BACK?**
IS HE **GONE FOREVER?**
WHAT WILL WE DO?

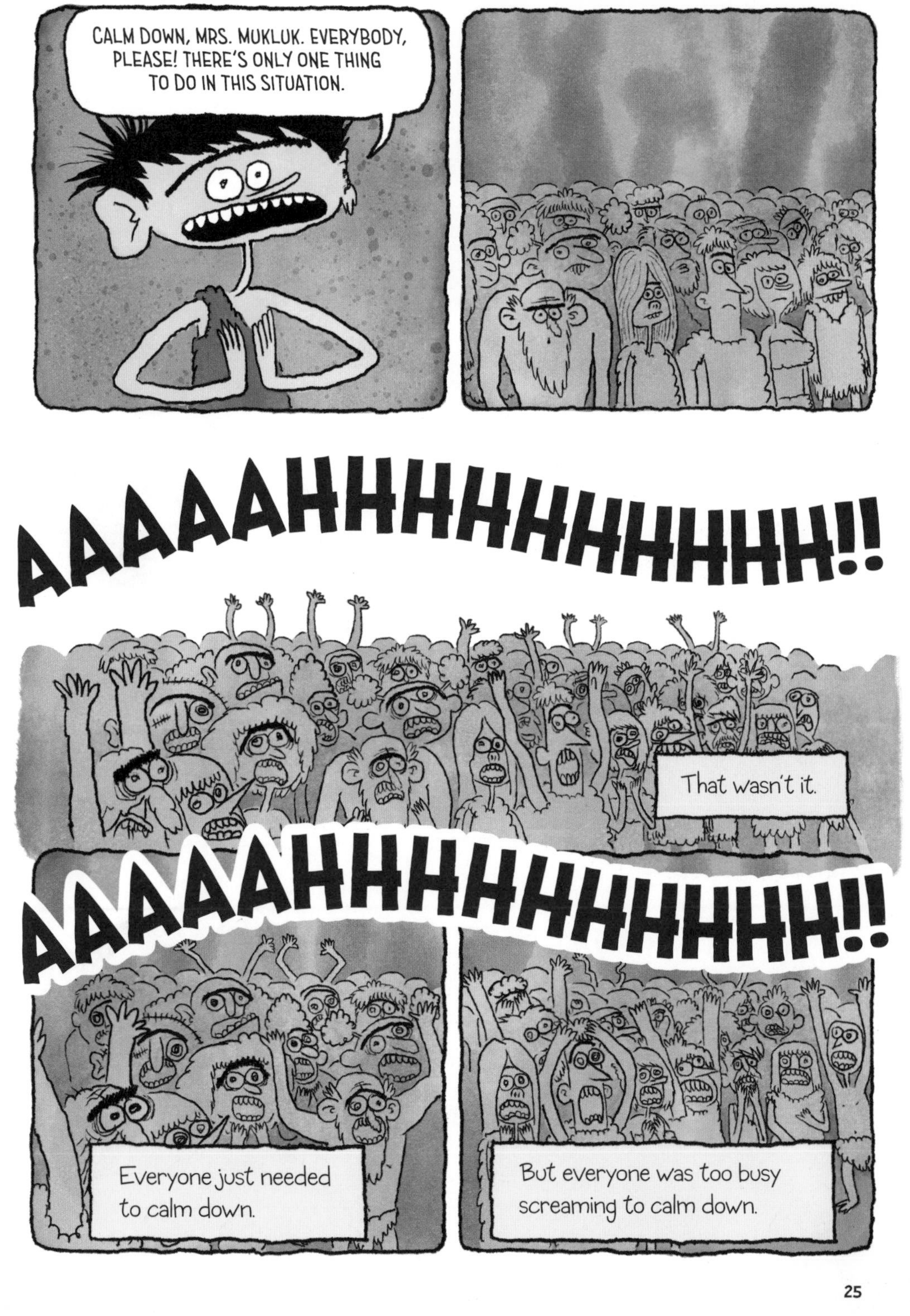
CALM DOWN, MRS. MUKLUK. EVERYBODY, PLEASE! THERE'S ONLY ONE THING TO DO IN THIS SITUATION.
AAAAAHHHHHHHHHHH!!
That wasn't it.
AAAAAHHHHHHHHHHH!!
Everyone just needed to calm down.
But everyone was too busy screaming to calm down.

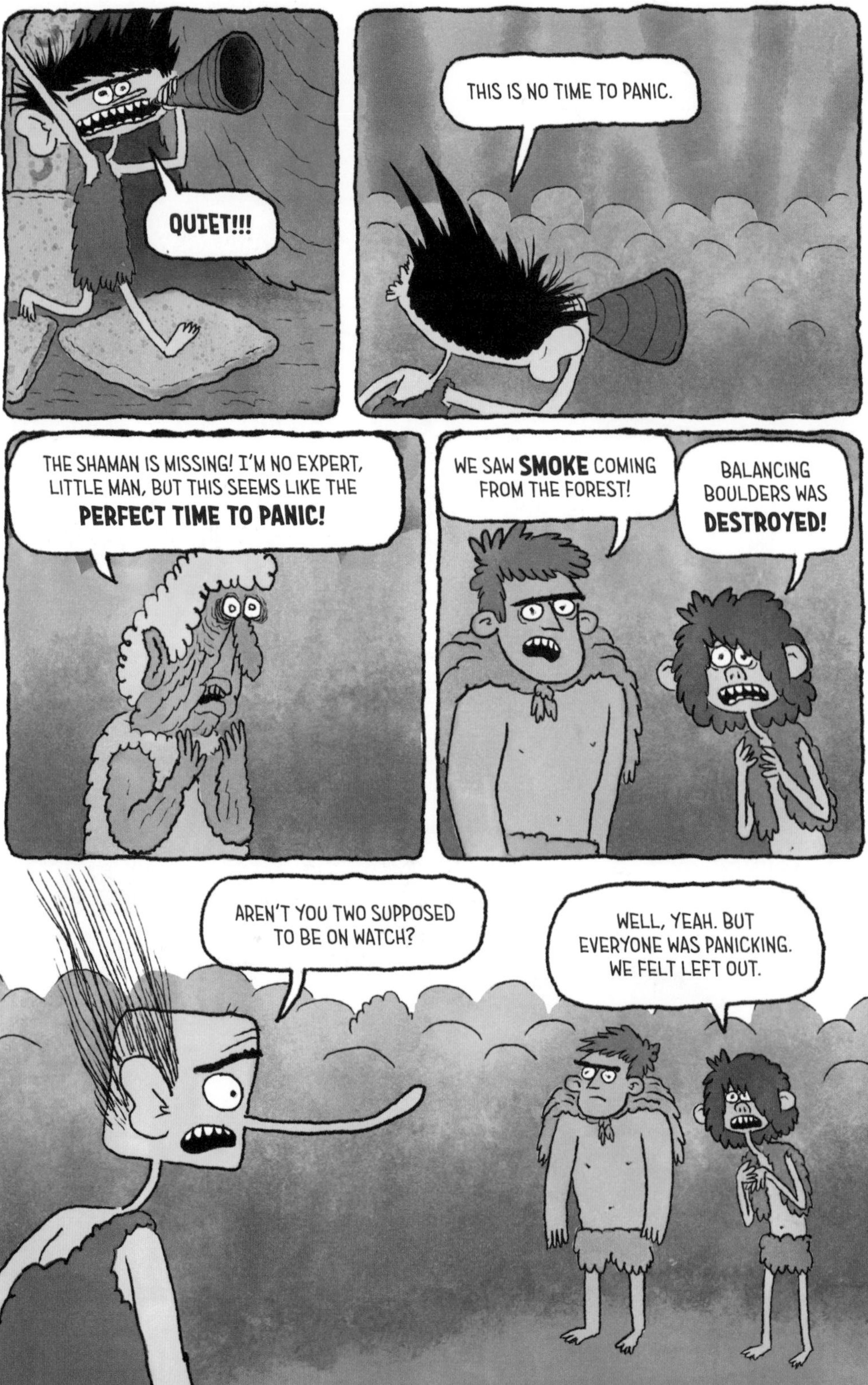
QUIET!!!
THIS IS NO TIME TO PANIC.
THE SHAMAN IS MISSING! I'M NO EXPERT, LITTLE MAN, BUT THIS SEEMS LIKE THE PERFECT TIME TO PANIC!
WE SAW SMOKE COMING FROM THE FOREST!
BALANCING BOULDERS WAS DESTROYED!
AREN'T YOU TWO SUPPOSED TO BE ON WATCH?
WELL, YEAH. BUT EVERYONE WAS PANICKING. WE FELT LEFT OUT.

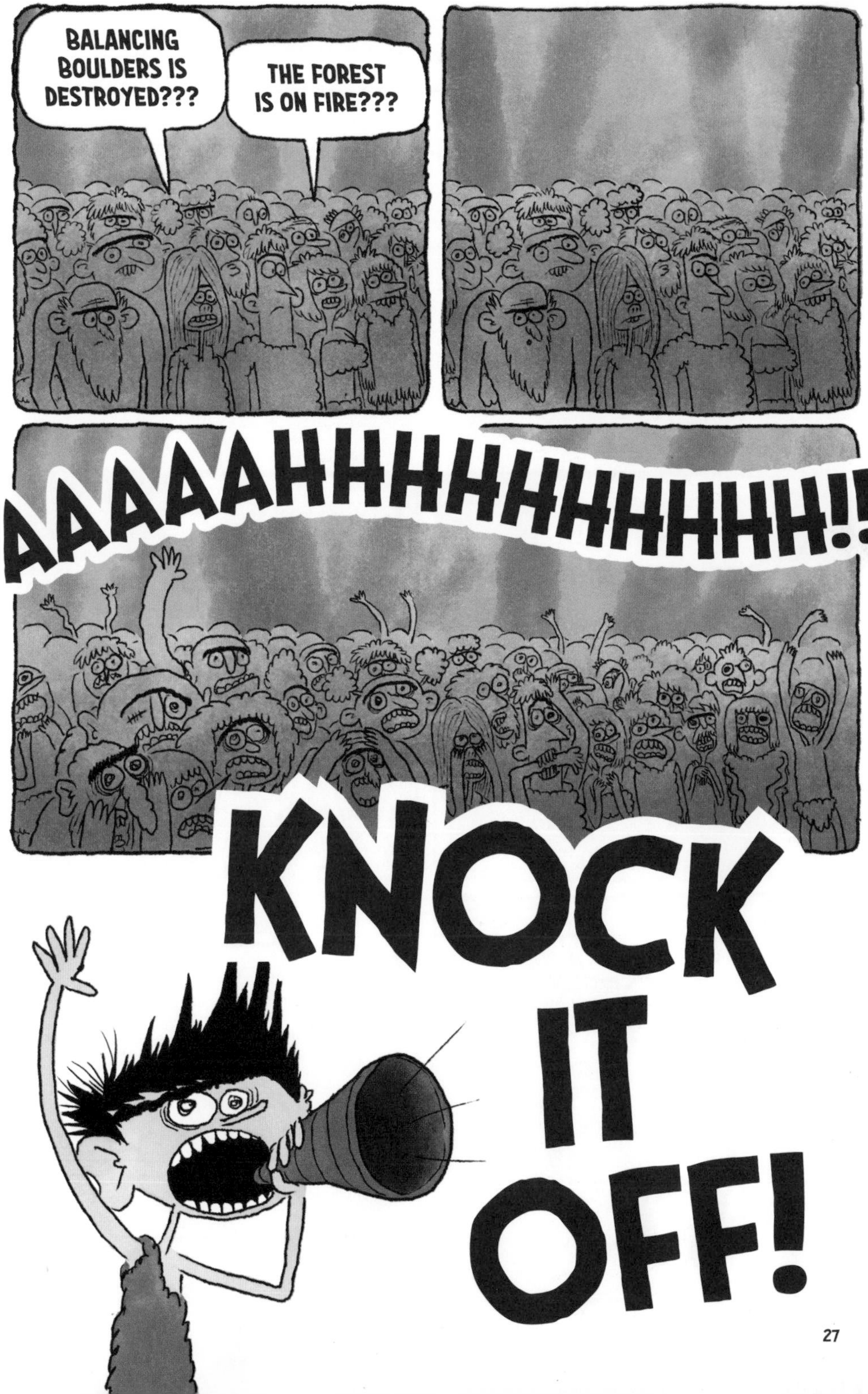
BALANCING BOULDERS IS DESTROYED???
THE FOREST IS ON FIRE???
AAAAAHHHHHHHHHH!!
KNOCK IT OFF!

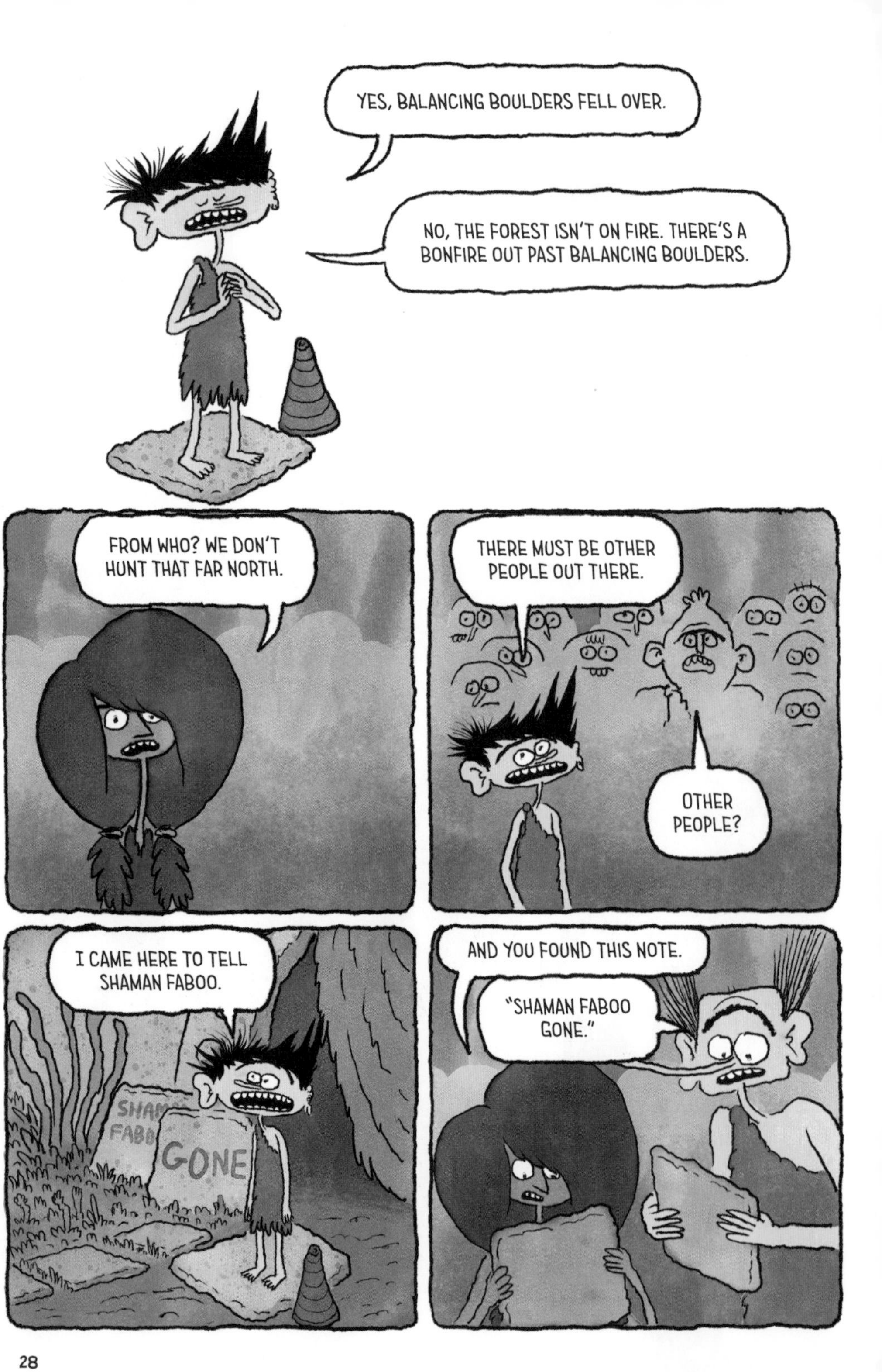
YES, BALANCING BOULDERS FELL OVER.
NO, THE FOREST ISN'T ON FIRE. THERE'S A BONFIRE OUT PAST BALANCING BOULDERS.
FROM WHO? WE DON'T HUNT THAT FAR NORTH.
THERE MUST BE OTHER PEOPLE OUT THERE.
OTHER PEOPLE?
I CAME HERE TO TELL SHAMAN FABOO.
GONE
AND YOU FOUND THIS NOTE.
"SHAMAN FABOO GONE."

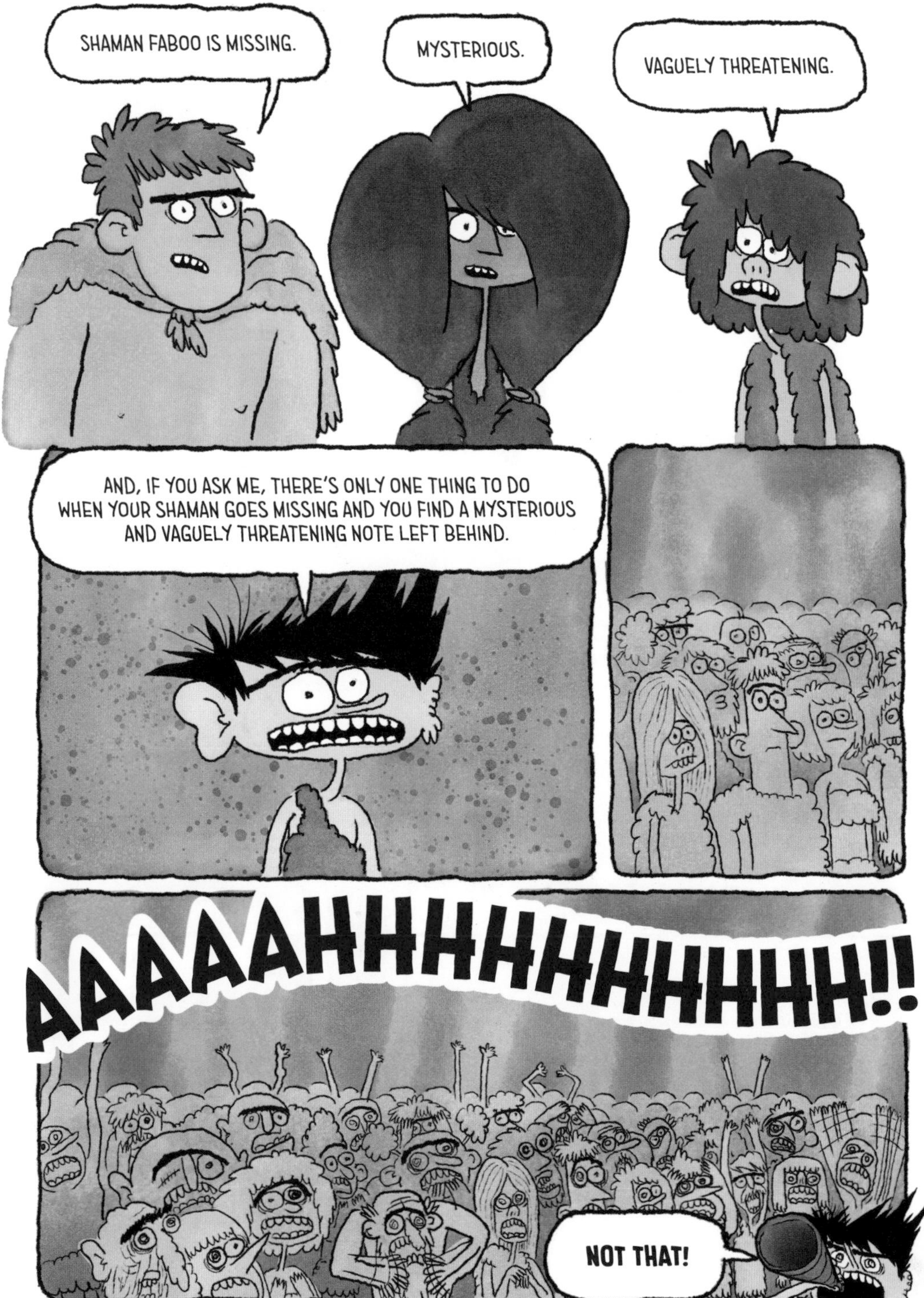
SHAMAN FABOO IS MISSING.
MYSTERIOUS.
VAGUELY THREATENING.
AND, IF YOU ASK ME, THERE'S ONLY ONE THING TO DO WHEN YOUR SHAMAN GOES MISSING AND YOU FIND A MYSTERIOUS AND VAGUELY THREATENING NOTE LEFT BEHIND.
AAAAAHHHHHHHHHHH!!
NOT THAT!

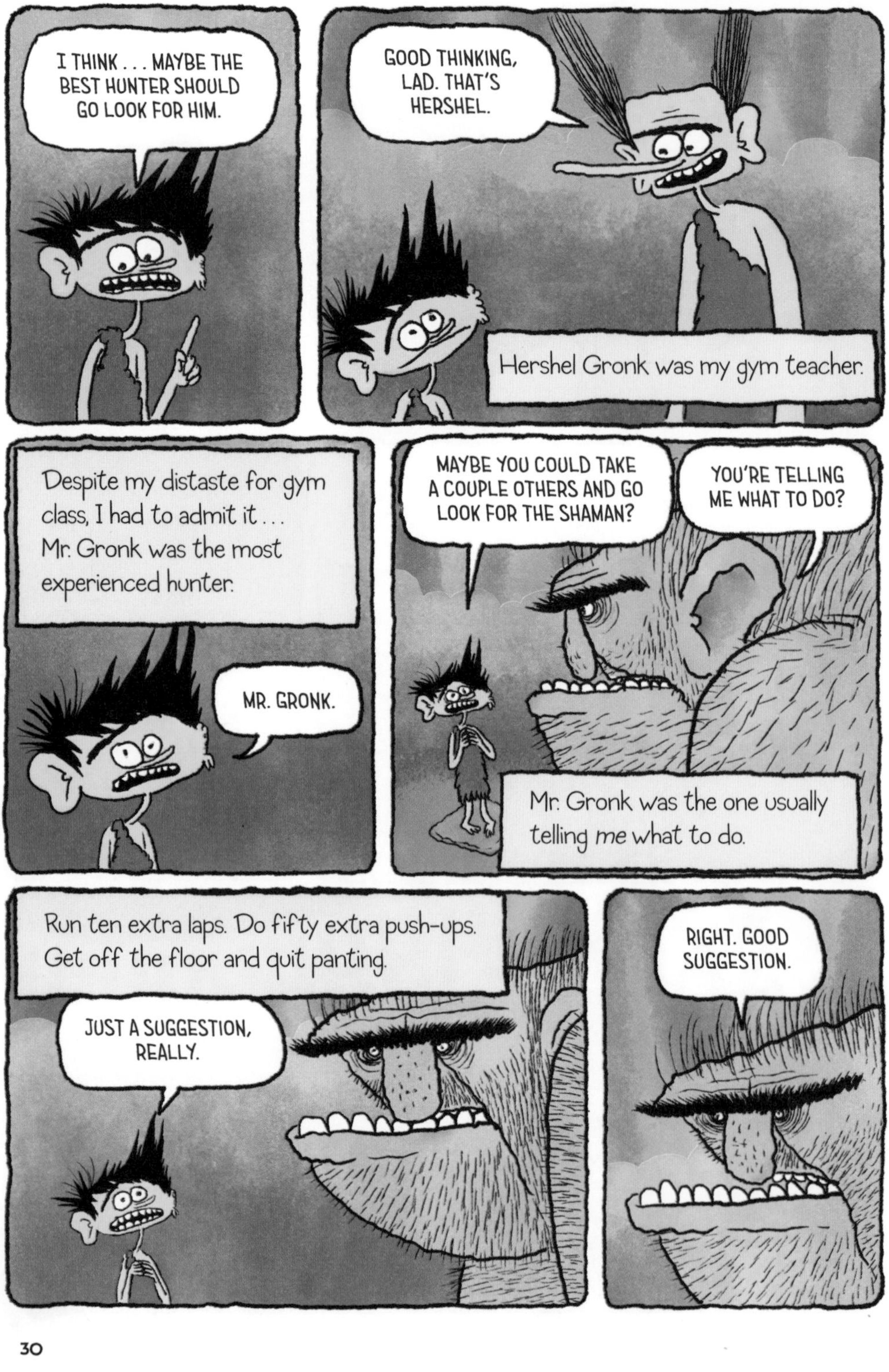
I THINK . . . MAYBE THE BEST HUNTER SHOULD GO LOOK FOR HIM.
GOOD THINKING, LAD. THAT'S HERSHEL.
Hershel Gronk was my gym teacher.
Despite my distaste for gym class, I had to admit it . . . Mr. Gronk was the most experienced hunter.
MR. GRONK.
MAYBE YOU COULD TAKE A COUPLE OTHERS AND GO LOOK FOR THE SHAMAN?
YOU'RE TELLING ME WHAT TO DO?
Mr. Gronk was the one usually telling *me* what to do.
Run ten extra laps. Do fifty extra push-ups. Get off the floor and quit panting.
JUST A SUGGESTION, REALLY.
RIGHT. GOOD SUGGESTION.

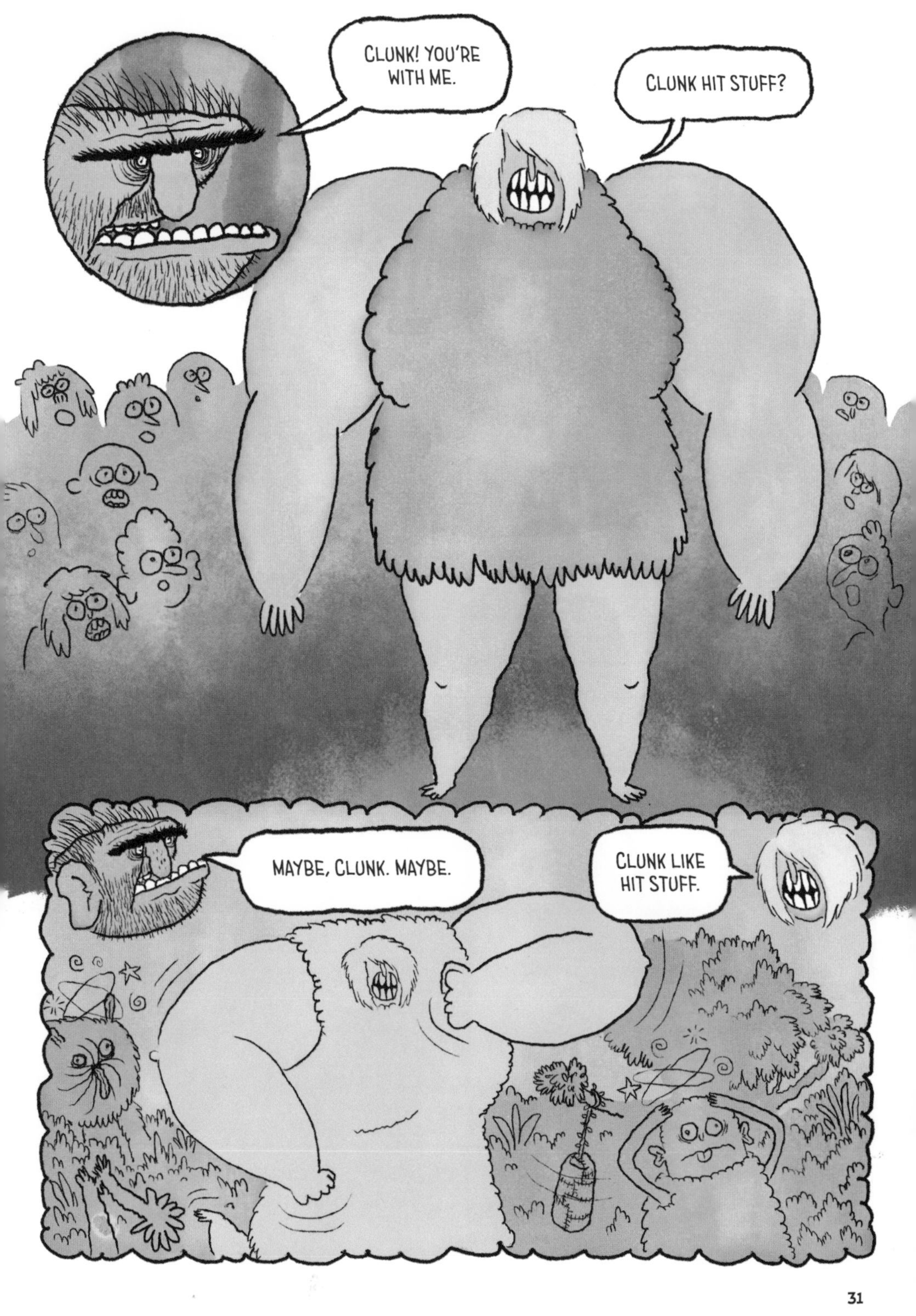
CLUNK! YOU'RE WITH ME.
CLUNK HIT STUFF?
MAYBE, CLUNK. MAYBE.
CLUNK LIKE HIT STUFF.

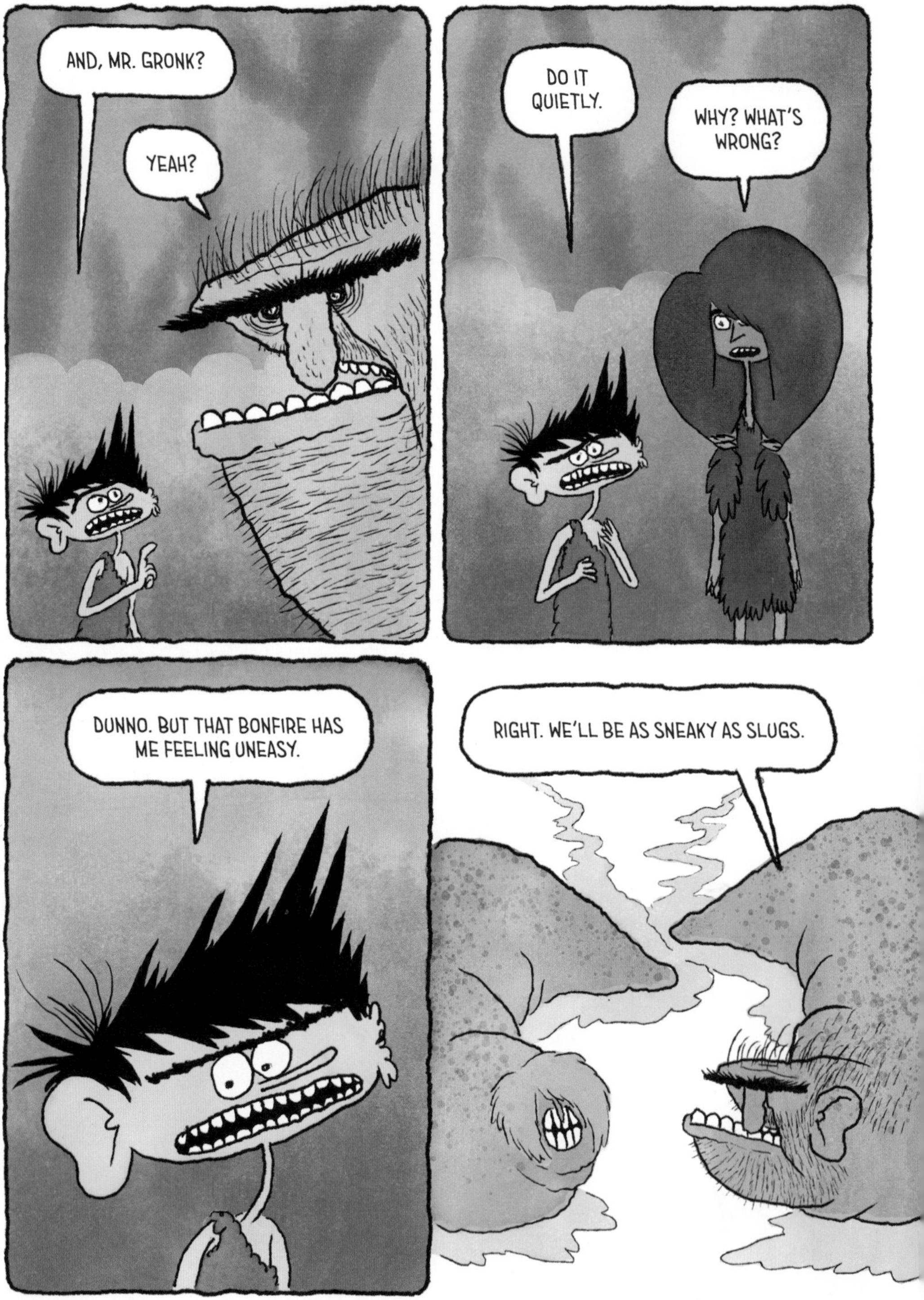
AND, MR. GRONK?
YEAH?
DO IT QUIETLY.
WHY? WHAT'S WRONG?
DUNNO. BUT THAT BONFIRE HAS ME FEELING UNEASY.
RIGHT. WE'LL BE AS SNEAKY AS SLUGS.

33

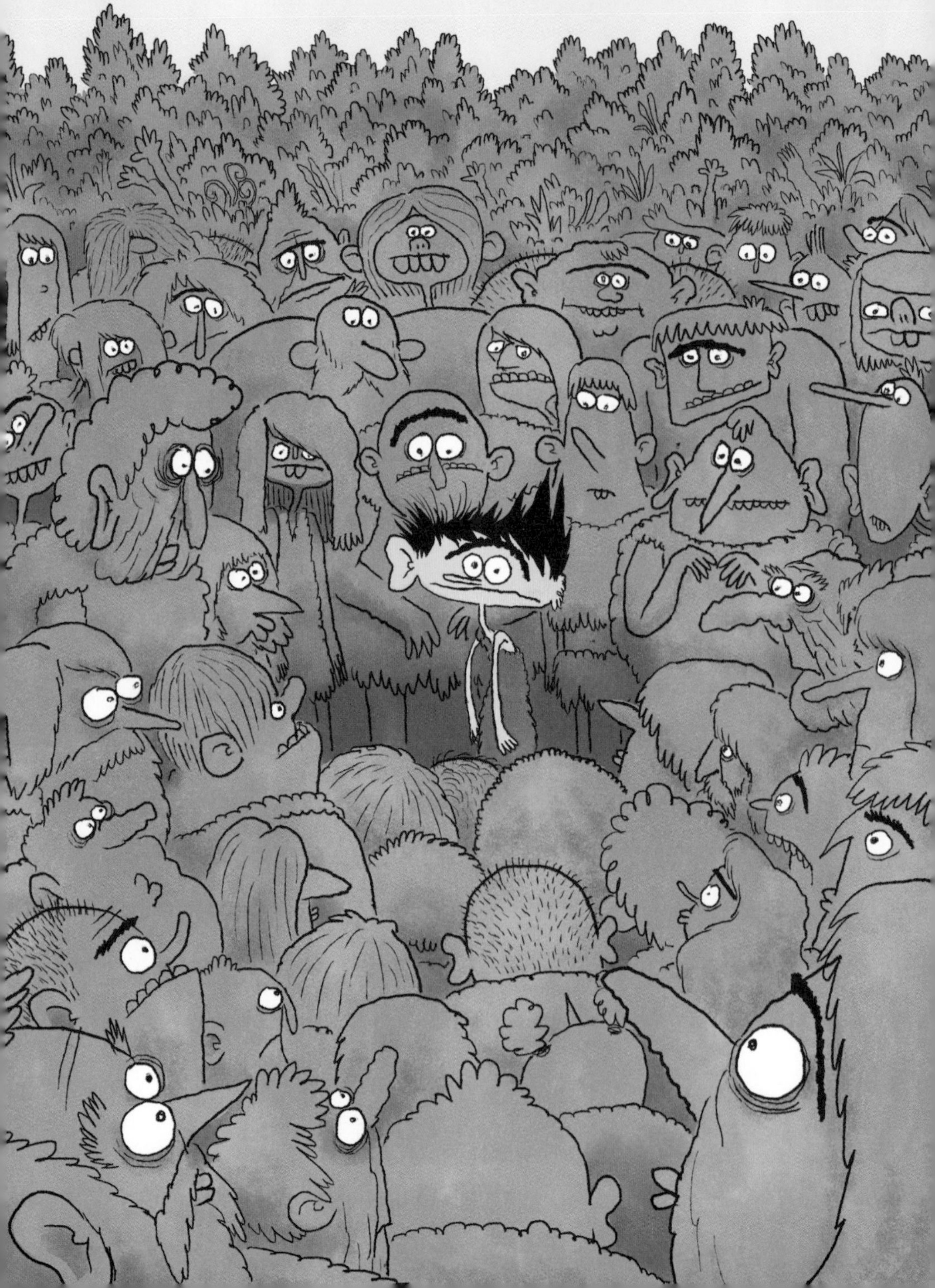

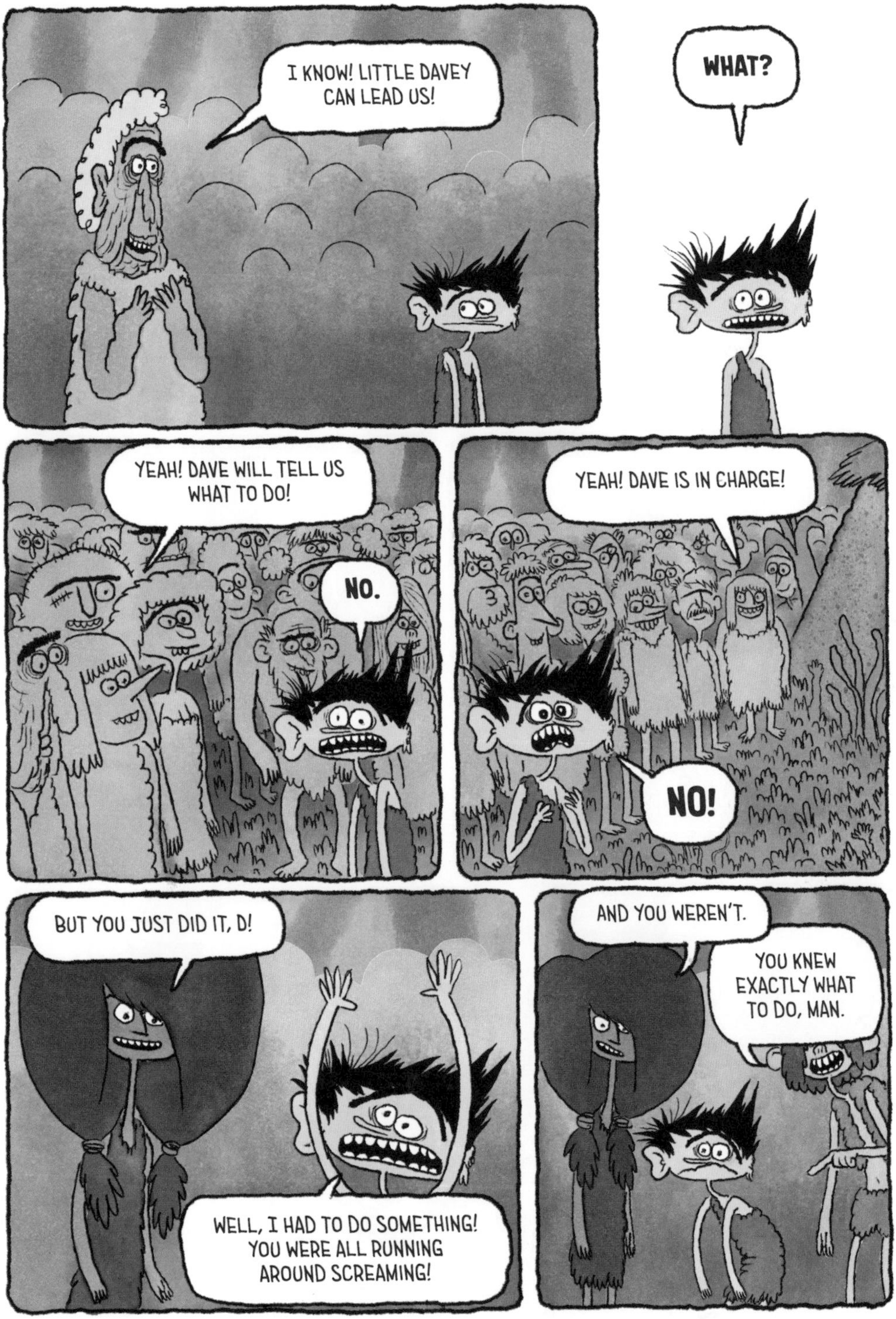
I KNOW! LITTLE DAVEY CAN LEAD US!
WHAT?
YEAH! DAVE WILL TELL US WHAT TO DO!
NO.
YEAH! DAVE IS IN CHARGE!
NO!
BUT YOU JUST DID IT, D!
WELL, I HAD TO DO SOMETHING! YOU WERE ALL RUNNING AROUND SCREAMING!
AND YOU WEREN'T.
YOU KNEW EXACTLY WHAT TO DO, MAN.

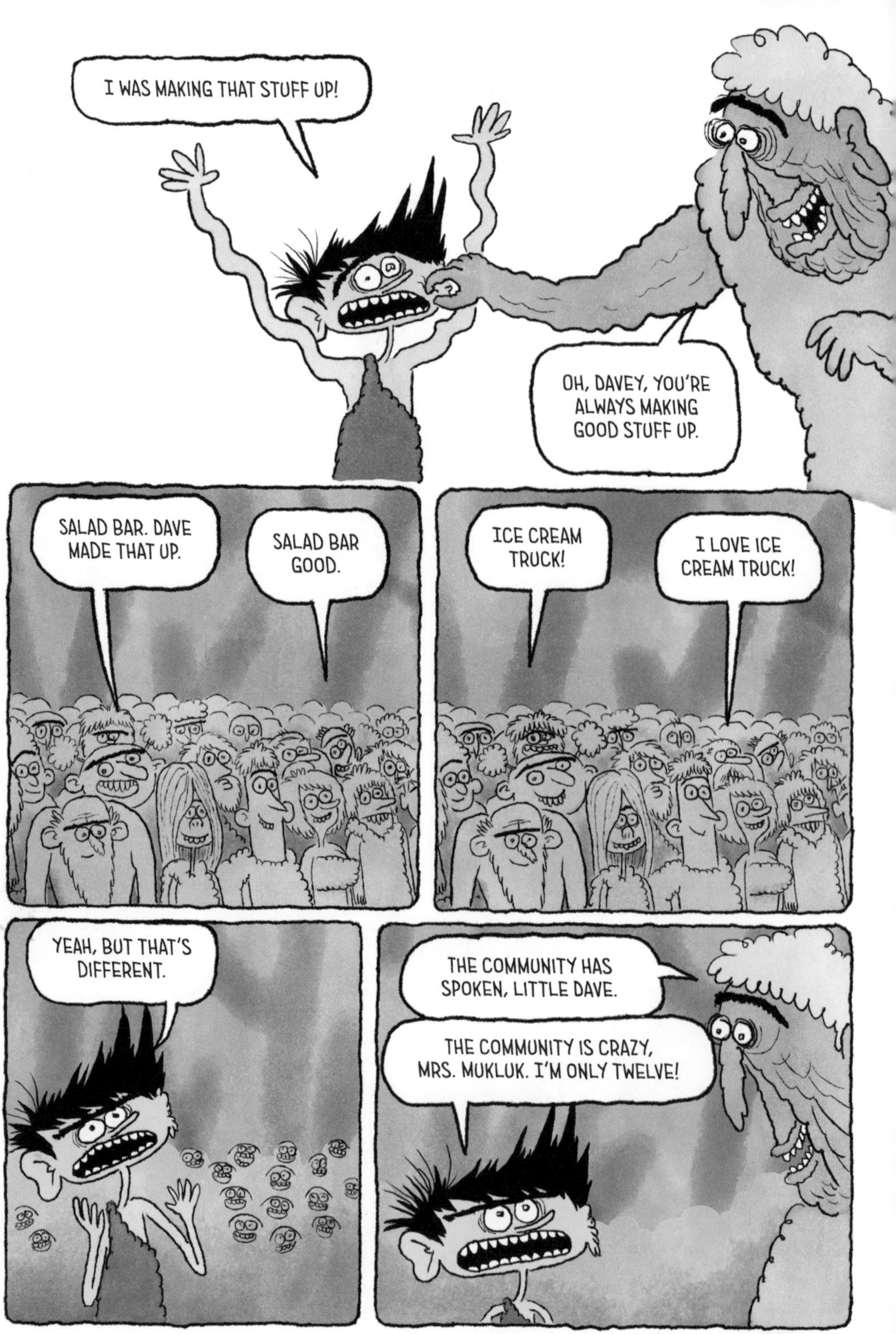
I WAS MAKING THAT STUFF UP!
OH, DAVEY, YOU'RE ALWAYS MAKING GOOD STUFF UP.
SALAD BAR. DAVE MADE THAT UP.
SALAD BAR GOOD.
ICE CREAM TRUCK!
I LOVE ICE CREAM TRUCK!
YEAH, BUT THAT'S DIFFERENT.
THE COMMUNITY HAS SPOKEN, LITTLE DAVE.
THE COMMUNITY IS CRAZY, MRS. MUKLUK. I'M ONLY TWELVE!

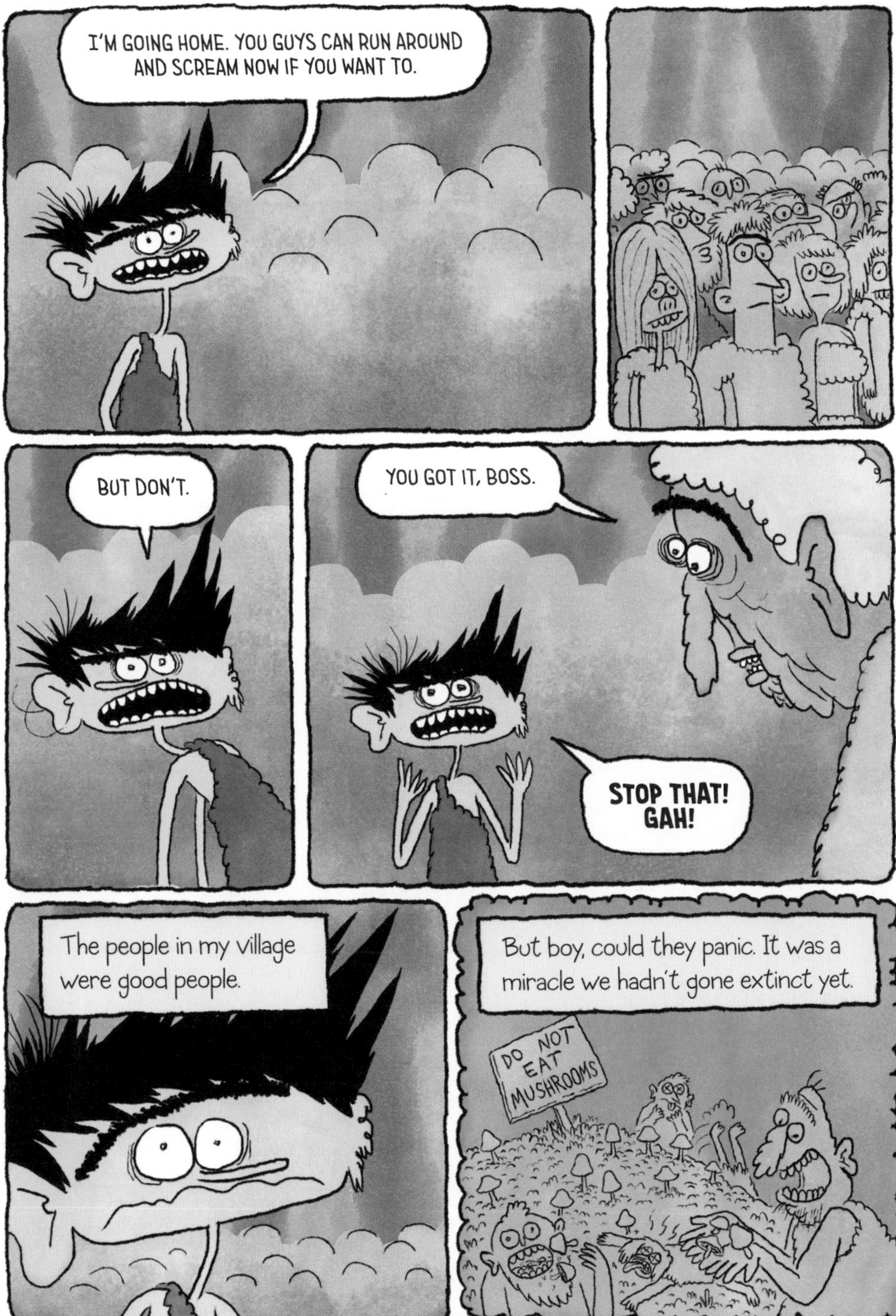
I'M GOING HOME. YOU GUYS CAN RUN AROUND AND SCREAM NOW IF YOU WANT TO.
BUT DON'T.
YOU GOT IT, BOSS.
STOP THAT! GAH!
The people in my village were good people.
But boy, could they panic. It was a miracle we hadn't gone extinct yet.
DO NOT EAT MUSHROOMS

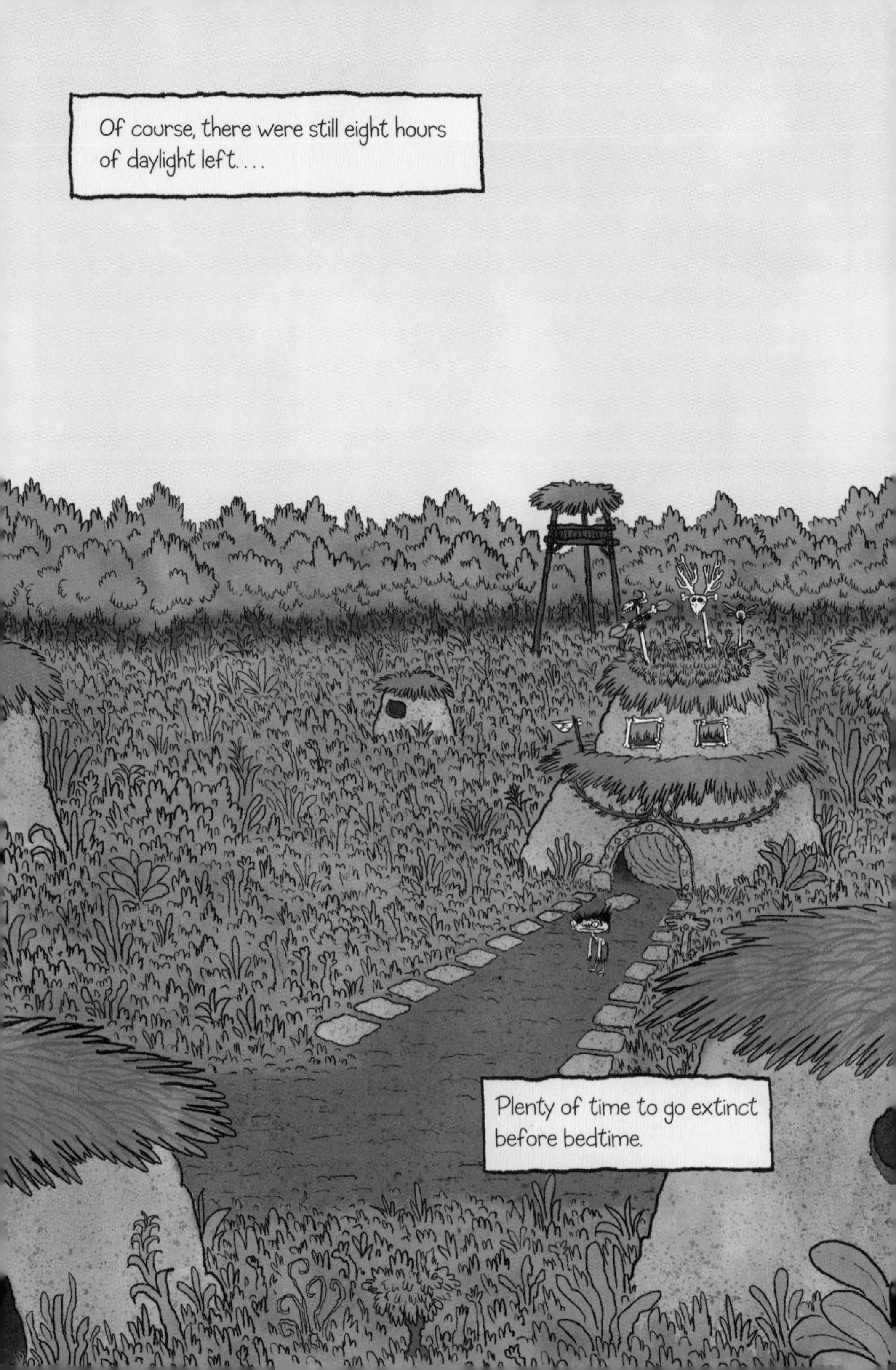
Of course, there were still eight hours of daylight left. . . .
Plenty of time to go extinct before bedtime.

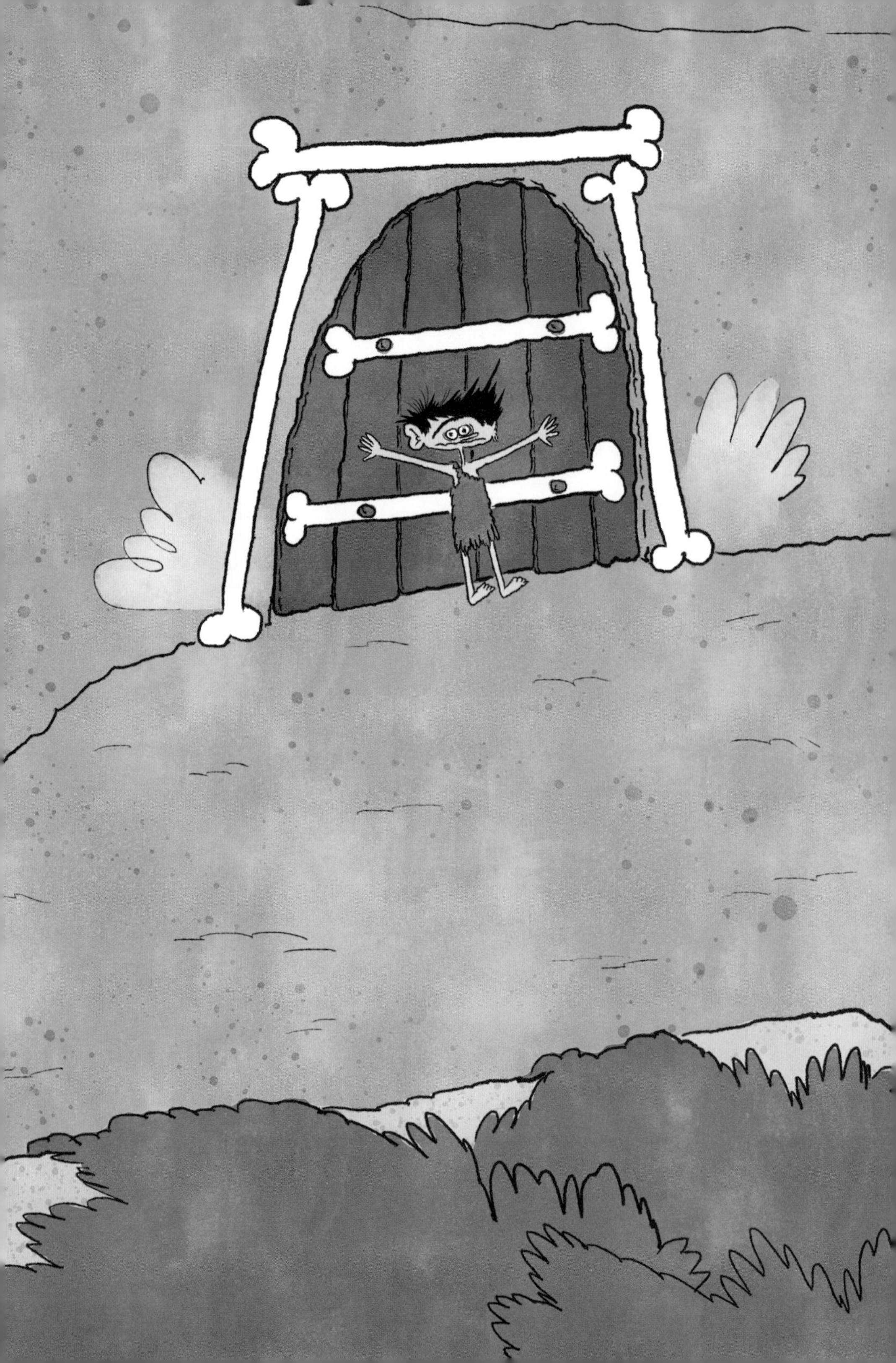

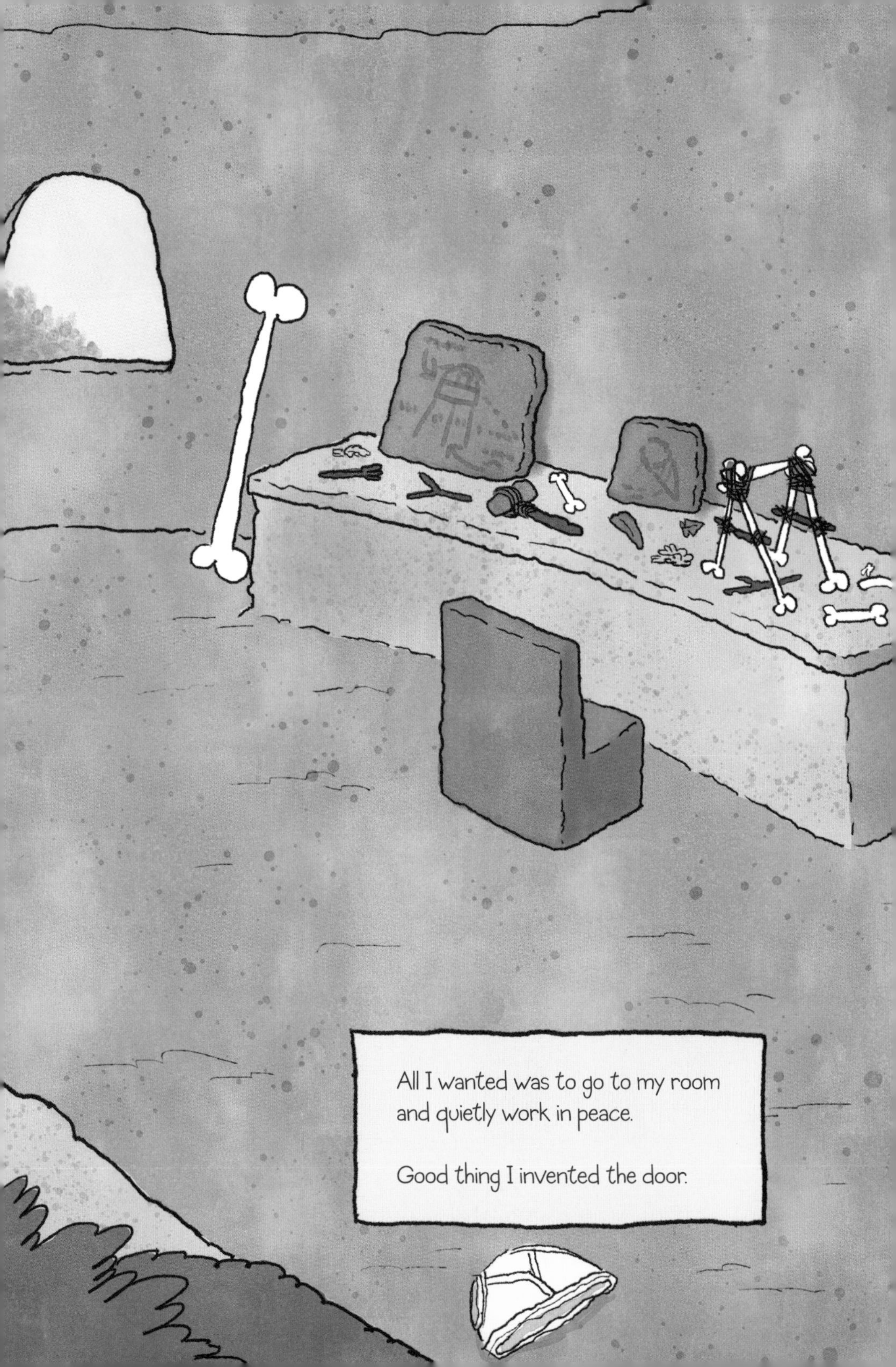
All I wanted was to go to my room and quietly work in peace.
Good thing I invented the door.

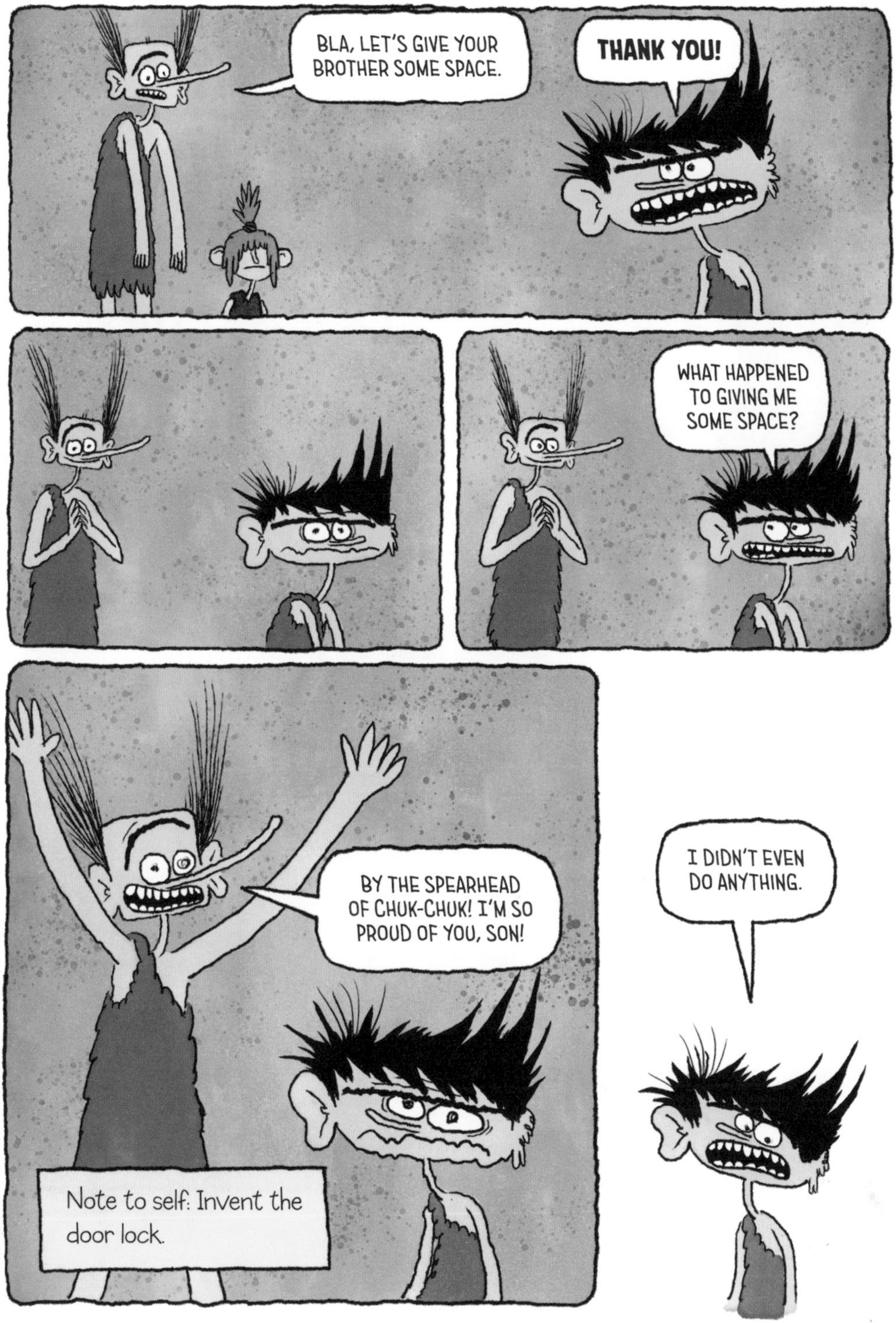
BLA, LET'S GIVE YOUR BROTHER SOME SPACE.
THANK YOU!
WHAT HAPPENED TO GIVING ME SOME SPACE?
BY THE SPEARHEAD OF CHUK-CHUK! I'M SO PROUD OF YOU, SON!
Note to self: Invent the door lock.
I DIDN'T EVEN DO ANYTHING.

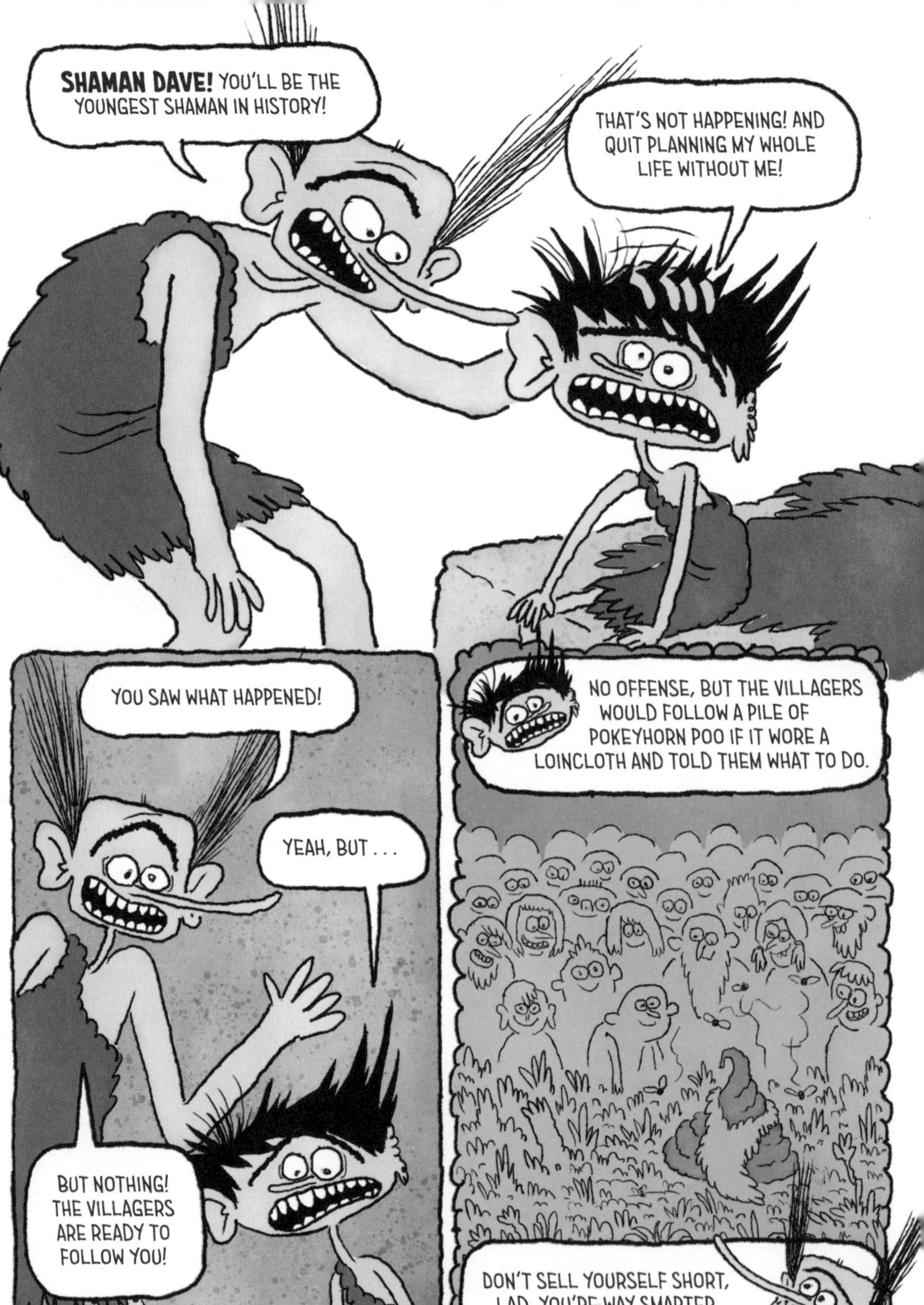
SHAMAN DAVE! YOU'LL BE THE YOUNGEST SHAMAN IN HISTORY!
THAT'S NOT HAPPENING! AND QUIT PLANNING MY WHOLE LIFE WITHOUT ME!
YOU SAW WHAT HAPPENED!
YEAH, BUT . . .
BUT NOTHING! THE VILLAGERS ARE READY TO FOLLOW YOU!
NO OFFENSE, BUT THE VILLAGERS WOULD FOLLOW A PILE OF POKEYHORN POO IF IT WORE A LOINCLOTH AND TOLD THEM WHAT TO DO.
DON'T SELL YOURSELF SHORT, LAD. YOU'RE WAY SMARTER THAN POKEYHORN POO.

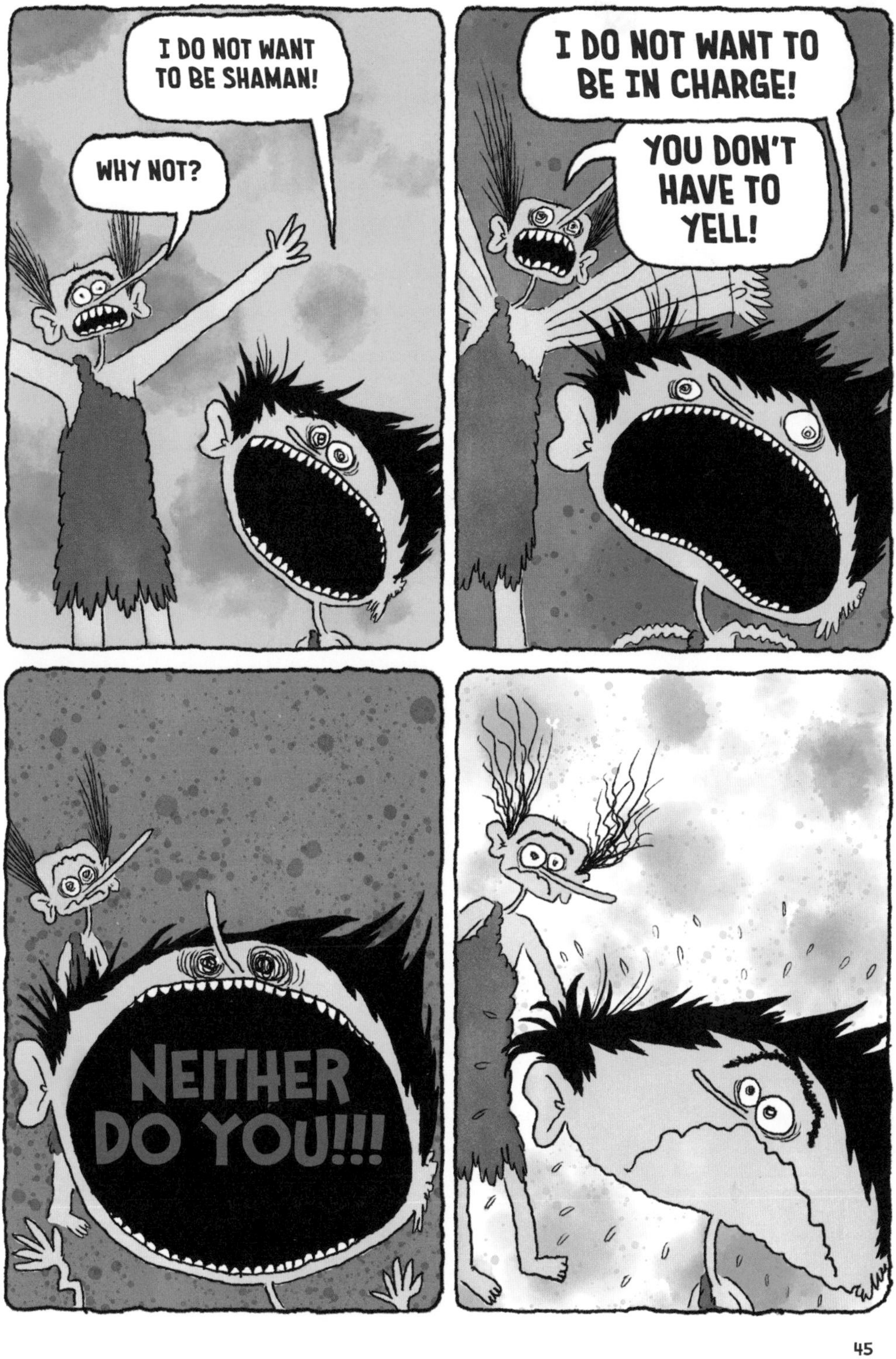
I DO NOT WANT TO BE SHAMAN!
WHY NOT?
I DO NOT WANT TO BE IN CHARGE!
YOU DON'T HAVE TO YELL!
NEITHER DO YOU!!!

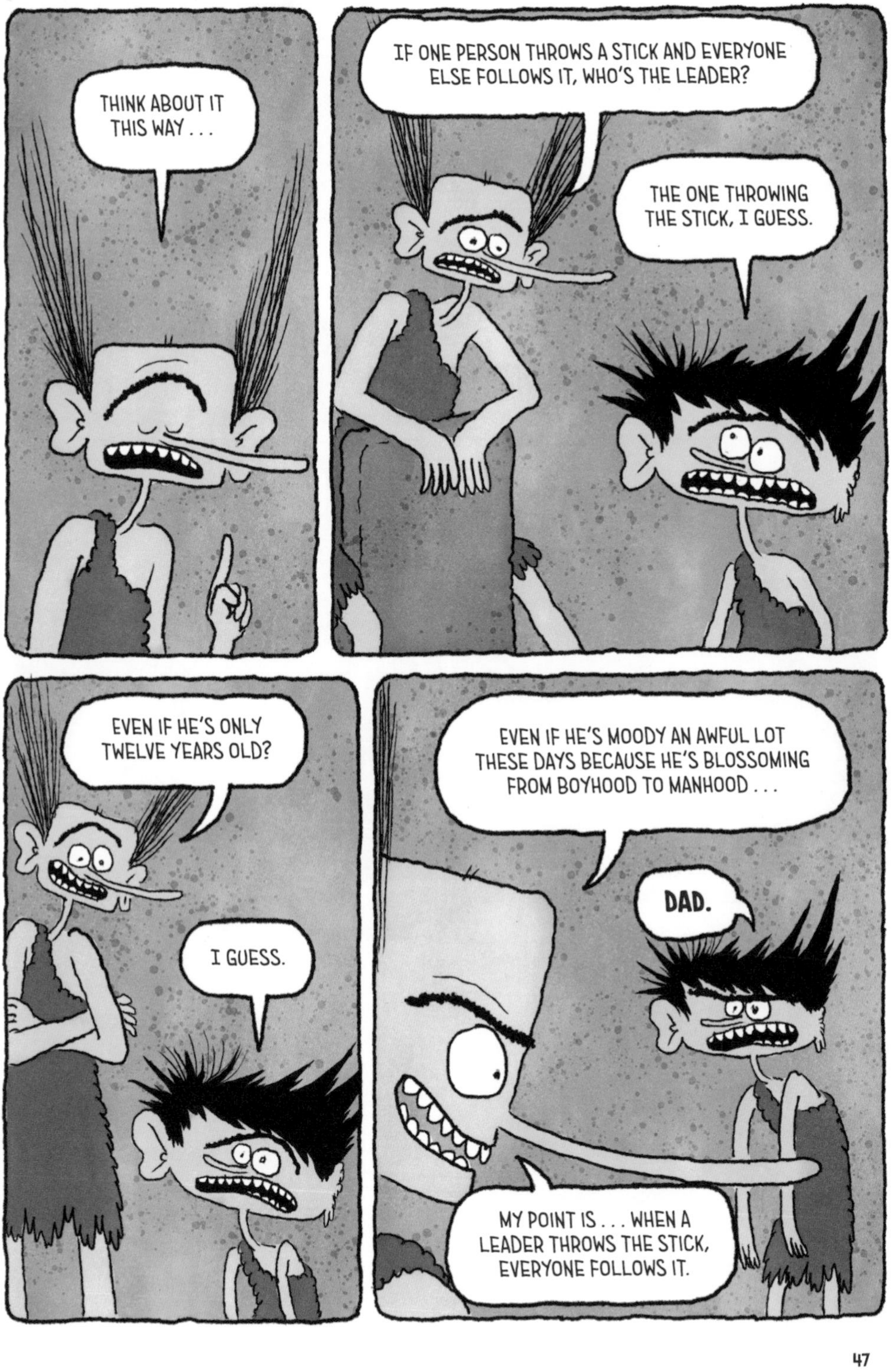
THINK ABOUT IT THIS WAY . . .
IF ONE PERSON THROWS A STICK AND EVERYONE ELSE FOLLOWS IT, WHO'S THE LEADER?
THE ONE THROWING THE STICK, I GUESS.
EVEN IF HE'S ONLY TWELVE YEARS OLD?
I GUESS.
EVEN IF HE'S MOODY AN AWFUL LOT THESE DAYS BECAUSE HE'S BLOSSOMING FROM BOYHOOD TO MANHOOD . . .
DAD.
MY POINT IS . . . WHEN A LEADER THROWS THE STICK, EVERYONE FOLLOWS IT.

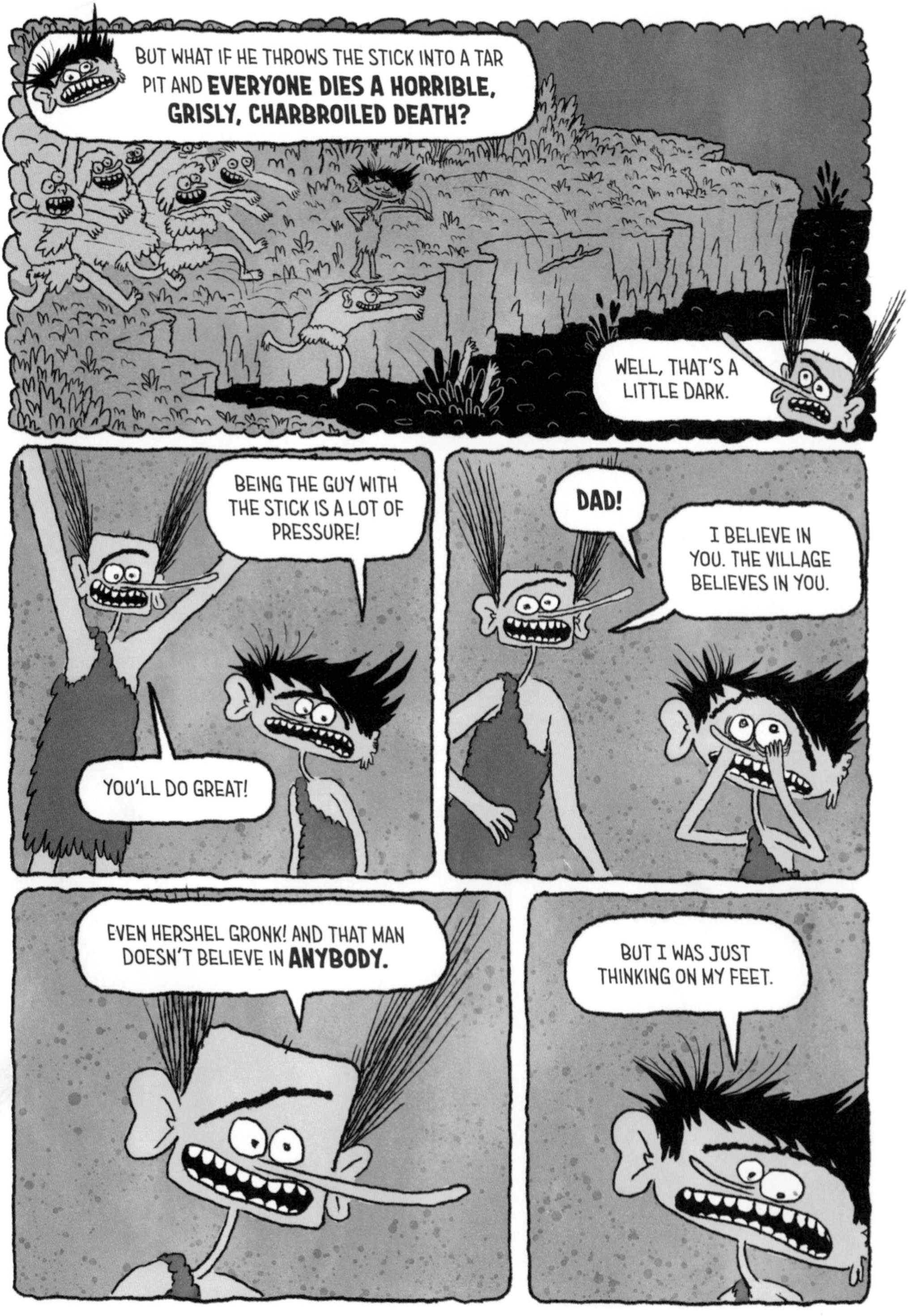

BUT WHAT IF HE THROWS THE STICK INTO A TAR PIT AND **EVERYONE DIES A HORRIBLE, GRISLY, CHARBROILED DEATH?**
WELL, THAT'S A LITTLE DARK.
BEING THE GUY WITH THE STICK IS A LOT OF PRESSURE!
YOU'LL DO GREAT!
DAD!
I BELIEVE IN YOU. THE VILLAGE BELIEVES IN YOU.
EVEN HERSHEL GRONK! AND THAT MAN DOESN'T BELIEVE IN **ANYBODY.**
BUT I WAS JUST THINKING ON MY FEET.

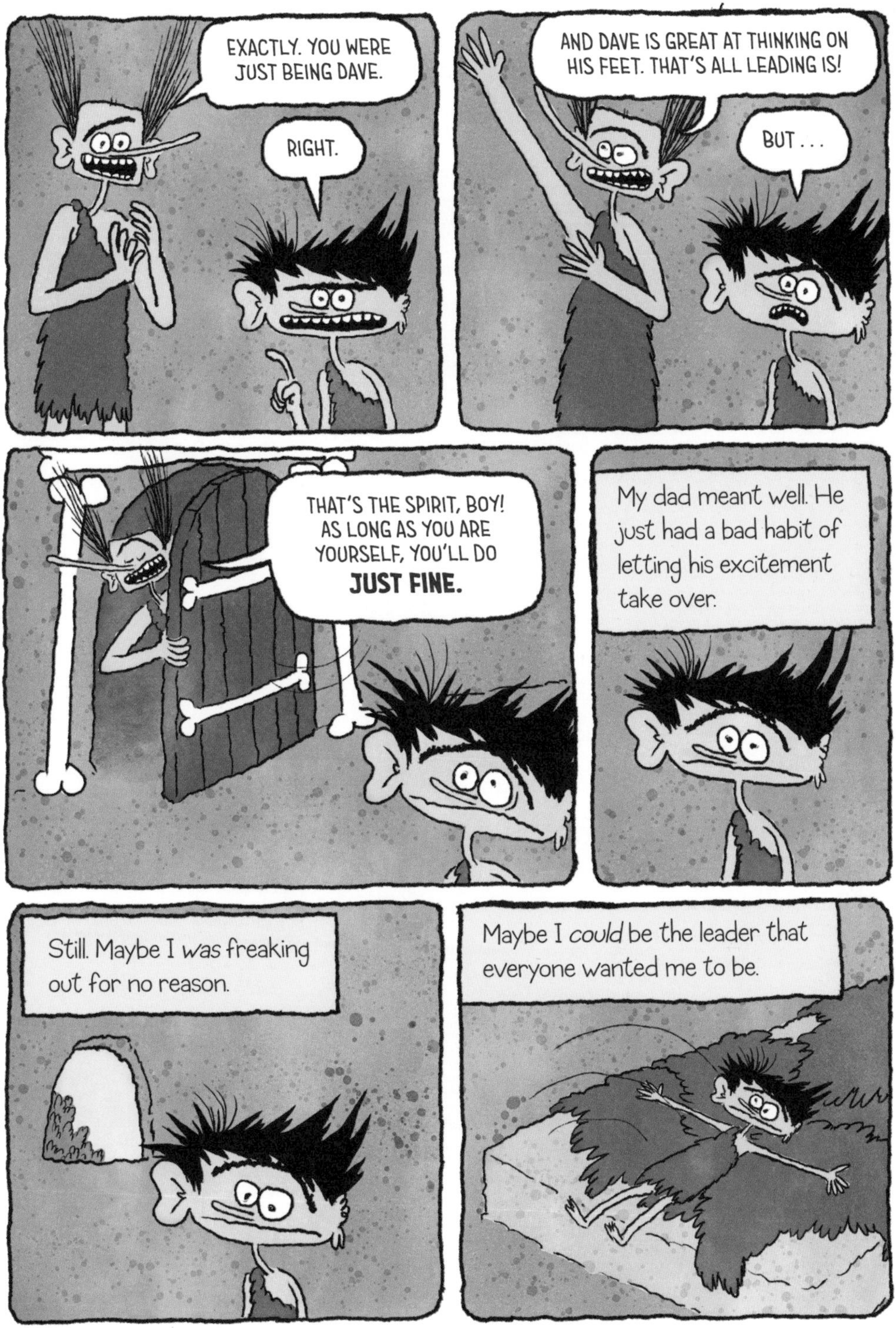
EXACTLY. YOU WERE JUST BEING DAVE.
RIGHT.
AND DAVE IS GREAT AT THINKING ON HIS FEET. THAT'S ALL LEADING IS!
BUT . . .
THAT'S THE SPIRIT, BOY! AS LONG AS YOU ARE YOURSELF, YOU'LL DO **JUST FINE.**
My dad meant well. He just had a bad habit of letting his excitement take over.
Still. Maybe I *was* freaking out for no reason.
Maybe I *could* be the leader that everyone wanted me to be.

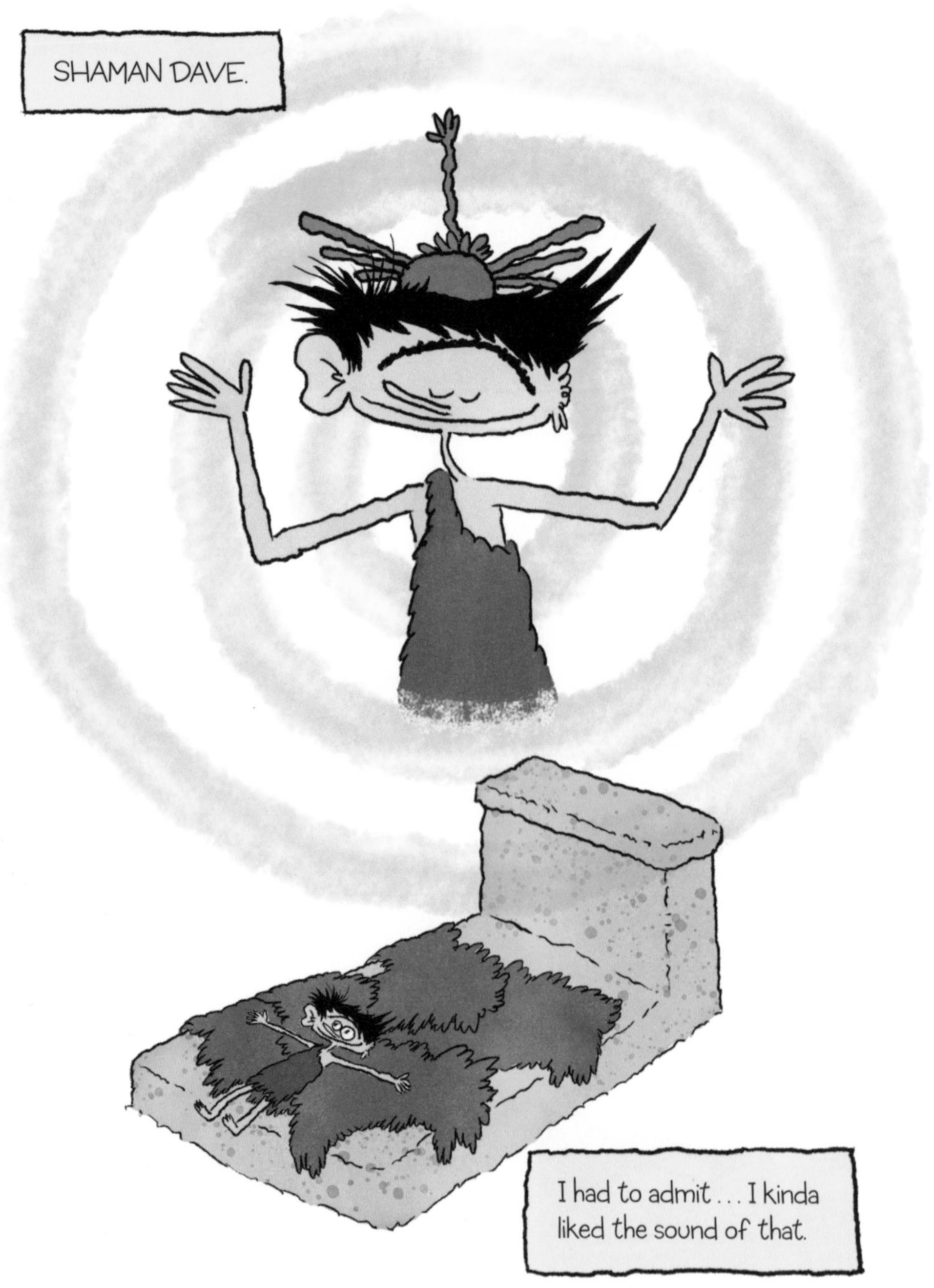
SHAMAN DAVE.
I had to admit . . . I kinda liked the sound of that.

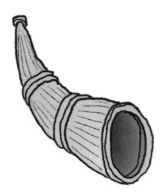

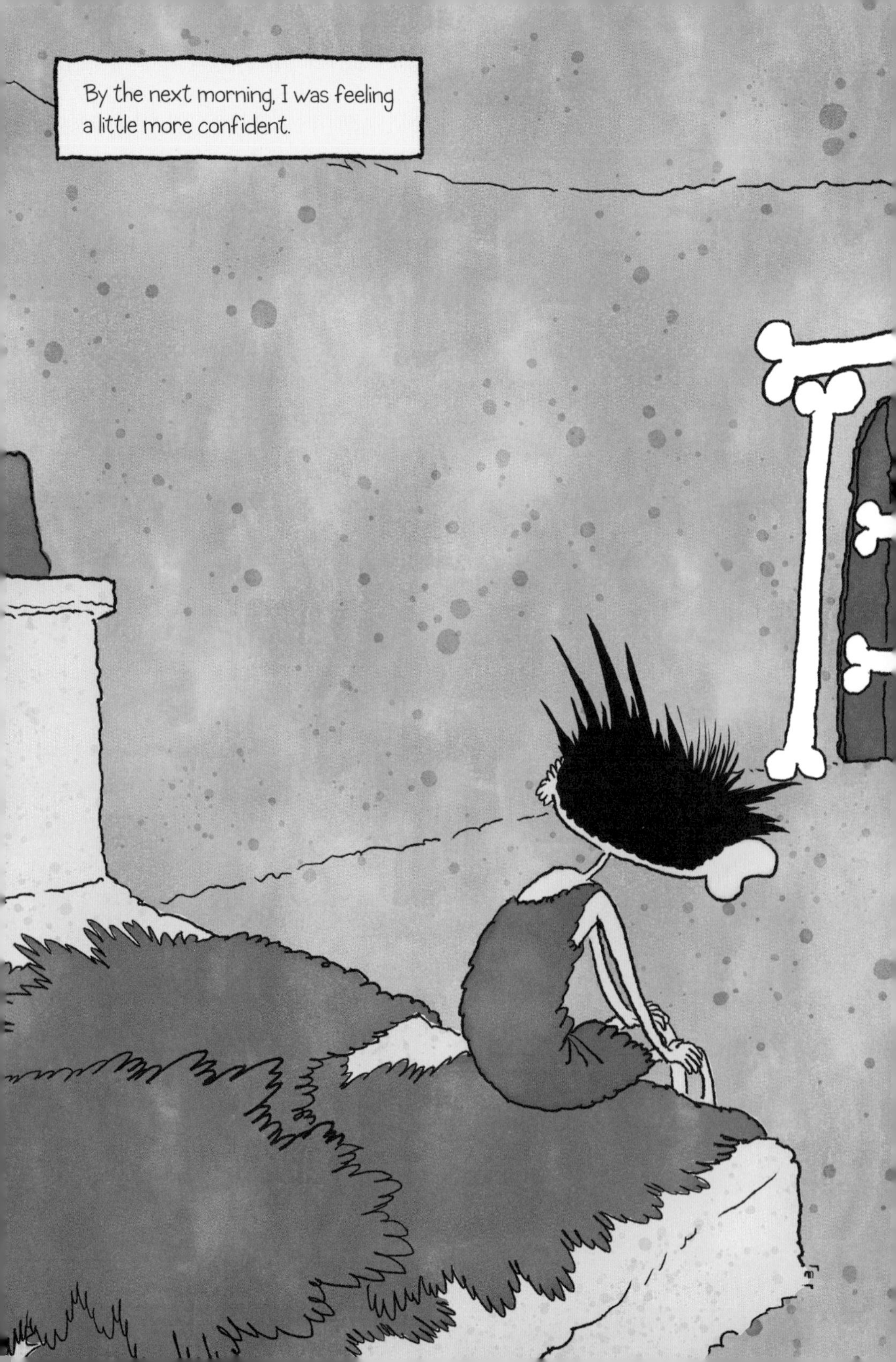
By the next morning, I was feeling a little more confident.

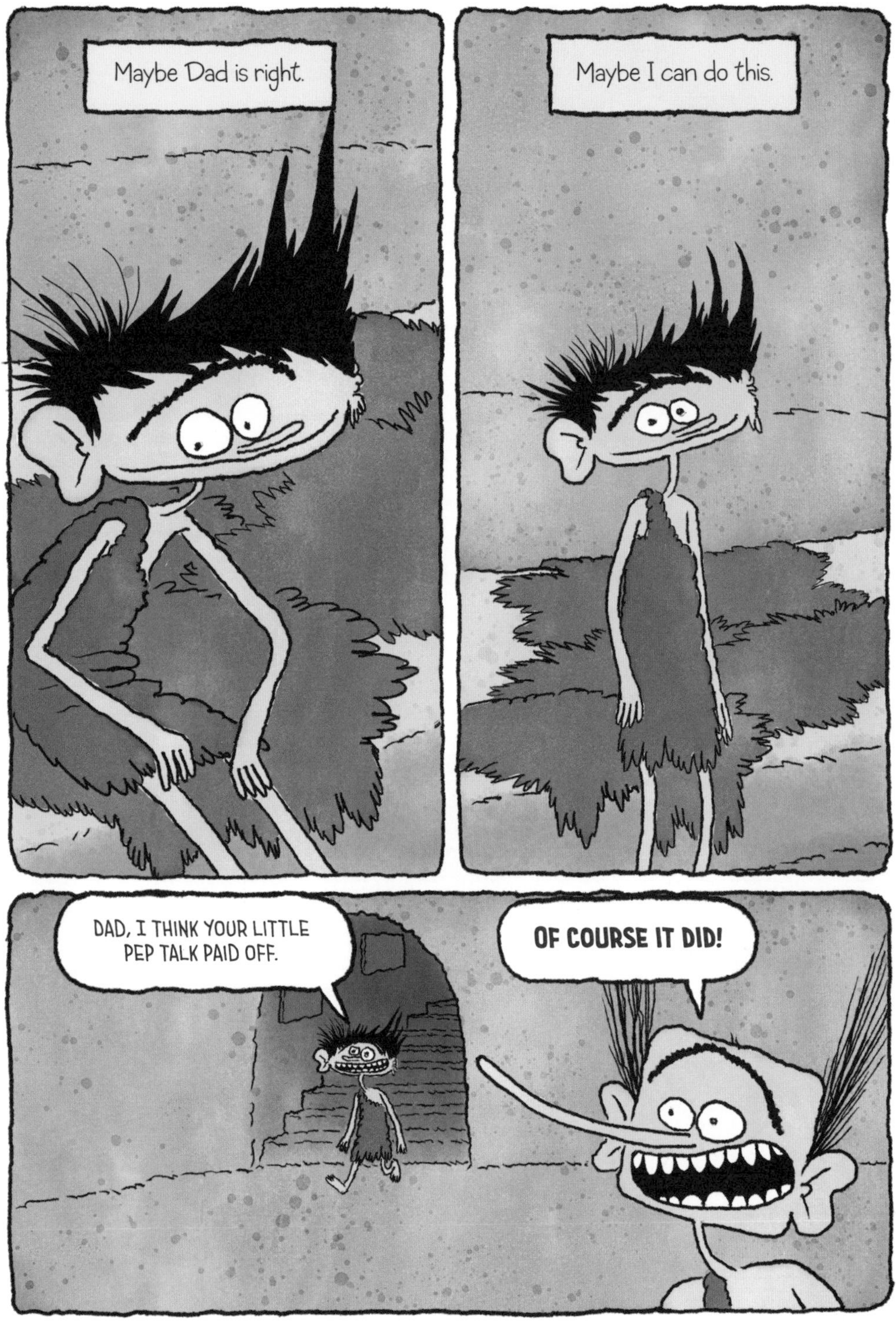
Maybe Dad is right.
Maybe I can do this.
DAD, I THINK YOUR LITTLE PEP TALK PAID OFF.
OF COURSE IT DID!

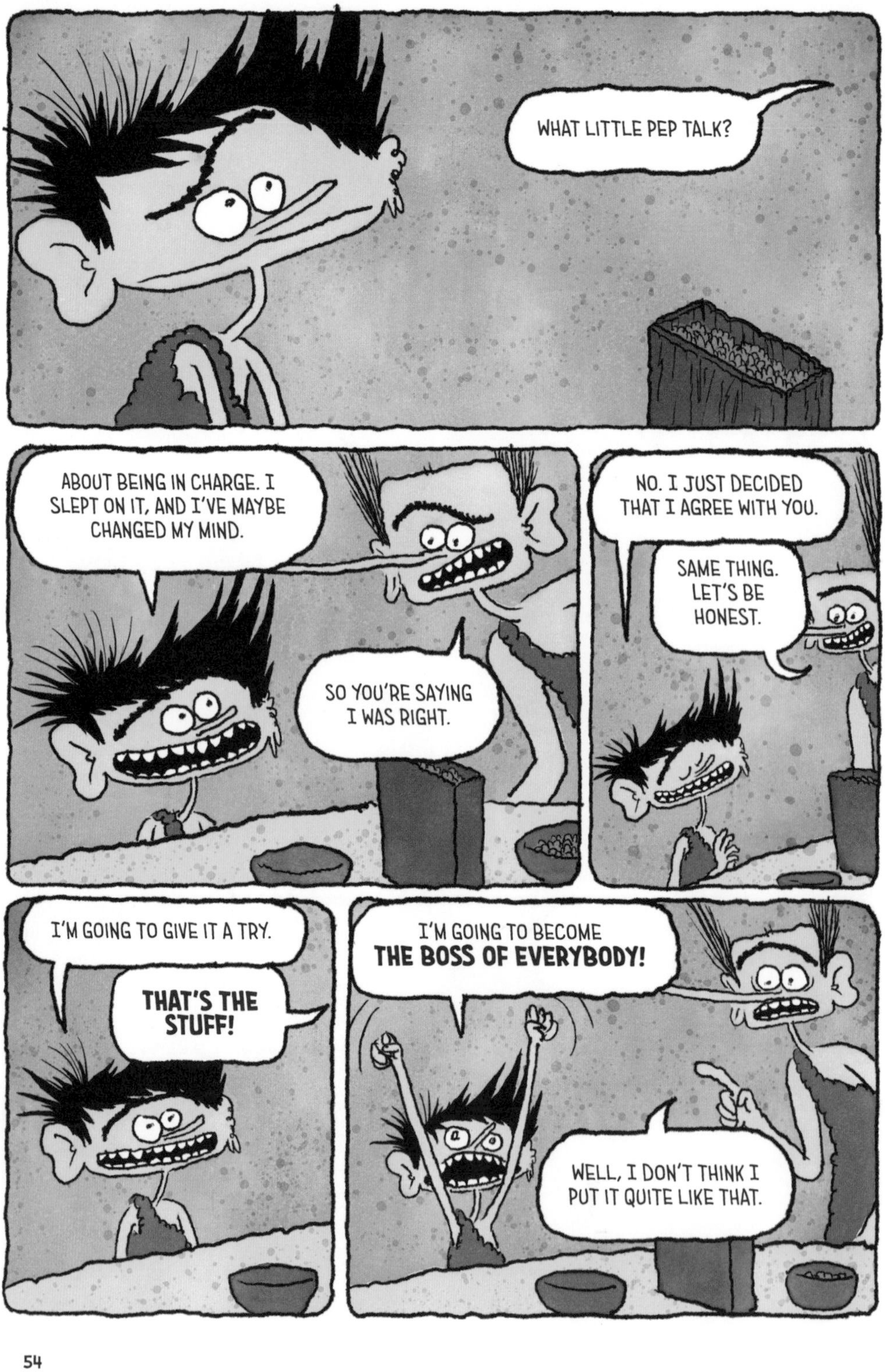
WHAT LITTLE PEP TALK?
ABOUT BEING IN CHARGE. I SLEPT ON IT, AND I'VE MAYBE CHANGED MY MIND.
SO YOU'RE SAYING I WAS RIGHT.
NO. I JUST DECIDED THAT I AGREE WITH YOU.
SAME THING. LET'S BE HONEST.
I'M GOING TO GIVE IT A TRY.
THAT'S THE STUFF!
I'M GOING TO BECOME **THE BOSS OF EVERYBODY!**
WELL, I DON'T THINK I PUT IT QUITE LIKE THAT.

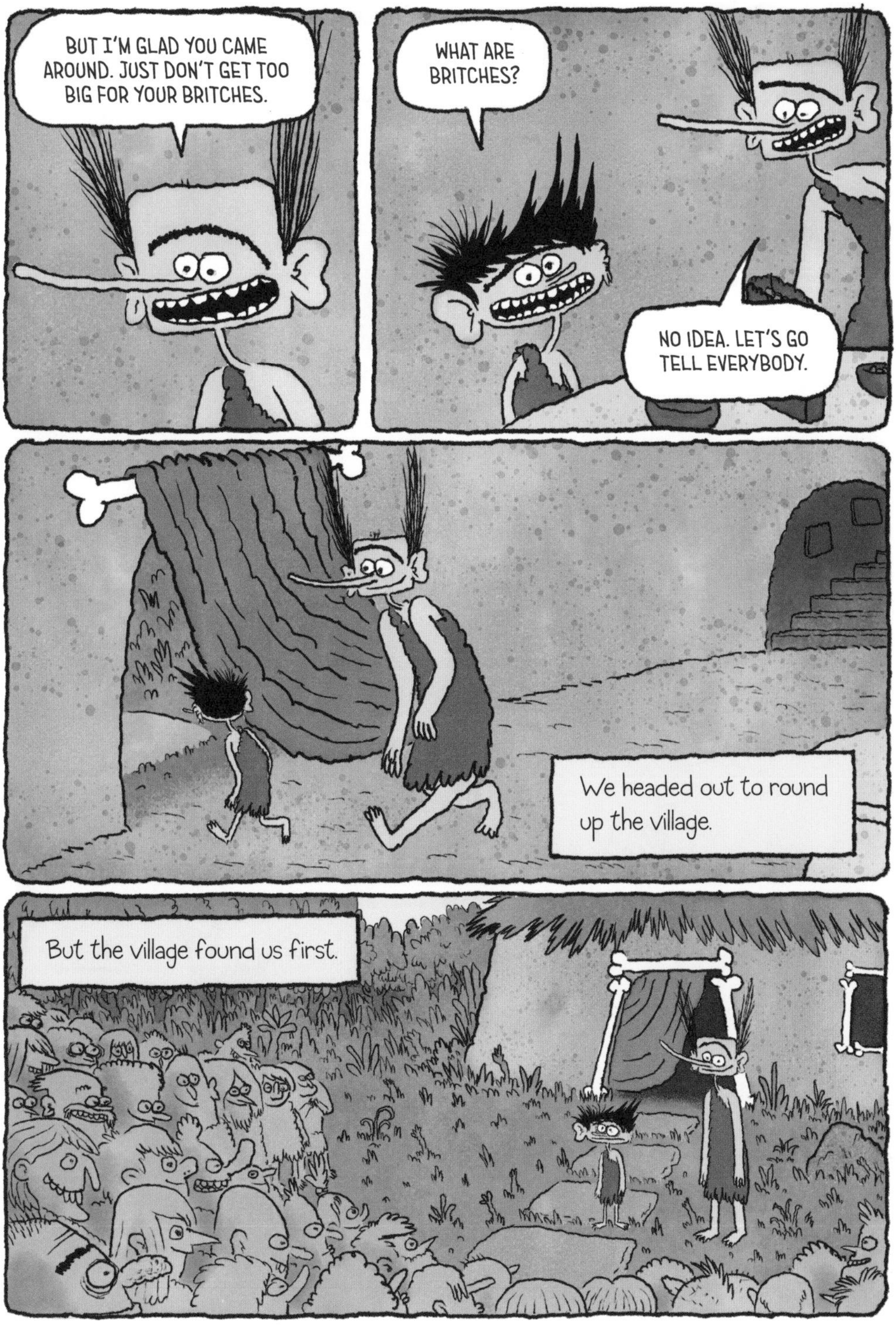
BUT I'M GLAD YOU CAME AROUND. JUST DON'T GET TOO BIG FOR YOUR BRITCHES.
WHAT ARE BRITCHES?
NO IDEA. LET'S GO TELL EVERYBODY.
We headed out to round up the village.
But the village found us first.

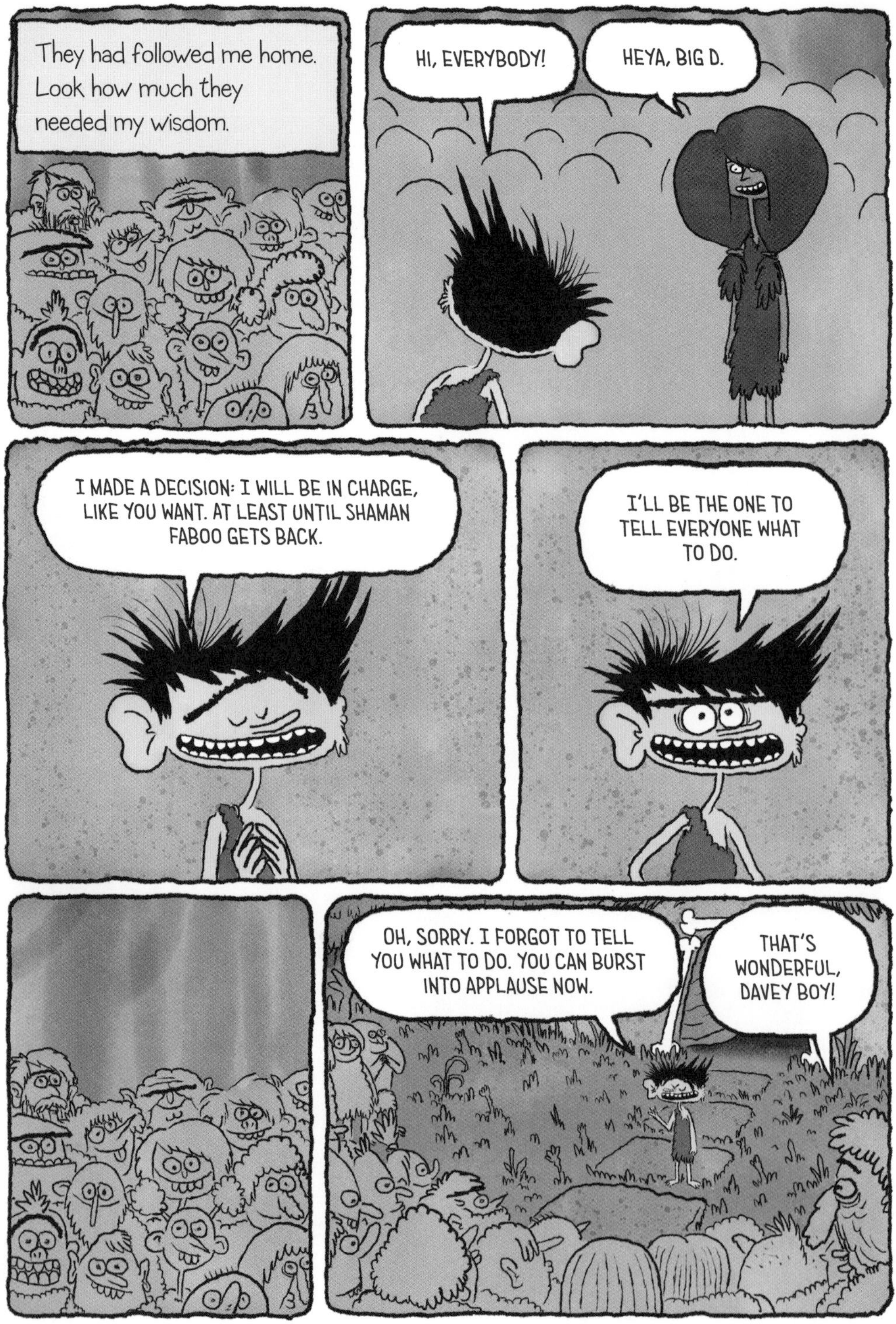
They had followed me home. Look how much they needed my wisdom.
HI, EVERYBODY!
HEYA, BIG D.
I MADE A DECISION: I WILL BE IN CHARGE, LIKE YOU WANT. AT LEAST UNTIL SHAMAN FABOO GETS BACK.
I'LL BE THE ONE TO TELL EVERYONE WHAT TO DO.
OH, SORRY. I FORGOT TO TELL YOU WHAT TO DO. YOU CAN BURST INTO APPLAUSE NOW.
THAT'S WONDERFUL, DAVEY BOY!

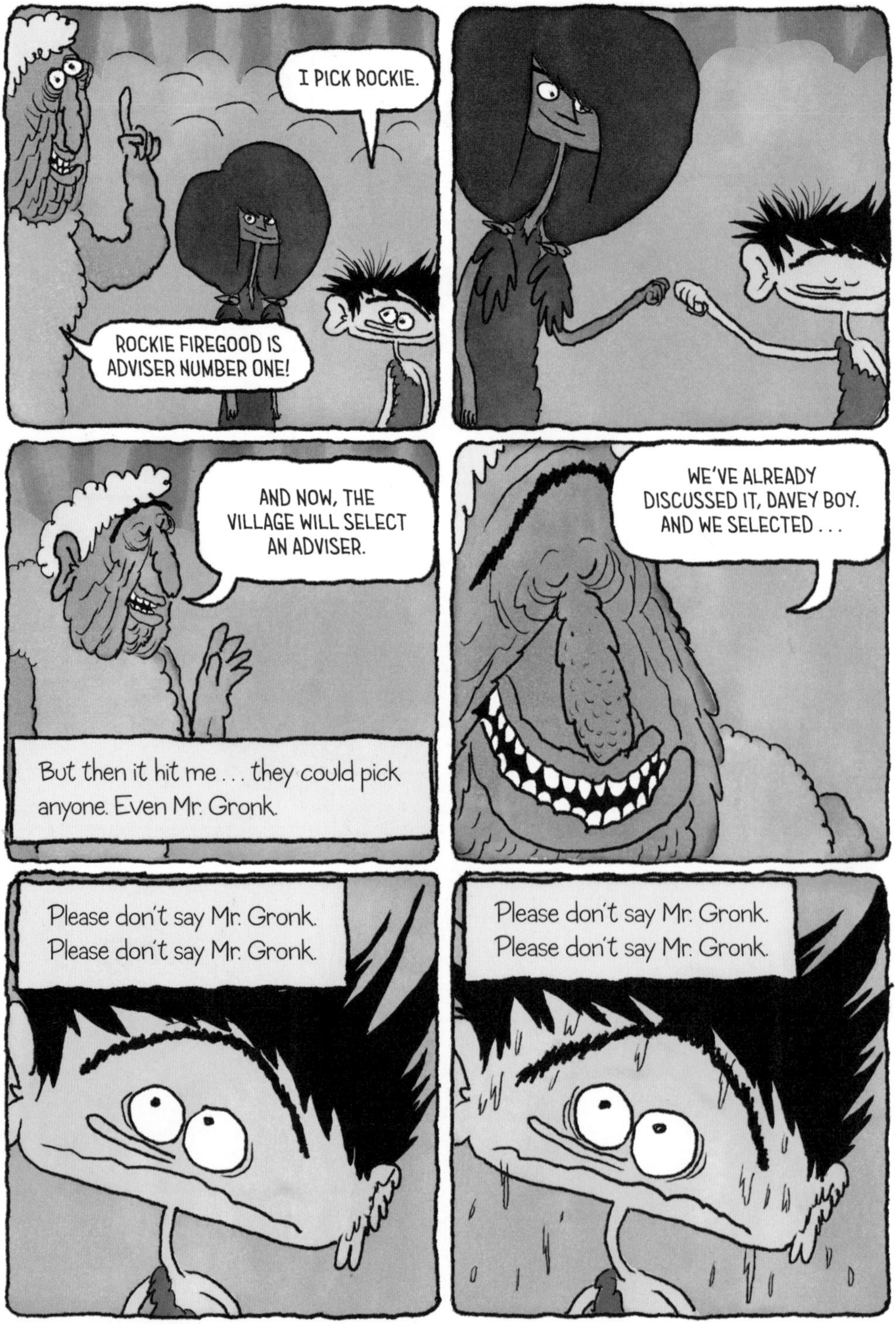
I PICK ROCKIE.
ROCKIE FIREGOOD IS ADVISER NUMBER ONE!
AND NOW, THE VILLAGE WILL SELECT AN ADVISER.
But then it hit me . . . they could pick anyone. Even Mr. Gronk.
WE'VE ALREADY DISCUSSED IT, DAVEY BOY. AND WE SELECTED . . .
Please don't say Mr. Gronk. Please don't say Mr. Gronk.
Please don't say Mr. Gronk. Please don't say Mr. Gronk.

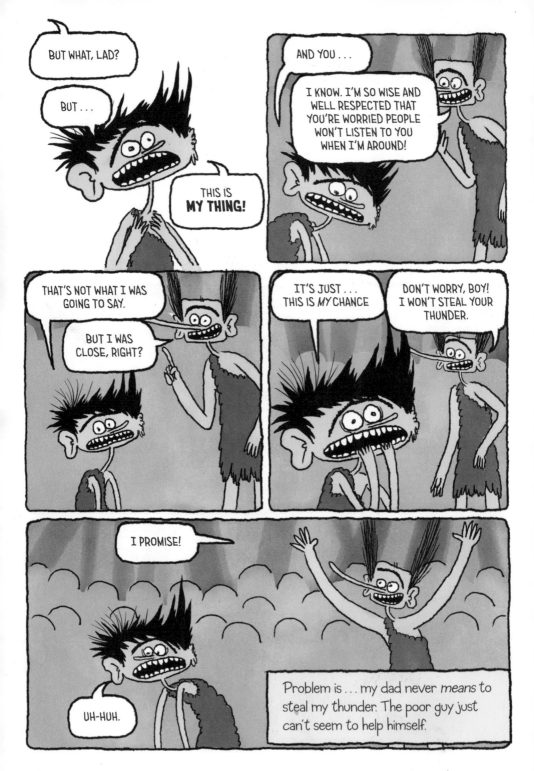

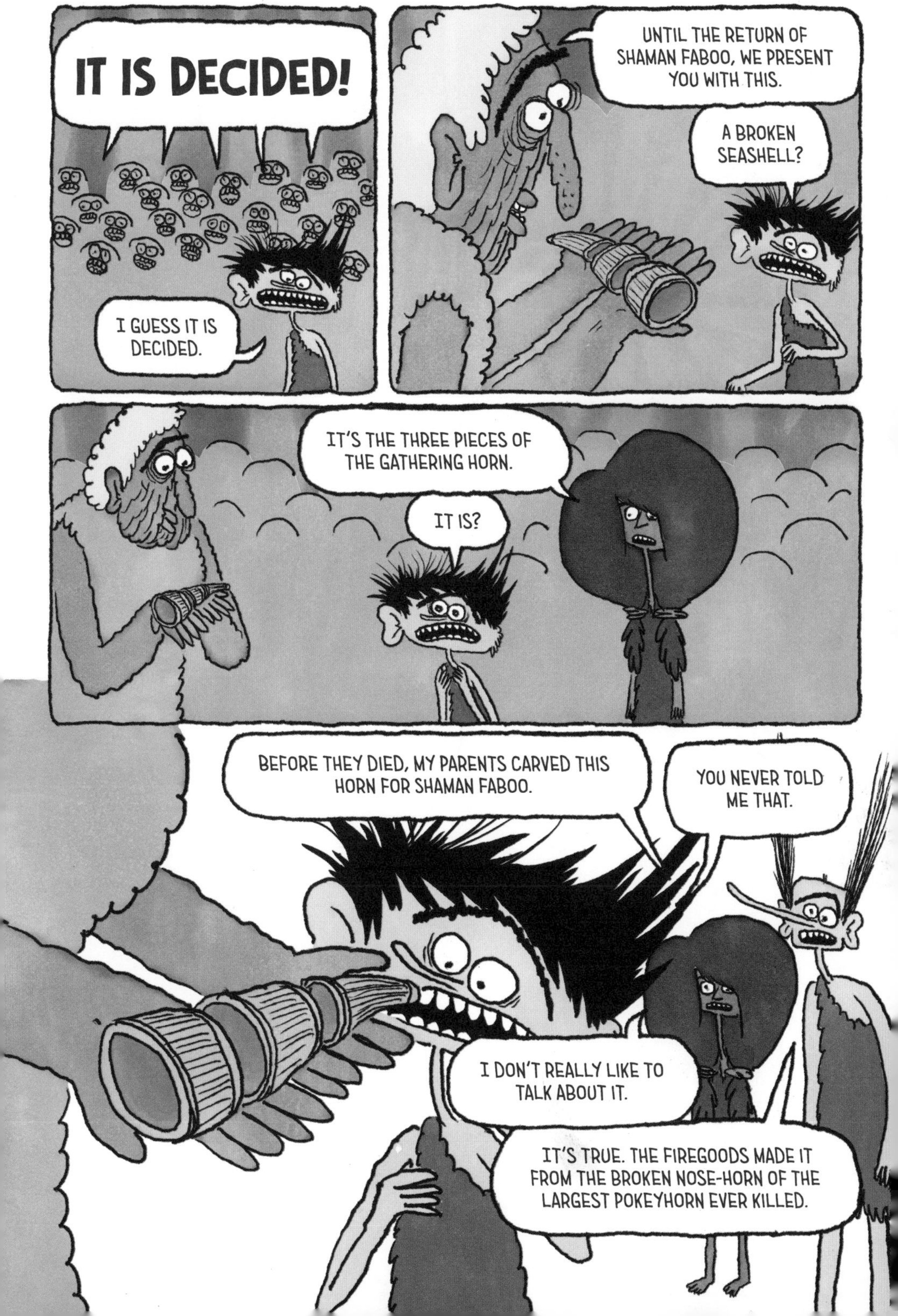
IT IS DECIDED!
I GUESS IT IS DECIDED.
UNTIL THE RETURN OF SHAMAN FABOO, WE PRESENT YOU WITH THIS.
A BROKEN SEASHELL?
IT'S THE THREE PIECES OF THE GATHERING HORN.
IT IS?
BEFORE THEY DIED, MY PARENTS CARVED THIS HORN FOR SHAMAN FABOO.
YOU NEVER TOLD ME THAT.
I DON'T REALLY LIKE TO TALK ABOUT IT.
IT'S TRUE. THE FIREGOODS MADE IT FROM THE BROKEN NOSE-HORN OF THE LARGEST POKEYHORN EVER KILLED.

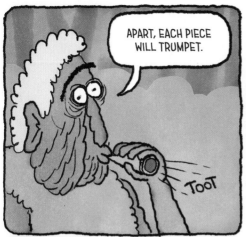

IT IS DECIDED!

Hmm. I was discovering that this whole "being the boss" thing might not be all it was cracked up to be.

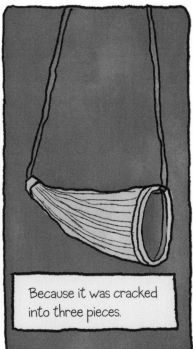

Because it was cracked into three pieces.

And Rockie had one.

And my dad had the other.

ISN'T THIS GREAT, LAD? FATHER AND SON, RULING THE WORLD TOGETHER!

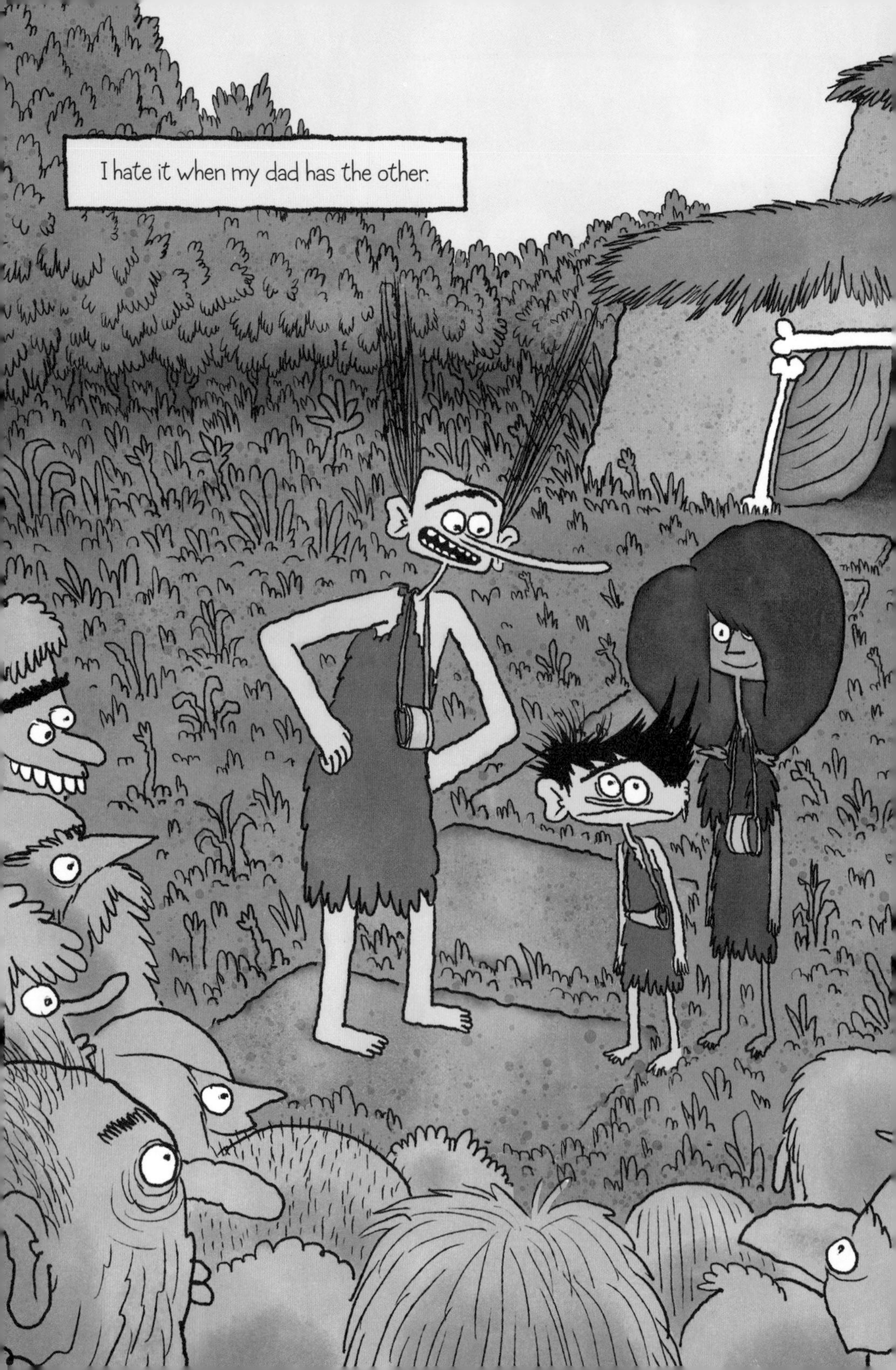
I hate it when my dad has the other.

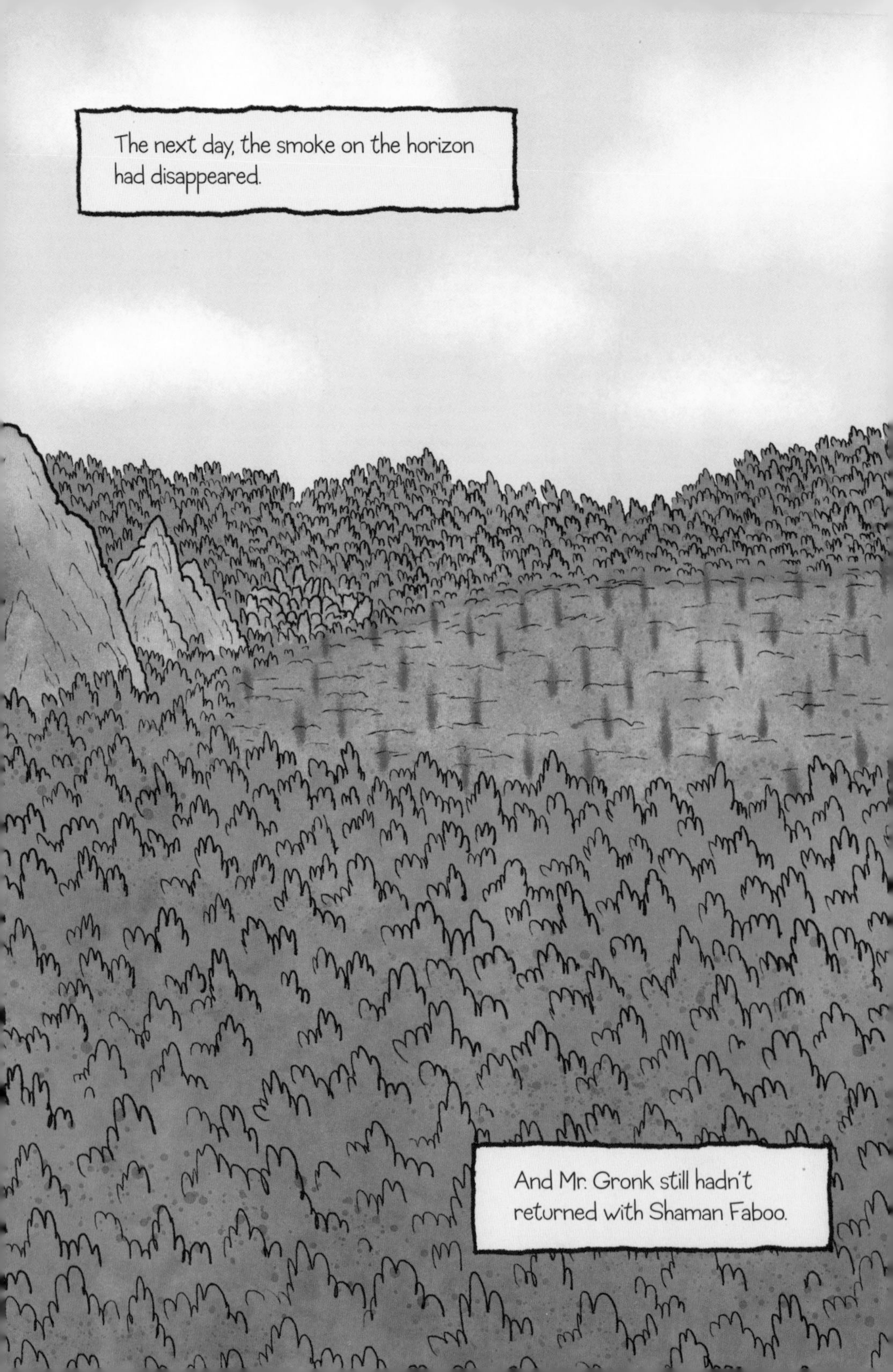
The next day, the smoke on the horizon had disappeared.
And Mr. Gronk still hadn't returned with Shaman Faboo.

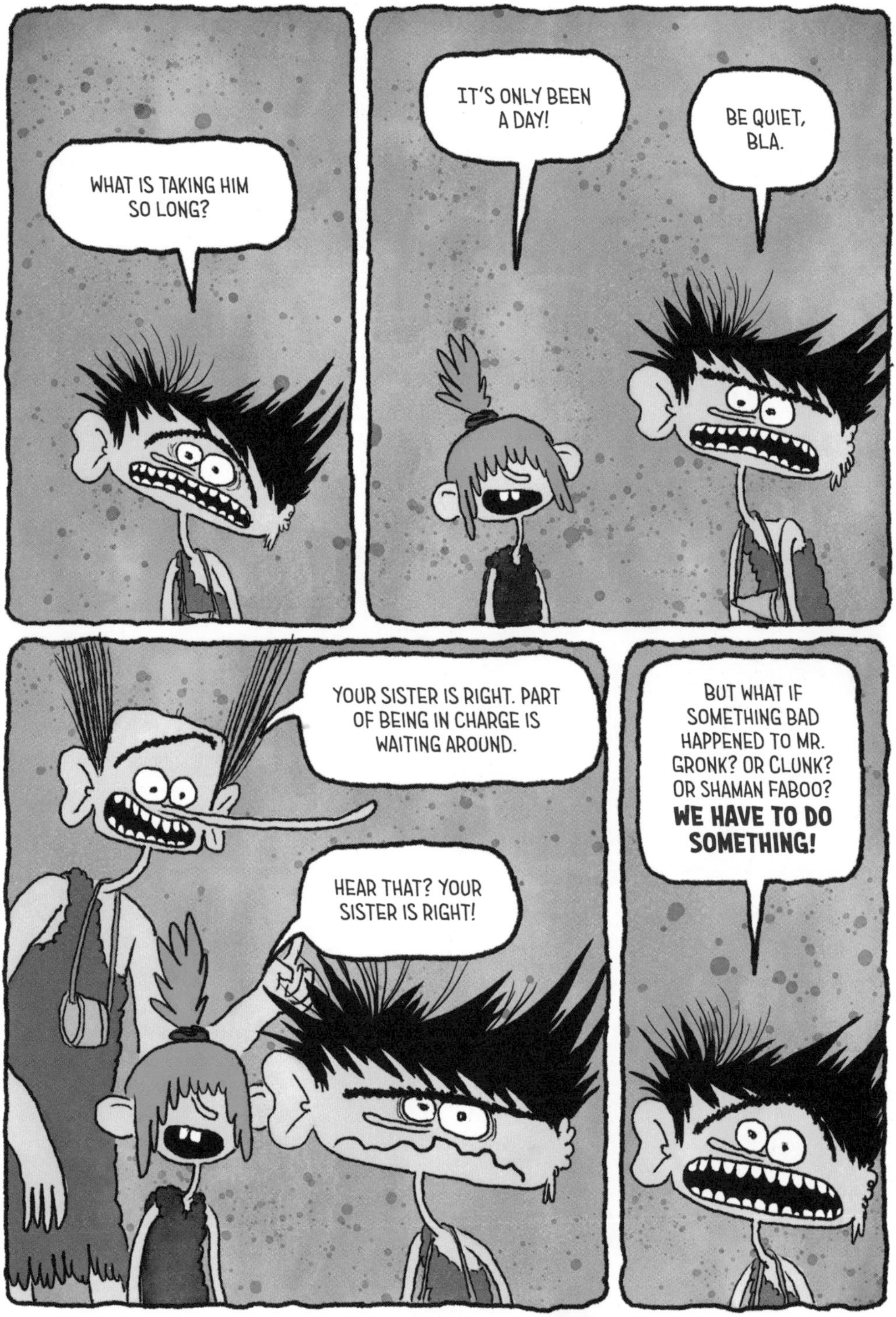
WHAT IS TAKING HIM SO LONG?
IT'S ONLY BEEN A DAY!
BE QUIET, BLA.
YOUR SISTER IS RIGHT. PART OF BEING IN CHARGE IS WAITING AROUND.
HEAR THAT? YOUR SISTER IS RIGHT!
BUT WHAT IF SOMETHING BAD HAPPENED TO MR. GRONK? OR CLUNK? OR SHAMAN FABOO? **WE HAVE TO DO SOMETHING!**

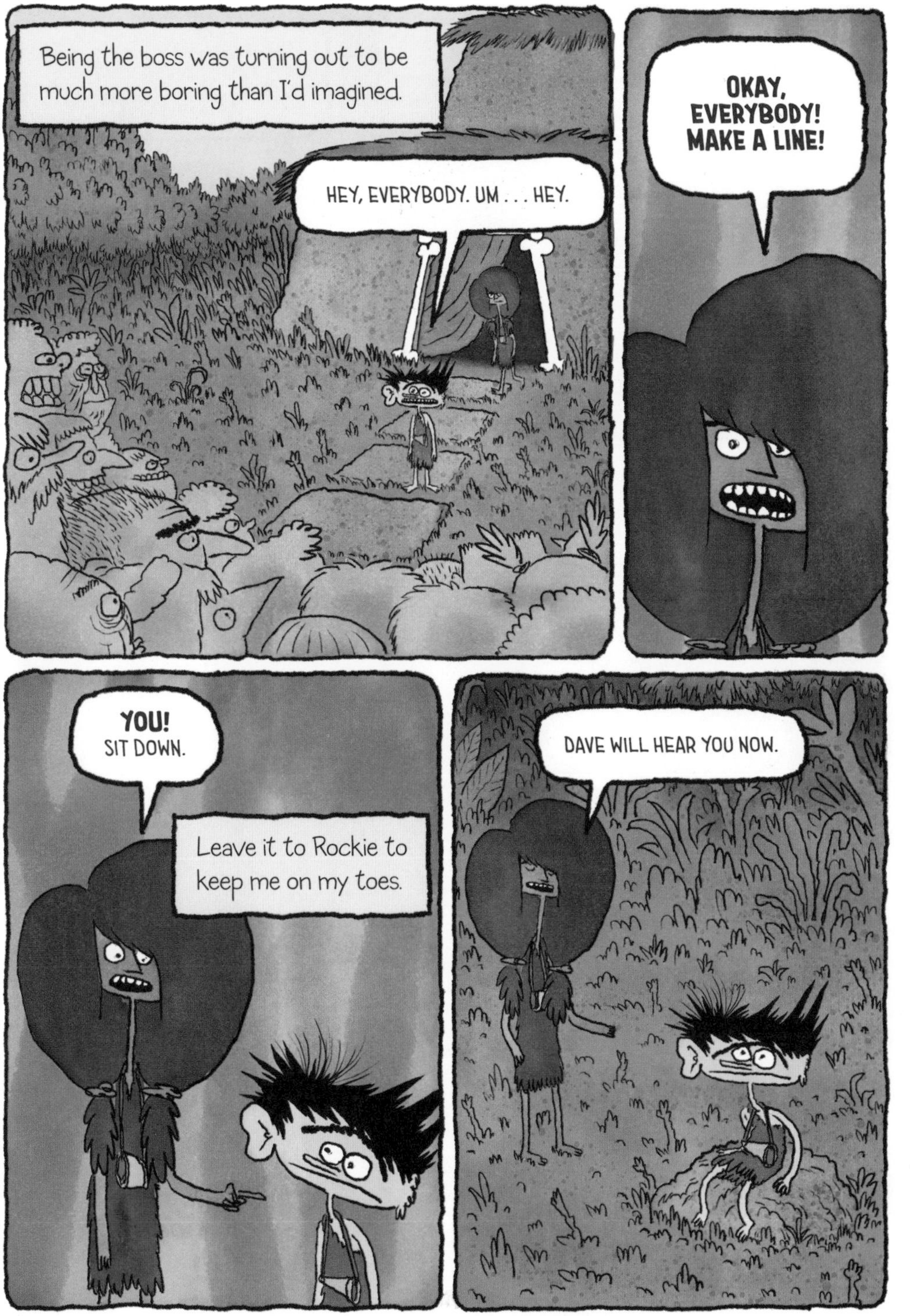
Being the boss was turning out to be much more boring than I'd imagined.
HEY, EVERYBODY. UM . . . HEY.
OKAY, EVERYBODY! MAKE A LINE!
YOU! SIT DOWN.
Leave it to Rockie to keep me on my toes.
DAVE WILL HEAR YOU NOW.

NO, SON. YOU HAVE TO PUNISH HIM.

WHAT? FOR MUSTACHES?

HE RUINED MR. STONEWALL'S PROPERTY.

YEAH, BUT IN A SLIGHTLY HILARIOUS WAY.

SO . . . ARE WE DONE WITH THIS ONE?

PLUS, HE FEELS TERRIBLE ABOUT IT. DON'T YOU, GAK?

TERRIBLE.

SEE?

IT'S YOUR JOB, BOY.

I DON'T KNOW. YOU'RE KIND OF THINKING LIKE A DAD, DAD.

BUT, DAVE!

LET'S ASK ROCKIE.

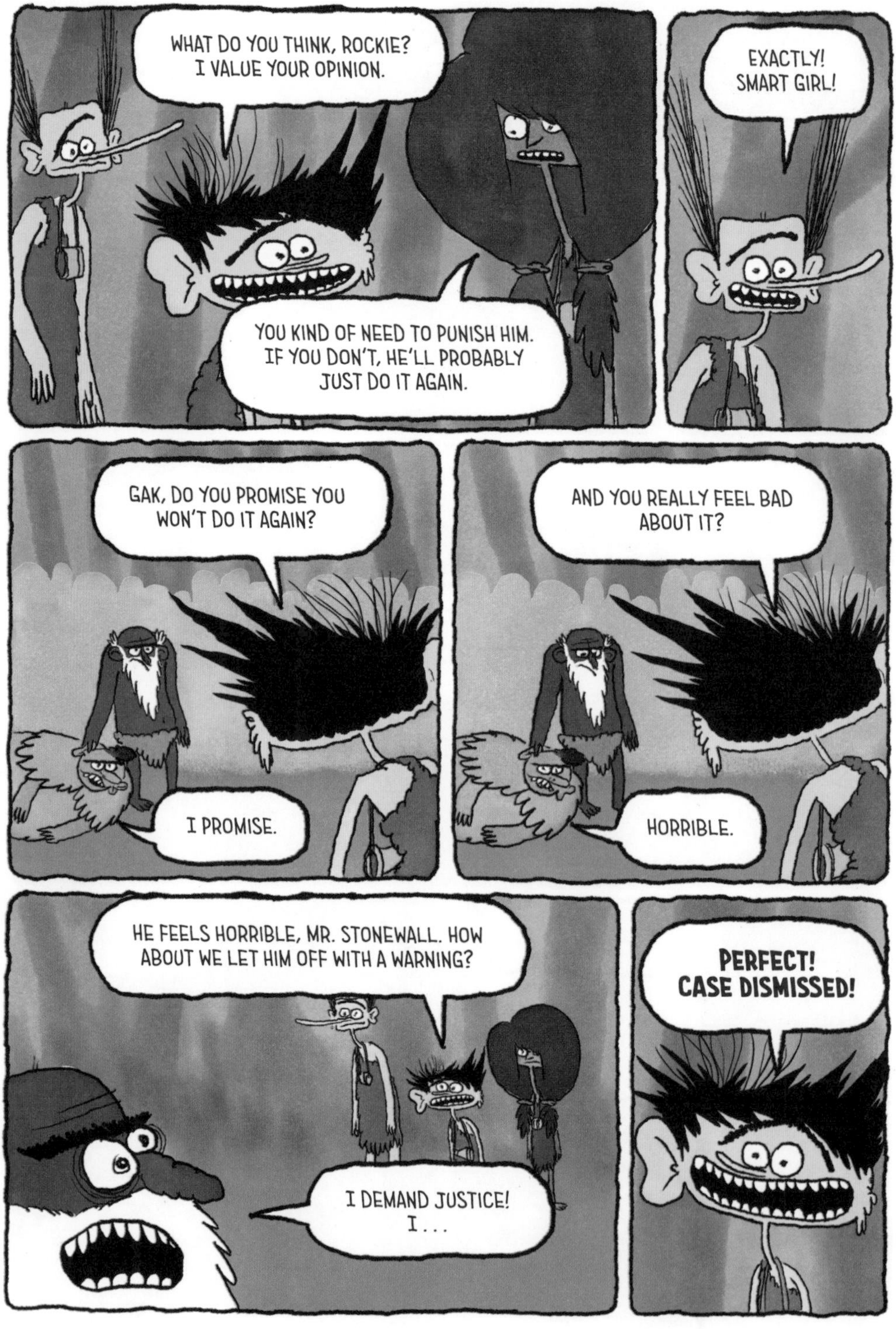
WHAT DO YOU THINK, ROCKIE?
I VALUE YOUR OPINION.
YOU KIND OF NEED TO PUNISH HIM. IF YOU DON'T, HE'LL PROBABLY JUST DO IT AGAIN.
EXACTLY! SMART GIRL!
GAK, DO YOU PROMISE YOU WON'T DO IT AGAIN?
I PROMISE.
AND YOU REALLY FEEL BAD ABOUT IT?
HORRIBLE.
HE FEELS HORRIBLE, MR. STONEWALL. HOW ABOUT WE LET HIM OFF WITH A WARNING?
I DEMAND JUSTICE! I . . .
PERFECT! CASE DISMISSED!

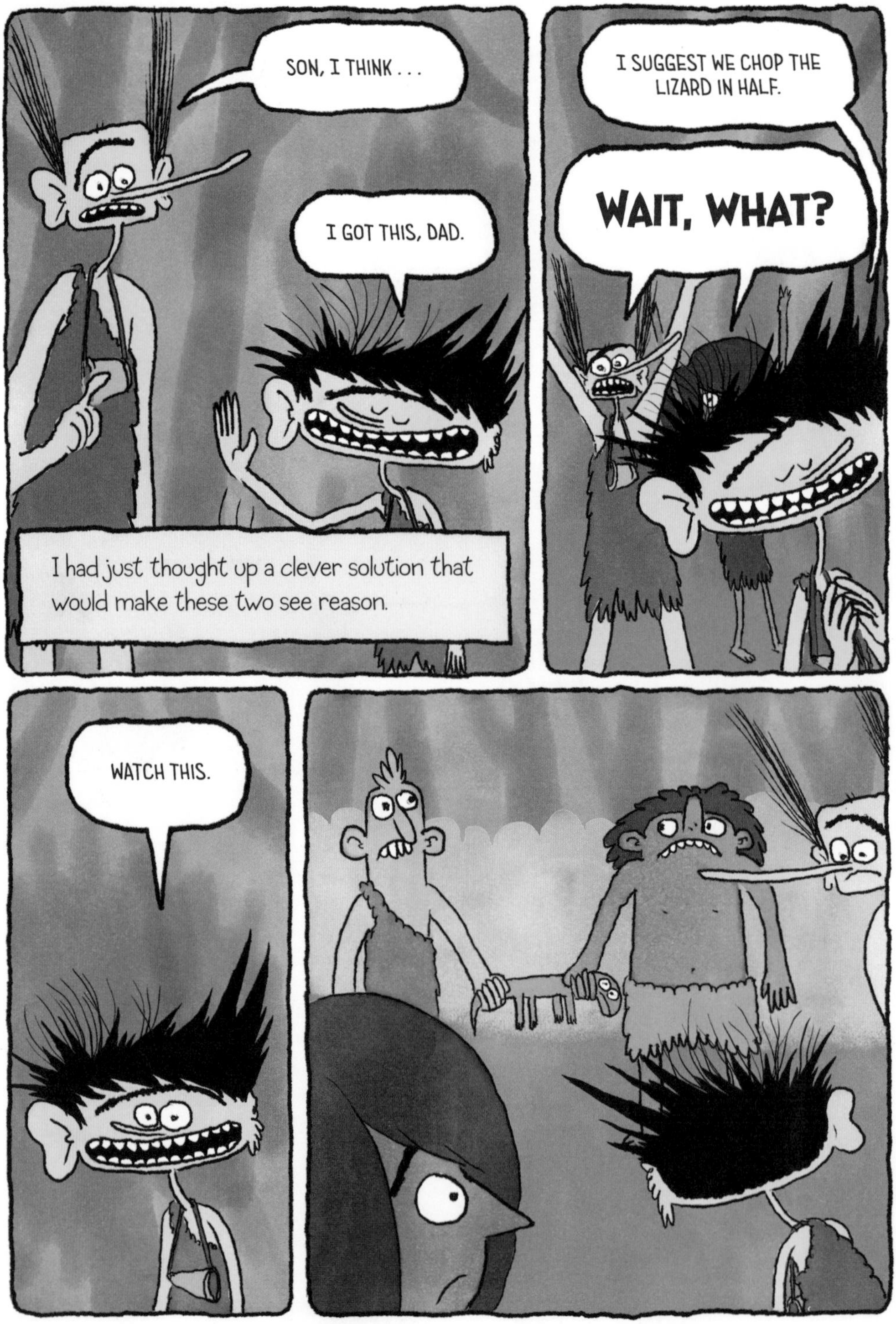

SON, I THINK . . .
I GOT THIS, DAD.
I had just thought up a clever solution that would make these two see reason.
I SUGGEST WE CHOP THE LIZARD IN HALF.
WAIT, WHAT?
WATCH THIS.

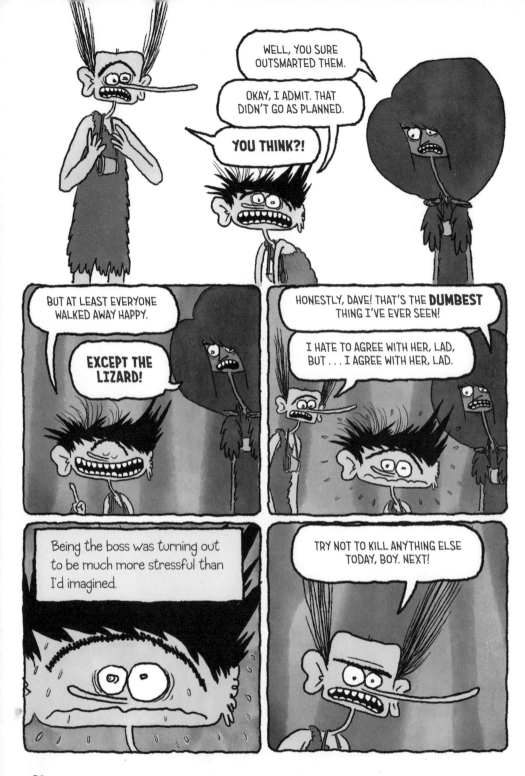

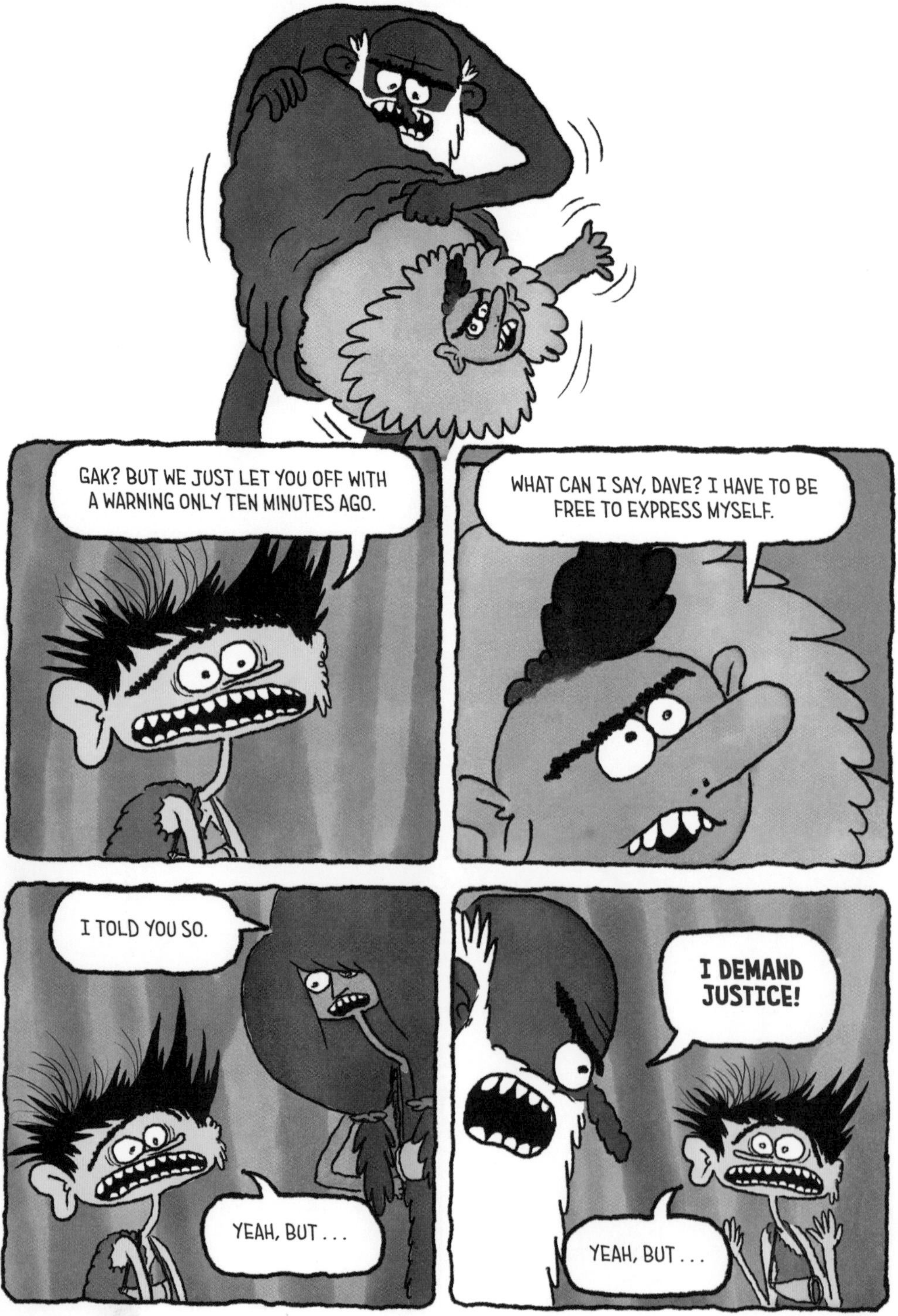
GAK? BUT WE JUST LET YOU OFF WITH A WARNING ONLY TEN MINUTES AGO.
WHAT CAN I SAY, DAVE? I HAVE TO BE FREE TO EXPRESS MYSELF.
I TOLD YOU SO.
YEAH, BUT . . .
I DEMAND JUSTICE!
YEAH, BUT . . .

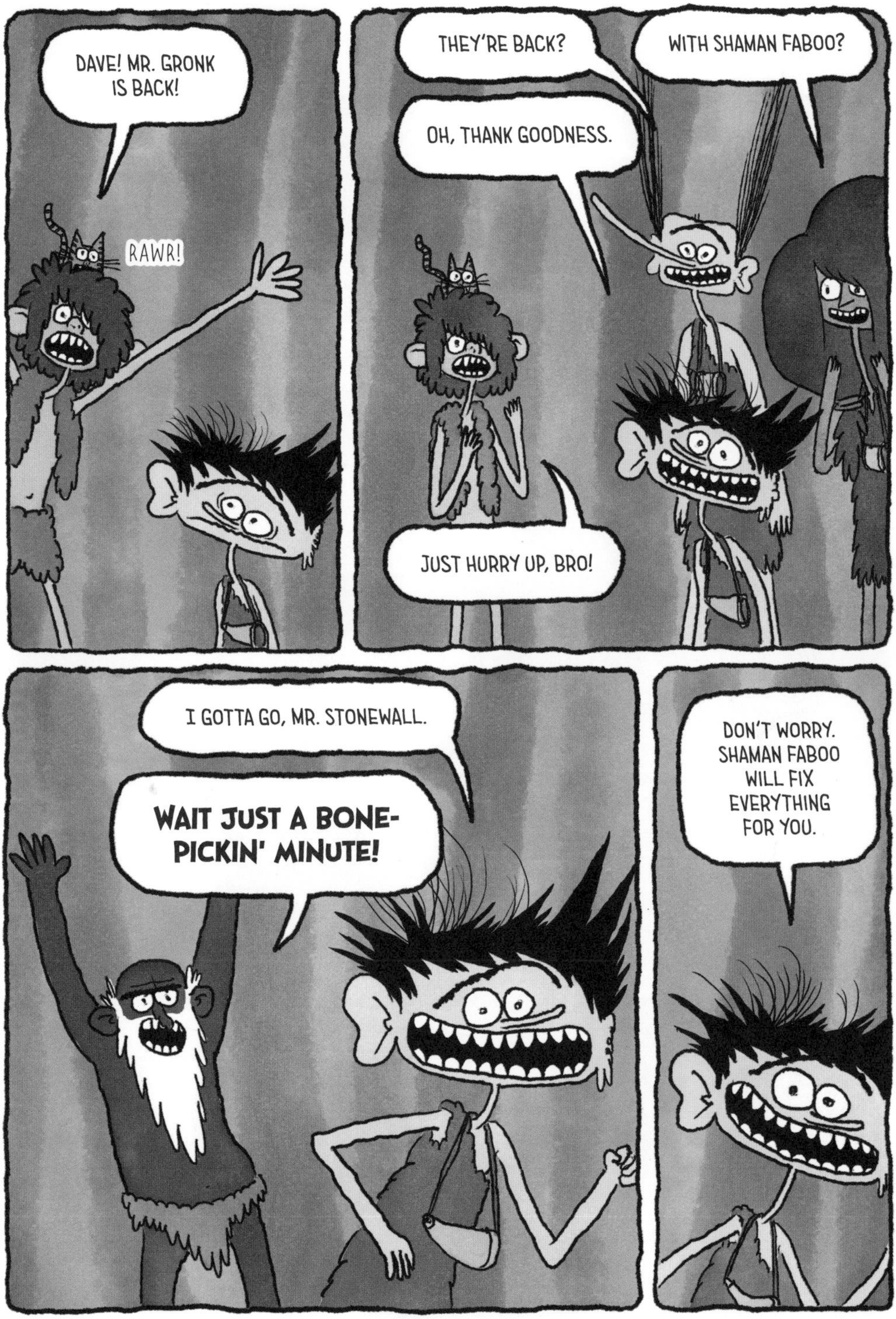
DAVE! MR. GRONK IS BACK!
RAWR!
THEY'RE BACK?
WITH SHAMAN FABOO?
OH, THANK GOODNESS.
JUST HURRY UP, BRO!
I GOTTA GO, MR. STONEWALL.
WAIT JUST A BONE-PICKIN' MINUTE!
DON'T WORRY. SHAMAN FABOO WILL FIX EVERYTHING FOR YOU.

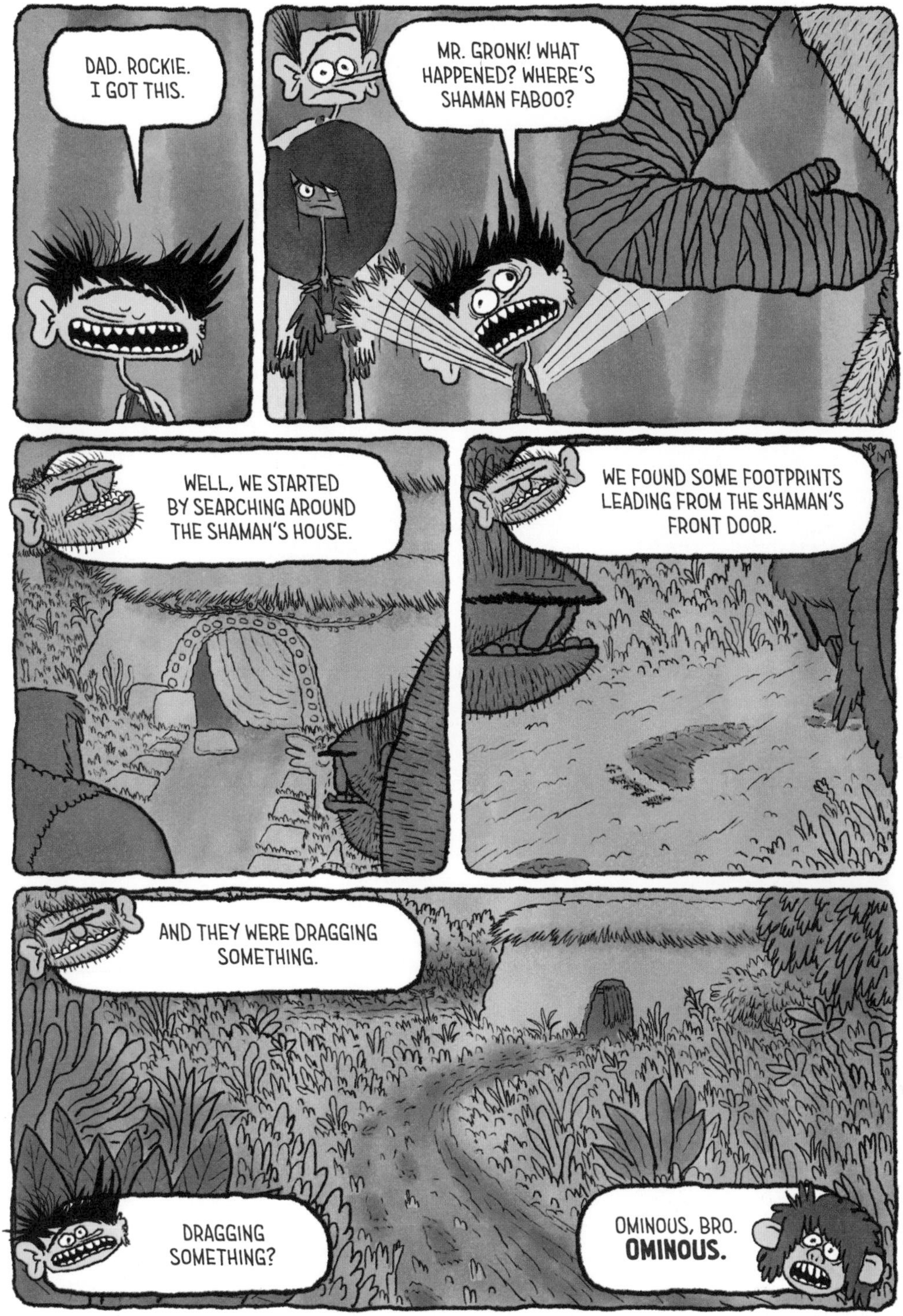
DAD. ROCKIE. I GOT THIS.
MR. GRONK! WHAT HAPPENED? WHERE'S SHAMAN FABOO?
WELL, WE STARTED BY SEARCHING AROUND THE SHAMAN'S HOUSE.
WE FOUND SOME FOOTPRINTS LEADING FROM THE SHAMAN'S FRONT DOOR.
AND THEY WERE DRAGGING SOMETHING.
DRAGGING SOMETHING?
OMINOUS, BRO. **OMINOUS.**

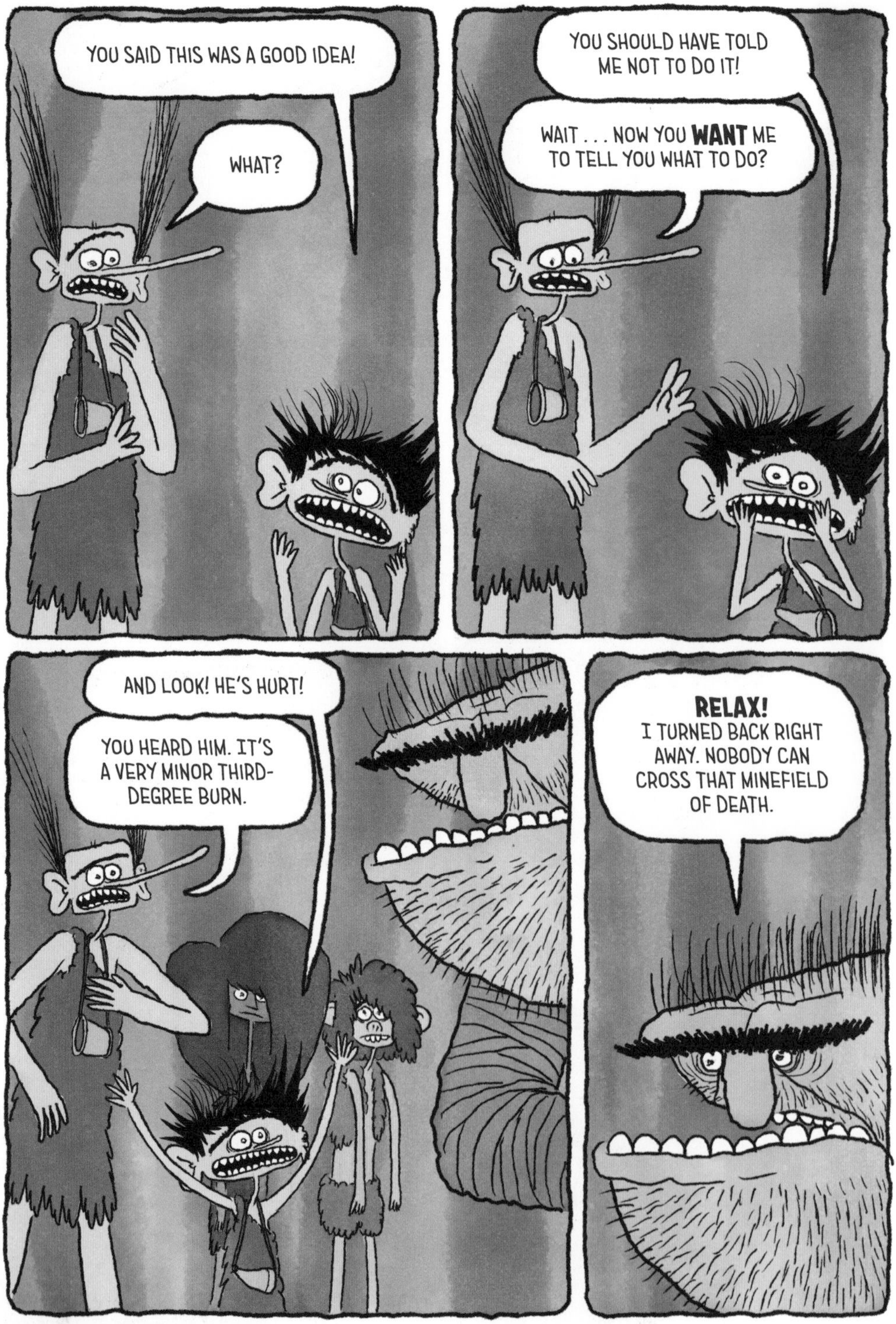
YOU SAID THIS WAS A GOOD IDEA!
WHAT?
YOU SHOULD HAVE TOLD ME NOT TO DO IT!
WAIT . . . NOW YOU **WANT** ME TO TELL YOU WHAT TO DO?
AND LOOK! HE'S HURT!
YOU HEARD HIM. IT'S A VERY MINOR THIRD-DEGREE BURN.
RELAX! I TURNED BACK RIGHT AWAY. NOBODY CAN CROSS THAT MINEFIELD OF DEATH.

91

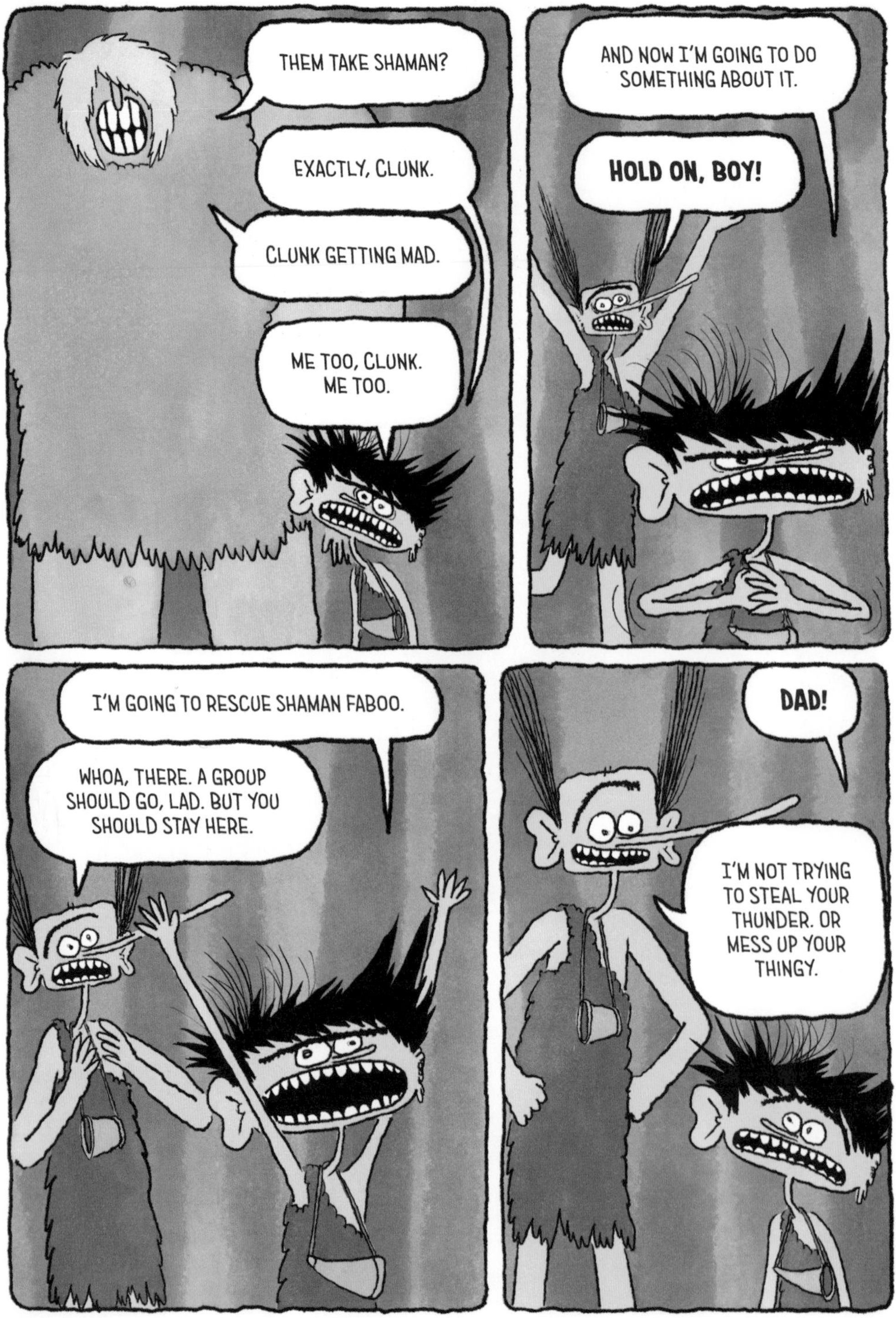

THEM TAKE SHAMAN?
EXACTLY, CLUNK.
CLUNK GETTING MAD.
ME TOO, CLUNK. ME TOO.
AND NOW I'M GOING TO DO SOMETHING ABOUT IT.
HOLD ON, BOY!
I'M GOING TO RESCUE SHAMAN FABOO.
WHOA, THERE. A GROUP SHOULD GO, LAD. BUT YOU SHOULD STAY HERE.
DAD!
I'M NOT TRYING TO STEAL YOUR THUNDER. OR MESS UP YOUR THINGY.

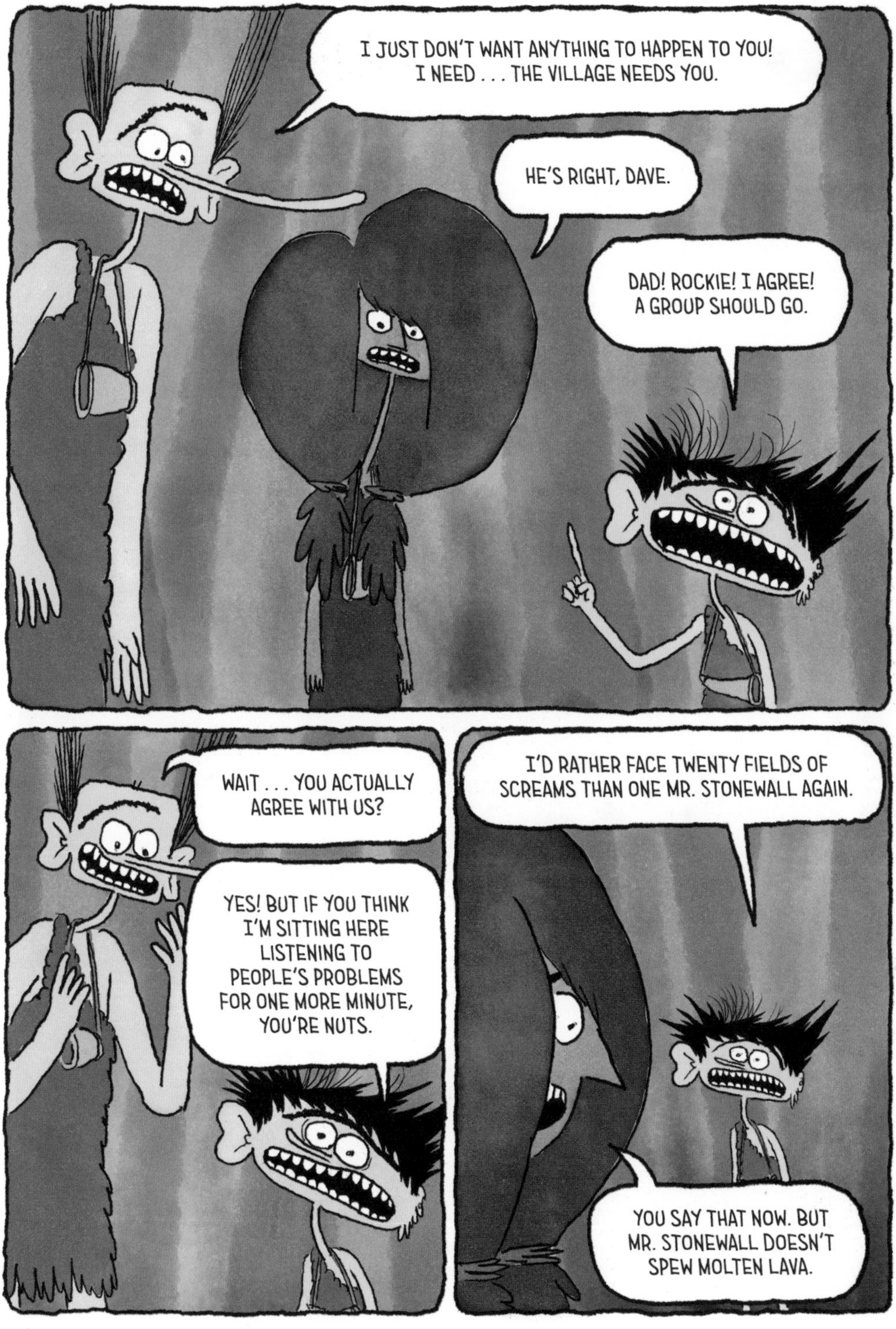
I JUST DON'T WANT ANYTHING TO HAPPEN TO YOU! I NEED . . . THE VILLAGE NEEDS YOU.
HE'S RIGHT, DAVE.
DAD! ROCKIE! I AGREE! A GROUP SHOULD GO.
WAIT . . . YOU ACTUALLY AGREE WITH US?
YES! BUT IF YOU THINK I'M SITTING HERE LISTENING TO PEOPLE'S PROBLEMS FOR ONE MORE MINUTE, YOU'RE NUTS.
I'D RATHER FACE TWENTY FIELDS OF SCREAMS THAN ONE MR. STONEWALL AGAIN.
YOU SAY THAT NOW. BUT MR. STONEWALL DOESN'T SPEW MOLTEN LAVA.

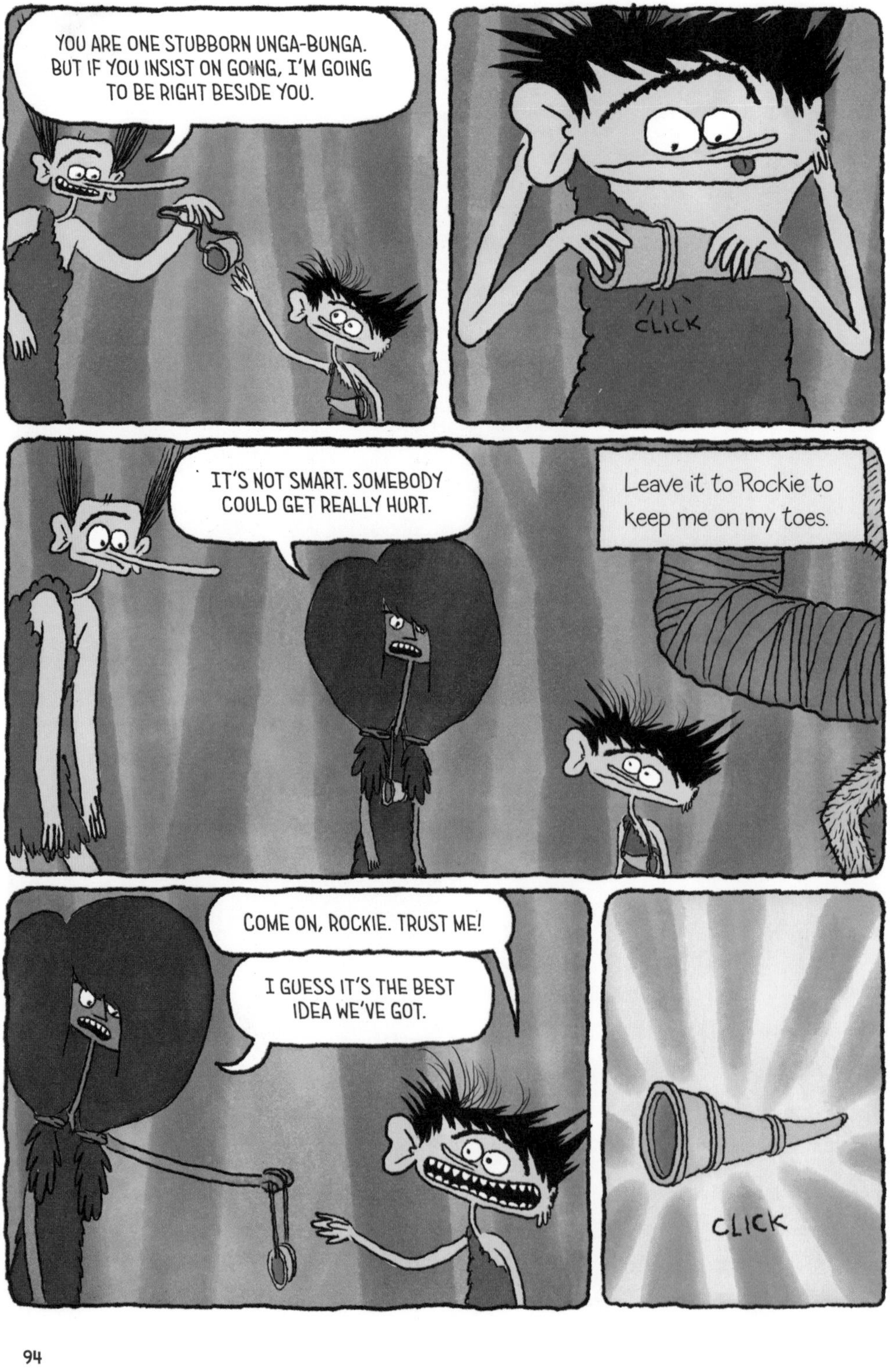
YOU ARE ONE STUBBORN UNGA-BUNGA. BUT IF YOU INSIST ON GOING, I'M GOING TO BE RIGHT BESIDE YOU.
CLICK
IT'S NOT SMART. SOMEBODY COULD GET REALLY HURT.
Leave it to Rockie to keep me on my toes.
COME ON, ROCKIE. TRUST ME!
I GUESS IT'S THE BEST IDEA WE'VE GOT.
CLICK

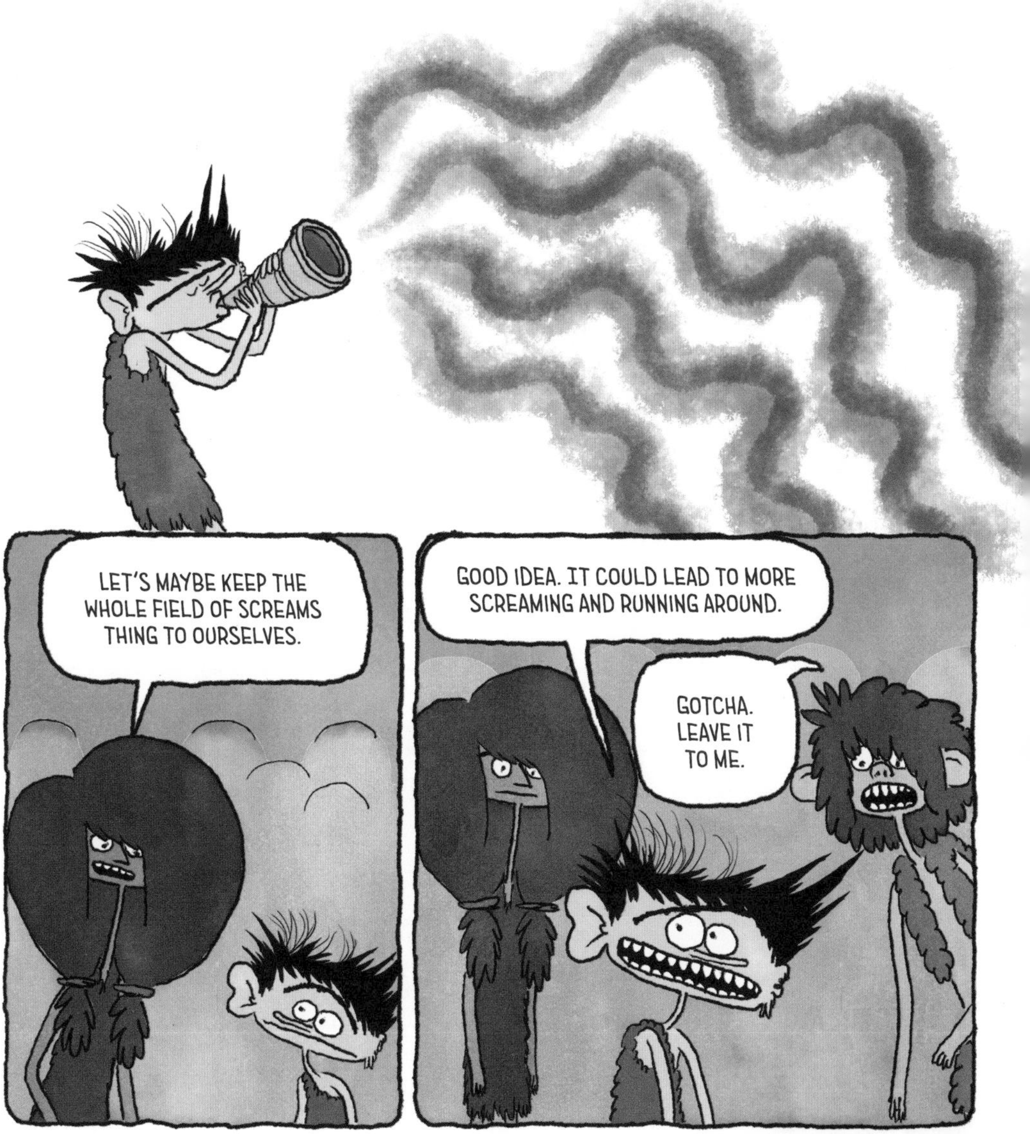
LET'S MAYBE KEEP THE WHOLE FIELD OF SCREAMS THING TO OURSELVES.
GOOD IDEA. IT COULD LEAD TO MORE SCREAMING AND RUNNING AROUND.
GOTCHA. LEAVE IT TO ME.

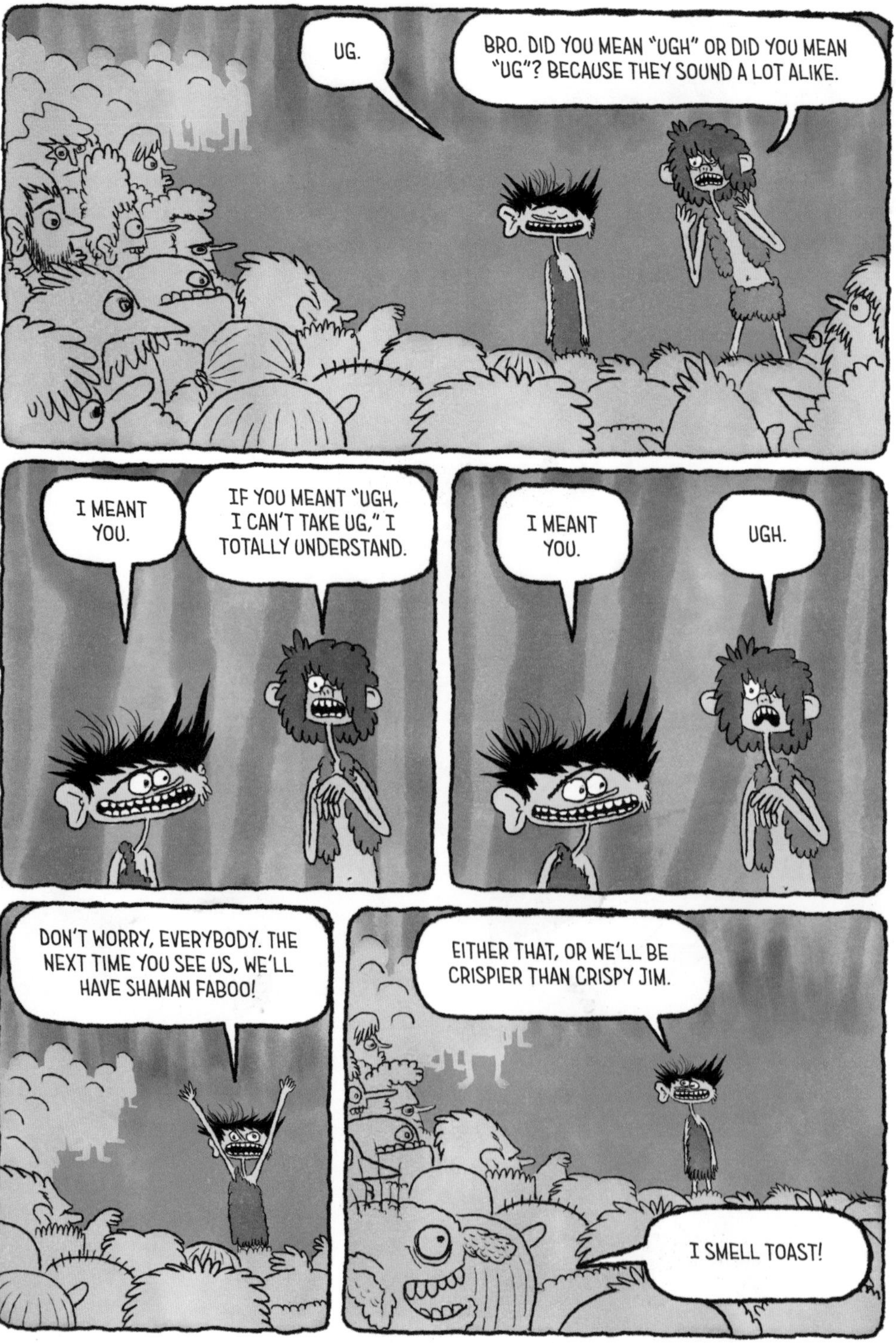
UG.
BRO. DID YOU MEAN "UGH" OR DID YOU MEAN "UG"? BECAUSE THEY SOUND A LOT ALIKE.
I MEANT YOU.
IF YOU MEANT "UGH, I CAN'T TAKE UG," I TOTALLY UNDERSTAND.
I MEANT YOU.
UGH.
DON'T WORRY, EVERYBODY. THE NEXT TIME YOU SEE US, WE'LL HAVE SHAMAN FABOO!
EITHER THAT, OR WE'LL BE CRISPIER THAN CRISPY JIM.
I SMELL TOAST!

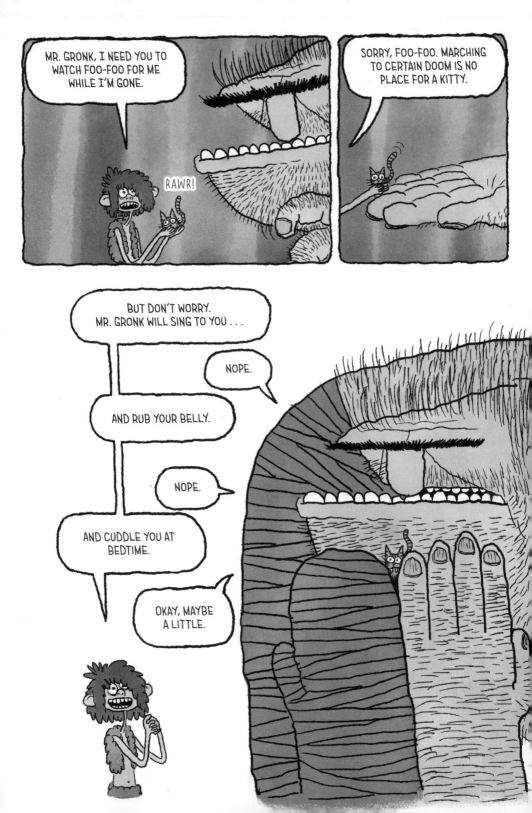

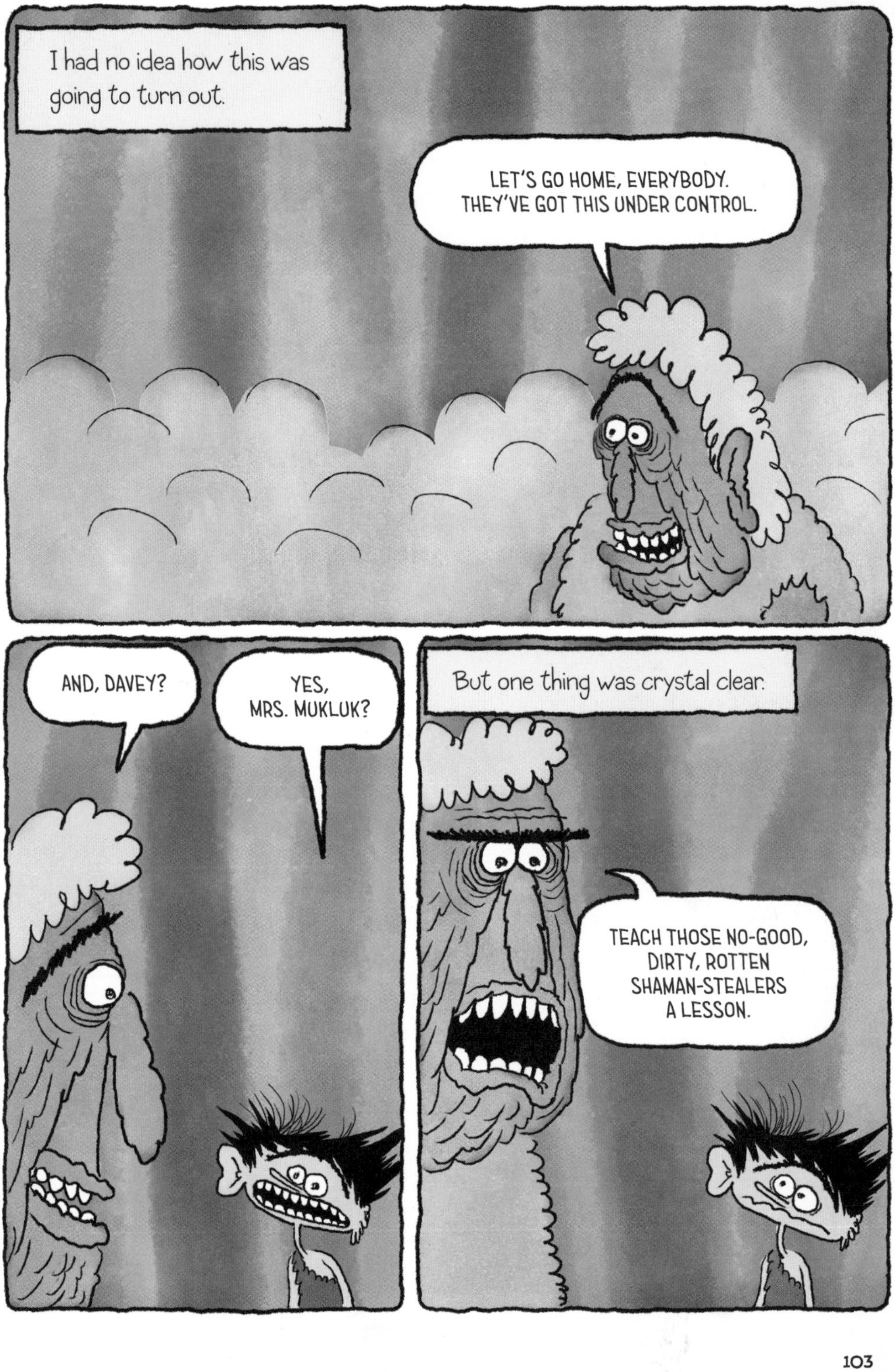
I had no idea how this was going to turn out.
LET'S GO HOME, EVERYBODY. THEY'VE GOT THIS UNDER CONTROL.
AND, DAVEY?
YES, MRS. MUKLUK?
But one thing was crystal clear.
TEACH THOSE NO-GOOD, DIRTY, ROTTEN SHAMAN-STEALERS A LESSON.

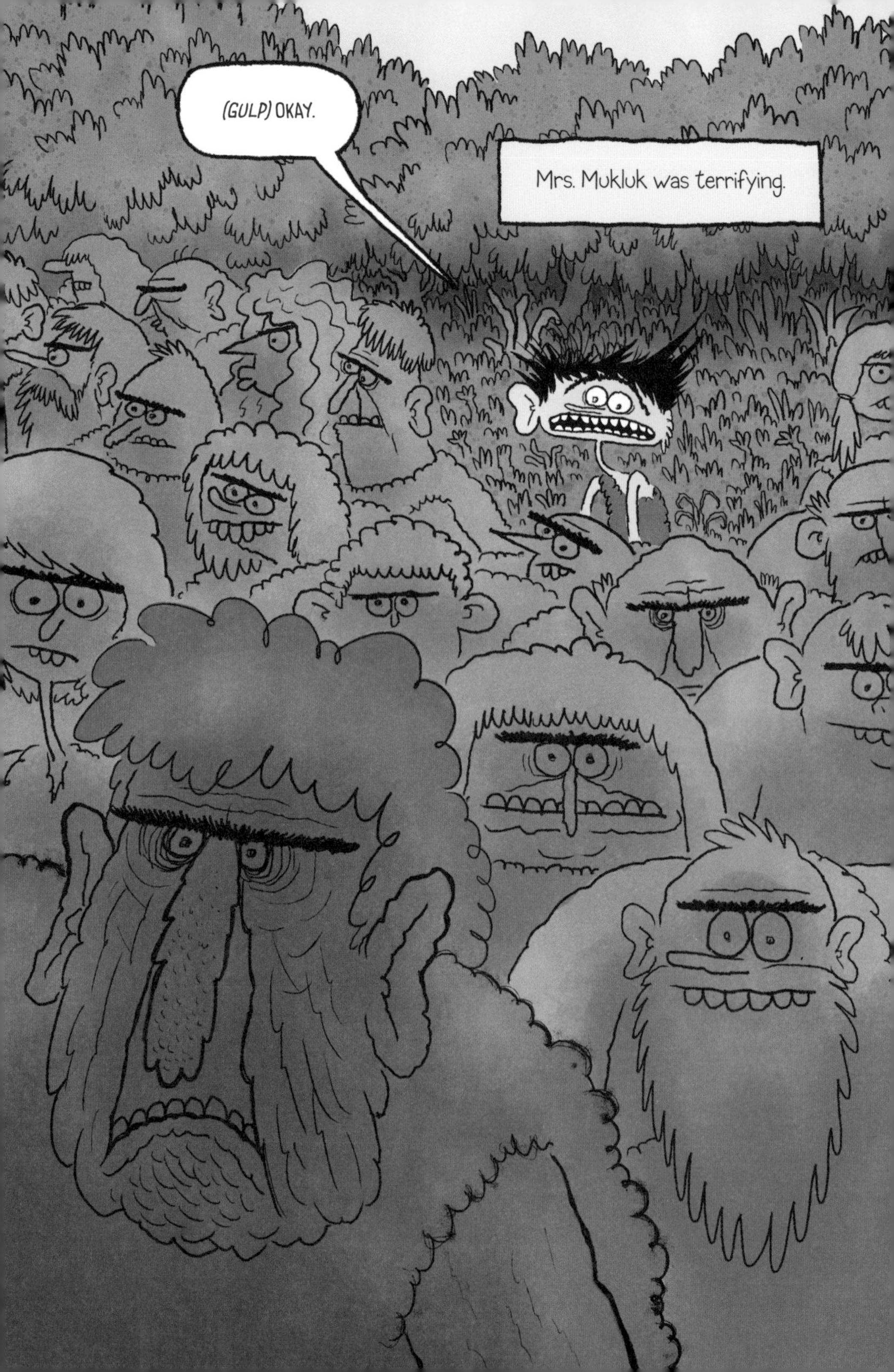
(GULP) OKAY.
Mrs. Mukluk was terrifying.

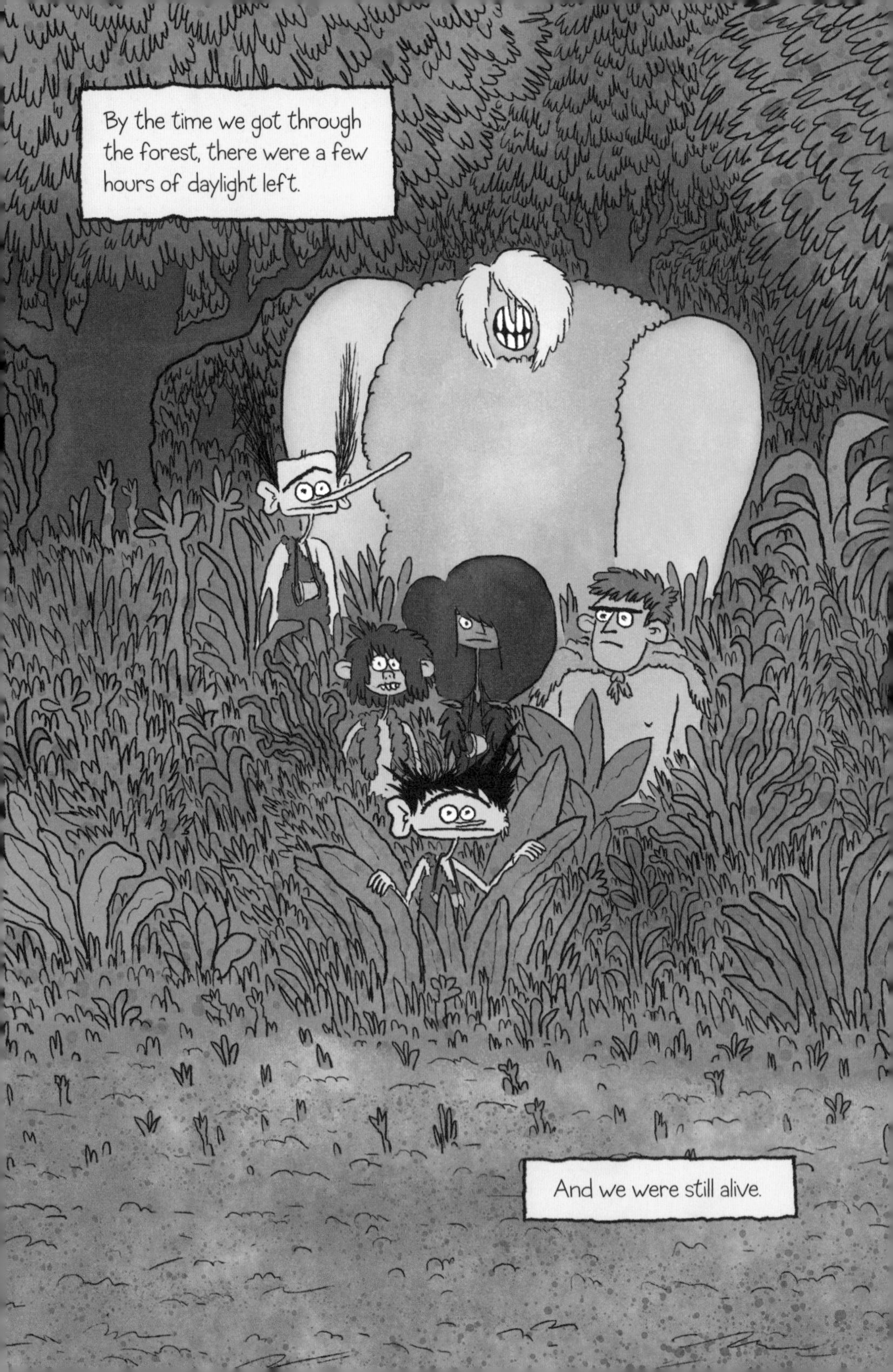
By the time we got through the forest, there were a few hours of daylight left.
And we were still alive.

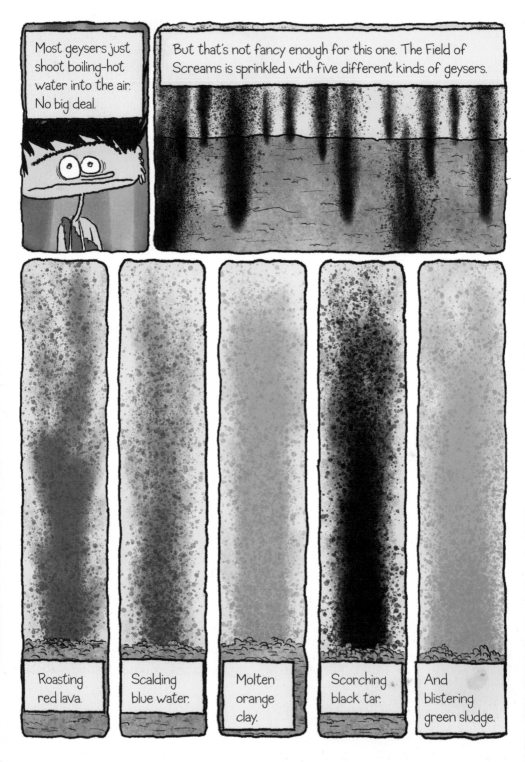

Most geysers just shoot boiling-hot water into the air. No big deal.

But that's not fancy enough for this one. The Field of Screams is sprinkled with five different kinds of geysers.

Roasting red lava.

Scalding blue water.

Molten orange clay.

Scorching black tar.

And blistering green sludge.

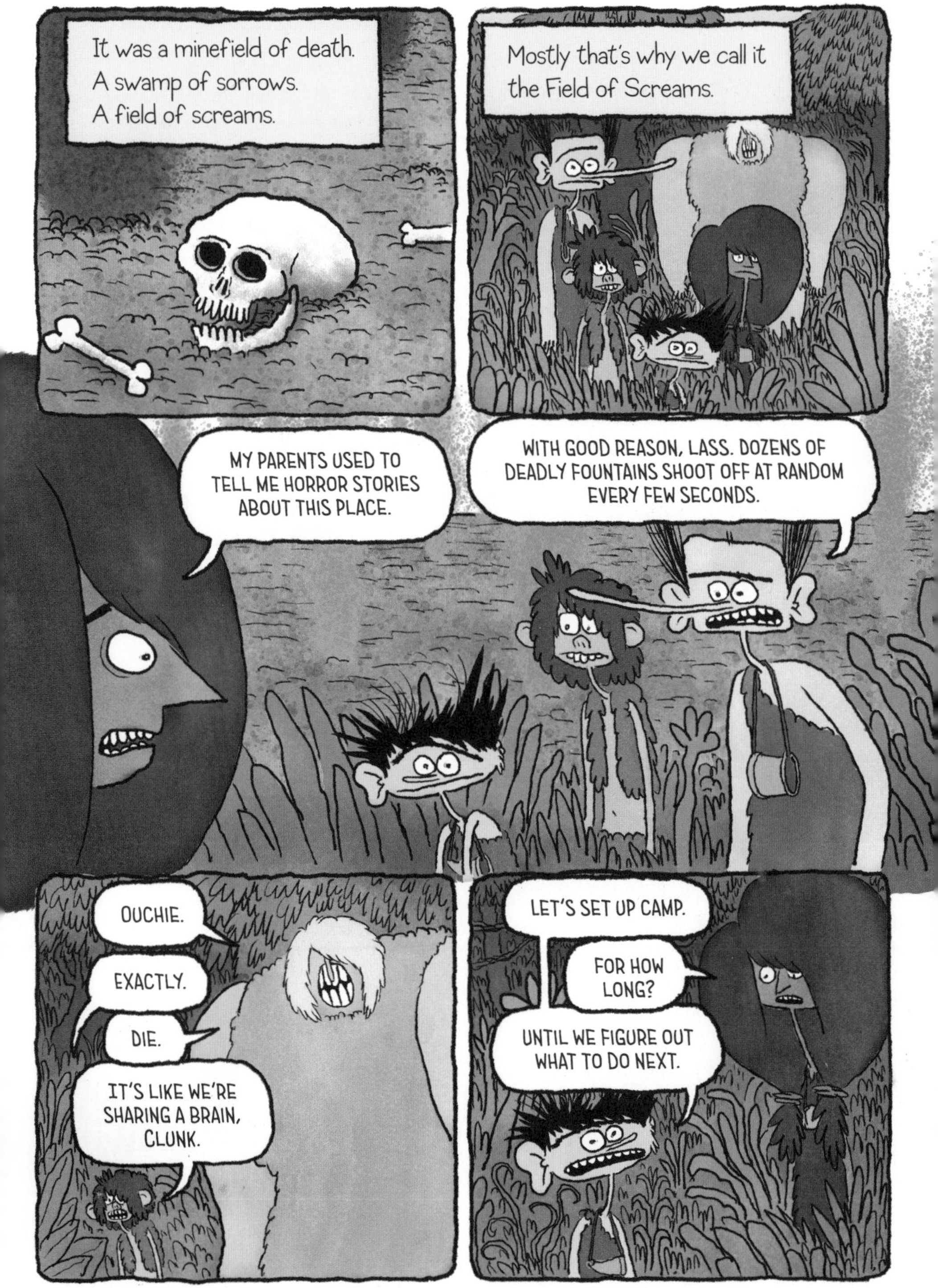
It was a minefield of death.
A swamp of sorrows.
A field of screams.
Mostly that's why we call it the Field of Screams.
MY PARENTS USED TO TELL ME HORROR STORIES ABOUT THIS PLACE.
WITH GOOD REASON, LASS. DOZENS OF DEADLY FOUNTAINS SHOOT OFF AT RANDOM EVERY FEW SECONDS.
OUCHIE.
EXACTLY.
DIE.
IT'S LIKE WE'RE SHARING A BRAIN, CLUNK.
LET'S SET UP CAMP.
FOR HOW LONG?
UNTIL WE FIGURE OUT WHAT TO DO NEXT.

I SAY WE GO AROUND.

AROUND? THAT WILL TAKE DAYS.

SITTING HERE IS TAKING DAYS.

MAYBE SHE'S RIGHT, MAN.

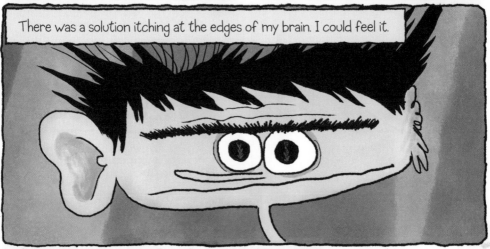

There was a solution itching at the edges of my brain. I could feel it.

Unless it was just dandruff.

LET'S GET REAL. THERE IS NO WAY WE'RE GOING TO MAKE IT ACROSS THIS THING.

THERE'S A WAY. I'LL FIGURE IT OUT.

I needed to think.

YOU JUST HAVE TO TRUST ME.

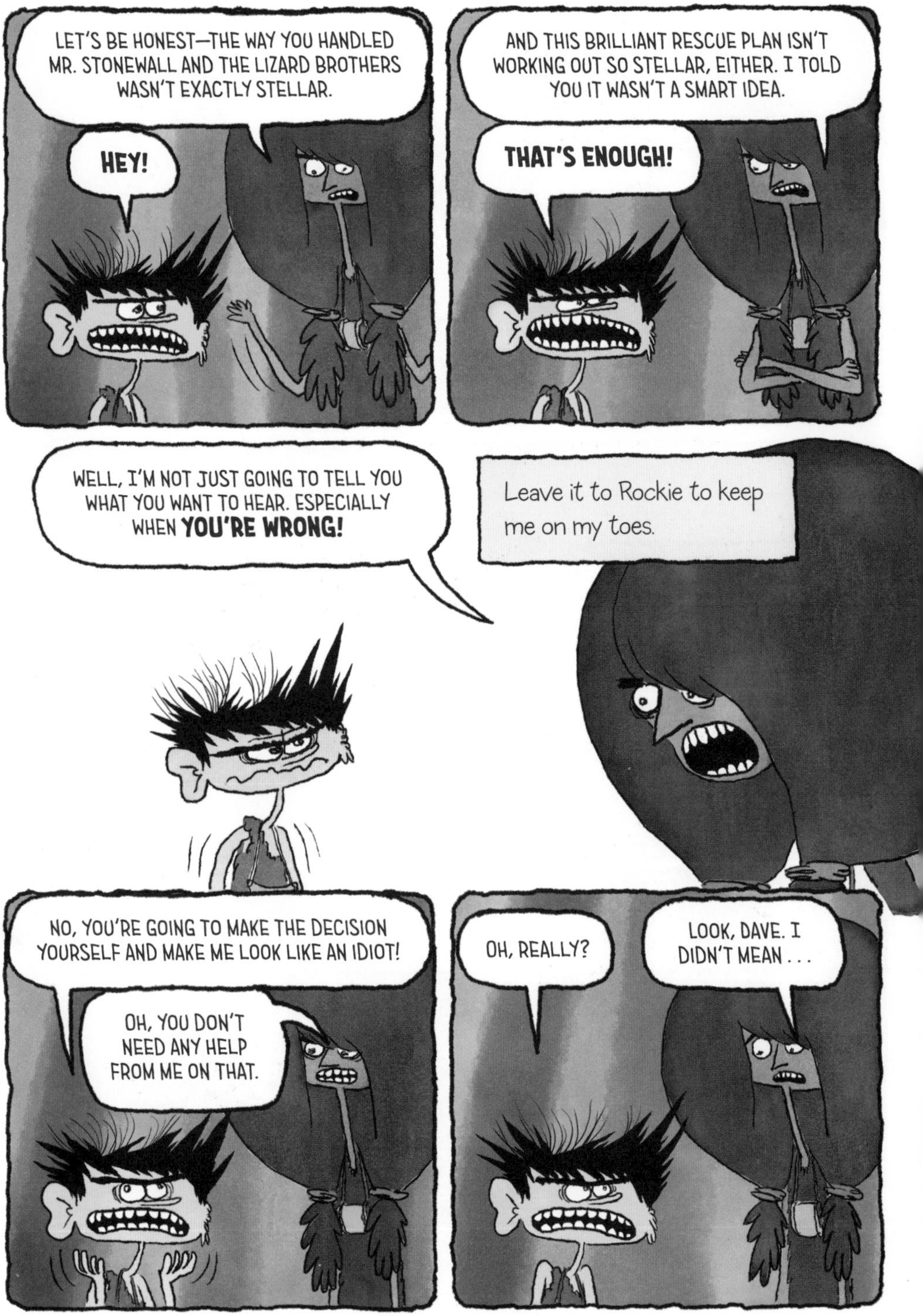

LET'S BE HONEST—THE WAY YOU HANDLED MR. STONEWALL AND THE LIZARD BROTHERS WASN'T EXACTLY STELLAR.
HEY!
AND THIS BRILLIANT RESCUE PLAN ISN'T WORKING OUT SO STELLAR, EITHER. I TOLD YOU IT WASN'T A SMART IDEA.
THAT'S ENOUGH!
WELL, I'M NOT JUST GOING TO TELL YOU WHAT YOU WANT TO HEAR. ESPECIALLY WHEN **YOU'RE WRONG!**
Leave it to Rockie to keep me on my toes.
NO, YOU'RE GOING TO MAKE THE DECISION YOURSELF AND MAKE ME LOOK LIKE AN IDIOT!
OH, YOU DON'T NEED ANY HELP FROM ME ON THAT.
OH, REALLY?
LOOK, DAVE. I DIDN'T MEAN . . .

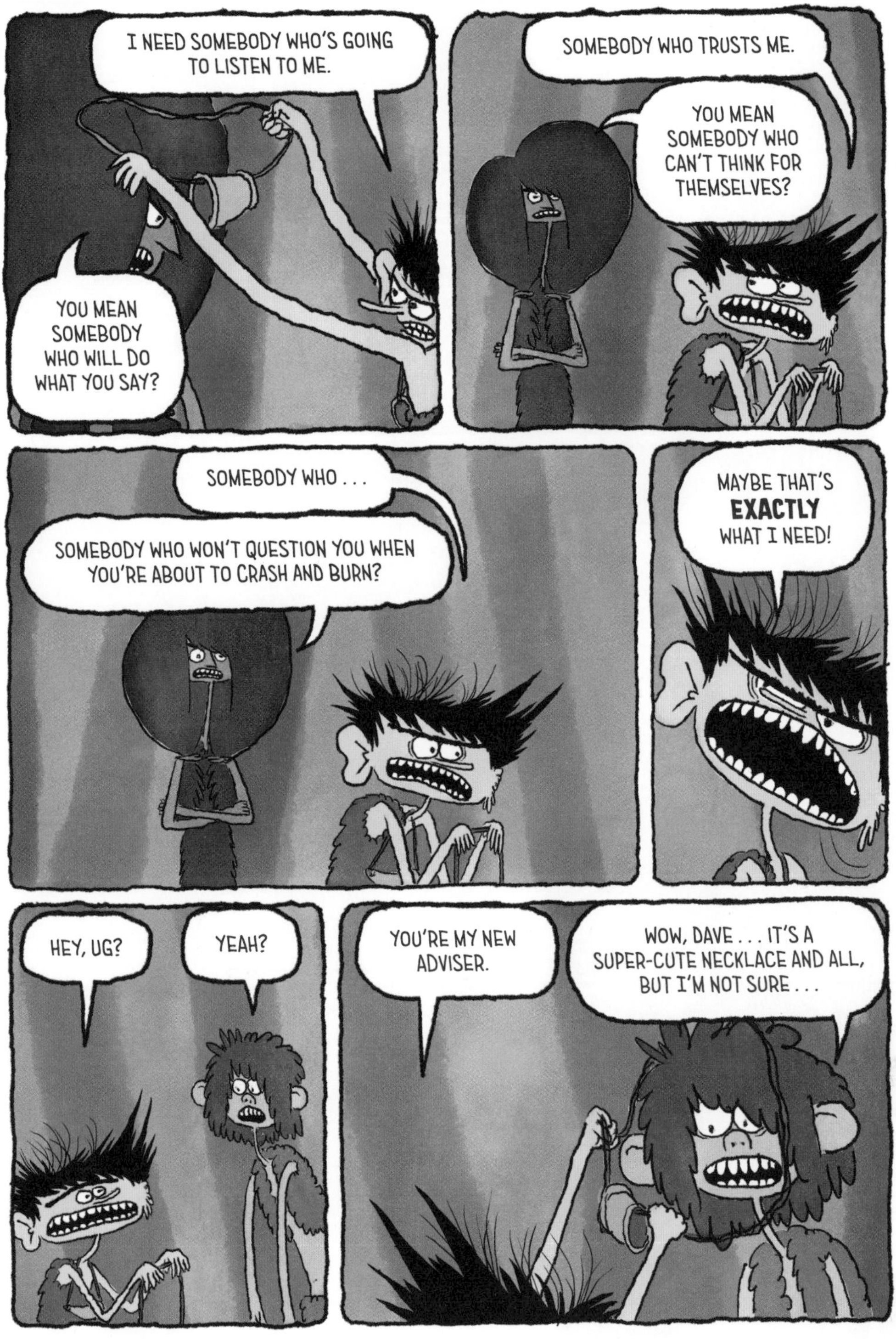
I NEED SOMEBODY WHO'S GOING TO LISTEN TO ME.
YOU MEAN SOMEBODY WHO WILL DO WHAT YOU SAY?
SOMEBODY WHO TRUSTS ME.
YOU MEAN SOMEBODY WHO CAN'T THINK FOR THEMSELVES?
SOMEBODY WHO . . .
SOMEBODY WHO WON'T QUESTION YOU WHEN YOU'RE ABOUT TO CRASH AND BURN?
MAYBE THAT'S **EXACTLY** WHAT I NEED!
HEY, UG?
YEAH?
YOU'RE MY NEW ADVISER.
WOW, DAVE . . . IT'S A SUPER-CUTE NECKLACE AND ALL, BUT I'M NOT SURE . . .

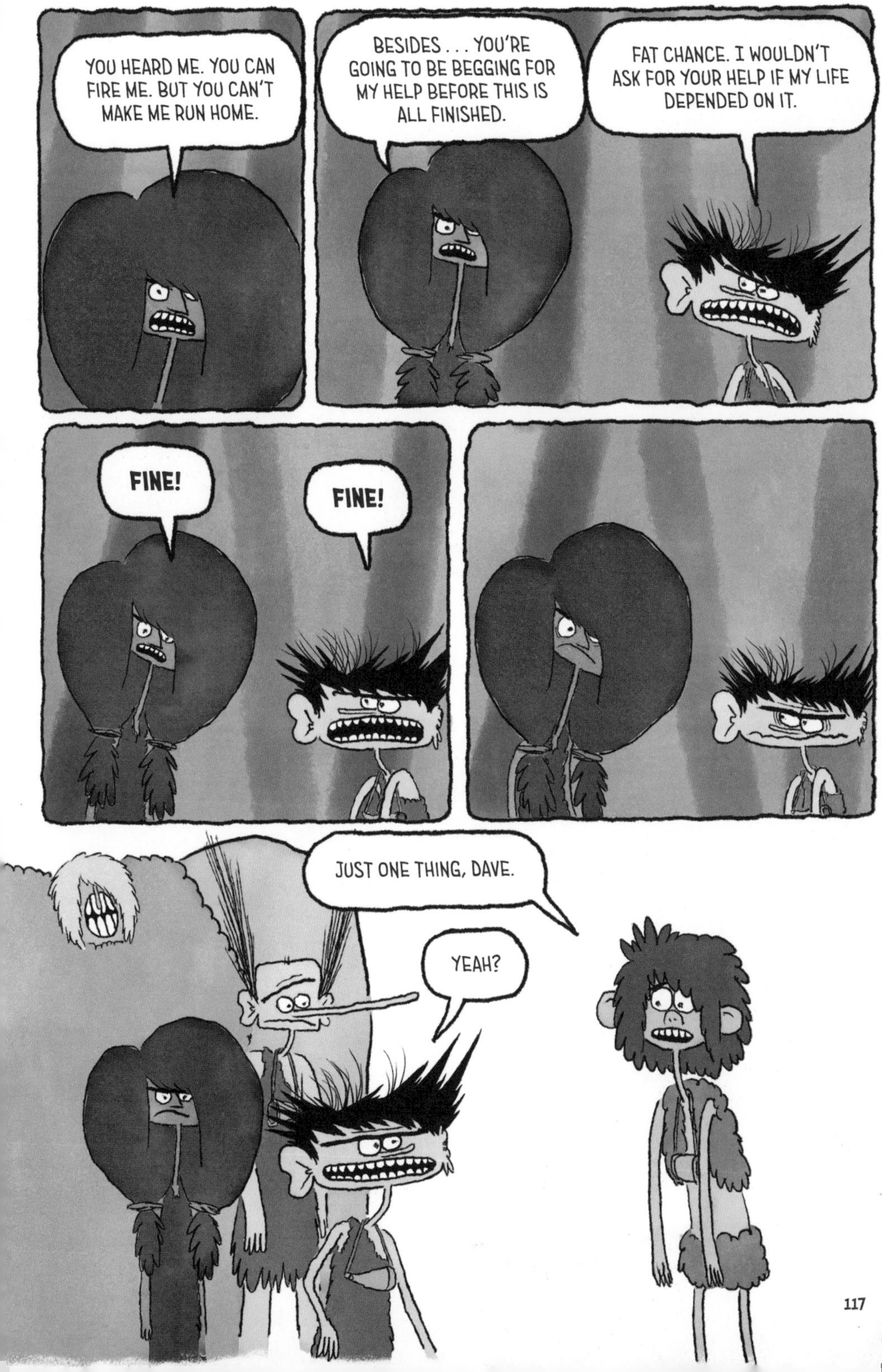
YOU HEARD ME. YOU CAN FIRE ME. BUT YOU CAN'T MAKE ME RUN HOME.
BESIDES . . . YOU'RE GOING TO BE BEGGING FOR MY HELP BEFORE THIS IS ALL FINISHED.
FAT CHANCE. I WOULDN'T ASK FOR YOUR HELP IF MY LIFE DEPENDED ON IT.
FINE!
FINE!
JUST ONE THING, DAVE.
YEAH?

121

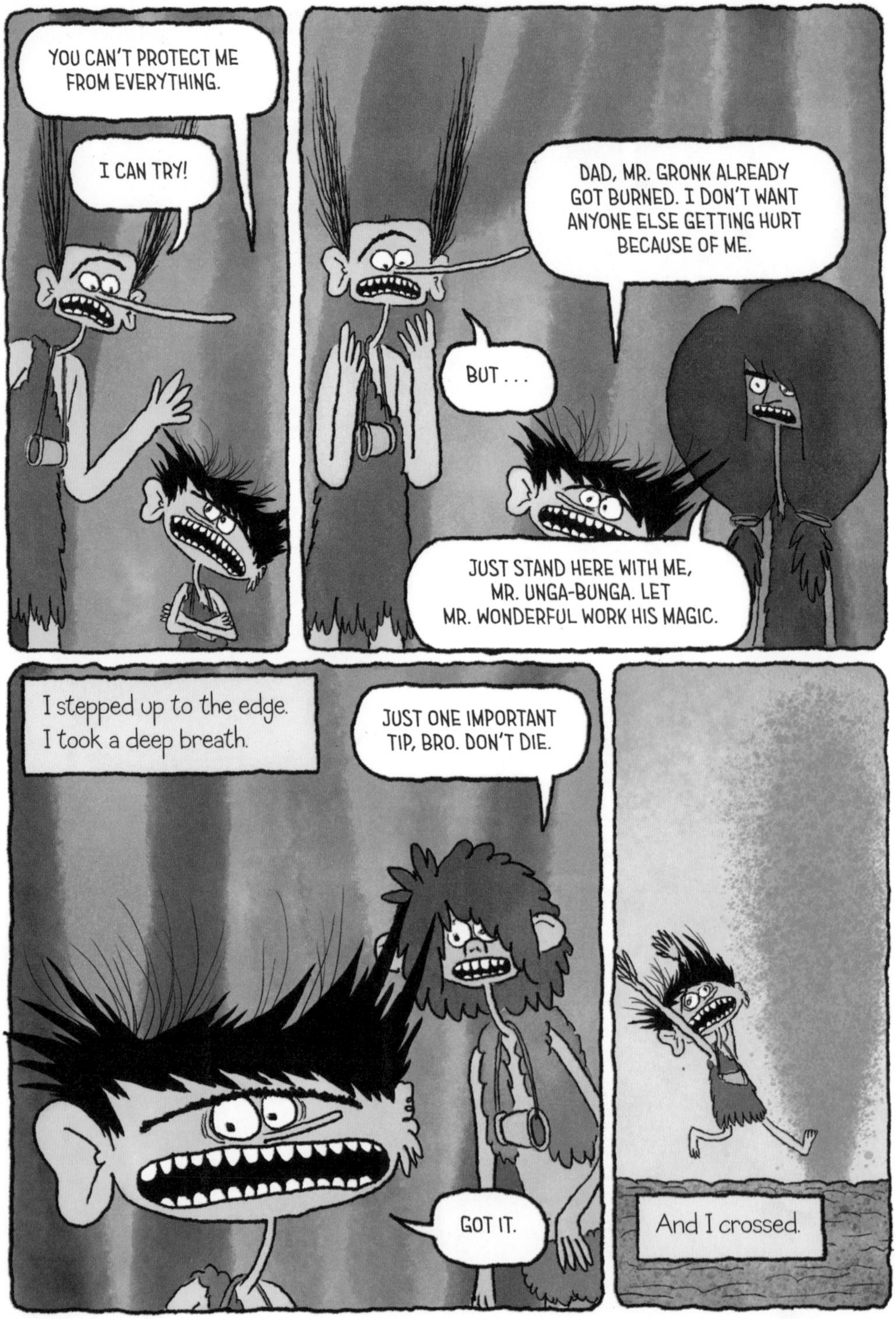
YOU CAN'T PROTECT ME FROM EVERYTHING.
I CAN TRY!
DAD, MR. GRONK ALREADY GOT BURNED. I DON'T WANT ANYONE ELSE GETTING HURT BECAUSE OF ME.
BUT . . .
JUST STAND HERE WITH ME, MR. UNGA-BUNGA. LET MR. WONDERFUL WORK HIS MAGIC.
I stepped up to the edge. I took a deep breath.
JUST ONE IMPORTANT TIP, BRO. DON'T DIE.
GOT IT.
And I crossed.

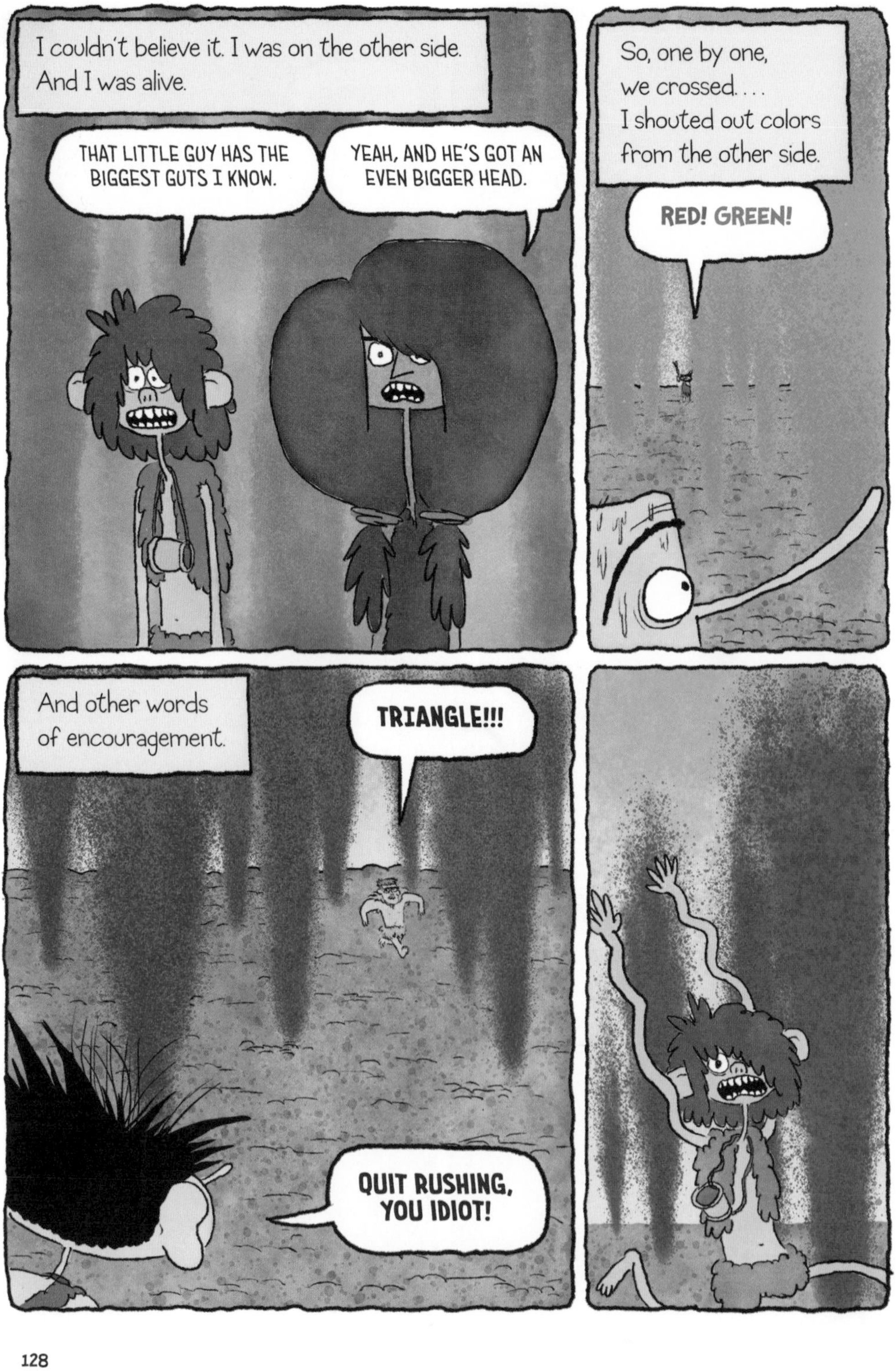

I couldn't believe it. I was on the other side. And I was alive.
THAT LITTLE GUY HAS THE BIGGEST GUTS I KNOW.
YEAH, AND HE'S GOT AN EVEN BIGGER HEAD.
So, one by one, we crossed. . . . I shouted out colors from the other side.
RED! GREEN!
And other words of encouragement.
TRIANGLE!!!
QUIT RUSHING, YOU IDIOT!

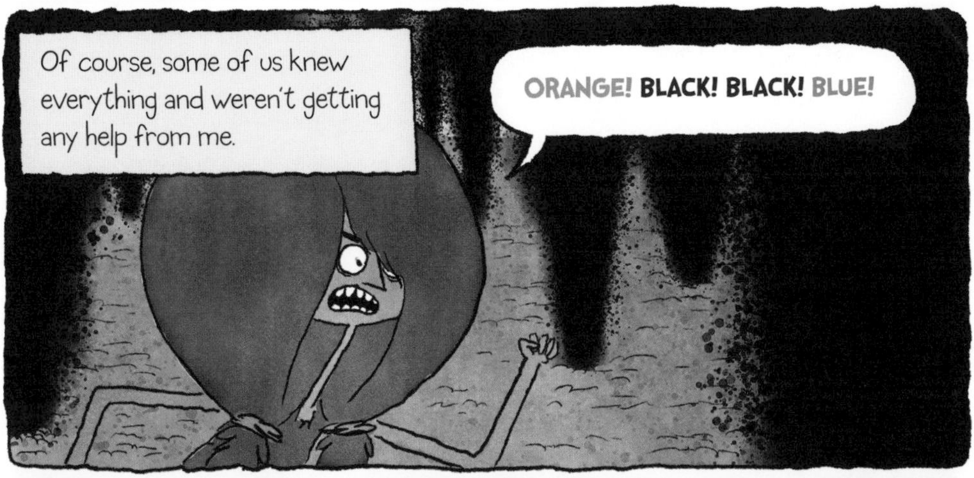
Of course, some of us knew everything and weren't getting any help from me.
ORANGE! BLACK! BLACK! BLUE!

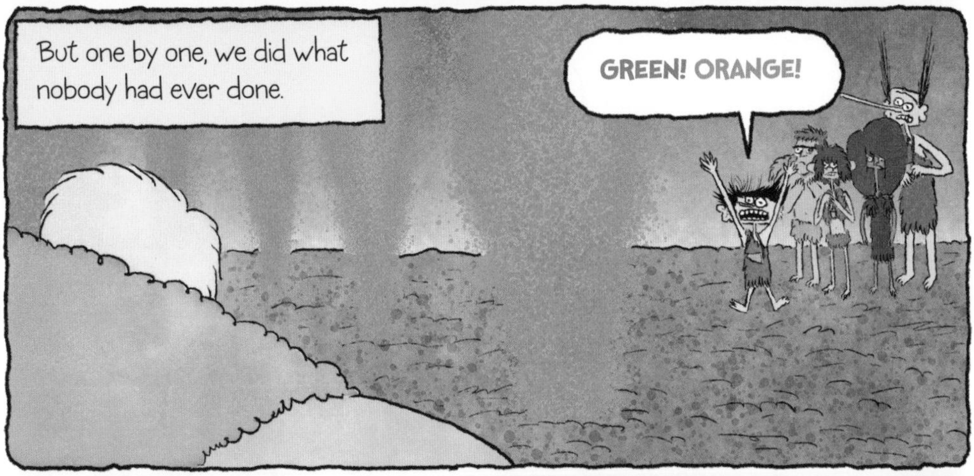
But one by one, we did what nobody had ever done.
GREEN! ORANGE!

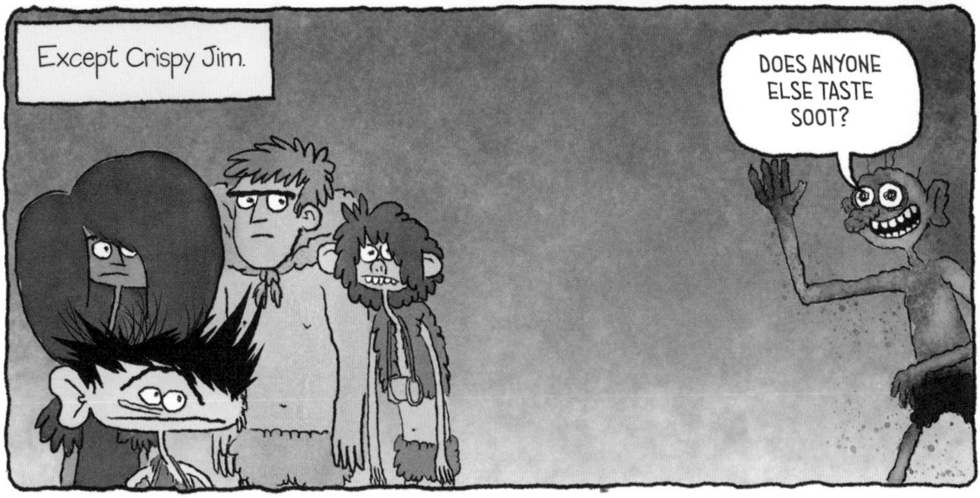
Except Crispy Jim.
DOES ANYONE ELSE TASTE SOOT?

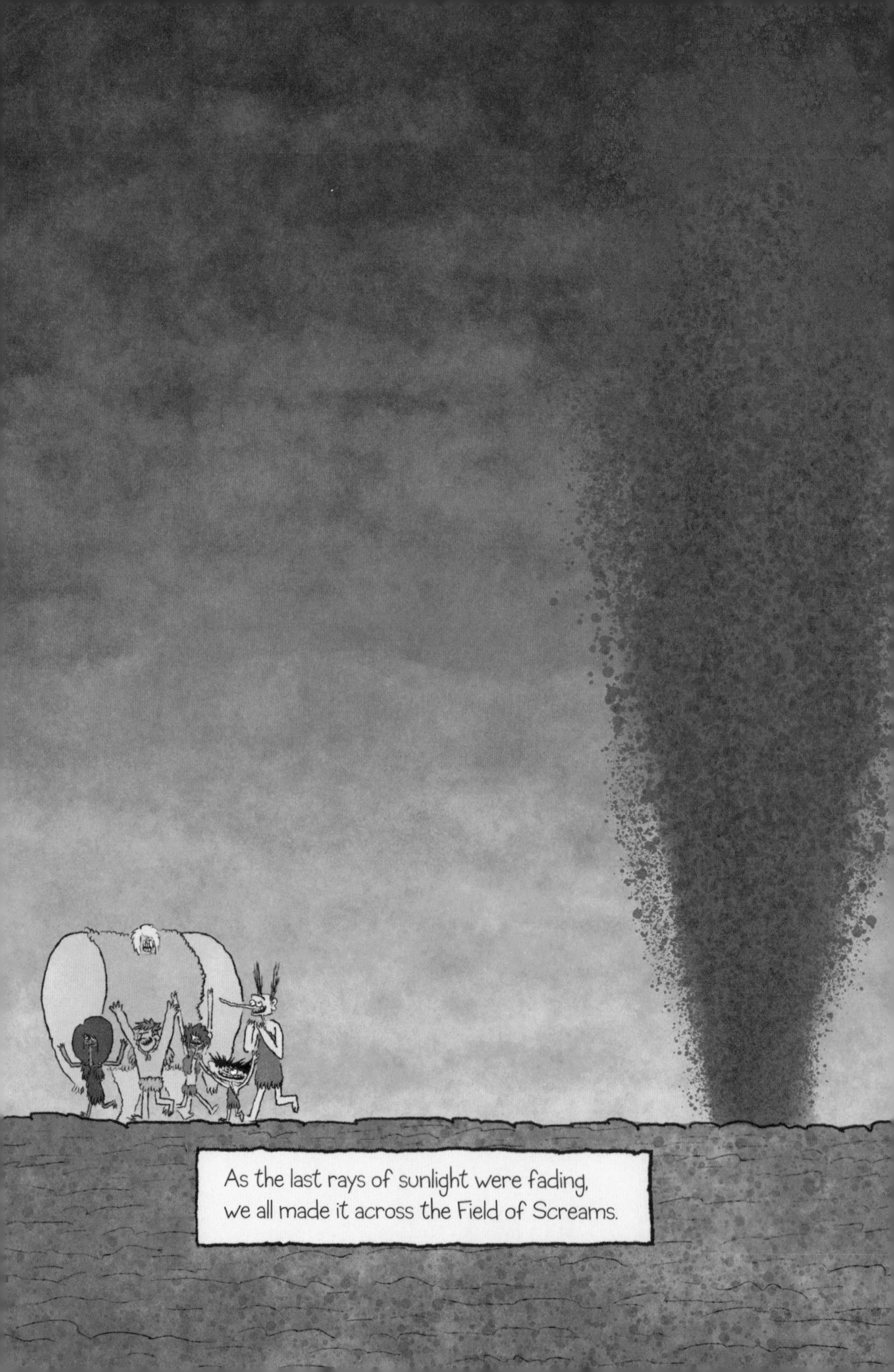
As the last rays of sunlight were fading, we all made it across the Field of Screams.

134

135

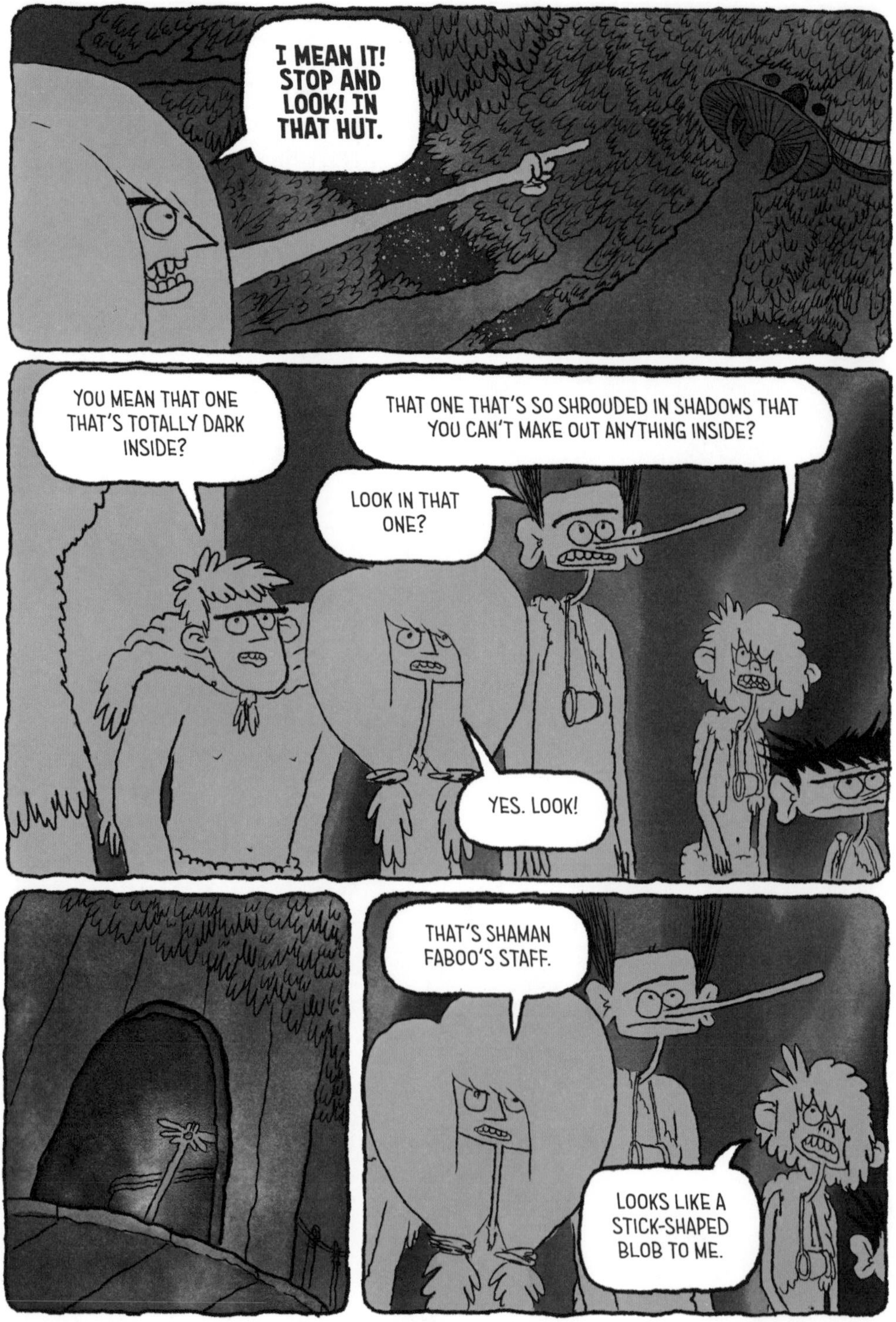
I MEAN IT! STOP AND LOOK! IN THAT HUT.
YOU MEAN THAT ONE THAT'S TOTALLY DARK INSIDE?
THAT ONE THAT'S SO SHROUDED IN SHADOWS THAT YOU CAN'T MAKE OUT ANYTHING INSIDE?
LOOK IN THAT ONE?
YES. LOOK!
THAT'S SHAMAN FABOO'S STAFF.
LOOKS LIKE A STICK-SHAPED BLOB TO ME.

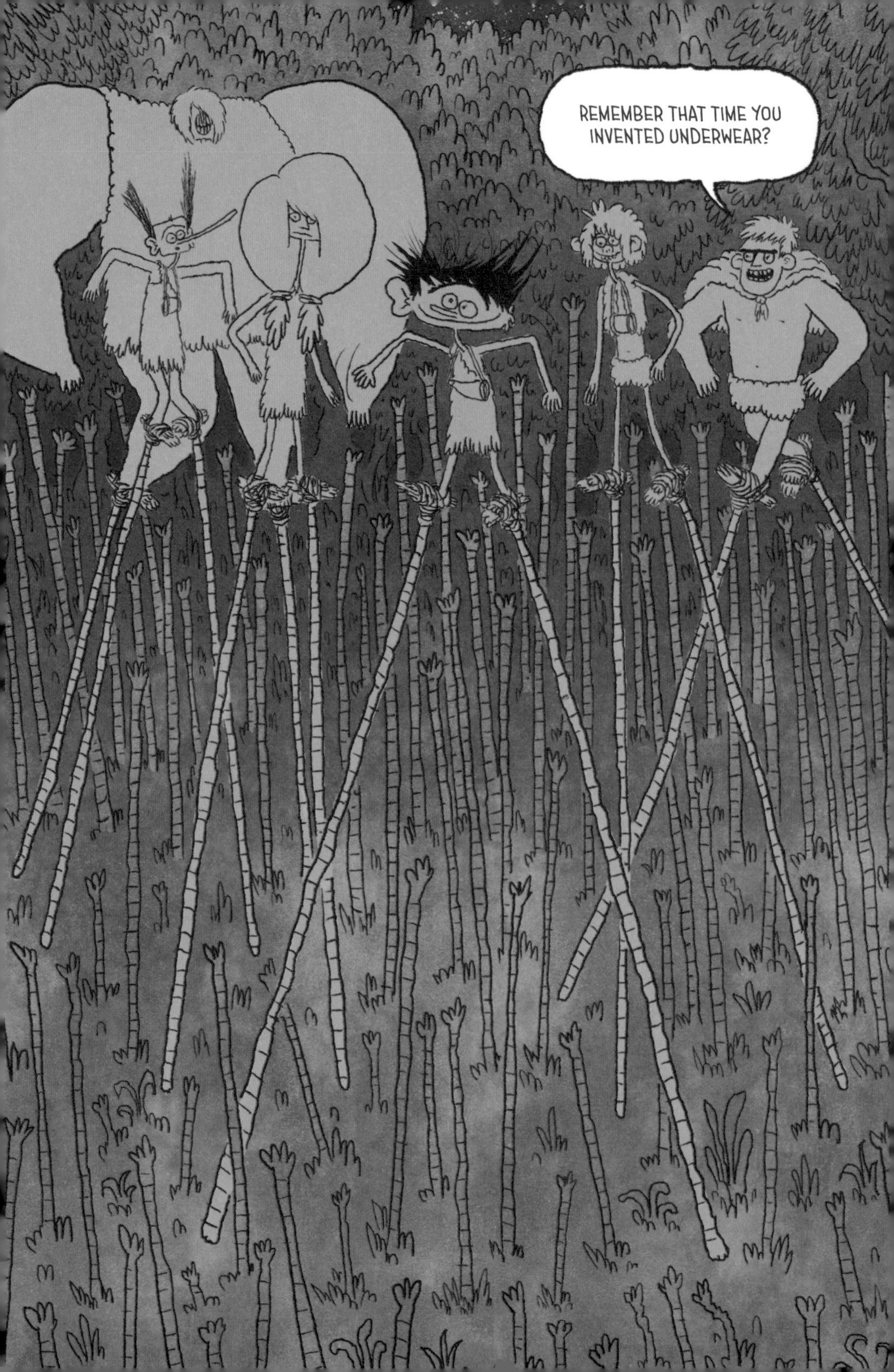
REMEMBER THAT TIME YOU INVENTED UNDERWEAR?

HEY, DAVE?

YOU CAN IGNORE ME ALL YOU WANT, BUT I'M STILL GOING TO SAY WHAT I NEED TO SAY.

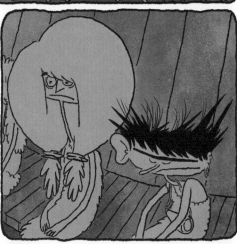

I LOST MY MOM WHEN I WAS YOUNGER. JUST LIKE YOU DID.

MY DAD, TOO. I WAS ABOUT SEVEN WHEN IT HAPPENED.

143

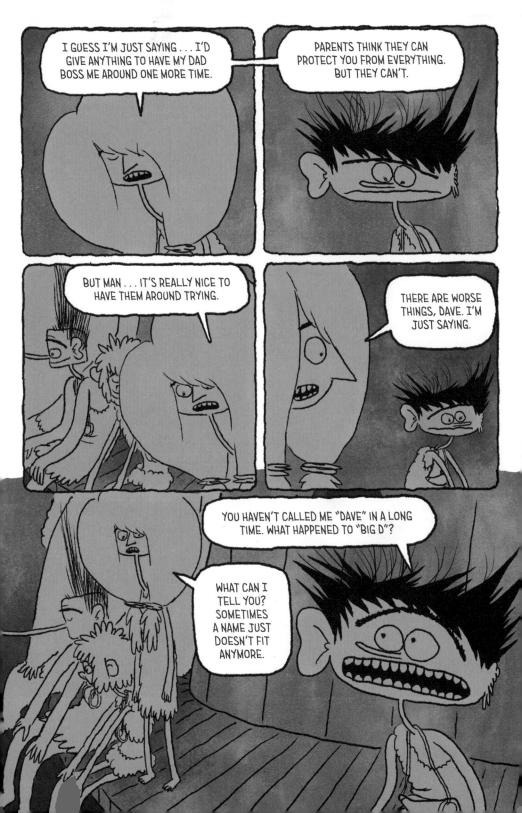

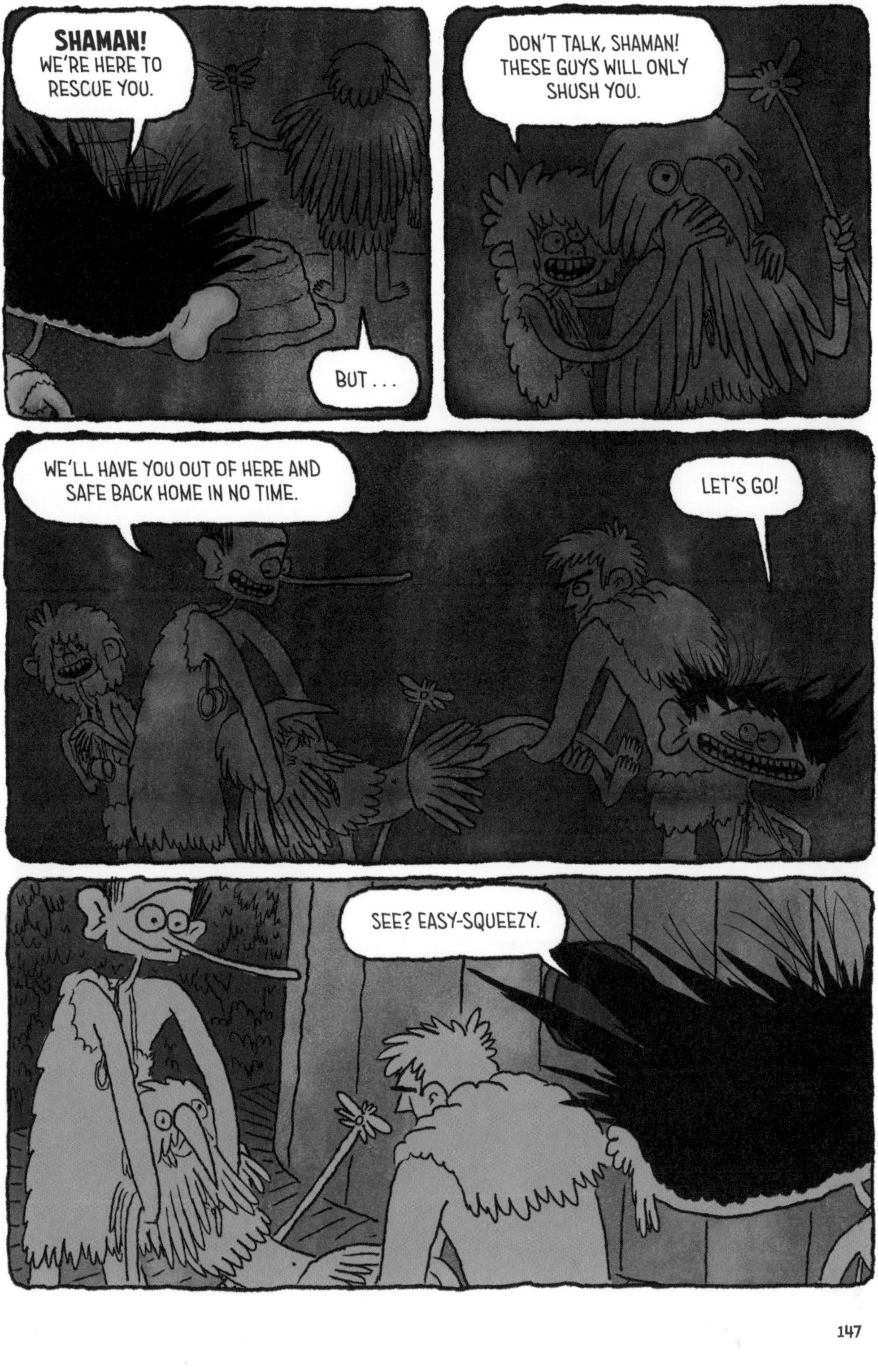
SHAMAN! WE'RE HERE TO RESCUE YOU.
BUT . . .
DON'T TALK, SHAMAN! THESE GUYS WILL ONLY SHUSH YOU.
WE'LL HAVE YOU OUT OF HERE AND SAFE BACK HOME IN NO TIME.
LET'S GO!
SEE? EASY-SQUEEZY.

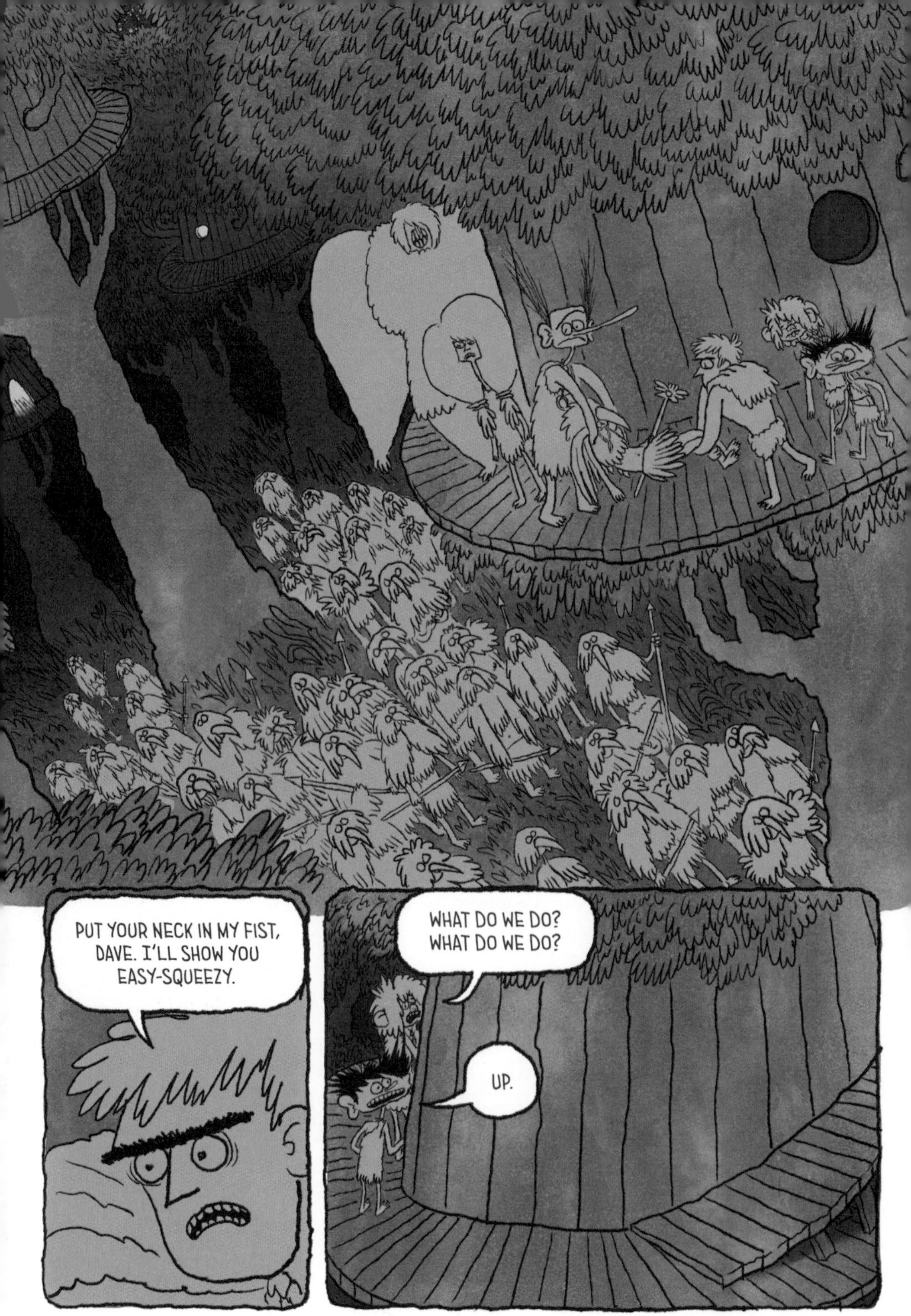
PUT YOUR NECK IN MY FIST, DAVE. I'LL SHOW YOU EASY-SQUEEZY.
WHAT DO WE DO? WHAT DO WE DO?
UP.

151

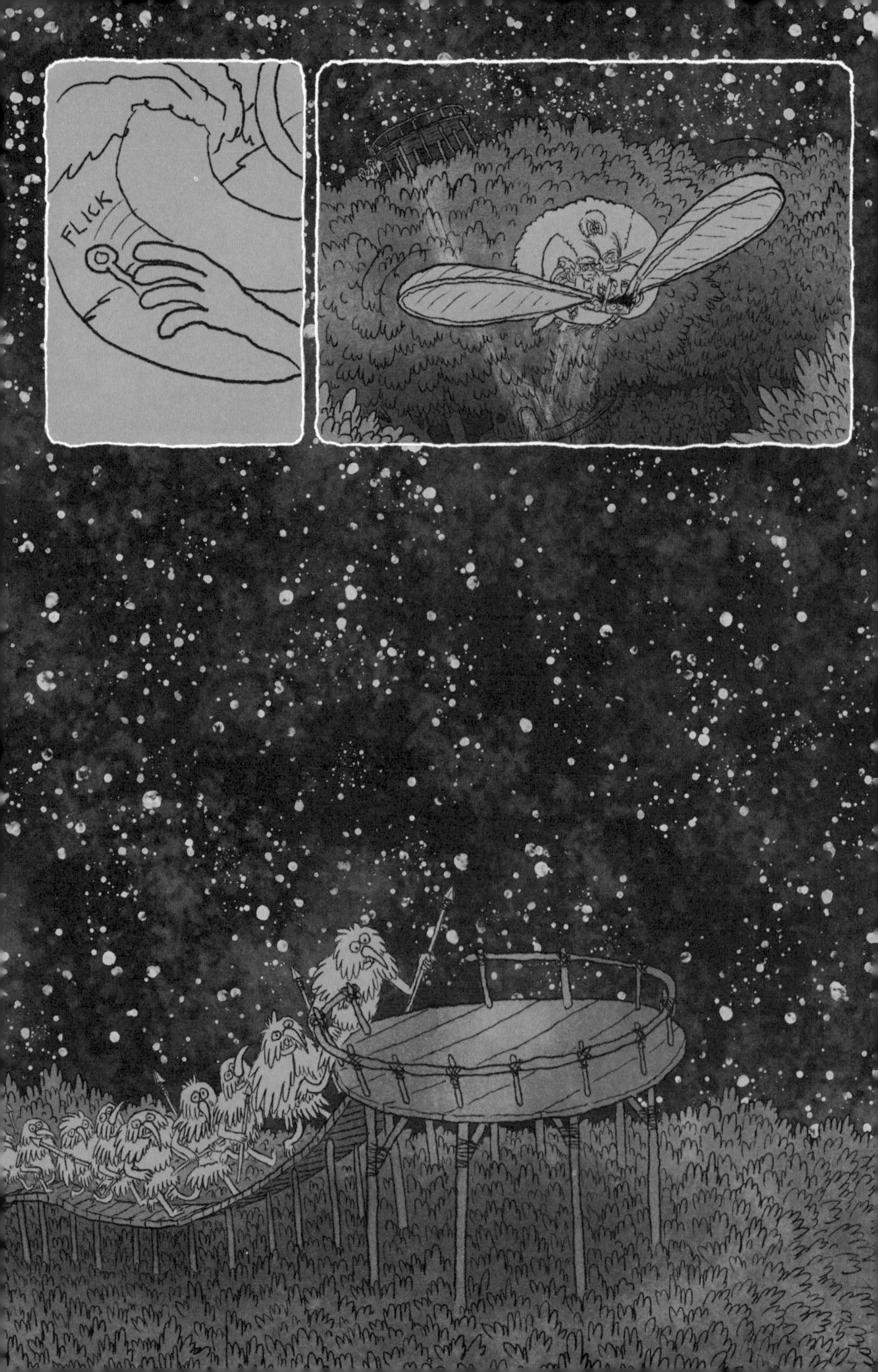
FLICK

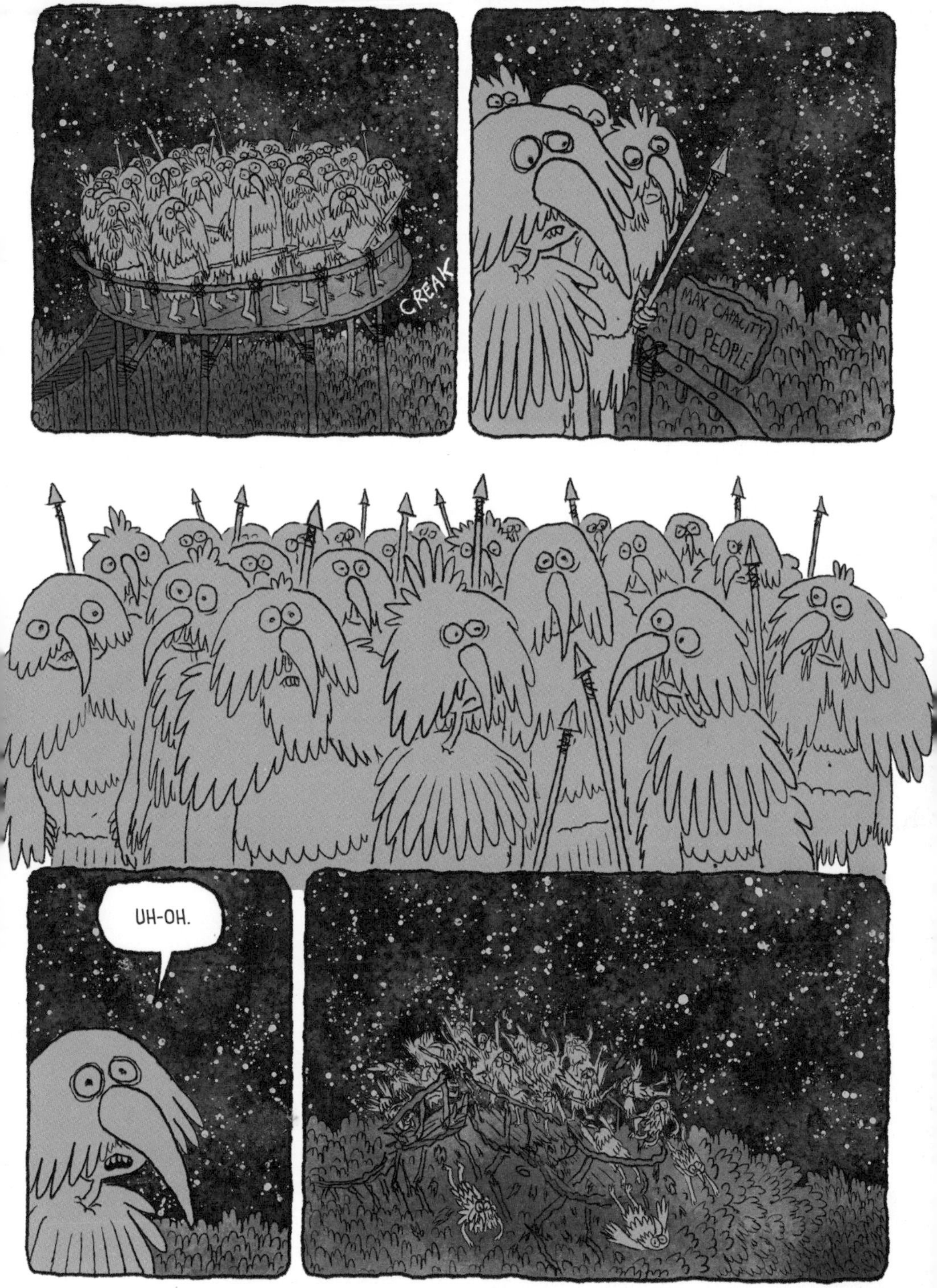
CREAK
MAX CAPACITY
10 PEOPLE
UH-OH.

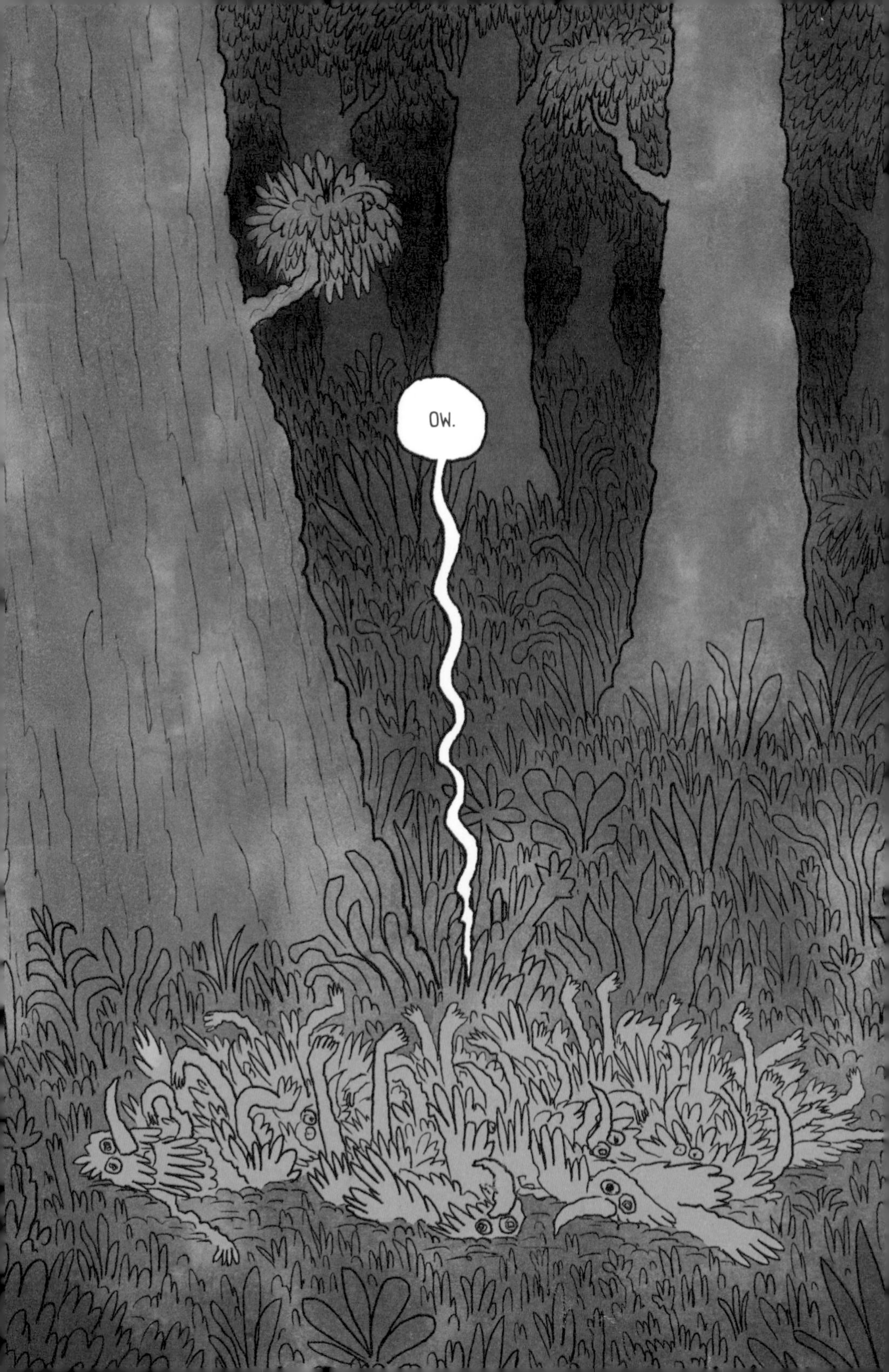
OW.

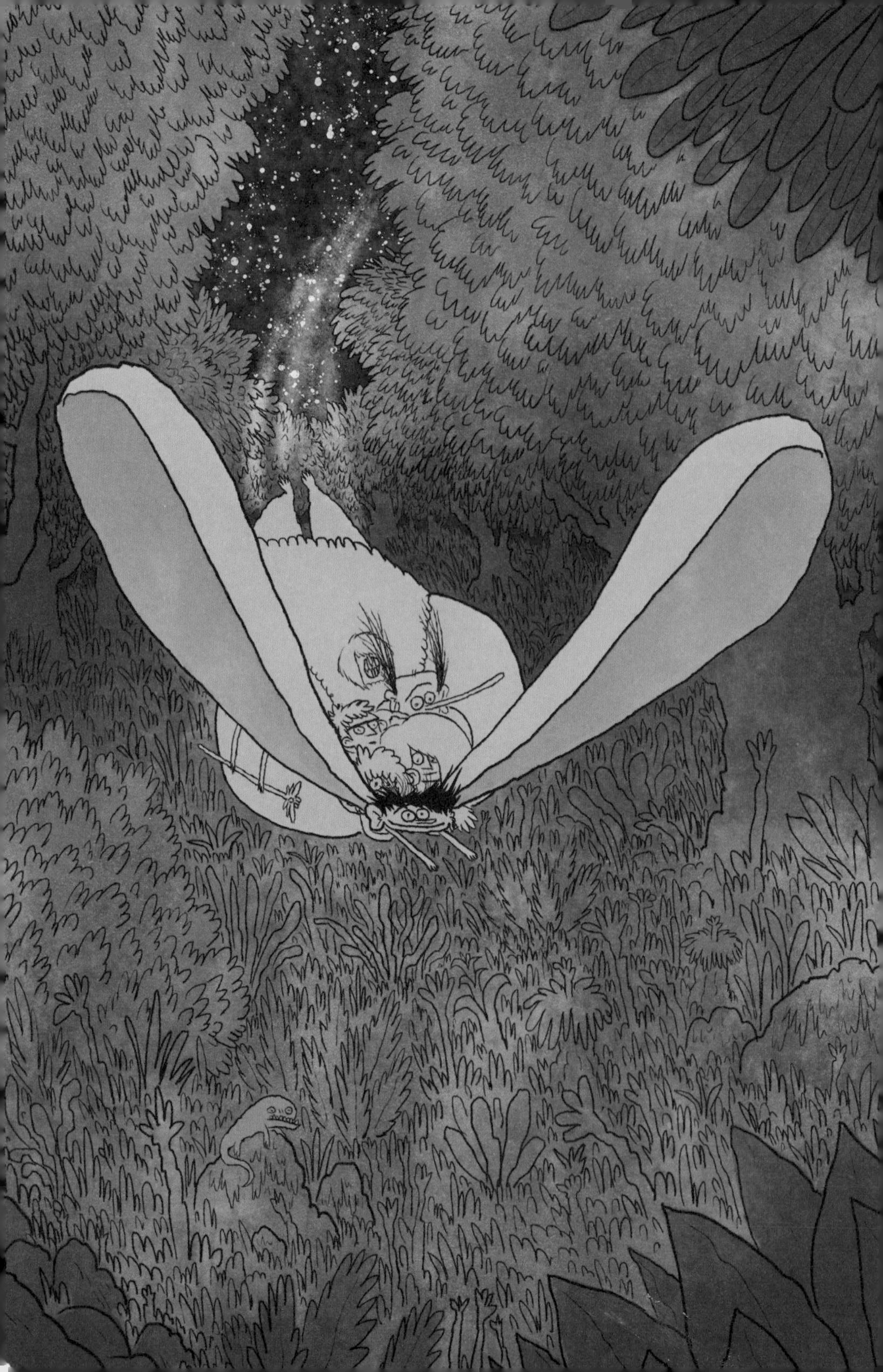

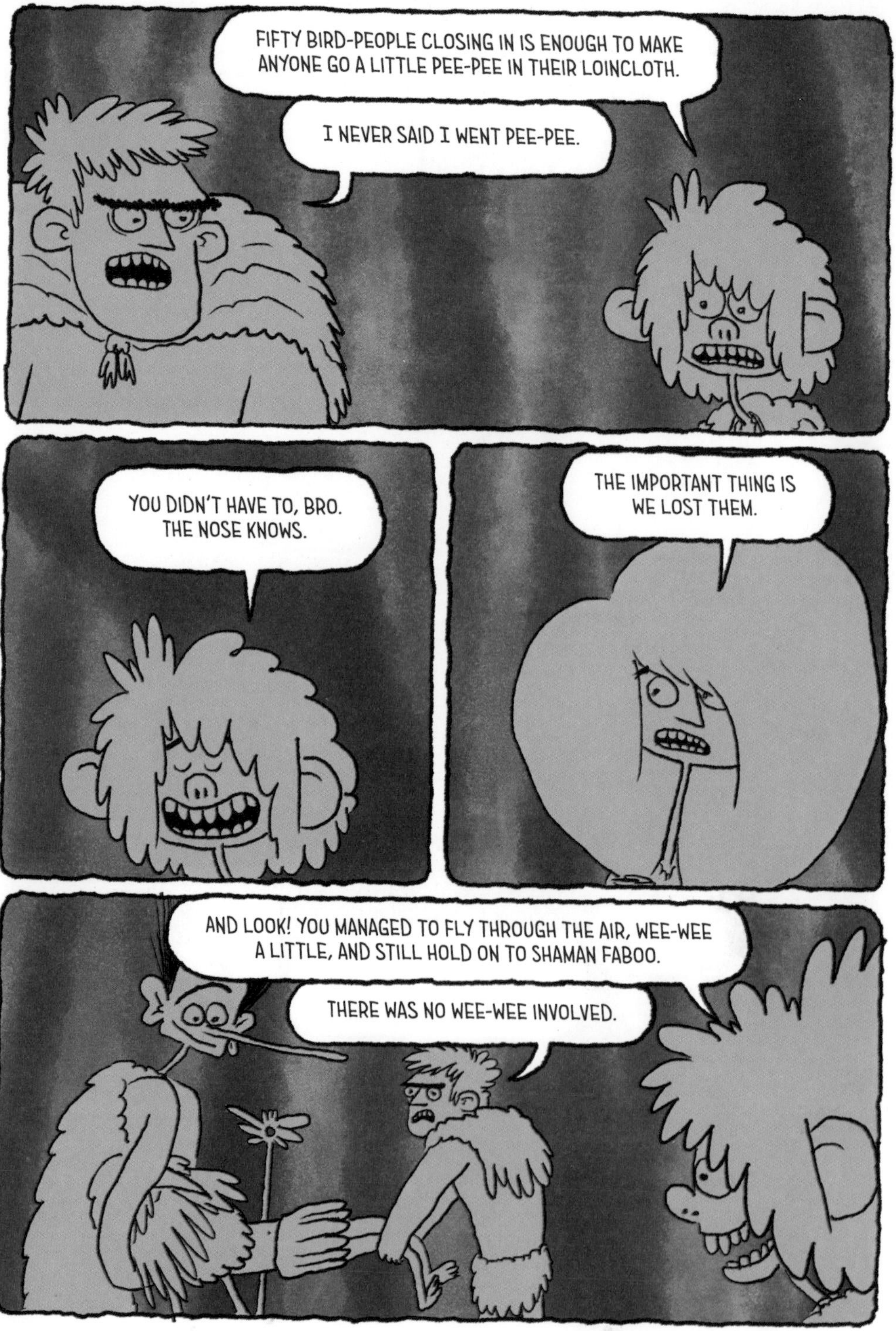
FIFTY BIRD-PEOPLE CLOSING IN IS ENOUGH TO MAKE ANYONE GO A LITTLE PEE-PEE IN THEIR LOINCLOTH.
I NEVER SAID I WENT PEE-PEE.
YOU DIDN'T HAVE TO, BRO. THE NOSE KNOWS.
THE IMPORTANT THING IS WE LOST THEM.
AND LOOK! YOU MANAGED TO FLY THROUGH THE AIR, WEE-WEE A LITTLE, AND STILL HOLD ON TO SHAMAN FABOO.
THERE WAS NO WEE-WEE INVOLVED.

159

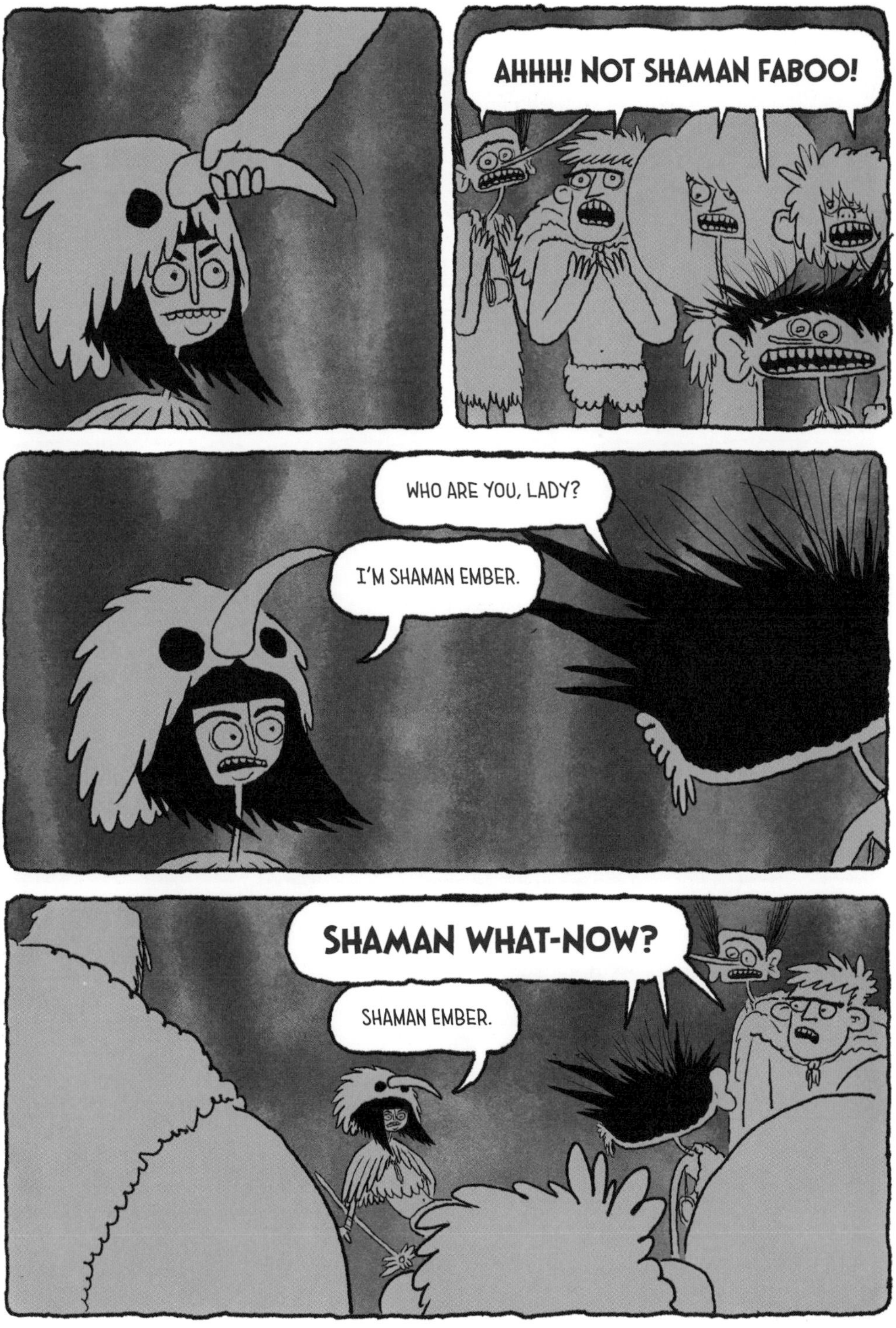
AHHH! NOT SHAMAN FABOO!
WHO ARE YOU, LADY?
I'M SHAMAN EMBER.
SHAMAN WHAT-NOW?
SHAMAN EMBER.

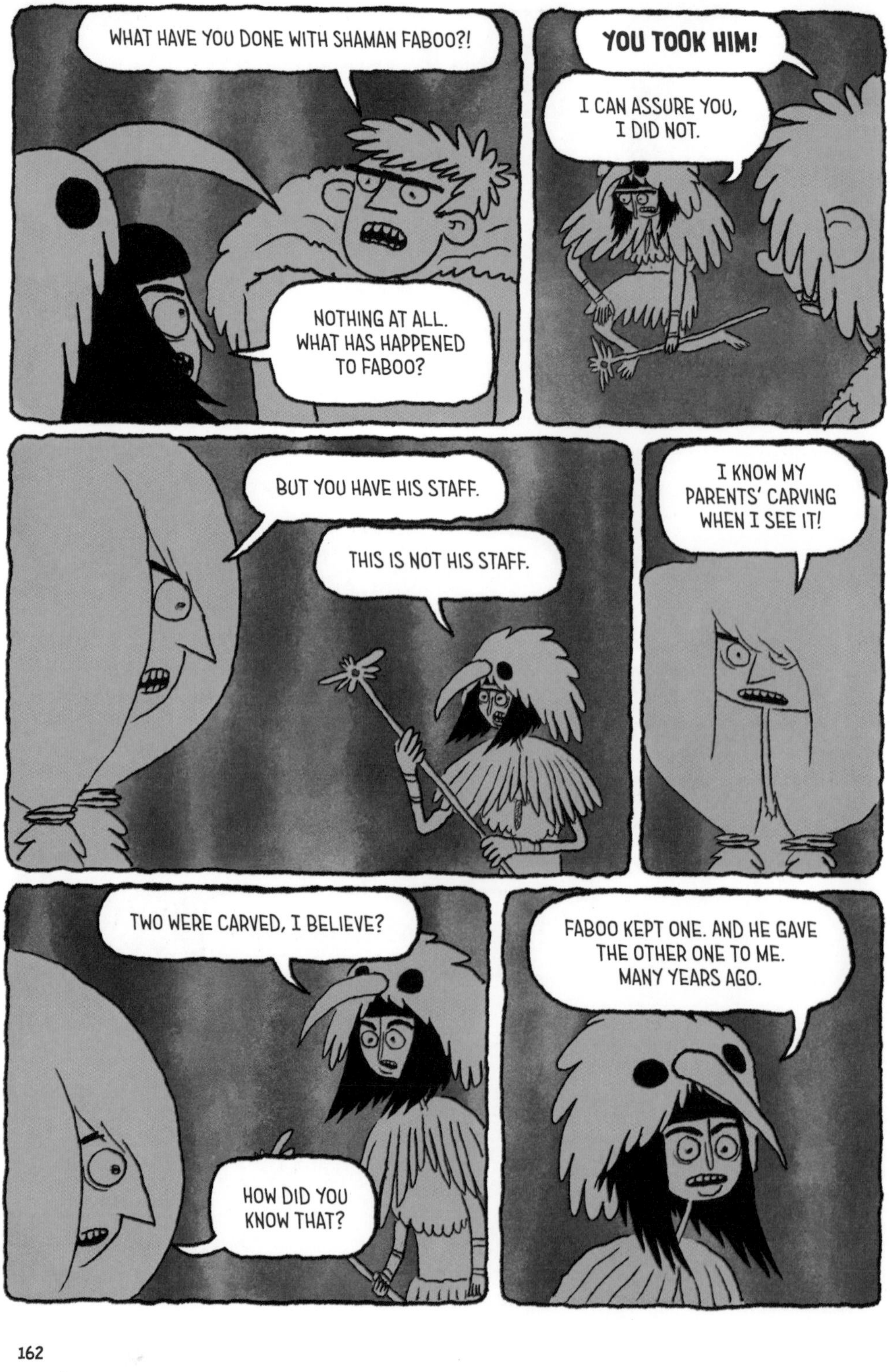
WHAT HAVE YOU DONE WITH SHAMAN FABOO?!
NOTHING AT ALL. WHAT HAS HAPPENED TO FABOO?
YOU TOOK HIM!
I CAN ASSURE YOU, I DID NOT.
BUT YOU HAVE HIS STAFF.
THIS IS NOT HIS STAFF.
I KNOW MY PARENTS' CARVING WHEN I SEE IT!
TWO WERE CARVED, I BELIEVE?
HOW DID YOU KNOW THAT?
FABOO KEPT ONE. AND HE GAVE THE OTHER ONE TO ME. MANY YEARS AGO.

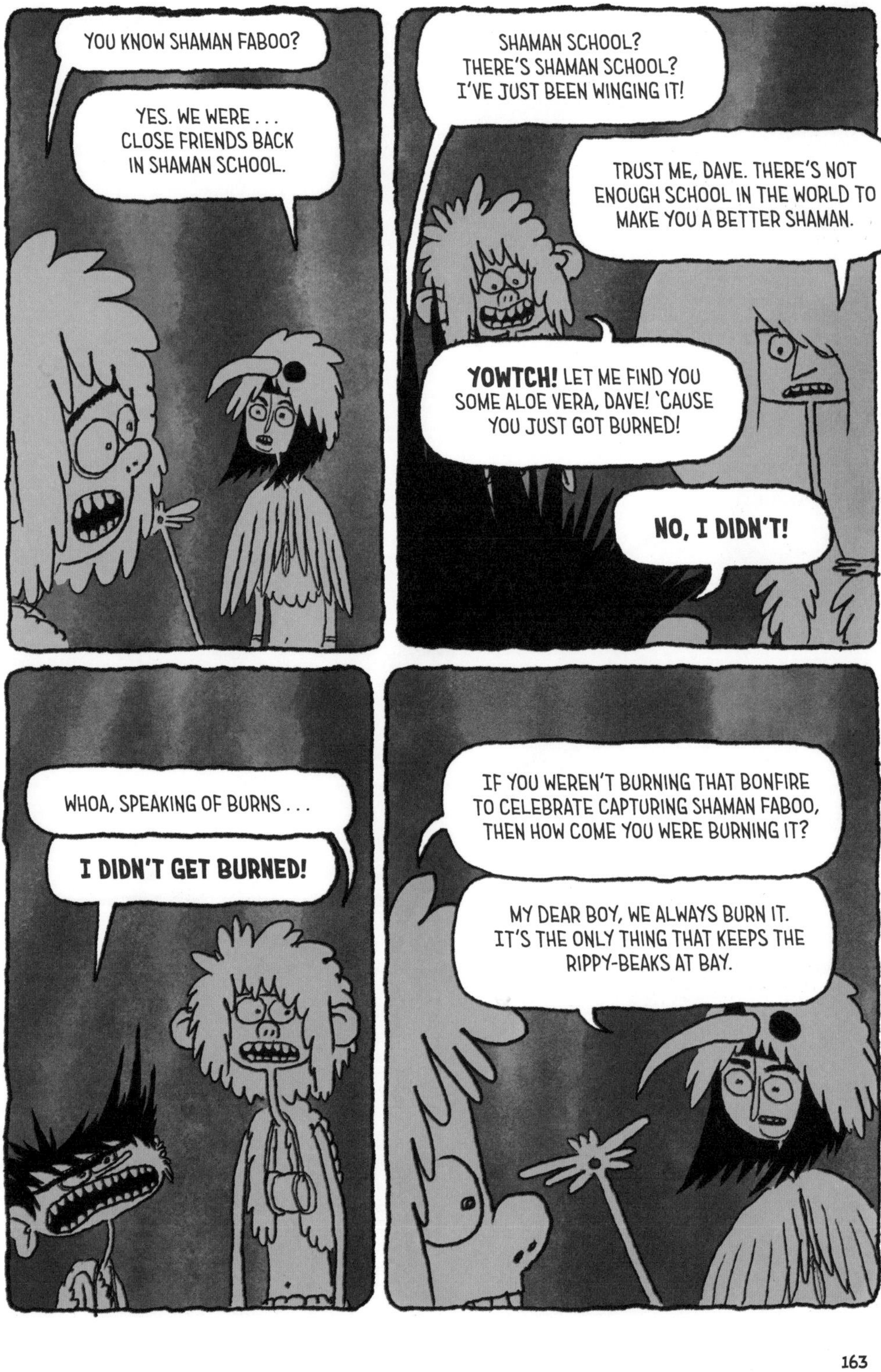

YOU KNOW SHAMAN FABOO?
YES. WE WERE . . . CLOSE FRIENDS BACK IN SHAMAN SCHOOL.
SHAMAN SCHOOL? THERE'S SHAMAN SCHOOL? I'VE JUST BEEN WINGING IT!
TRUST ME, DAVE. THERE'S NOT ENOUGH SCHOOL IN THE WORLD TO MAKE YOU A BETTER SHAMAN.
YOWTCH! LET ME FIND YOU SOME ALOE VERA, DAVE! 'CAUSE YOU JUST GOT BURNED!
NO, I DIDN'T!
WHOA, SPEAKING OF BURNS . . .
I DIDN'T GET BURNED!
IF YOU WEREN'T BURNING THAT BONFIRE TO CELEBRATE CAPTURING SHAMAN FABOO, THEN HOW COME YOU WERE BURNING IT?
MY DEAR BOY, WE ALWAYS BURN IT. IT'S THE ONLY THING THAT KEEPS THE RIPPY-BEAKS AT BAY.

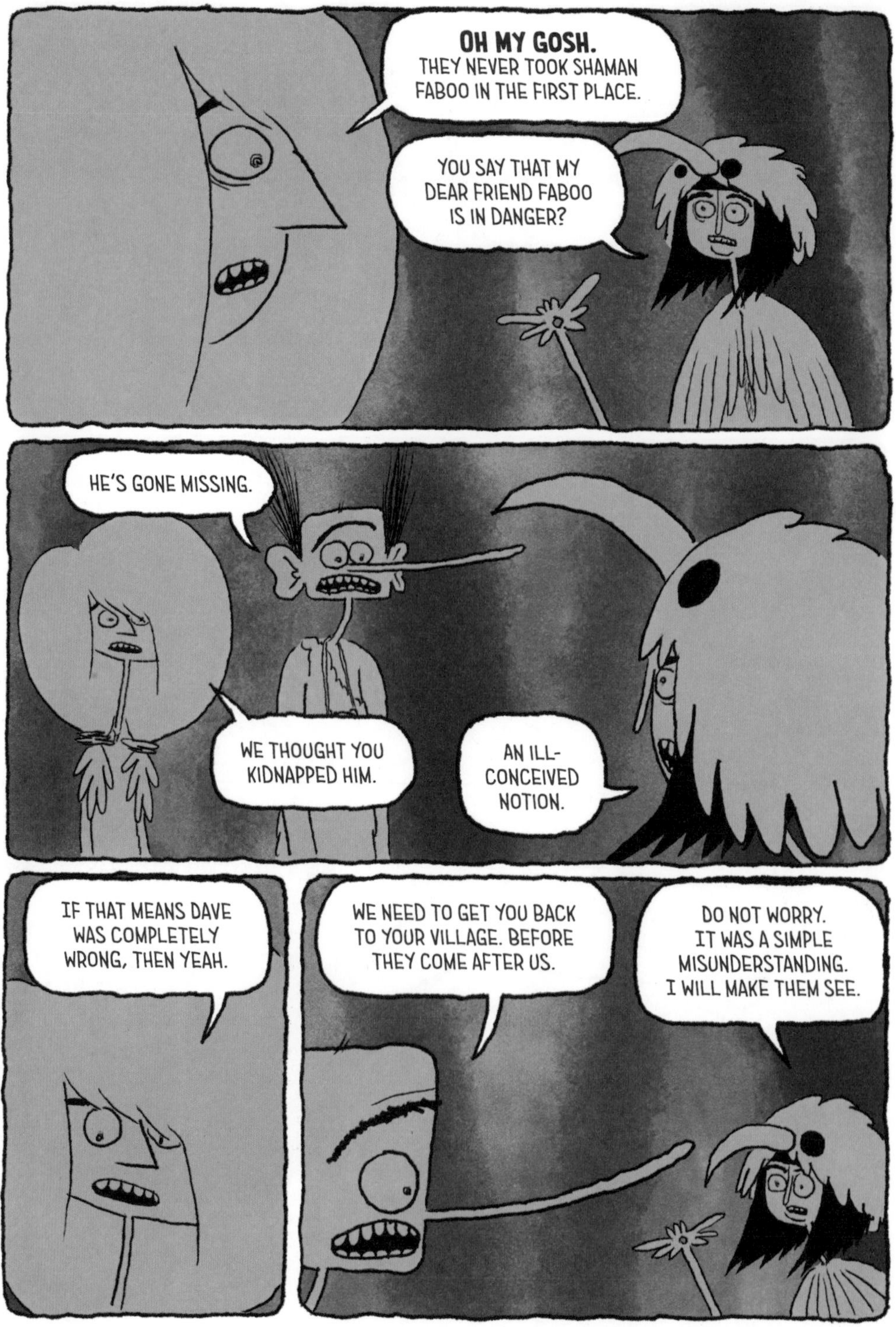

OH MY GOSH.
THEY NEVER TOOK SHAMAN FABOO IN THE FIRST PLACE.
YOU SAY THAT MY DEAR FRIEND FABOO IS IN DANGER?
HE'S GONE MISSING.
WE THOUGHT YOU KIDNAPPED HIM.
AN ILL-CONCEIVED NOTION.
IF THAT MEANS DAVE WAS COMPLETELY WRONG, THEN YEAH.
WE NEED TO GET YOU BACK TO YOUR VILLAGE. BEFORE THEY COME AFTER US.
DO NOT WORRY. IT WAS A SIMPLE MISUNDERSTANDING. I WILL MAKE THEM SEE.

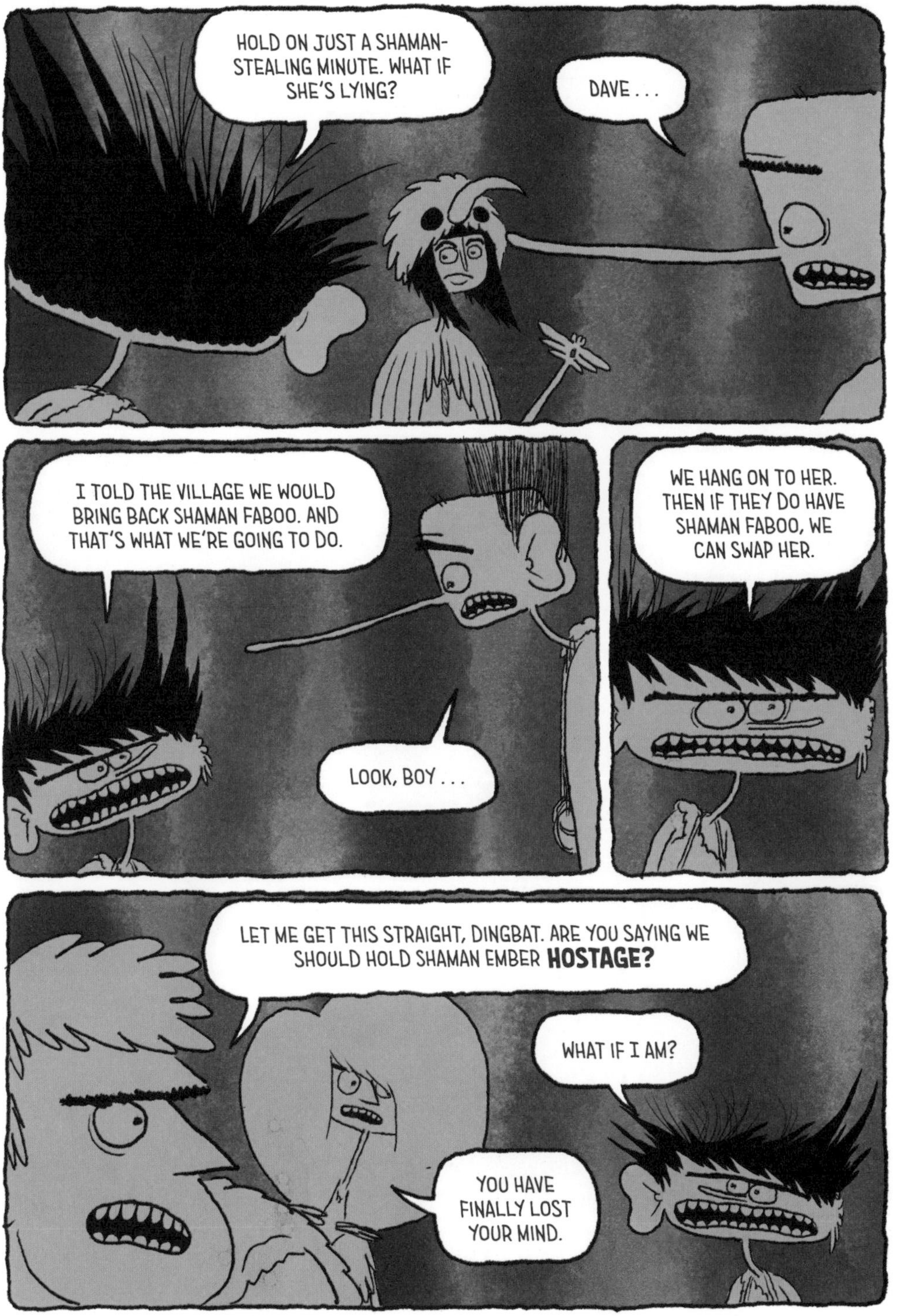
HOLD ON JUST A SHAMAN-STEALING MINUTE. WHAT IF SHE'S LYING?
DAVE . . .
I TOLD THE VILLAGE WE WOULD BRING BACK SHAMAN FABOO. AND THAT'S WHAT WE'RE GOING TO DO.
LOOK, BOY . . .
WE HANG ON TO HER. THEN IF THEY DO HAVE SHAMAN FABOO, WE CAN SWAP HER.
LET ME GET THIS STRAIGHT, DINGBAT. ARE YOU SAYING WE SHOULD HOLD SHAMAN EMBER **HOSTAGE?**
WHAT IF I AM?
YOU HAVE FINALLY LOST YOUR MIND.

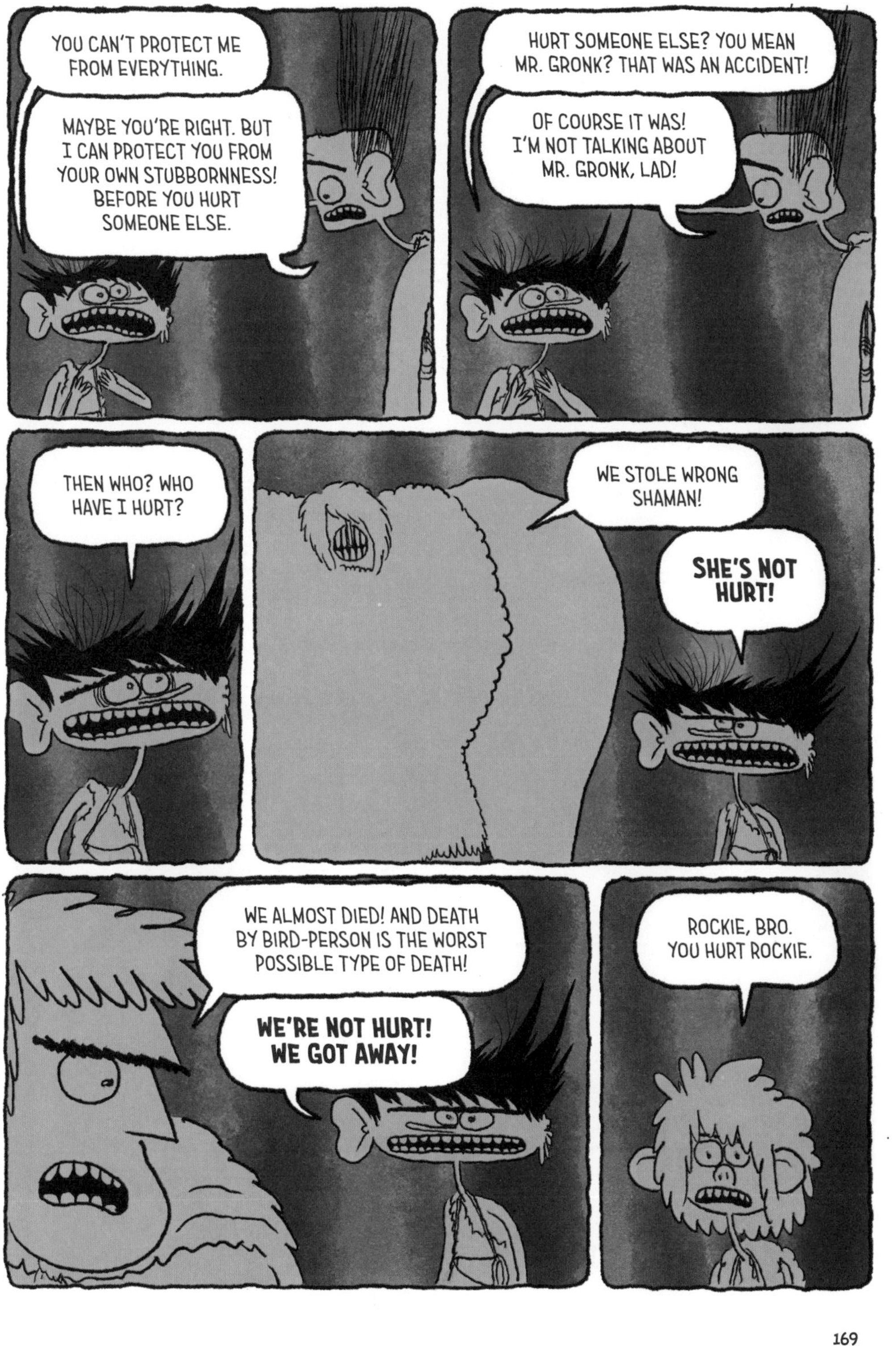
YOU CAN'T PROTECT ME FROM EVERYTHING.
MAYBE YOU'RE RIGHT. BUT I CAN PROTECT YOU FROM YOUR OWN STUBBORNNESS! BEFORE YOU HURT SOMEONE ELSE.
HURT SOMEONE ELSE? YOU MEAN MR. GRONK? THAT WAS AN ACCIDENT!
OF COURSE IT WAS! I'M NOT TALKING ABOUT MR. GRONK, LAD!
THEN WHO? WHO HAVE I HURT?
WE STOLE WRONG SHAMAN!
SHE'S NOT HURT!
WE ALMOST DIED! AND DEATH BY BIRD-PERSON IS THE WORST POSSIBLE TYPE OF DEATH!
WE'RE NOT HURT! WE GOT AWAY!
ROCKIE, BRO. YOU HURT ROCKIE.

171

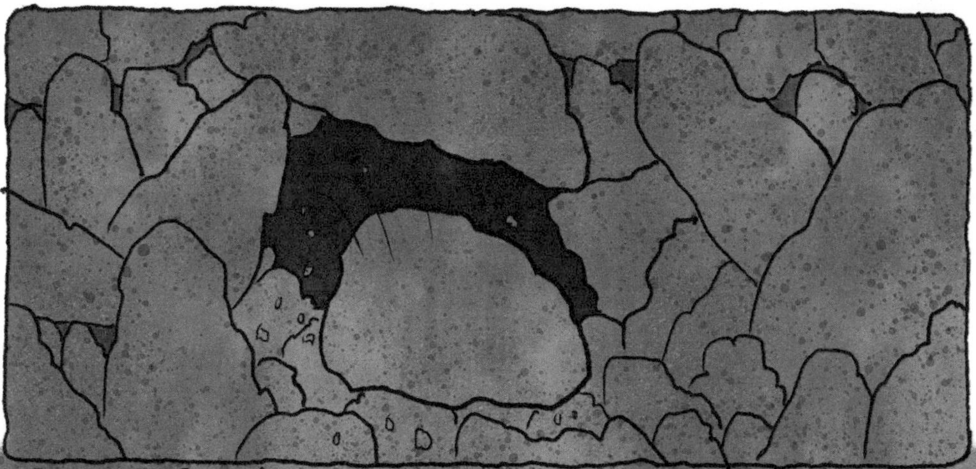

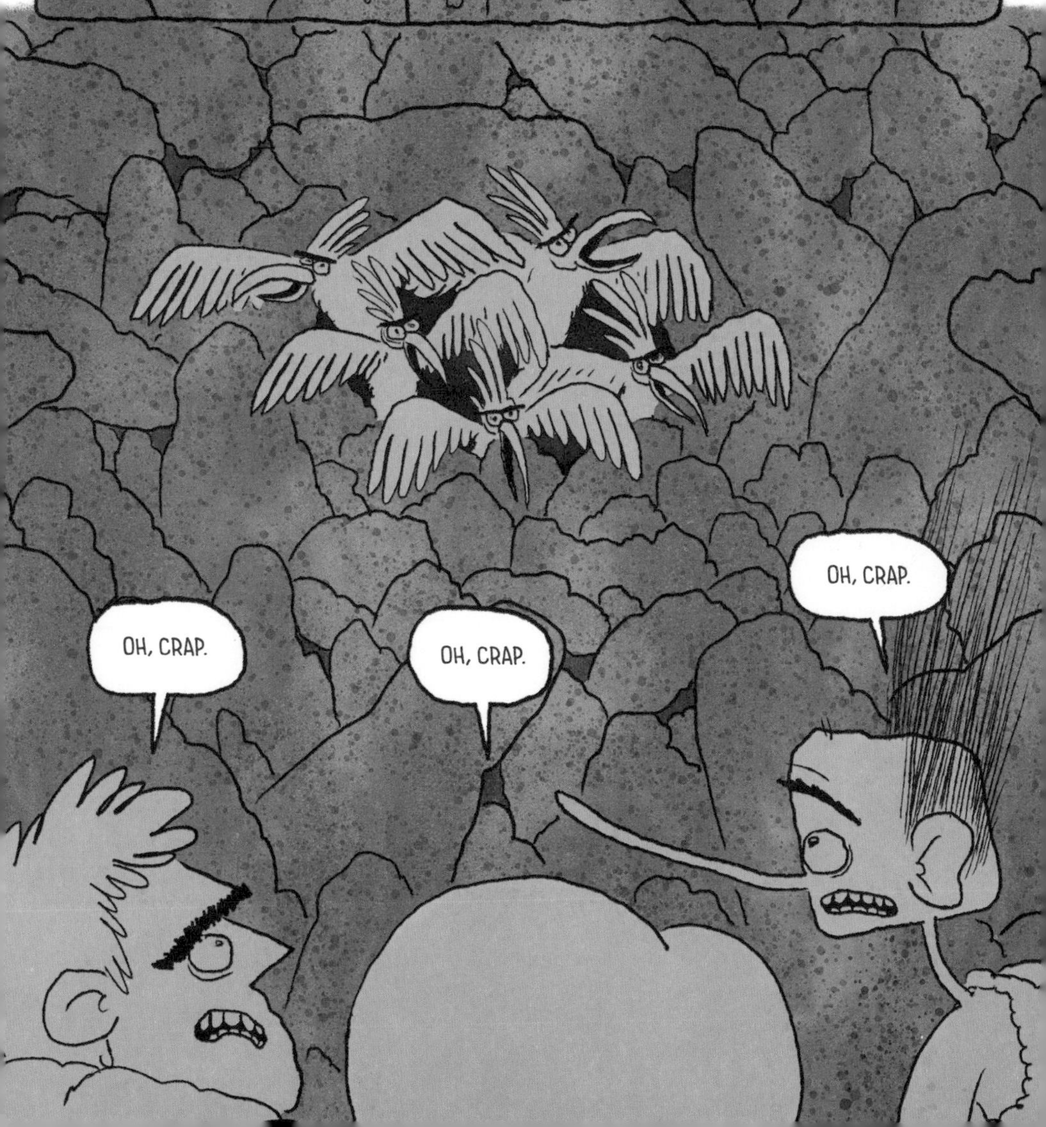
OH, CRAP.
OH, CRAP.
OH, CRAP.

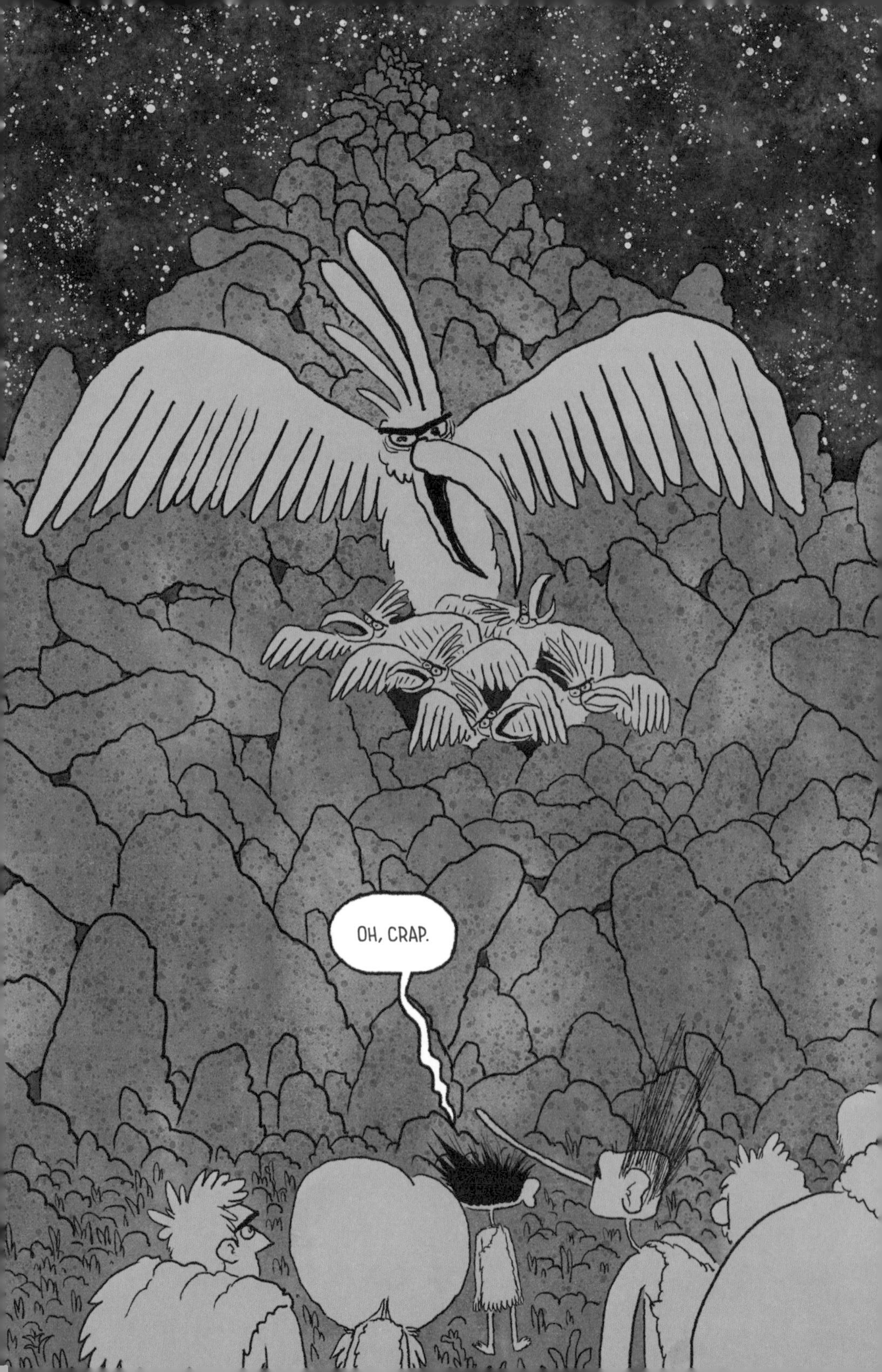
OH, CRAP.

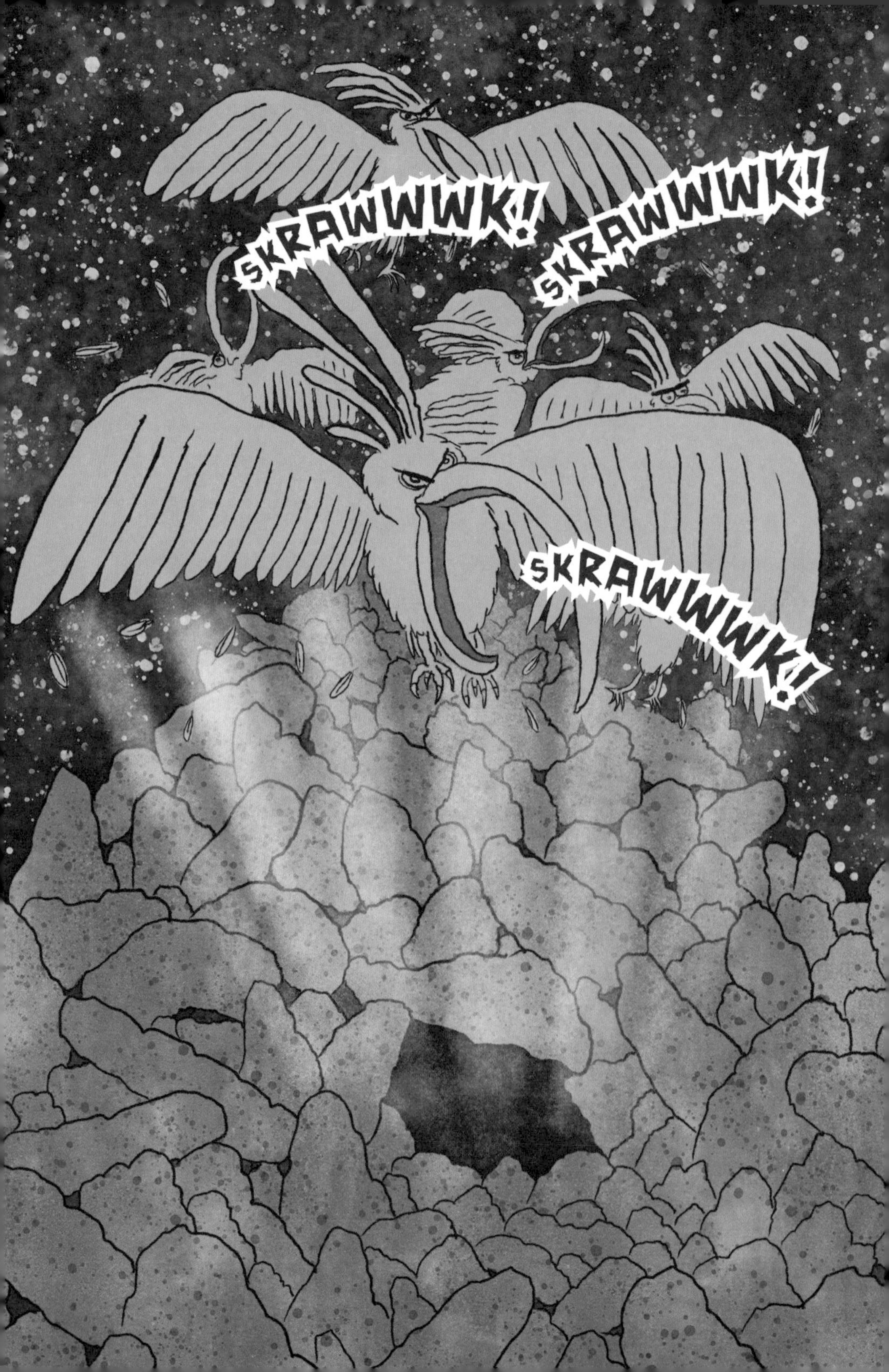
SKRAWWWK!
SKRAWWWK!
SKRAWWWK!

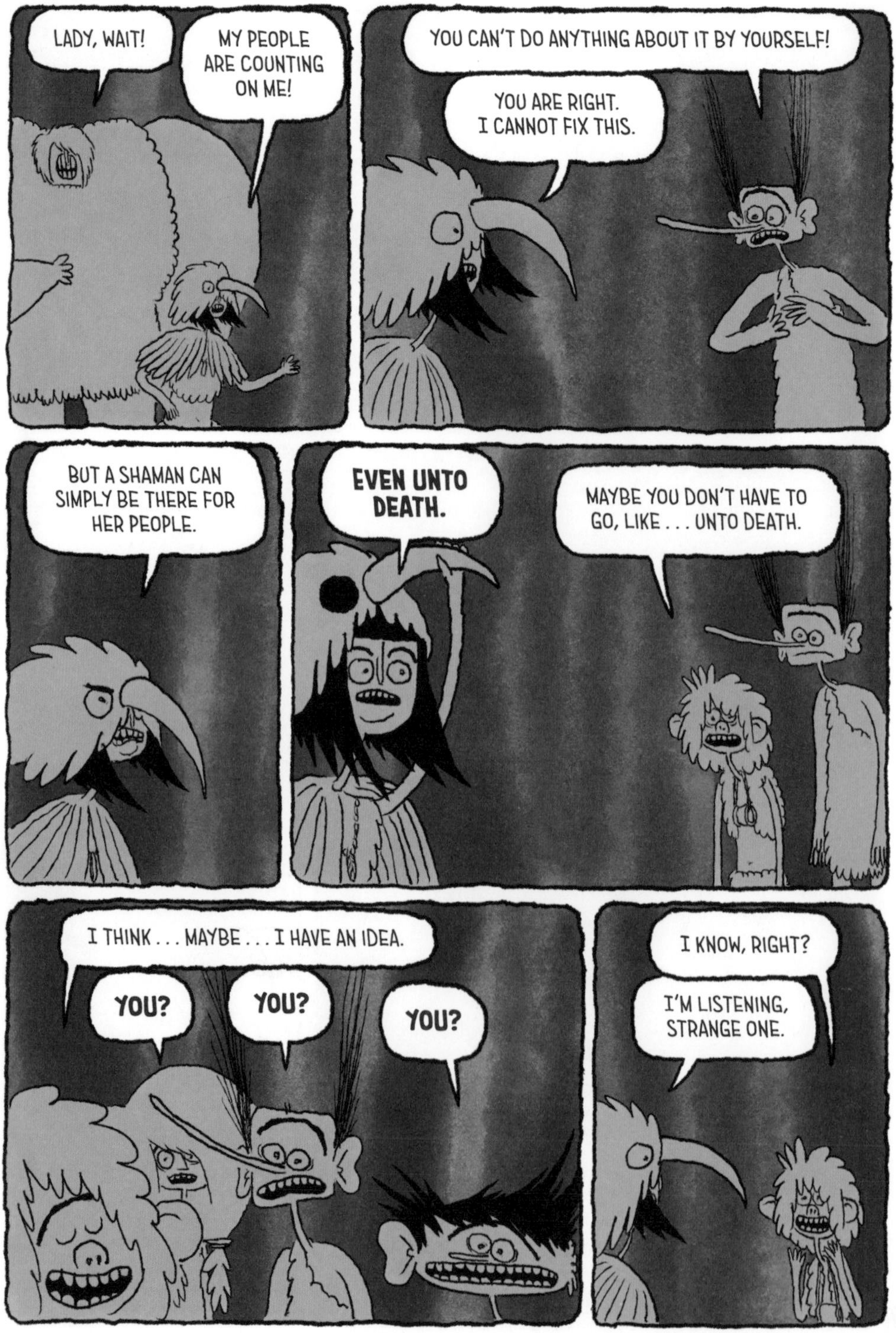

LADY, WAIT!
MY PEOPLE ARE COUNTING ON ME!
YOU CAN'T DO ANYTHING ABOUT IT BY YOURSELF!
YOU ARE RIGHT. I CANNOT FIX THIS.
BUT A SHAMAN CAN SIMPLY BE THERE FOR HER PEOPLE.
EVEN UNTO DEATH.
MAYBE YOU DON'T HAVE TO GO, LIKE . . . UNTO DEATH.
I THINK . . . MAYBE . . . I HAVE AN IDEA.
YOU?
YOU?
YOU?
I KNOW, RIGHT?
I'M LISTENING, STRANGE ONE.

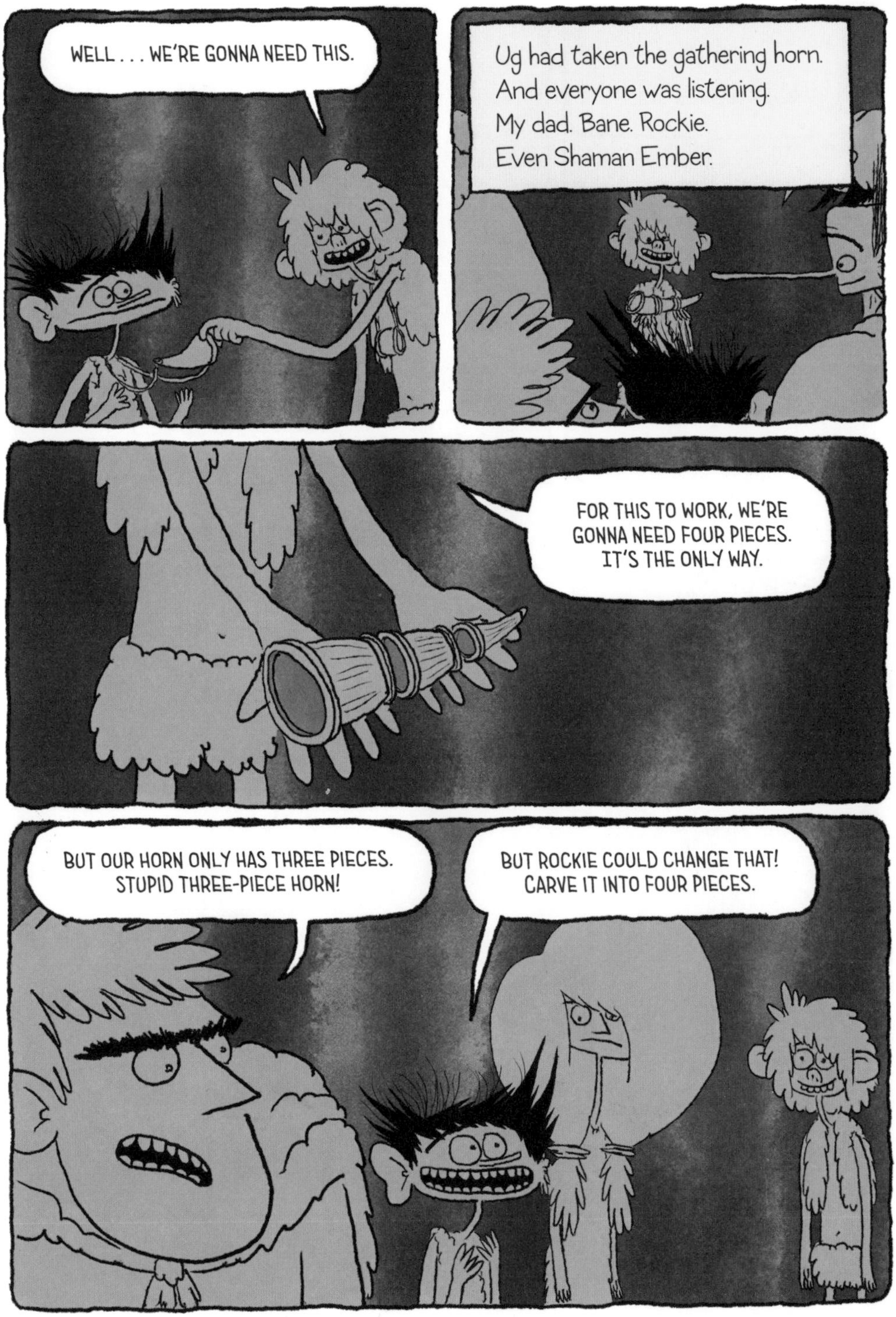
WELL . . . WE'RE GONNA NEED THIS.
Ug had taken the gathering horn.
And everyone was listening.
My dad. Bane. Rockie.
Even Shaman Ember.
FOR THIS TO WORK, WE'RE GONNA NEED FOUR PIECES. IT'S THE ONLY WAY.
BUT OUR HORN ONLY HAS THREE PIECES. STUPID THREE-PIECE HORN!
BUT ROCKIE COULD CHANGE THAT! CARVE IT INTO FOUR PIECES.

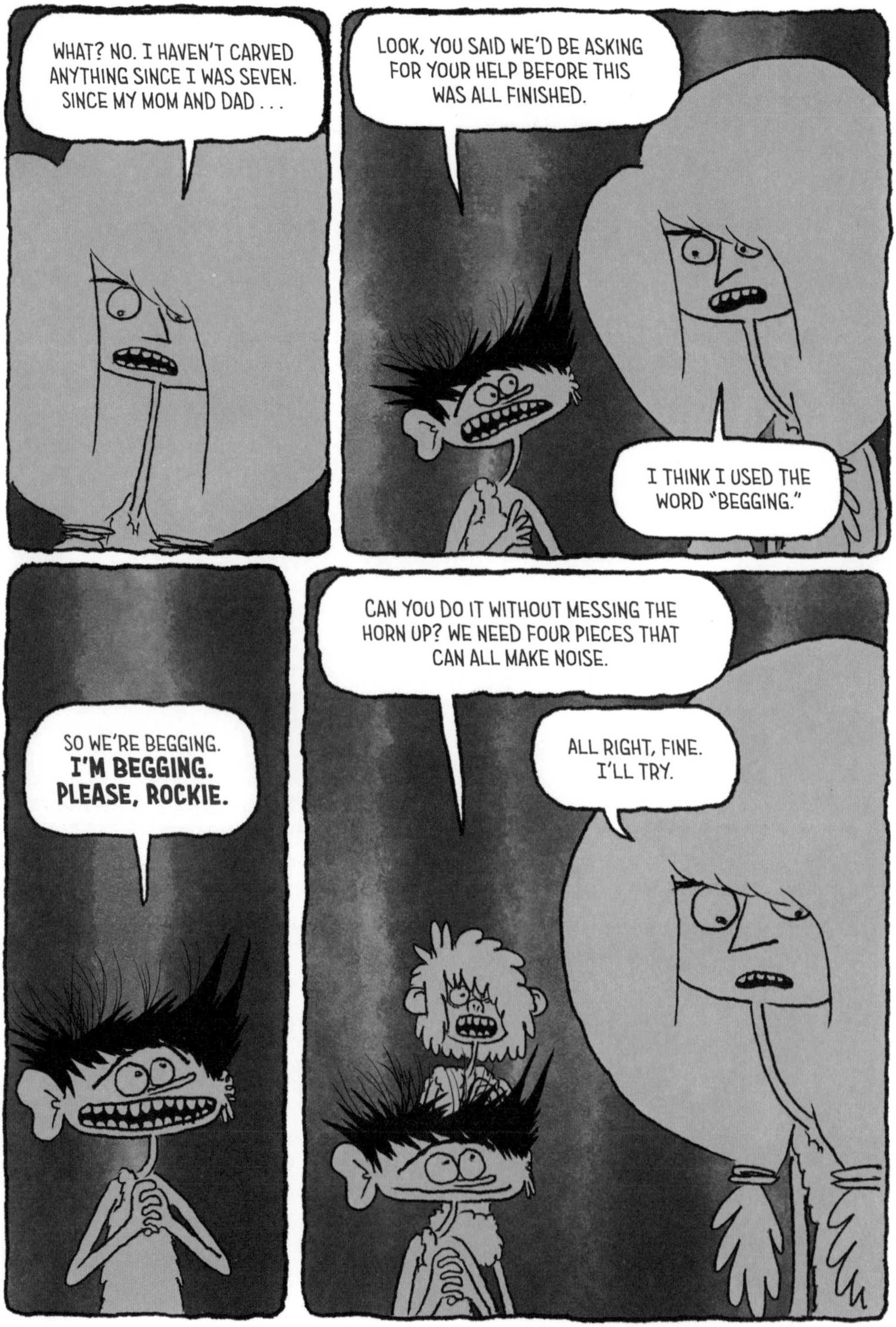
WHAT? NO. I HAVEN'T CARVED ANYTHING SINCE I WAS SEVEN. SINCE MY MOM AND DAD . . .
LOOK, YOU SAID WE'D BE ASKING FOR YOUR HELP BEFORE THIS WAS ALL FINISHED.
I THINK I USED THE WORD "BEGGING."
SO WE'RE BEGGING. I'M BEGGING. PLEASE, ROCKIE.
CAN YOU DO IT WITHOUT MESSING THE HORN UP? WE NEED FOUR PIECES THAT CAN ALL MAKE NOISE.
ALL RIGHT, FINE. I'LL TRY.

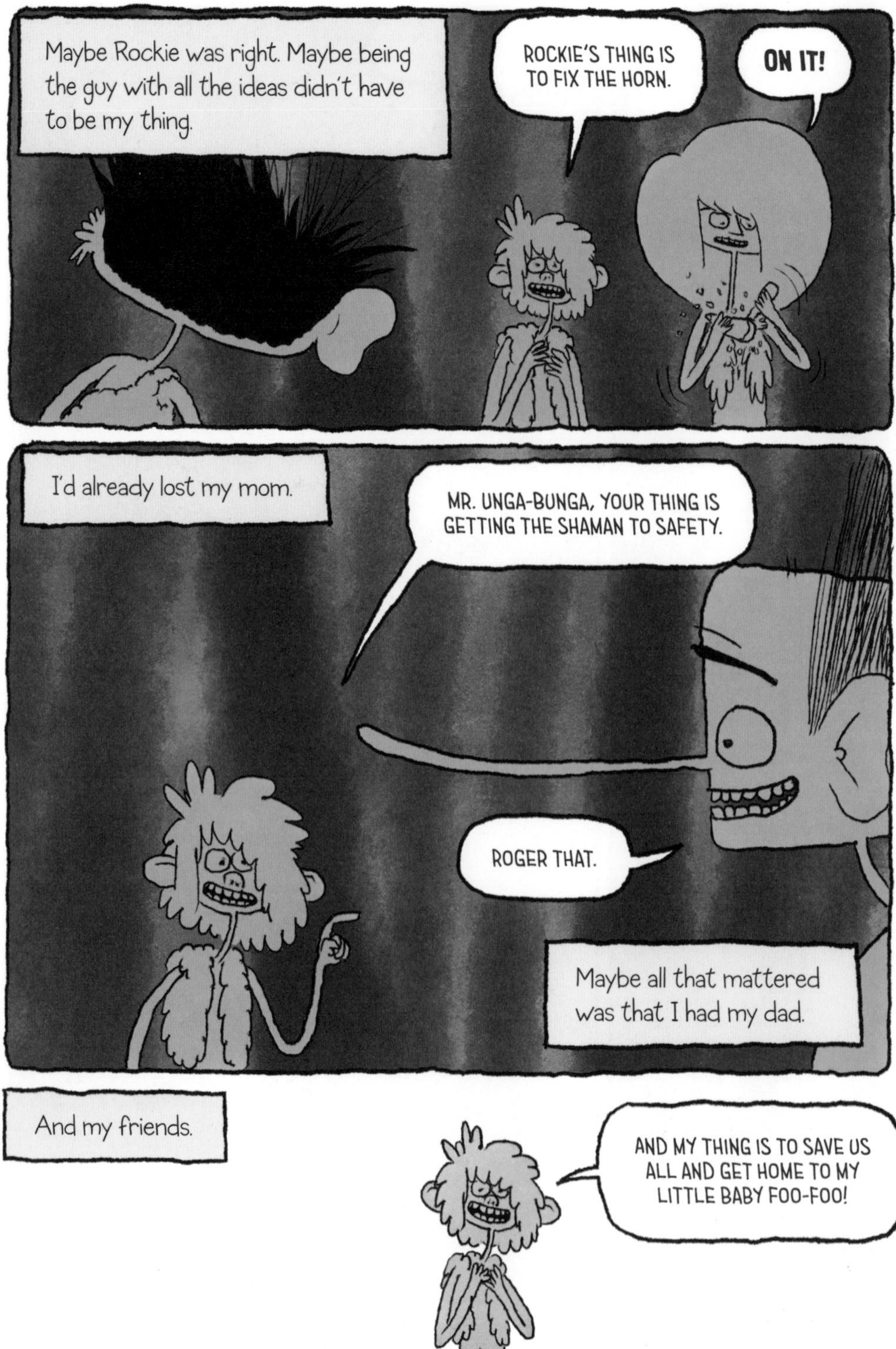

Maybe Rockie was right. Maybe being the guy with all the ideas didn't have to be my thing.
ROCKIE'S THING IS TO FIX THE HORN.
ON IT!
I'd already lost my mom.
MR. UNGA-BUNGA, YOUR THING IS GETTING THE SHAMAN TO SAFETY.
ROGER THAT.
Maybe all that mattered was that I had my dad.
And my friends.
AND MY THING IS TO SAVE US ALL AND GET HOME TO MY LITTLE BABY FOO-FOO!

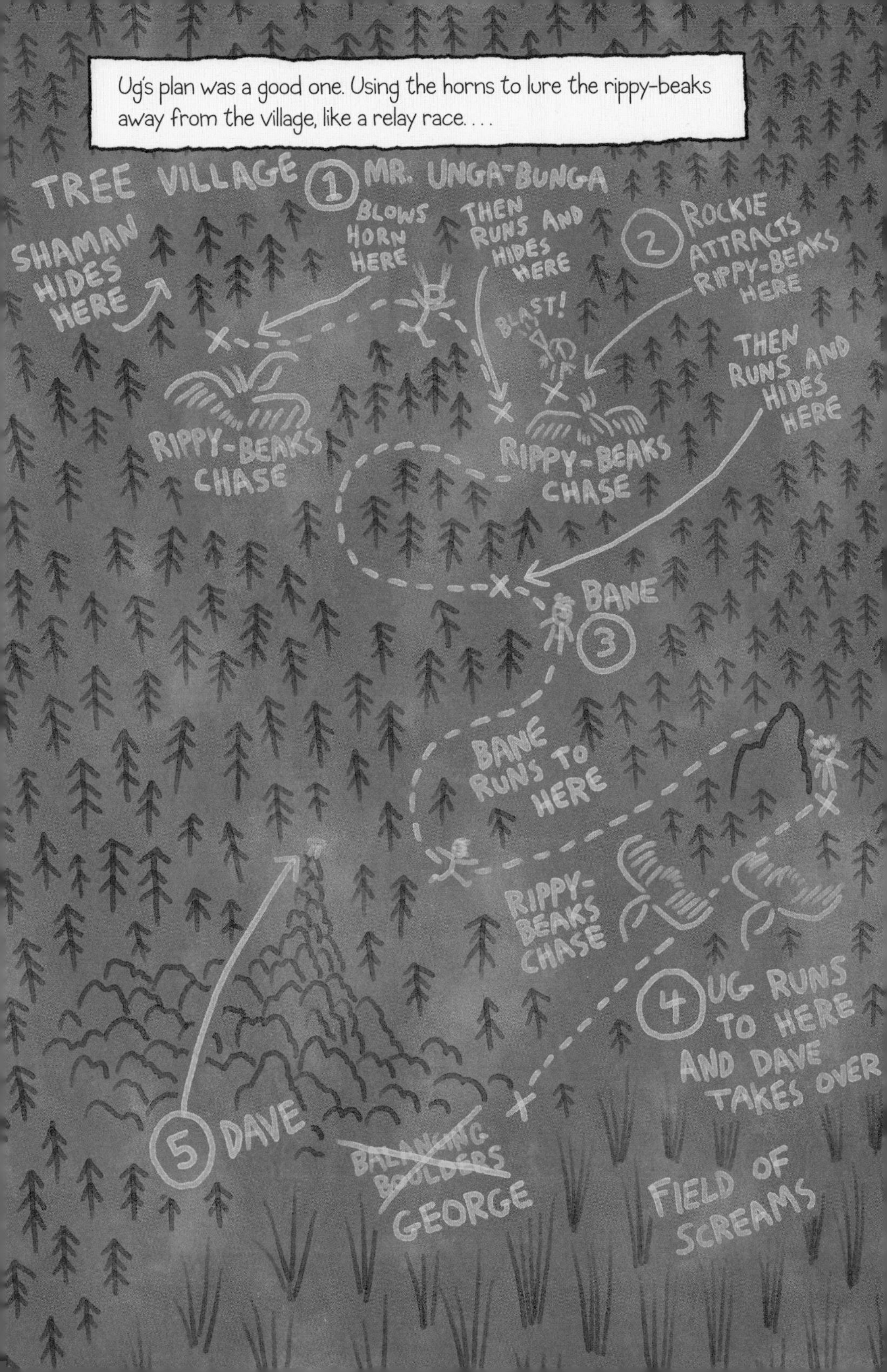
Ug's plan was a good one. Using the horns to lure the rippy-beaks away from the village, like a relay race. . . .
TREE VILLAGE
1 MR. UNGA-BUNGA
SHAMAN HIDES HERE
BLOWS HORN HERE
THEN RUNS AND HIDES HERE
2 ROCKIE ATTRACTS RIPPY-BEAKS HERE
BLAST!
THEN RUNS AND HIDES HERE
RIPPY-BEAKS CHASE
RIPPY-BEAKS CHASE
BANE
3
BANE RUNS TO HERE
RIPPY-BEAKS CHASE
4 UG RUNS TO HERE AND DAVE TAKES OVER
5 DAVE
~~BALANCING BOULDERS~~
GEORGE
FIELD OF SCREAMS

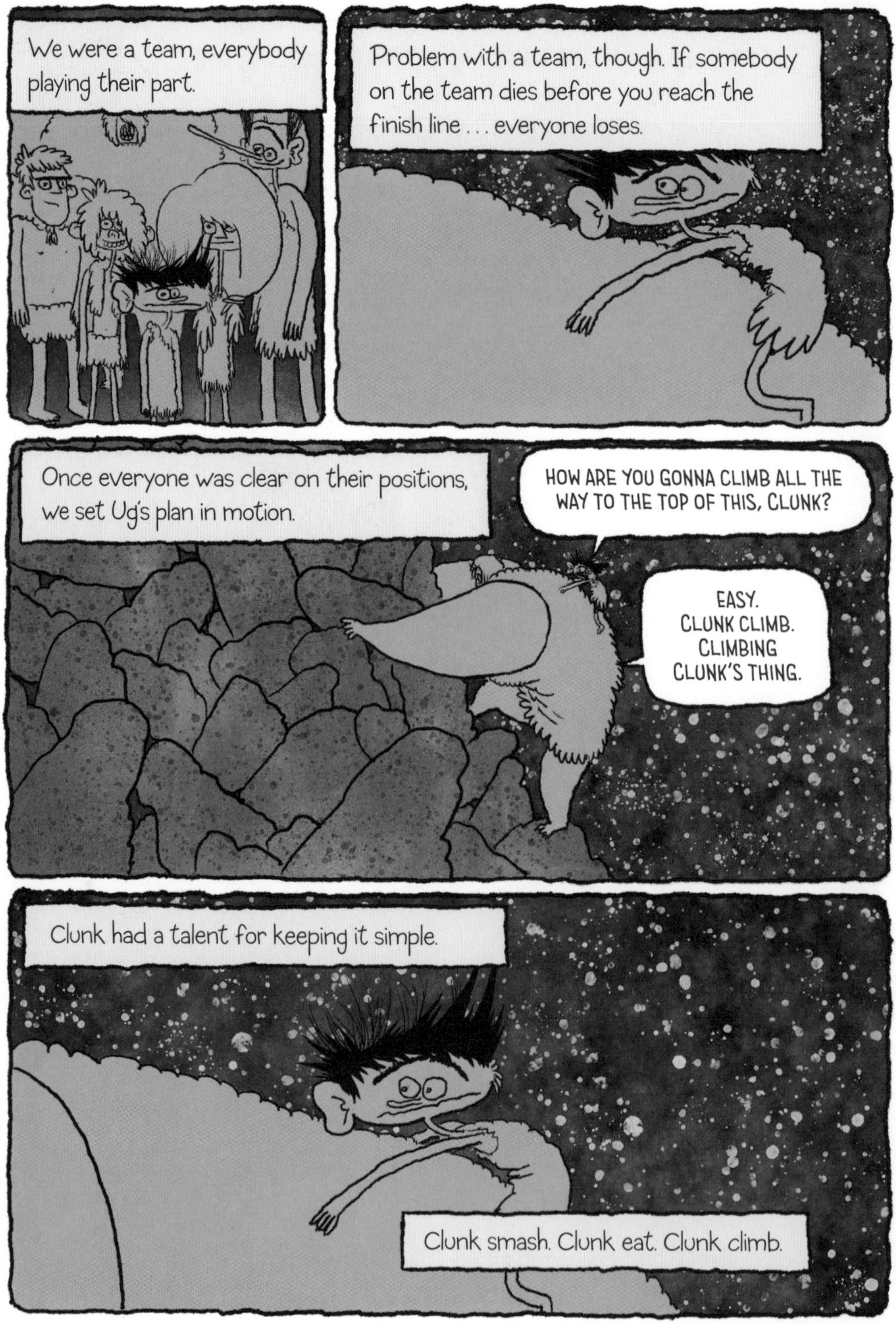
We were a team, everybody playing their part.
Problem with a team, though. If somebody on the team dies before you reach the finish line . . . everyone loses.
Once everyone was clear on their positions, we set Ug's plan in motion.
HOW ARE YOU GONNA CLIMB ALL THE WAY TO THE TOP OF THIS, CLUNK?
EASY. CLUNK CLIMB. CLIMBING CLUNK'S THING.
Clunk had a talent for keeping it simple.
Clunk smash. Clunk eat. Clunk climb.

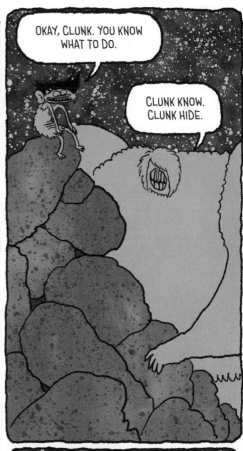

187

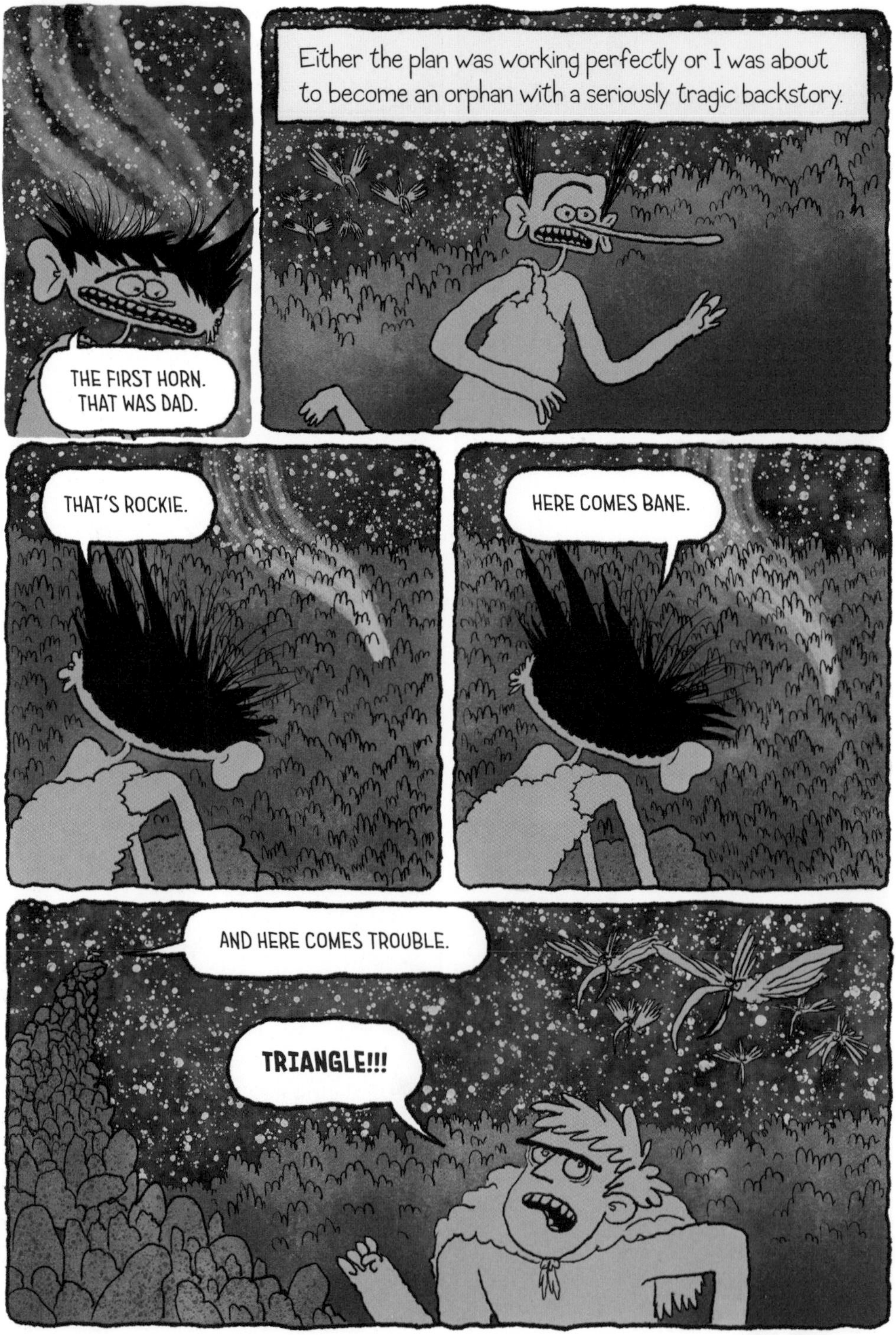
THE FIRST HORN. THAT WAS DAD.
Either the plan was working perfectly or I was about to become an orphan with a seriously tragic backstory.
THAT'S ROCKIE.
HERE COMES BANE.
AND HERE COMES TROUBLE.
TRIANGLE!!!

189

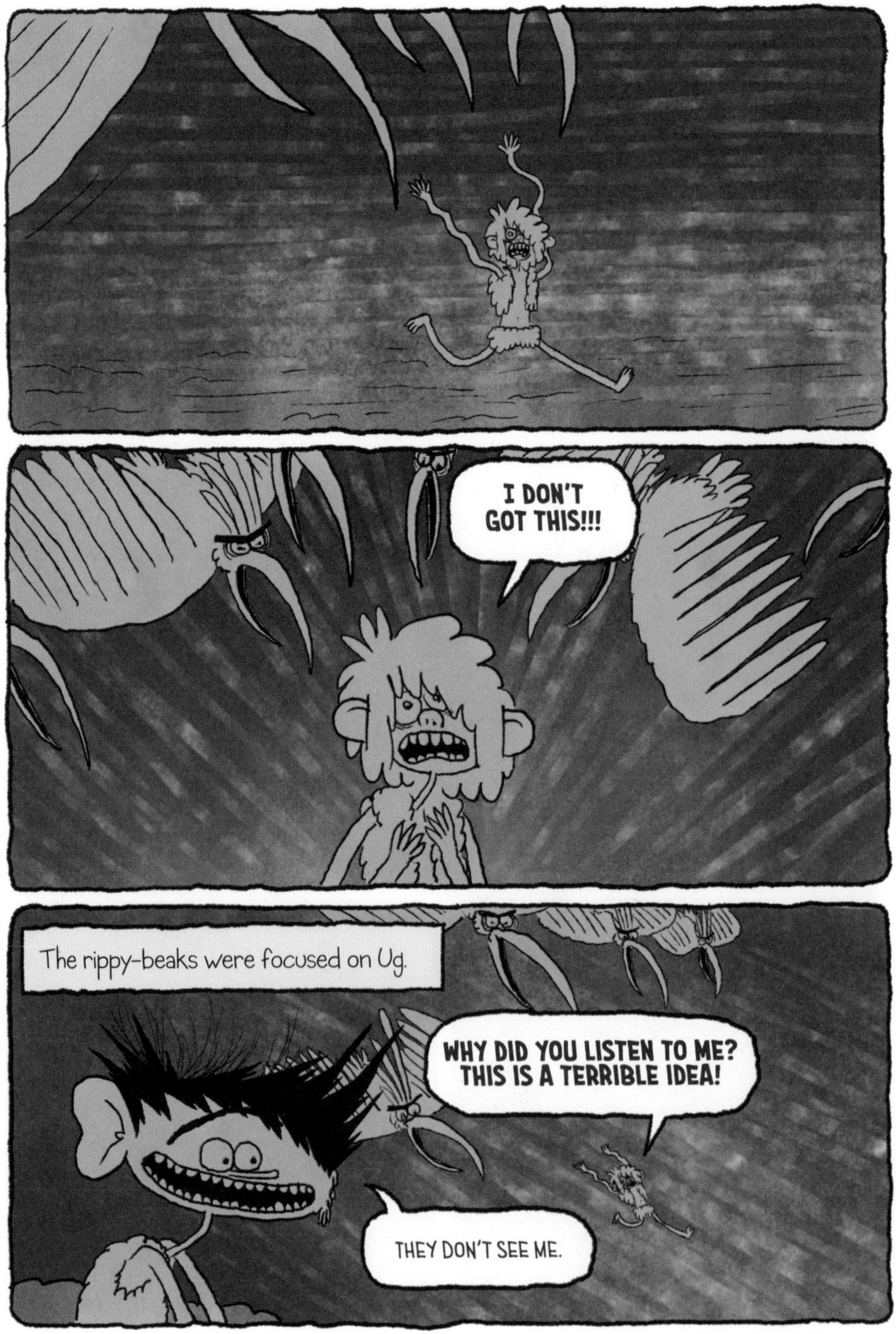
I DON'T GOT THIS!!!
The rippy-beaks were focused on Ug.
WHY DID YOU LISTEN TO ME? THIS IS A TERRIBLE IDEA!
THEY DON'T SEE ME.

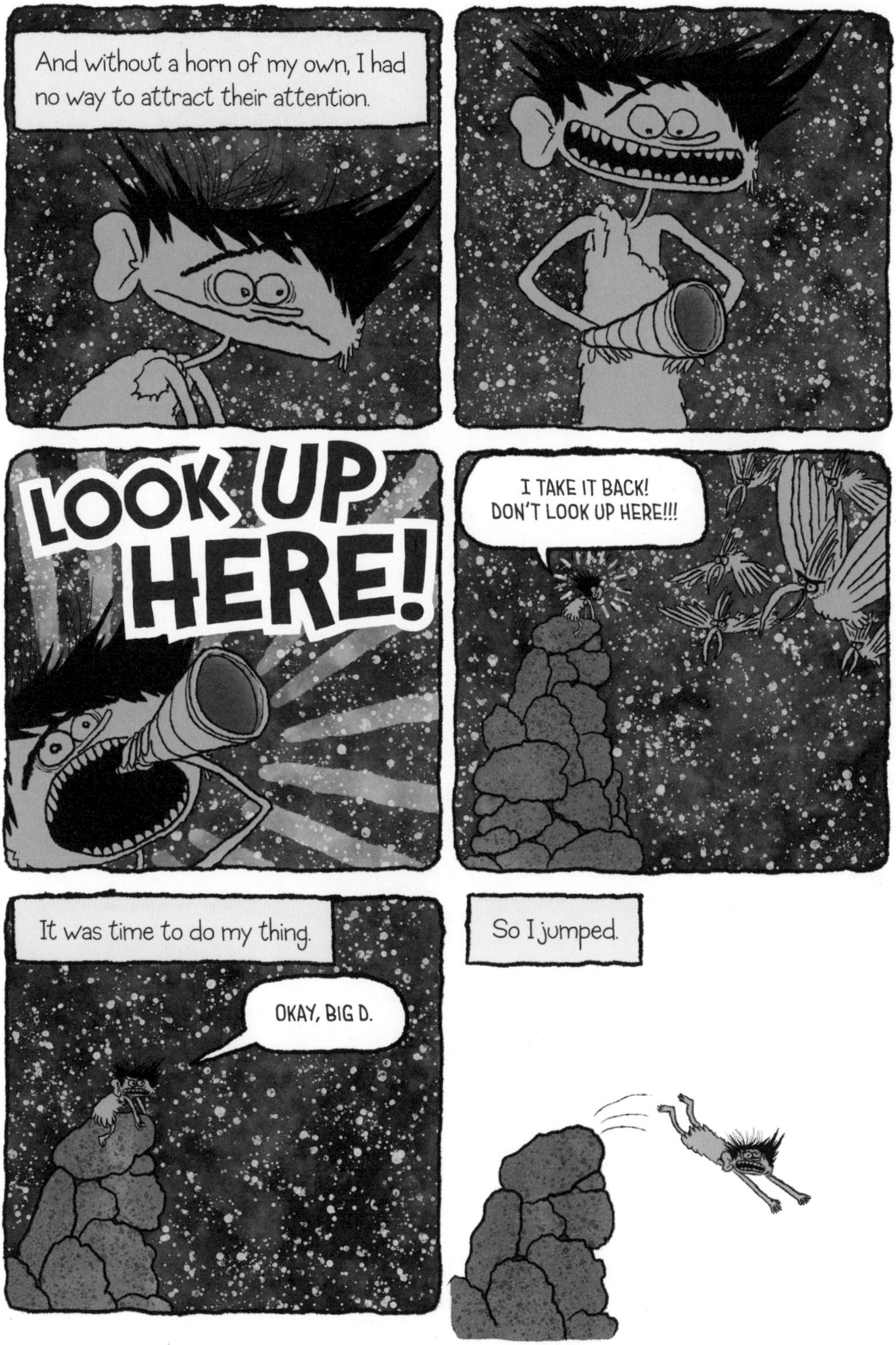
And without a horn of my own, I had no way to attract their attention.
LOOK UP HERE!
I TAKE IT BACK! DON'T LOOK UP HERE!!!
It was time to do my thing.
OKAY, BIG D.
So I jumped.

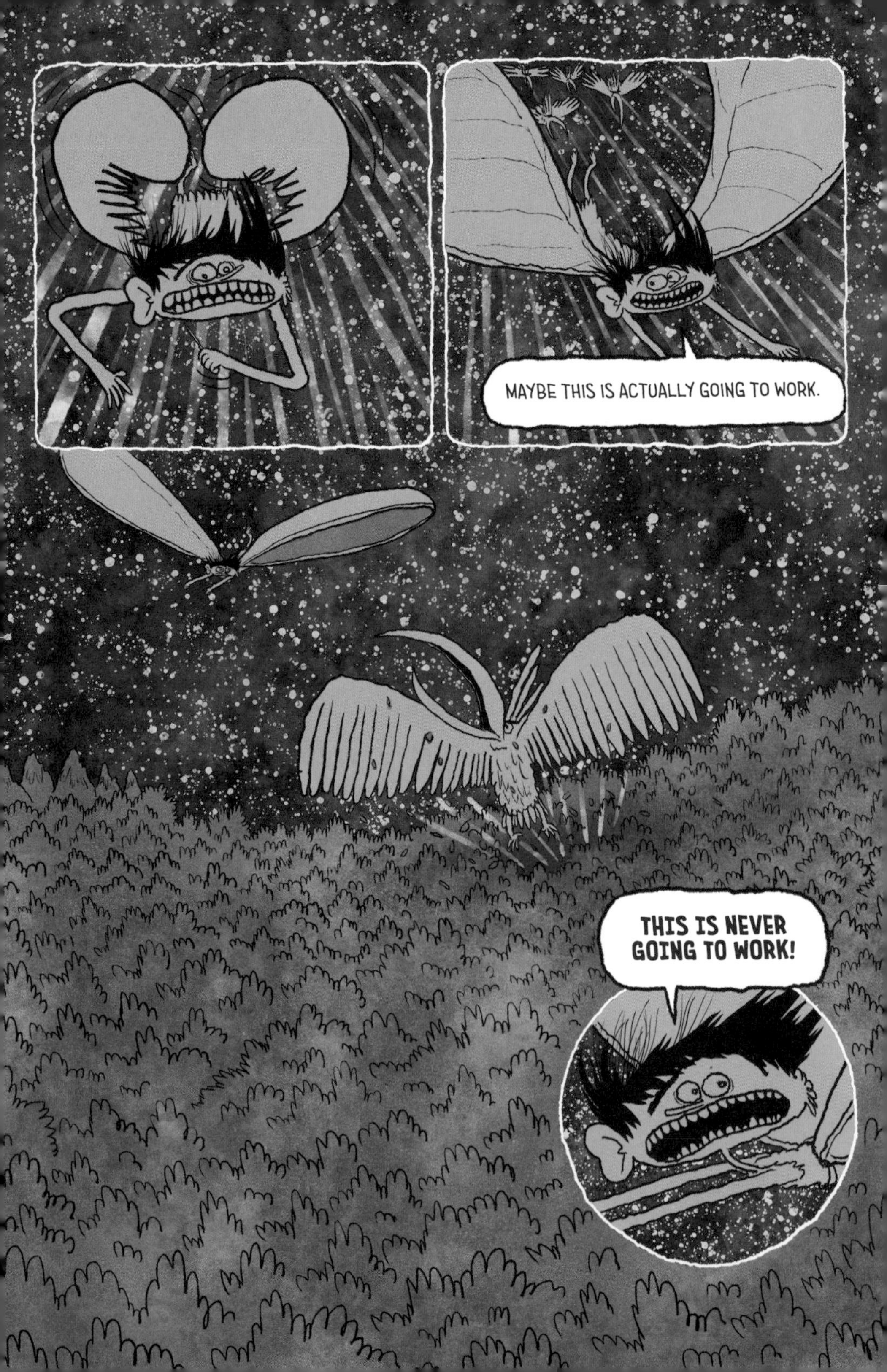
MAYBE THIS IS ACTUALLY GOING TO WORK.
THIS IS NEVER GOING TO WORK!

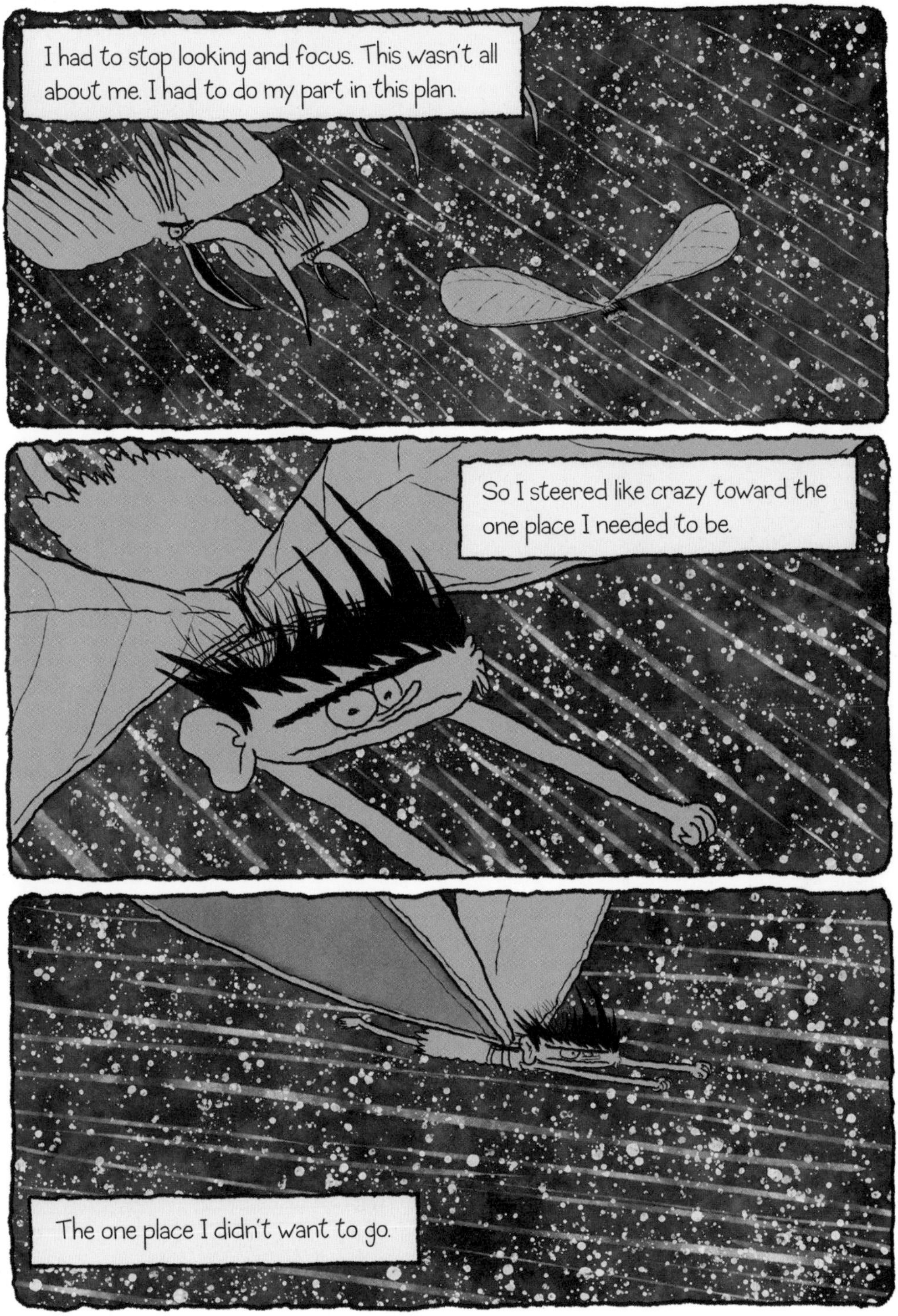
I had to stop looking and focus. This wasn't all about me. I had to do my part in this plan.
So I steered like crazy toward the one place I needed to be.
The one place I didn't want to go.

RED! GREEN! ORANGE! BLACK! BLACK! BLUE! GREEN! ORANGE!
I just had to remember the order and steer.

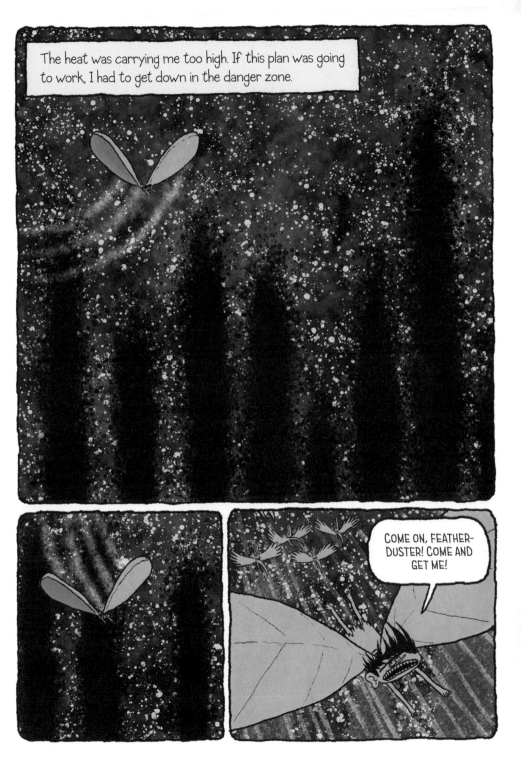

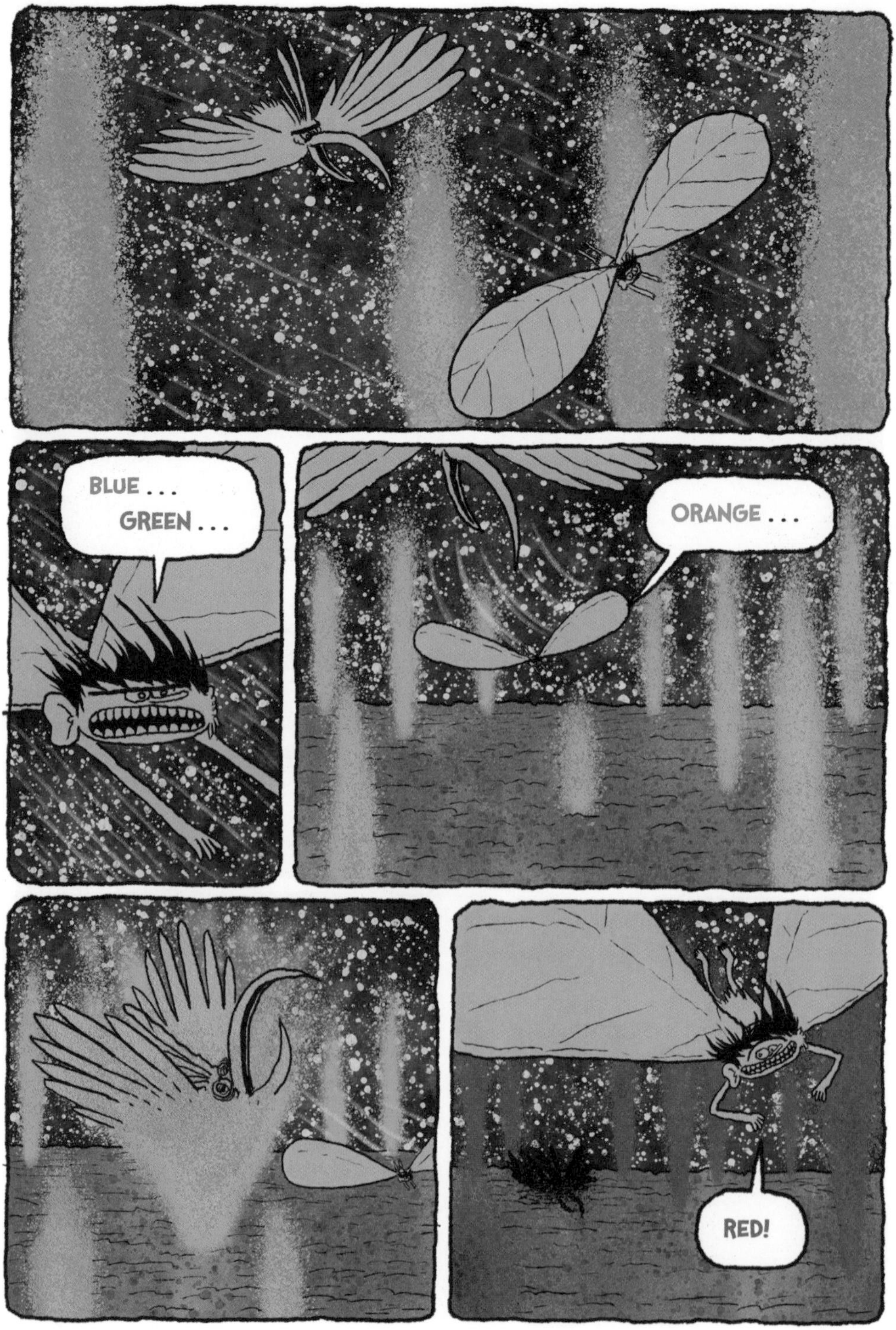
BLUE . . .
GREEN . . .
ORANGE . . .
RED!

199

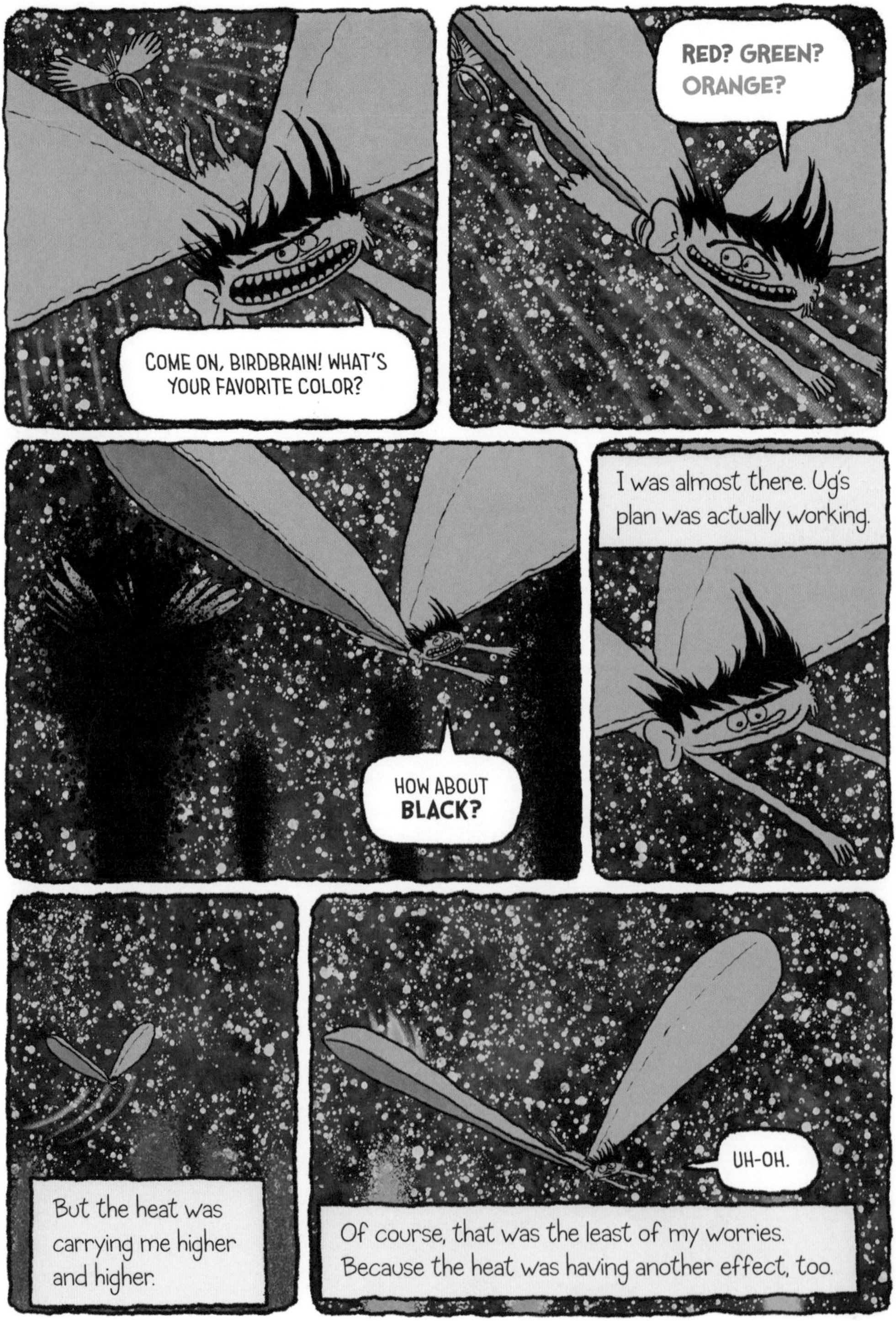
COME ON, BIRDBRAIN! WHAT'S YOUR FAVORITE COLOR?
RED? GREEN? ORANGE?
HOW ABOUT BLACK?
I was almost there. Ug's plan was actually working.
But the heat was carrying me higher and higher.
UH-OH.
Of course, that was the least of my worries. Because the heat was having another effect, too.

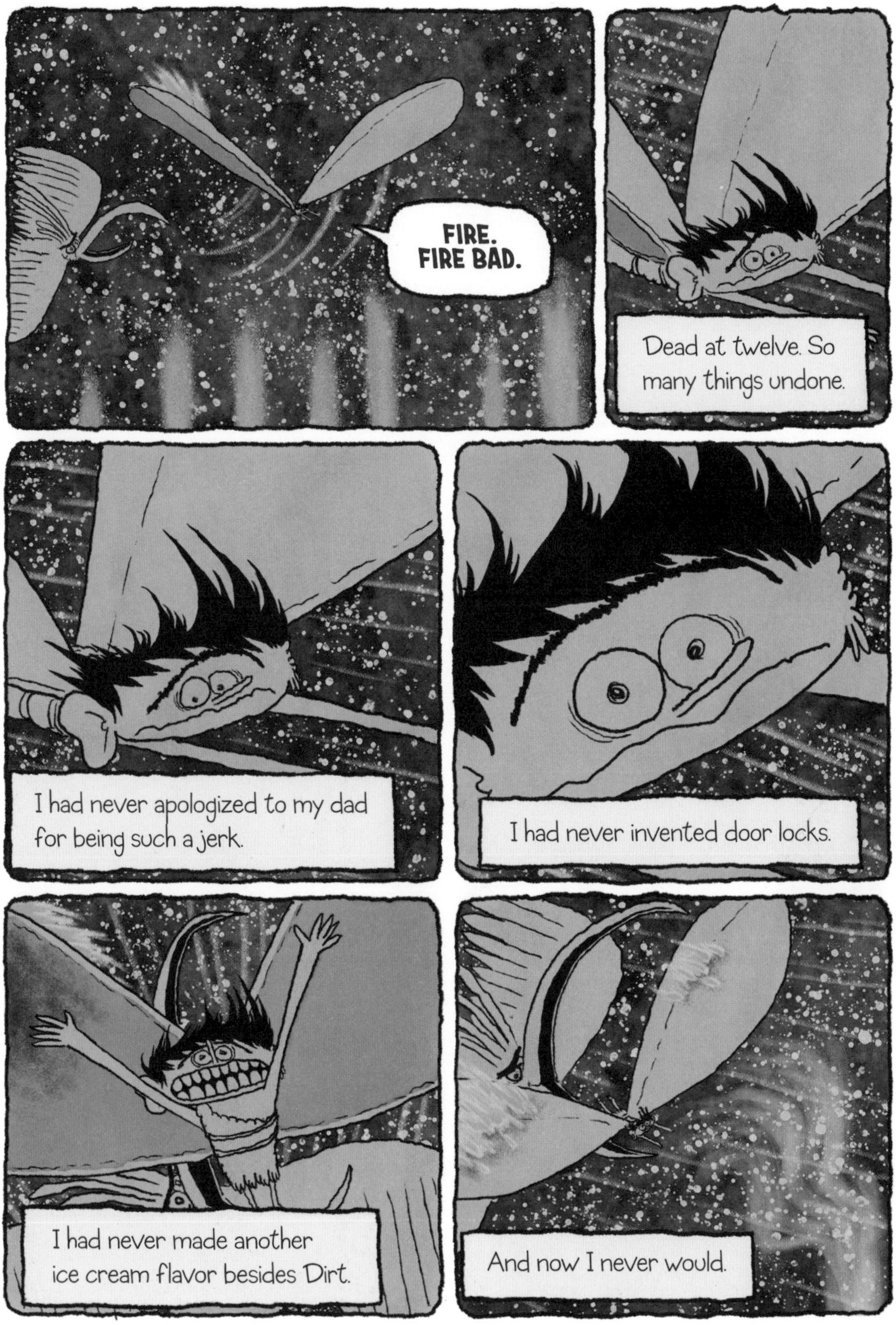
FIRE.
FIRE BAD.
Dead at twelve. So many things undone.
I had never apologized to my dad for being such a jerk.
I had never invented door locks.
I had never made another ice cream flavor besides Dirt.
And now I never would.

DAD!

Dad said I was trying so hard to do my own thing that I forgot to just be Dave.

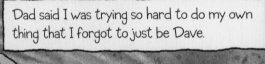

And he was right.

If there's one thing Dave knew how to do, it was think on his feet.

EJECT

So that's what I did.

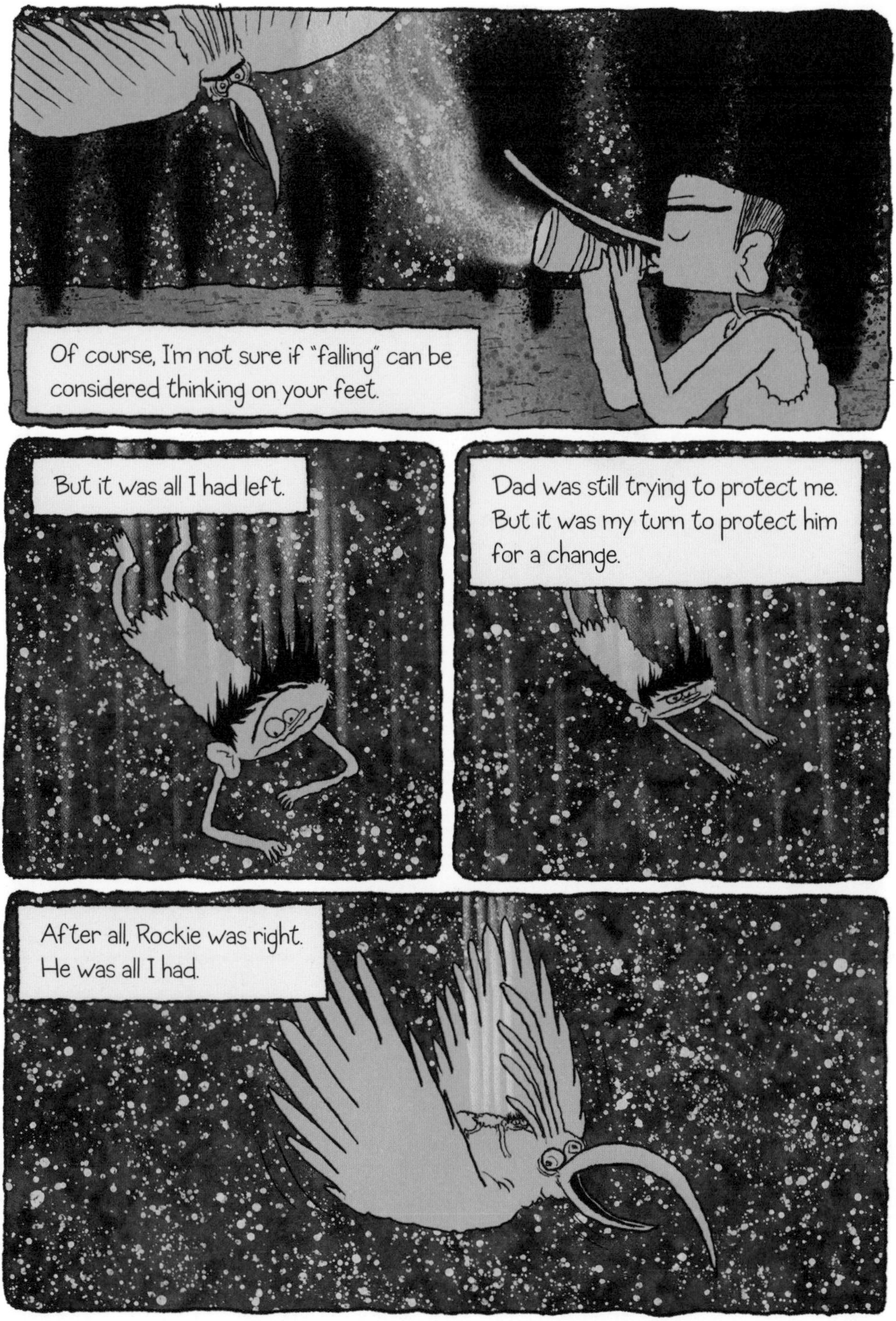
Of course, I'm not sure if "falling" can be considered thinking on your feet.
But it was all I had left.
Dad was still trying to protect me. But it was my turn to protect him for a change.
After all, Rockie was right. He was all I had.

I was doing the one thing left to do.

The one thing that would make sure Dad and the others got away safely.

The one thing Rockie predicted I would do. Crash and burn.

A shaman didn't always need to have all the answers.

A good shaman listened.

And sometimes a shaman could just be there for his people.

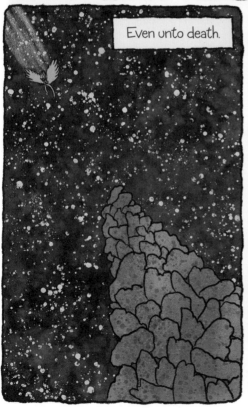

Even unto death.

Hopefully I hadn't realized it too late.

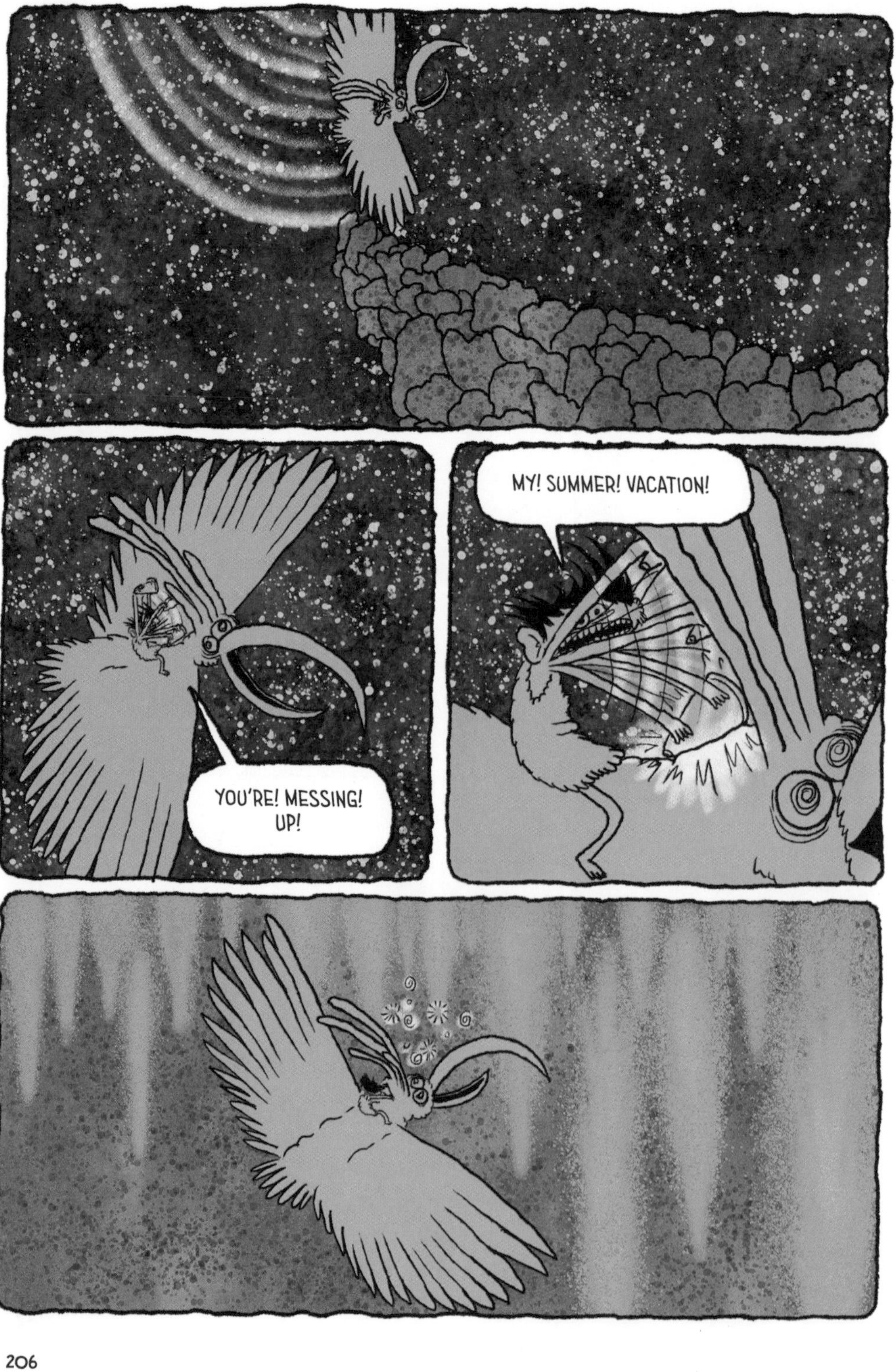
YOU'RE! MESSING! UP!
MY! SUMMER! VACATION!

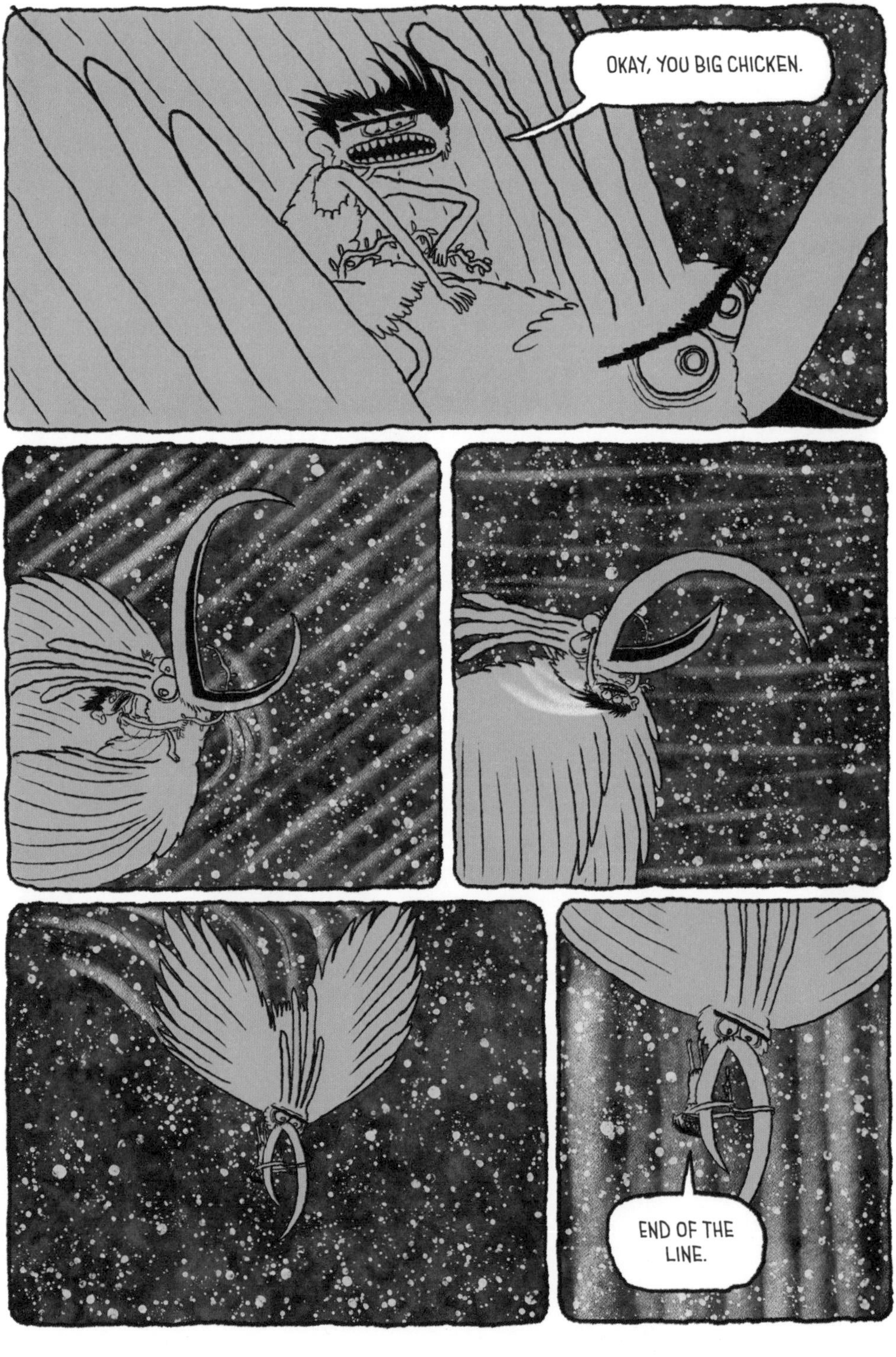
OKAY, YOU BIG CHICKEN.
END OF THE LINE.

Nothing left to do but jump and enjoy the ride.

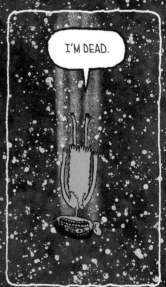

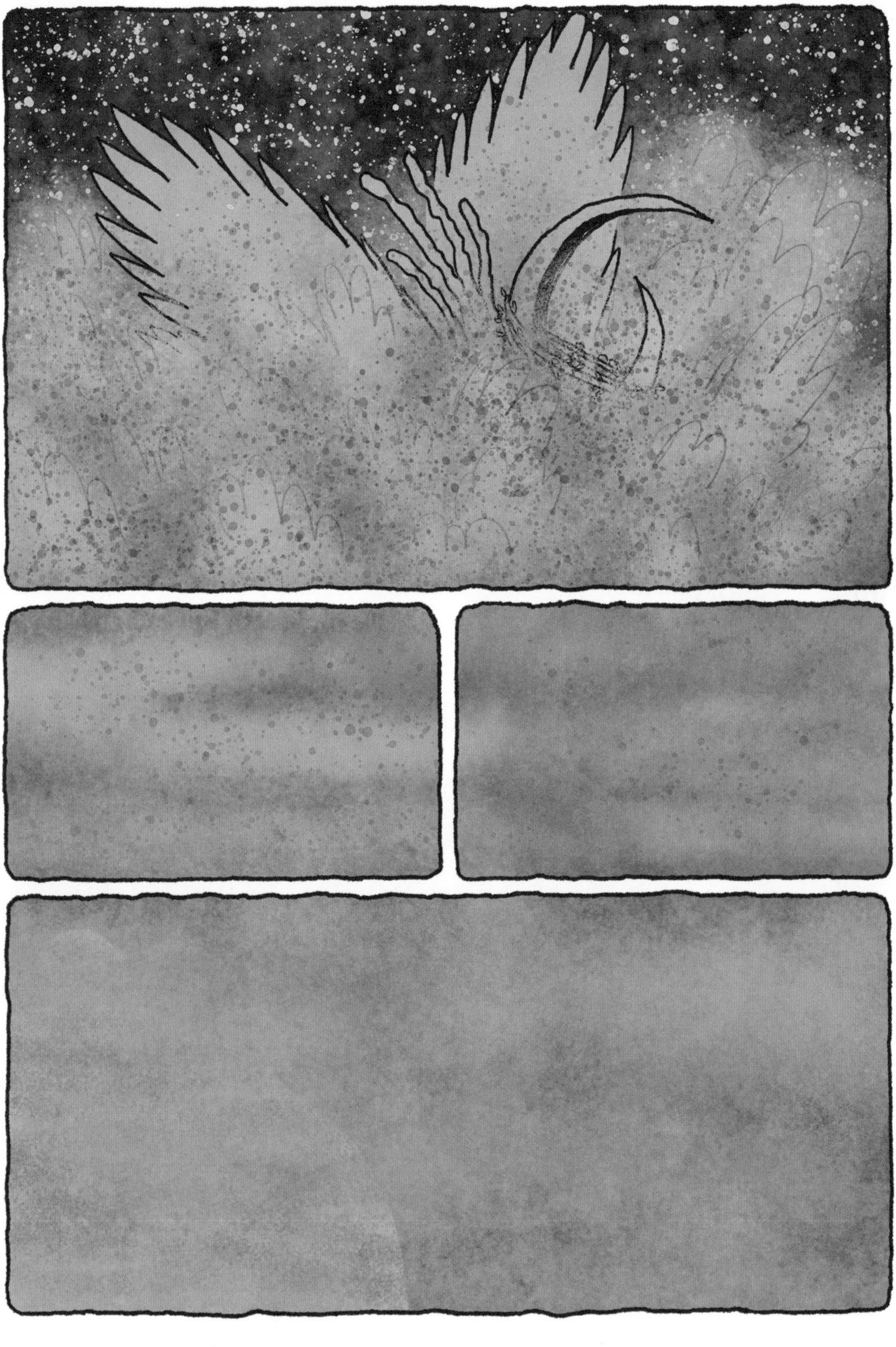

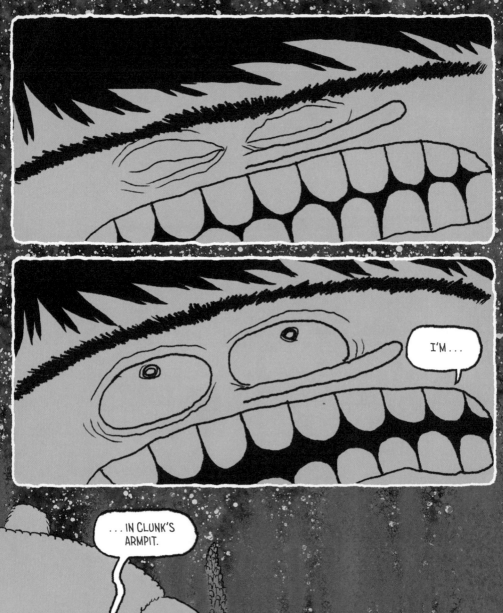

I'M . . .

. . . IN CLUNK'S ARMPIT.

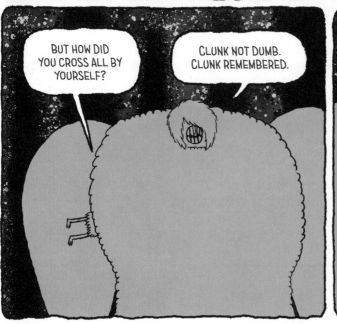

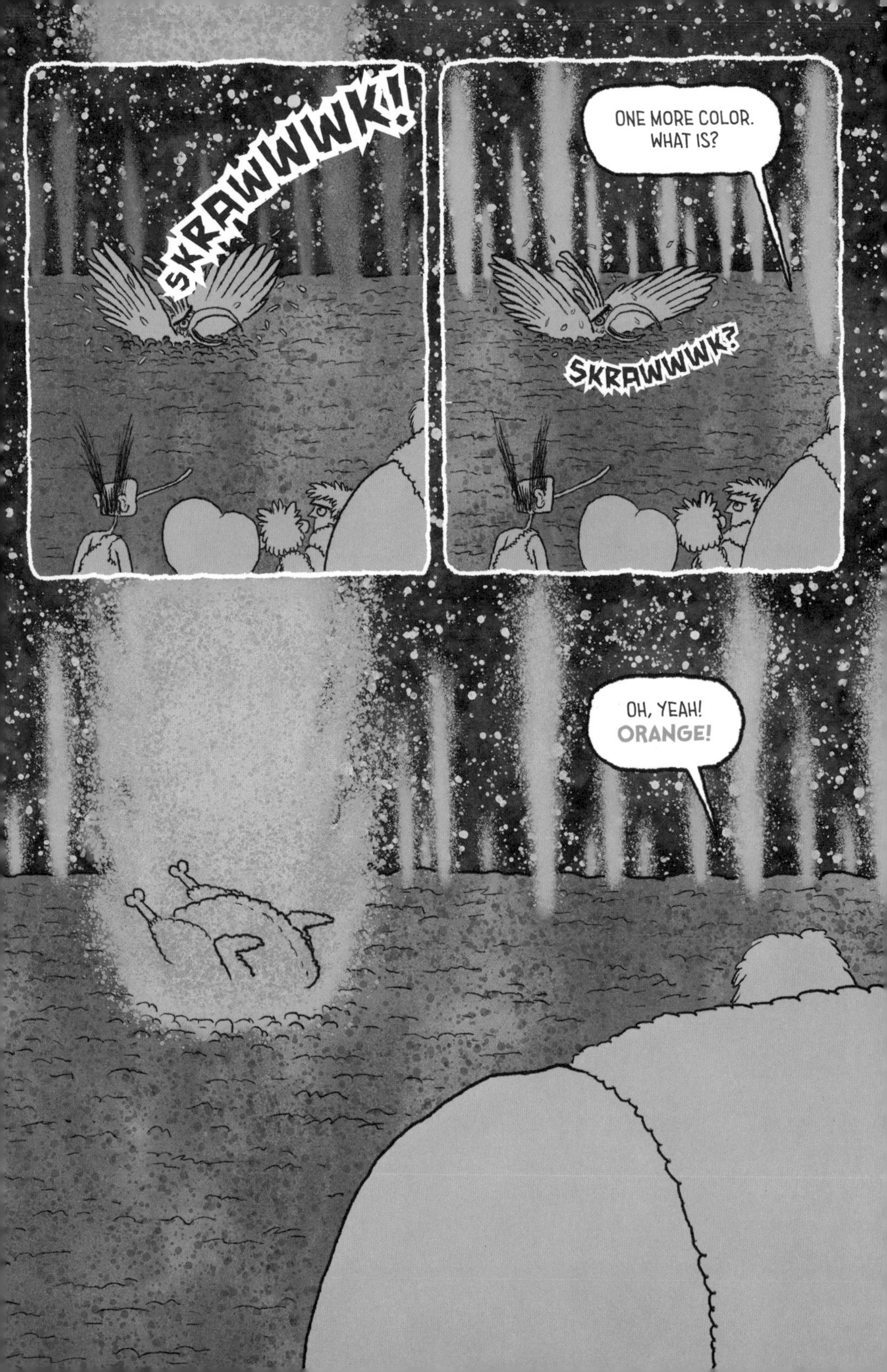
SKRAWWWK!
ONE MORE COLOR. WHAT IS?
SKRAWWWK?
OH, YEAH! ORANGE!

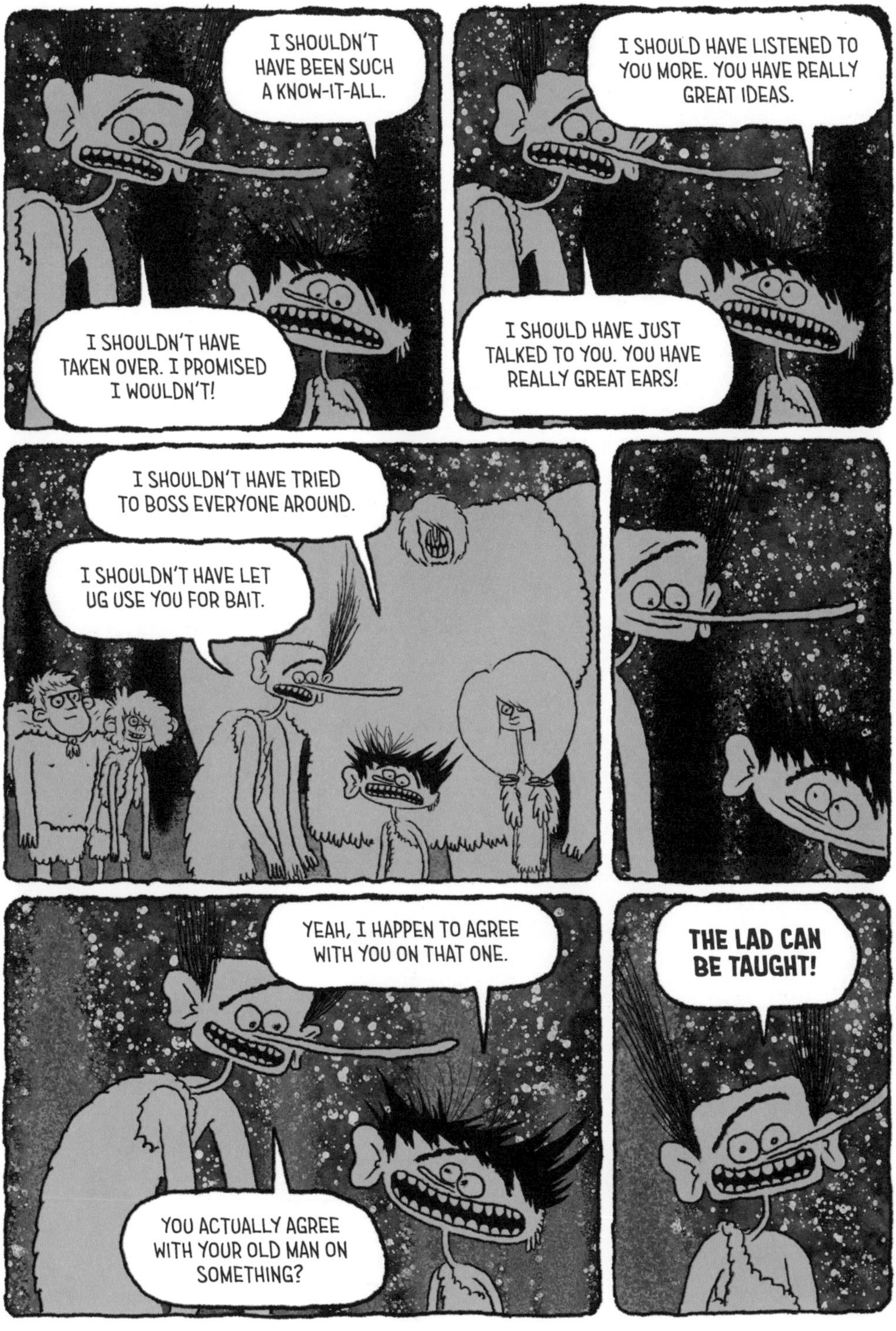
I SHOULDN'T HAVE BEEN SUCH A KNOW-IT-ALL.
I SHOULDN'T HAVE TAKEN OVER. I PROMISED I WOULDN'T!
I SHOULD HAVE LISTENED TO YOU MORE. YOU HAVE REALLY GREAT IDEAS.
I SHOULD HAVE JUST TALKED TO YOU. YOU HAVE REALLY GREAT EARS!
I SHOULDN'T HAVE TRIED TO BOSS EVERYONE AROUND.
I SHOULDN'T HAVE LET UG USE YOU FOR BAIT.
YEAH, I HAPPEN TO AGREE WITH YOU ON THAT ONE.
YOU ACTUALLY AGREE WITH YOUR OLD MAN ON SOMETHING?
THE LAD CAN BE TAUGHT!

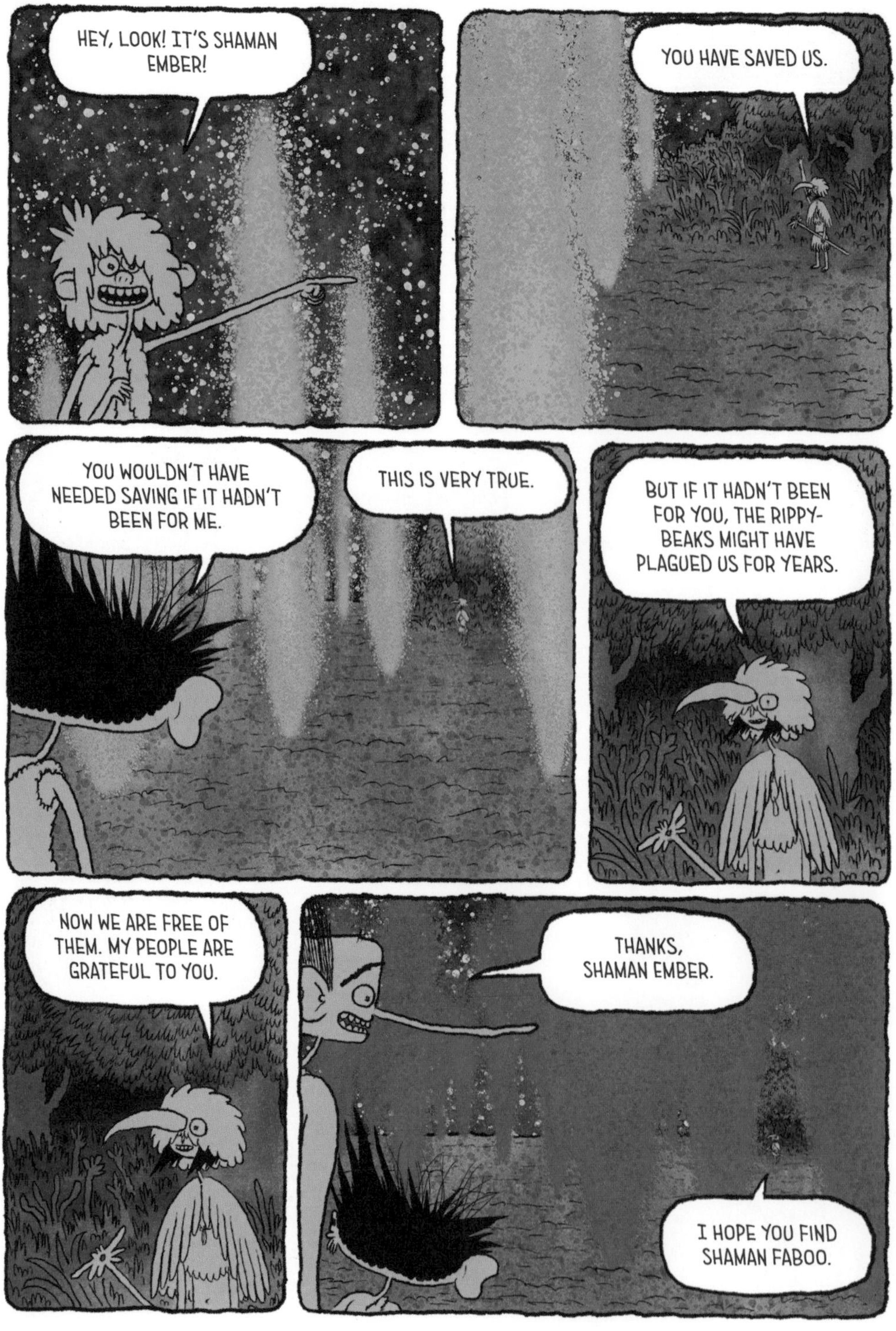
HEY, LOOK! IT'S SHAMAN EMBER!
YOU HAVE SAVED US.
YOU WOULDN'T HAVE NEEDED SAVING IF IT HADN'T BEEN FOR ME.
THIS IS VERY TRUE.
BUT IF IT HADN'T BEEN FOR YOU, THE RIPPY-BEAKS MIGHT HAVE PLAGUED US FOR YEARS.
NOW WE ARE FREE OF THEM. MY PEOPLE ARE GRATEFUL TO YOU.
THANKS, SHAMAN EMBER.
I HOPE YOU FIND SHAMAN FABOO.

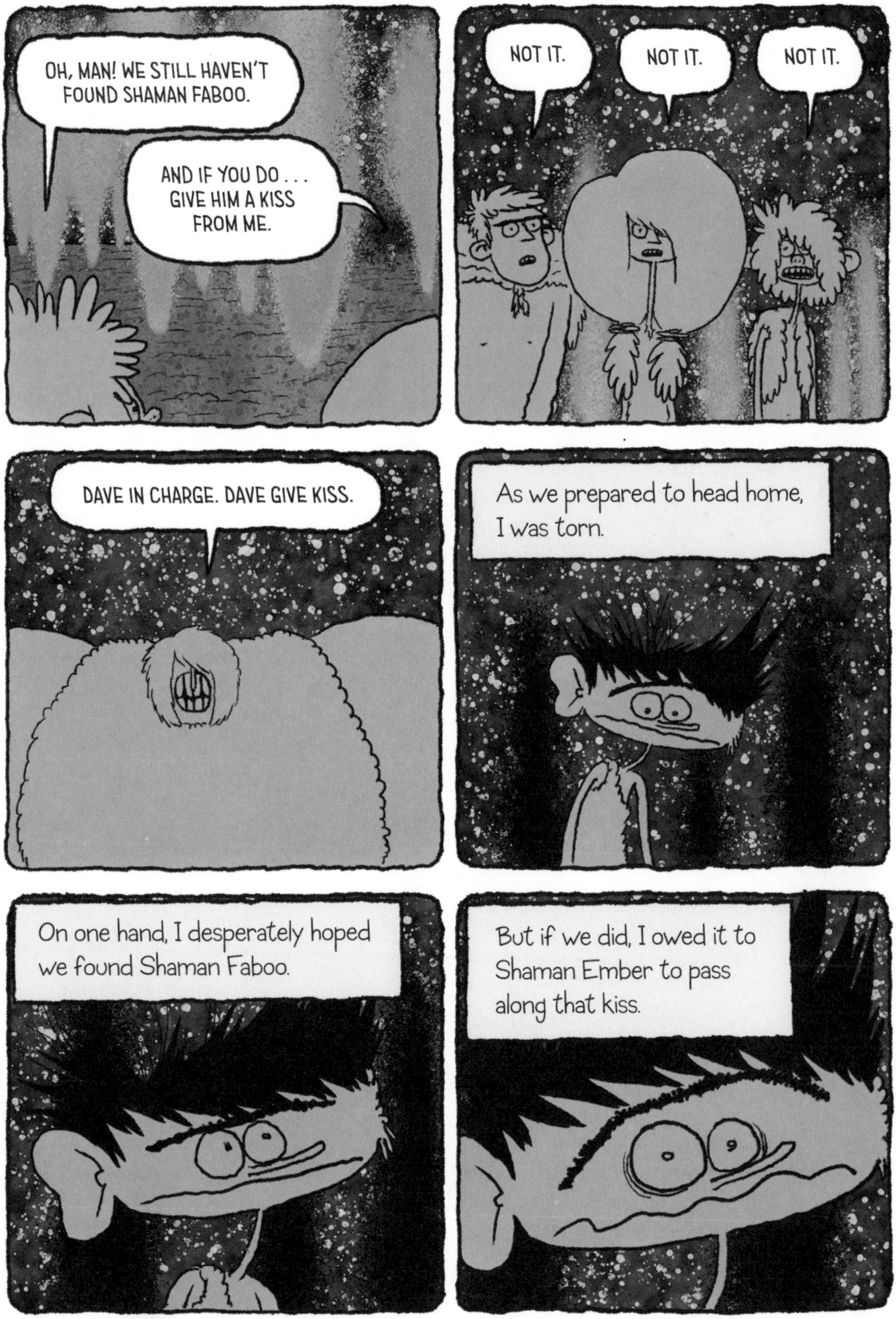
OH, MAN! WE STILL HAVEN'T FOUND SHAMAN FABOO.
AND IF YOU DO . . . GIVE HIM A KISS FROM ME.
NOT IT.
NOT IT.
NOT IT.
DAVE IN CHARGE. DAVE GIVE KISS.
As we prepared to head home, I was torn.
On one hand, I desperately hoped we found Shaman Faboo.
But if we did, I owed it to Shaman Ember to pass along that kiss.

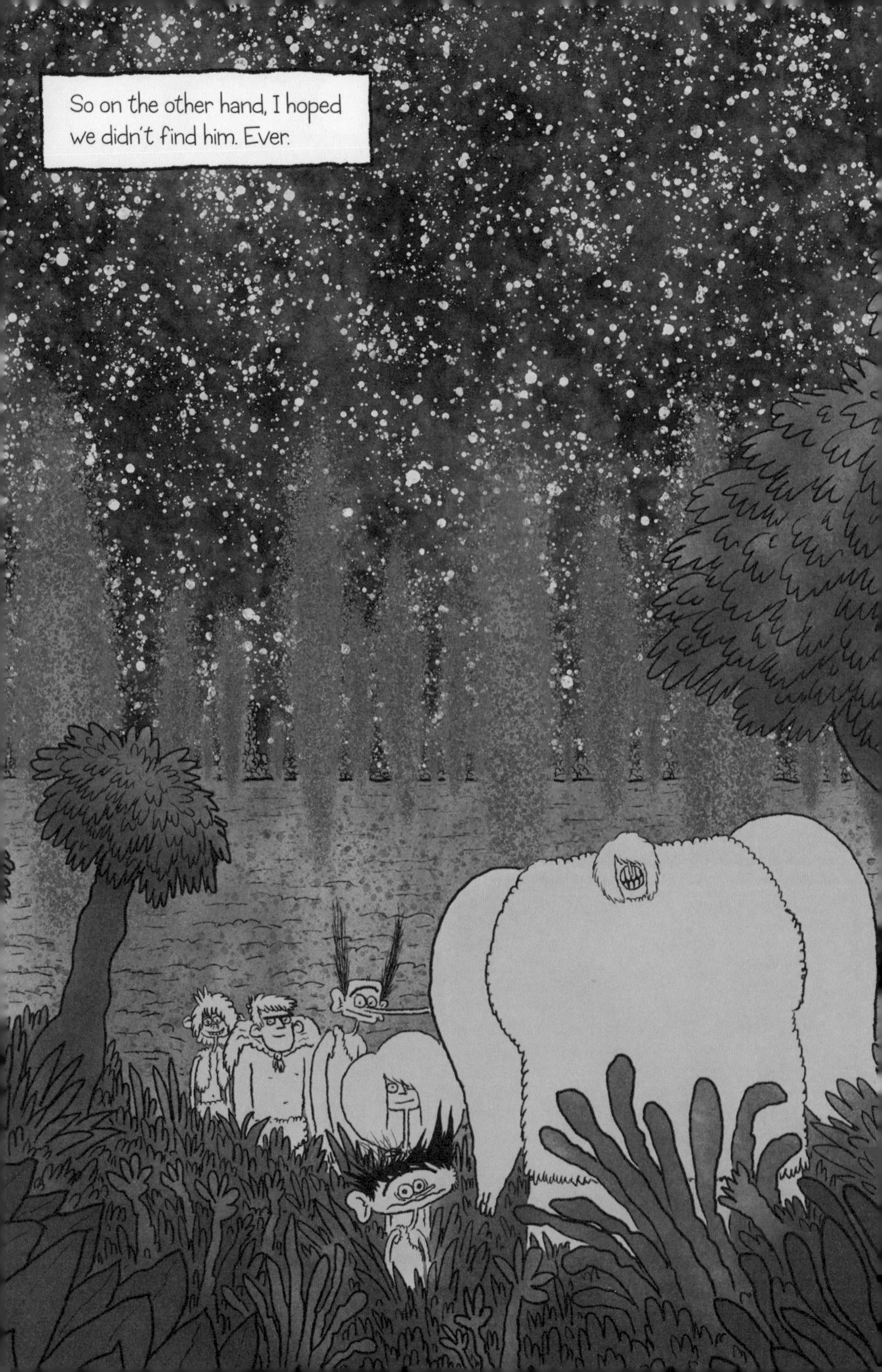
So on the other hand, I hoped we didn't find him. Ever.

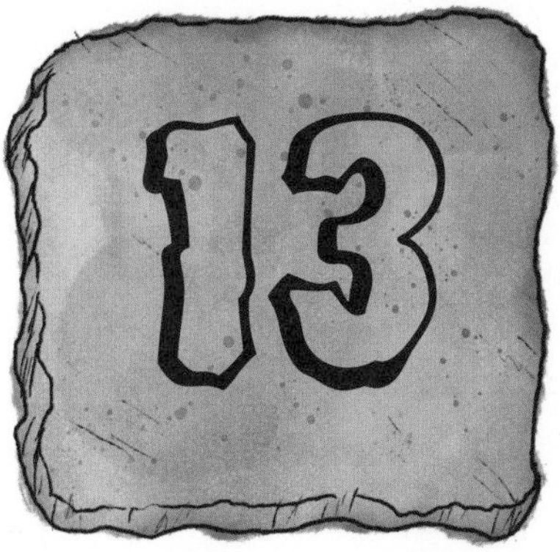
13

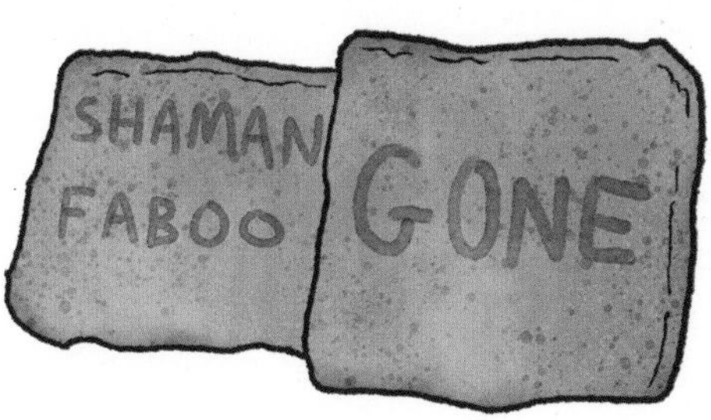
SHAMAN
FABOO
GONE

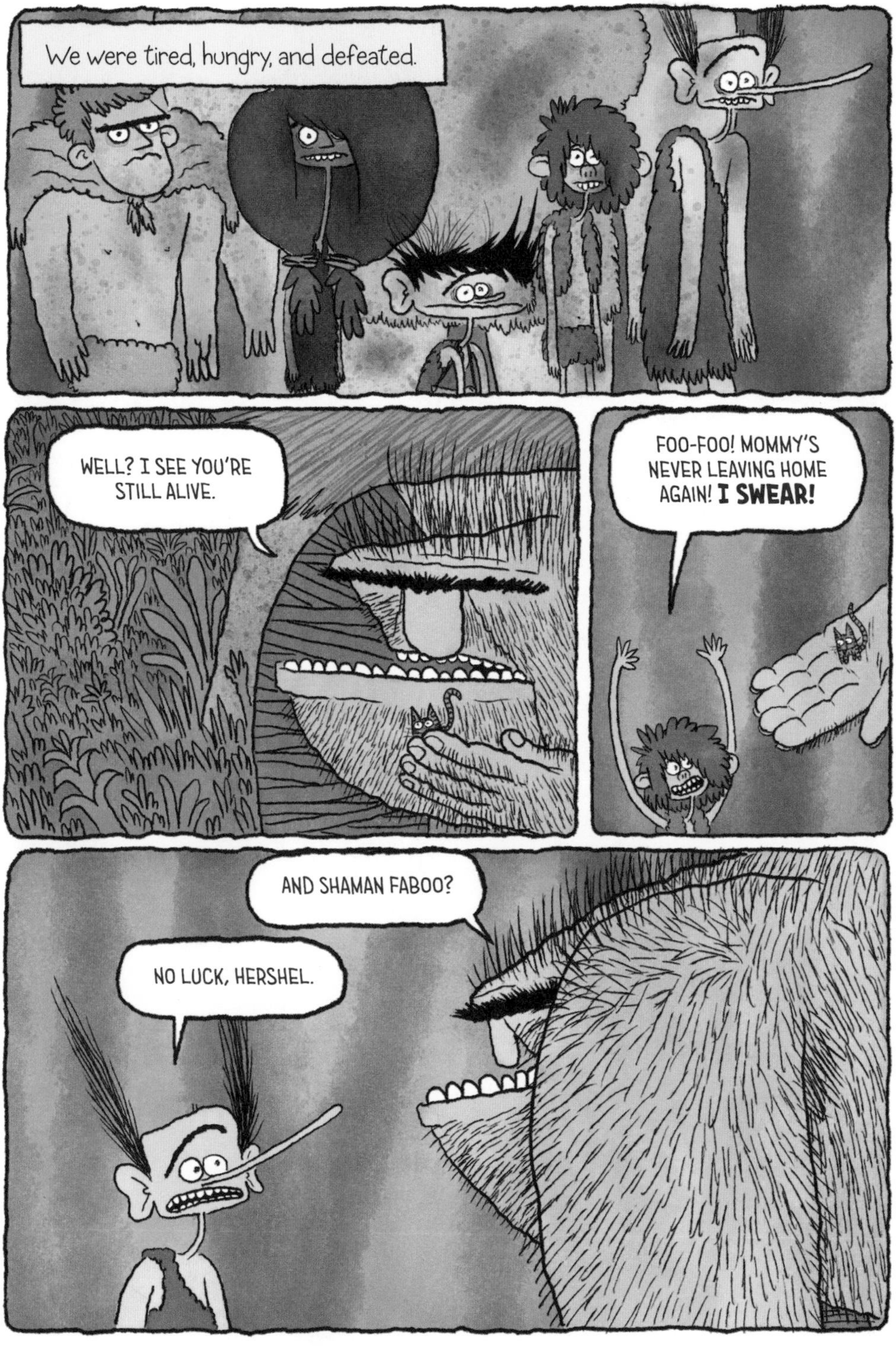
We were tired, hungry, and defeated.
WELL? I SEE YOU'RE STILL ALIVE.
FOO-FOO! MOMMY'S NEVER LEAVING HOME AGAIN! **I SWEAR!**
AND SHAMAN FABOO?
NO LUCK, HERSHEL.

ALL I KNOW IS "SHAMAN FABOO GONE." MAYBE FOR GOOD.

SHAM
FABO

GONE

YOU KNOW WHAT THAT MEANS, DON'T YOU, BOY?

NO.

SHAM
FABO

GONE

IT MEANS YOU MAY NEED TO TAKE CHARGE FOR GOOD.

So much for simplifying my life. I was doomed.

225

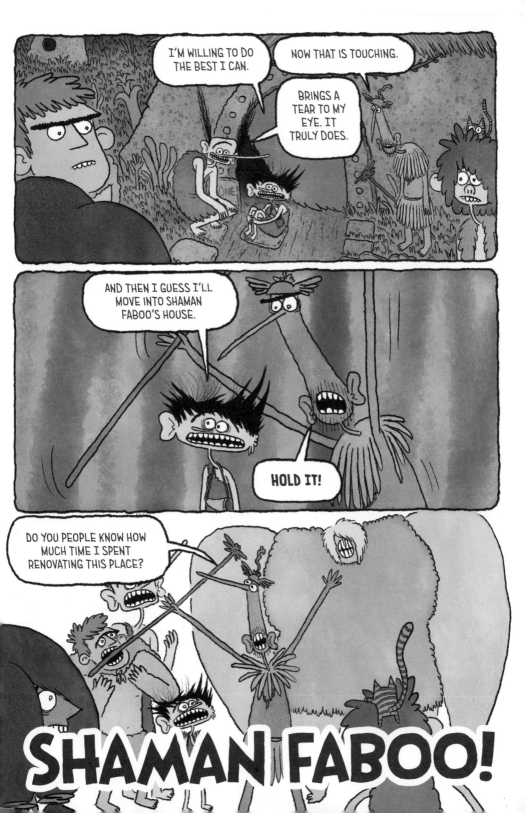

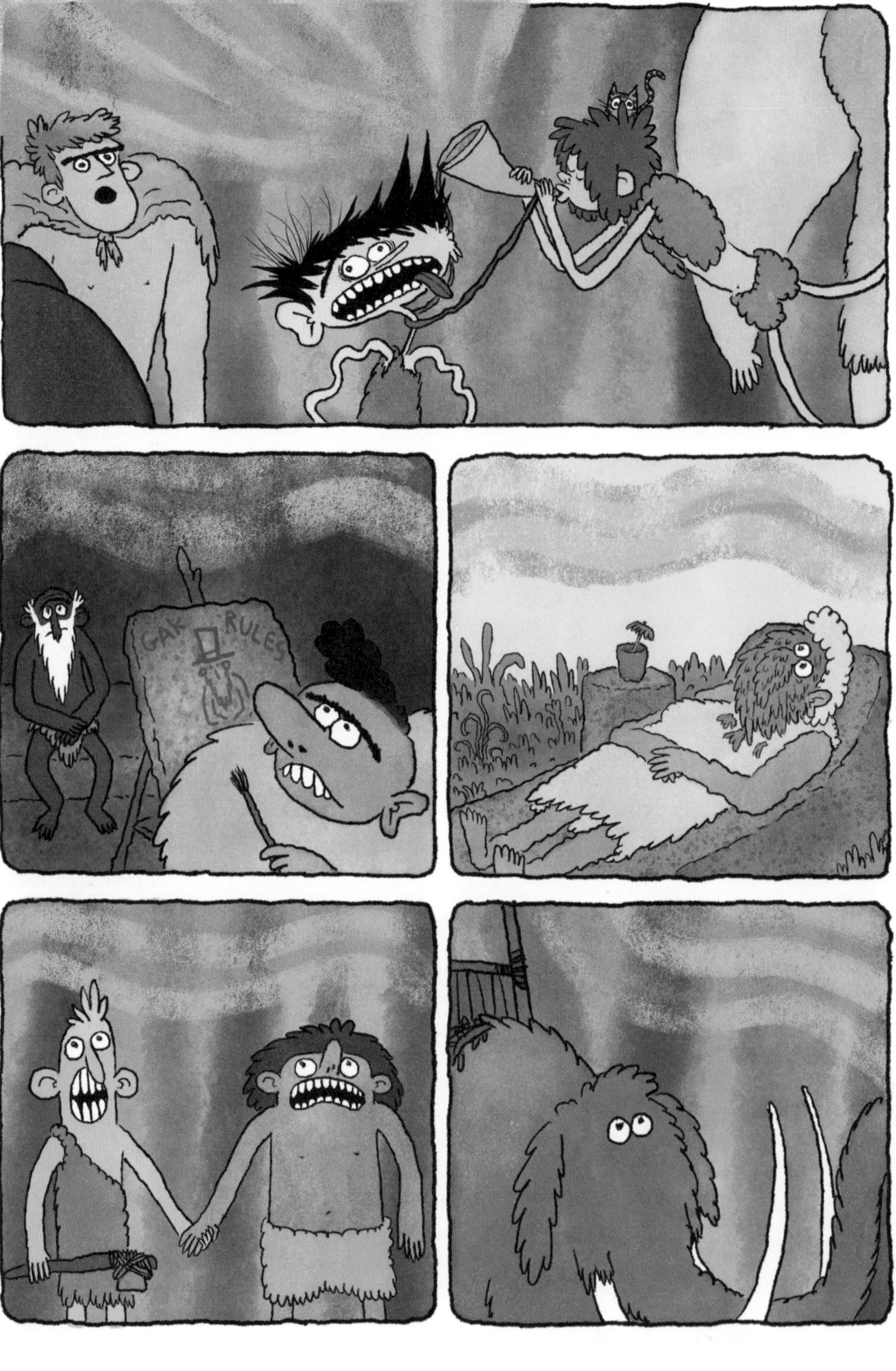
GAK RULES

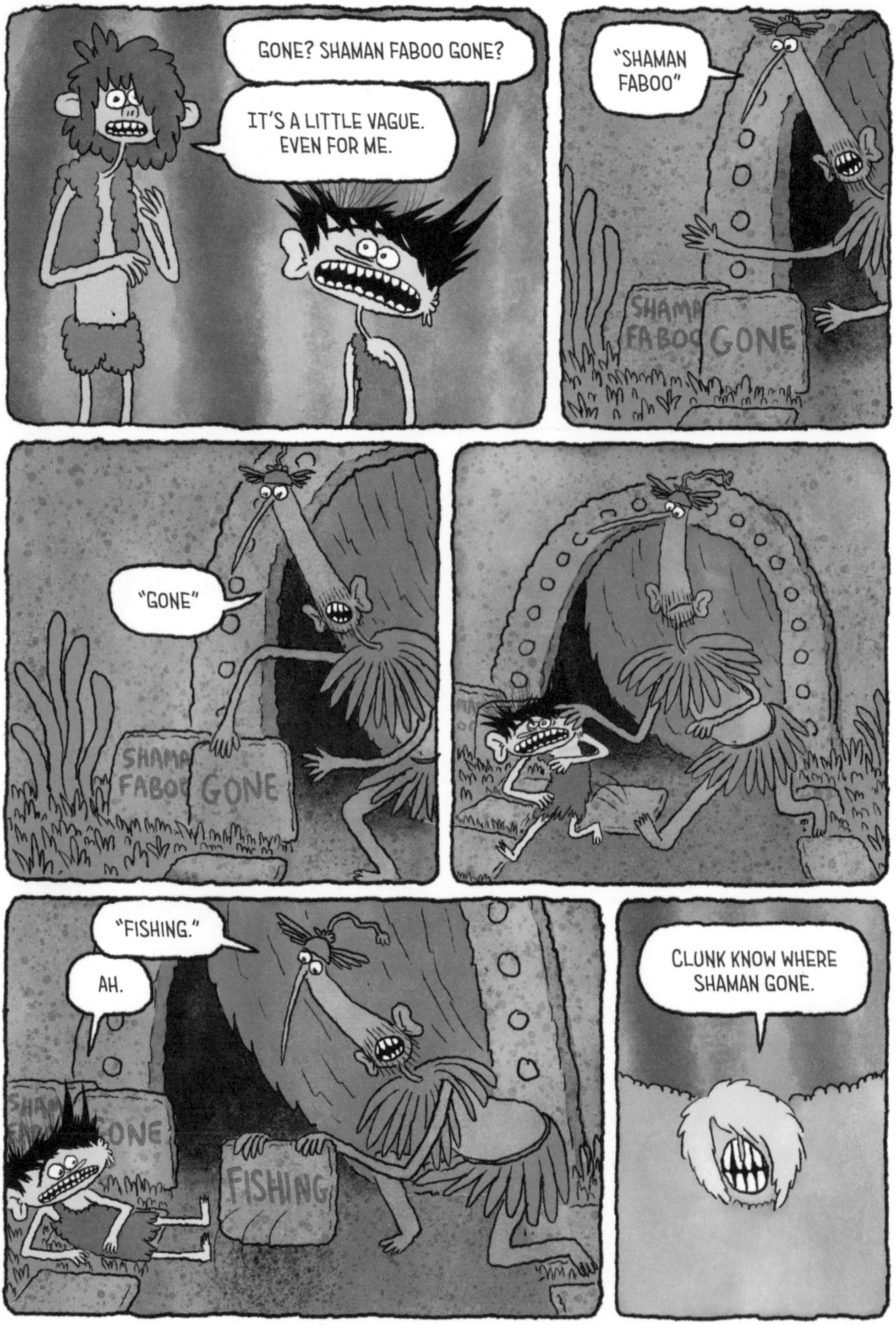
GONE? SHAMAN FABOO GONE?
IT'S A LITTLE VAGUE. EVEN FOR ME.
"SHAMAN FABOO"
SHAMA FABOO
GONE
"GONE"
SHAMA FABOO
GONE
"FISHING."
AH.
FISHING
CLUNK KNOW WHERE SHAMAN GONE.

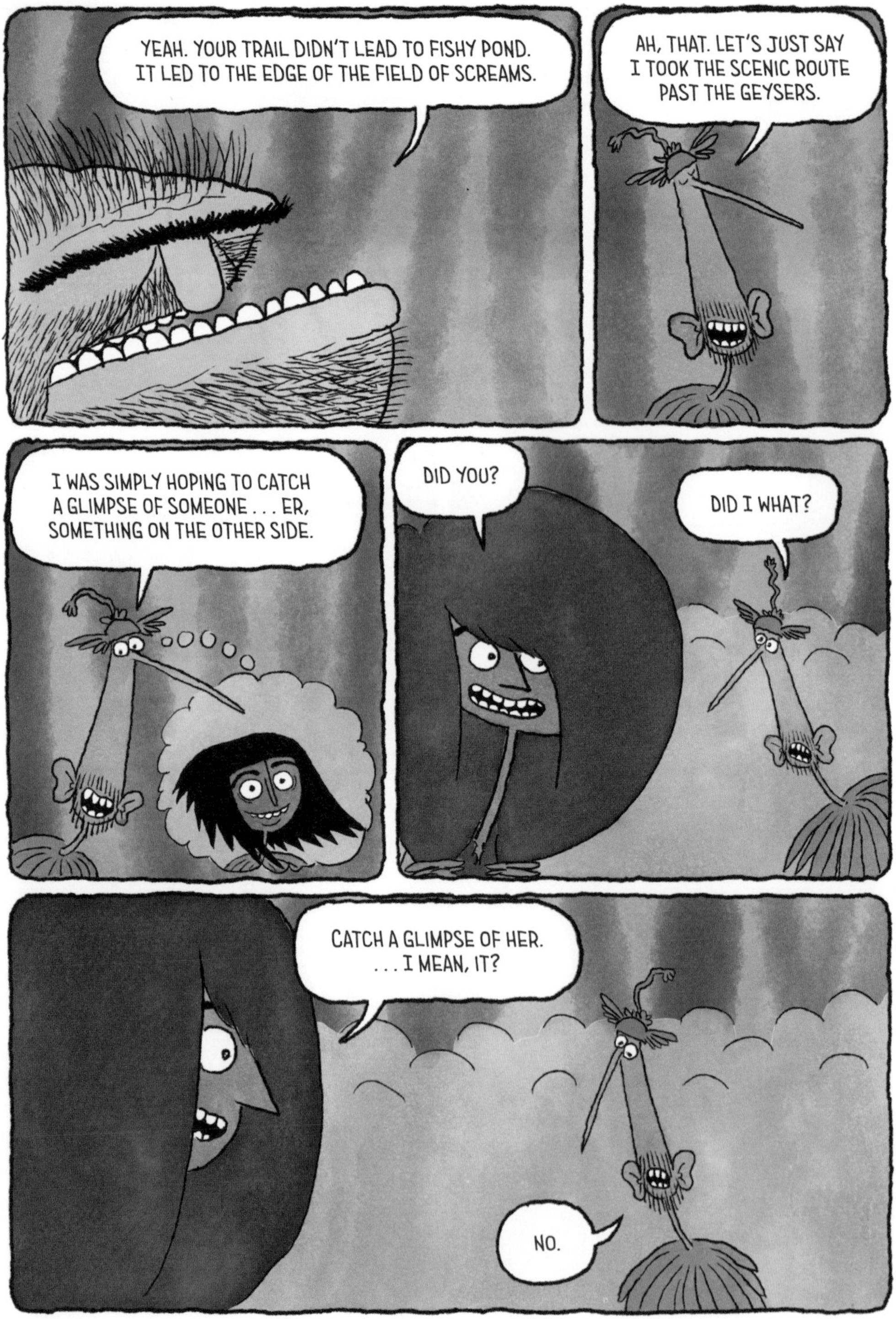
YEAH. YOUR TRAIL DIDN'T LEAD TO FISHY POND. IT LED TO THE EDGE OF THE FIELD OF SCREAMS.
AH, THAT. LET'S JUST SAY I TOOK THE SCENIC ROUTE PAST THE GEYSERS.
I WAS SIMPLY HOPING TO CATCH A GLIMPSE OF SOMEONE . . . ER, SOMETHING ON THE OTHER SIDE.
DID YOU?
DID I WHAT?
CATCH A GLIMPSE OF HER. . . . I MEAN, IT?
NO.

235

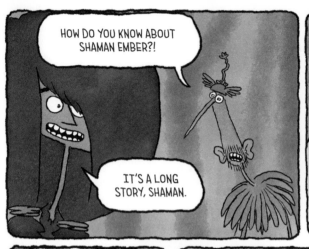

HOW DO YOU KNOW ABOUT SHAMAN EMBER?!

IT'S A LONG STORY, SHAMAN.

I'LL MAKE US A CUP OF SLUDGEWATER TEA AND TELL YOU ALL ABOUT IT.

COME ON, EVERYBODY. LET'S GET THAT BONFIRE STARTED.

WE CELEBRATE WITH FISH TONIGHT!

CLUNK NOT LIKE FISH. TASTES LIKE FISH.

YOU'LL EAT IT AND YOU'LL LIKE IT.

CLUNK EAT. CLUNK NOT LIKE.

237

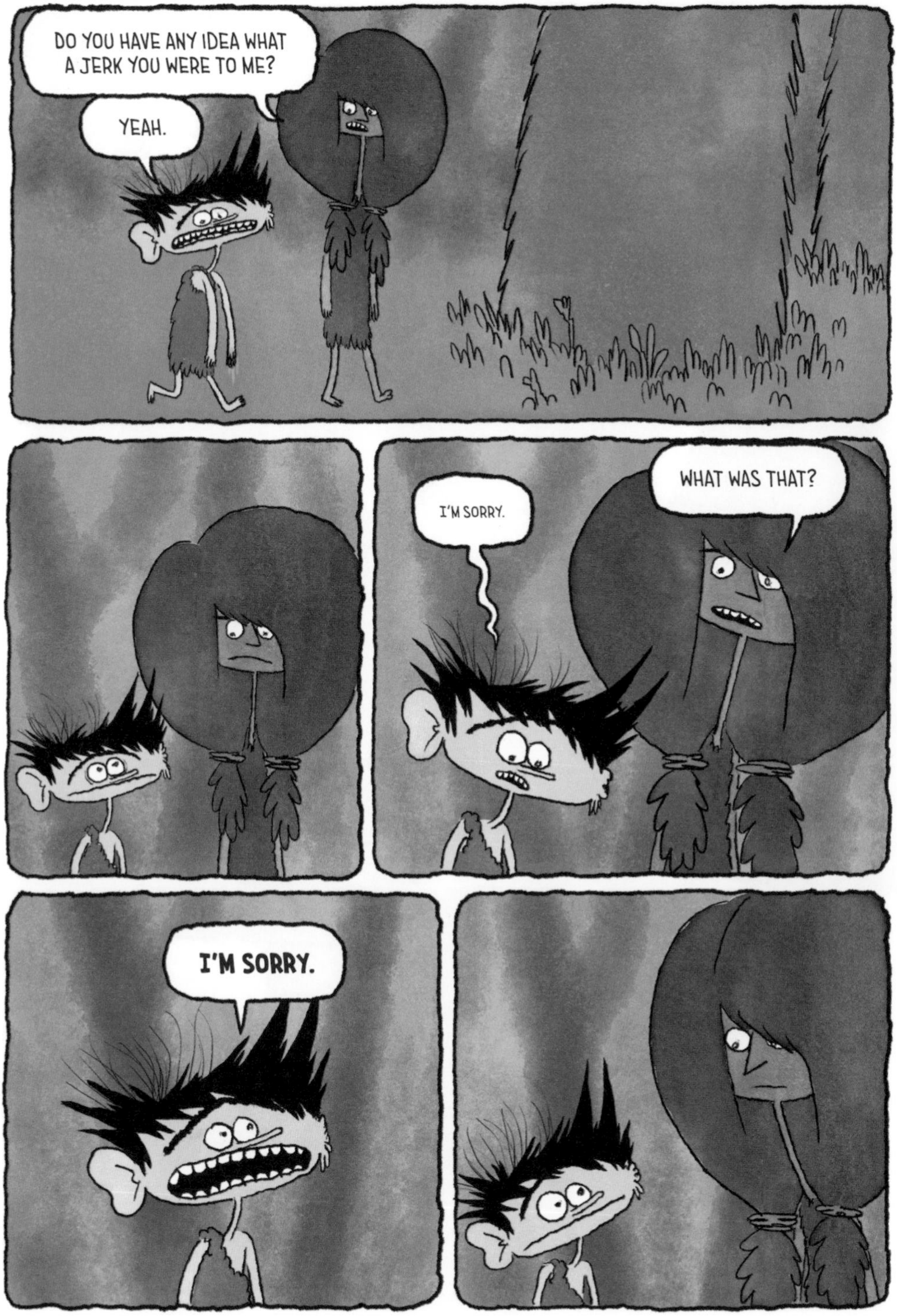
DO YOU HAVE ANY IDEA WHAT A JERK YOU WERE TO ME?
YEAH.
I'M SORRY.
WHAT WAS THAT?
I'M SORRY.

240

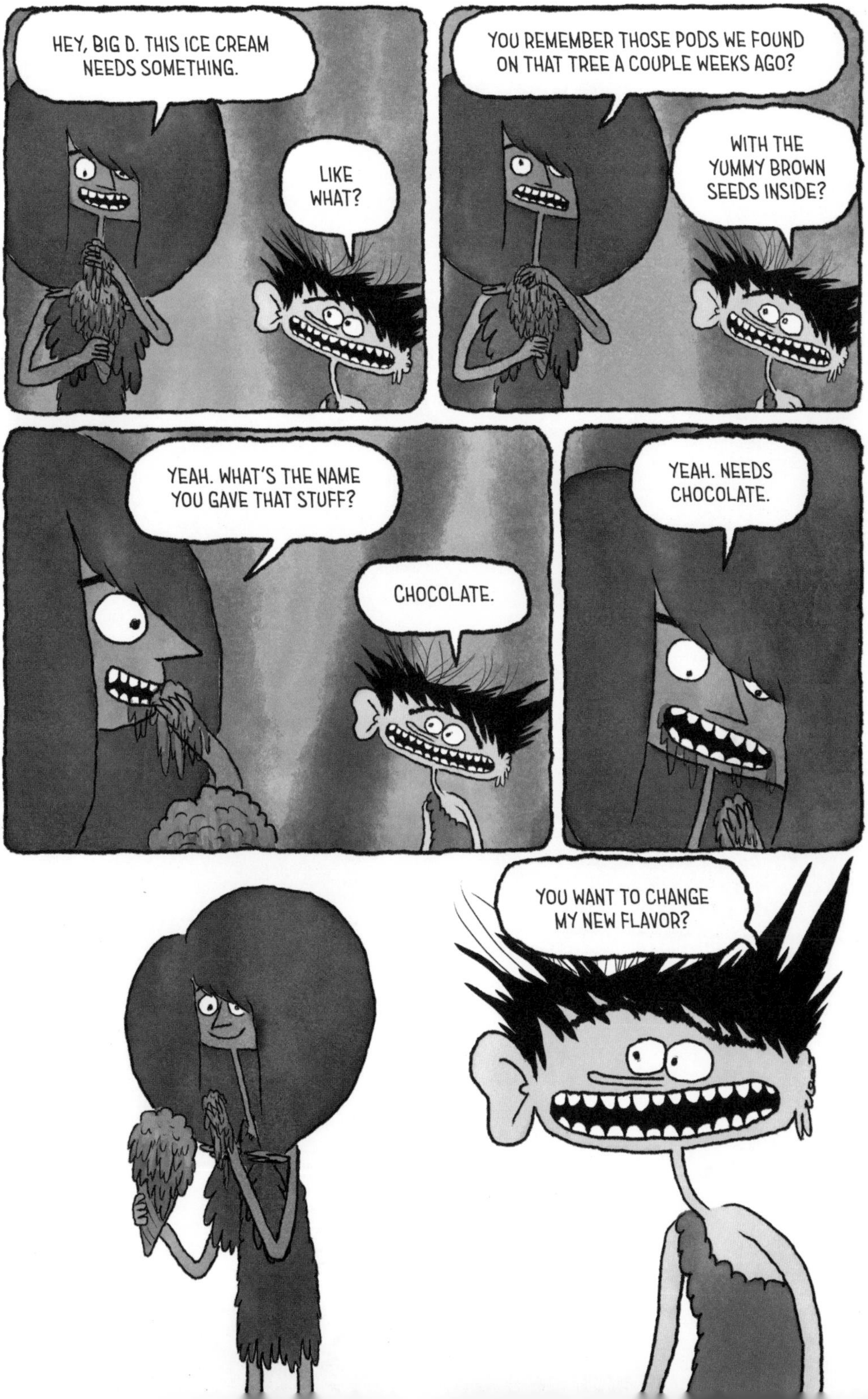
HEY, BIG D. THIS ICE CREAM NEEDS SOMETHING.
LIKE WHAT?
YOU REMEMBER THOSE PODS WE FOUND ON THAT TREE A COUPLE WEEKS AGO?
WITH THE YUMMY BROWN SEEDS INSIDE?
YEAH. WHAT'S THE NAME YOU GAVE THAT STUFF?
CHOCOLATE.
YEAH. NEEDS CHOCOLATE.
YOU WANT TO CHANGE MY NEW FLAVOR?

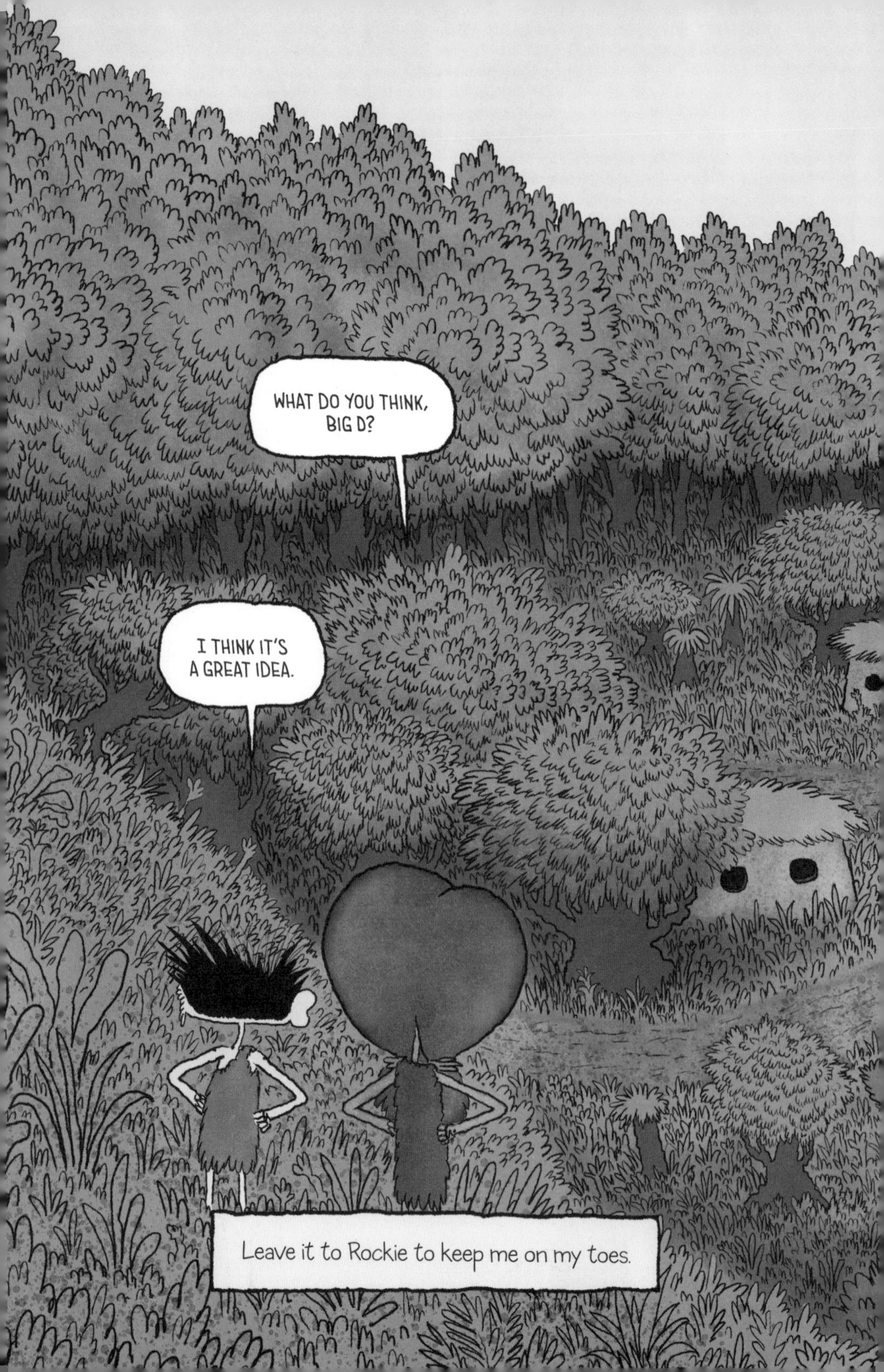
WHAT DO YOU THINK, BIG D?
I THINK IT'S A GREAT IDEA.
Leave it to Rockie to keep me on my toes.

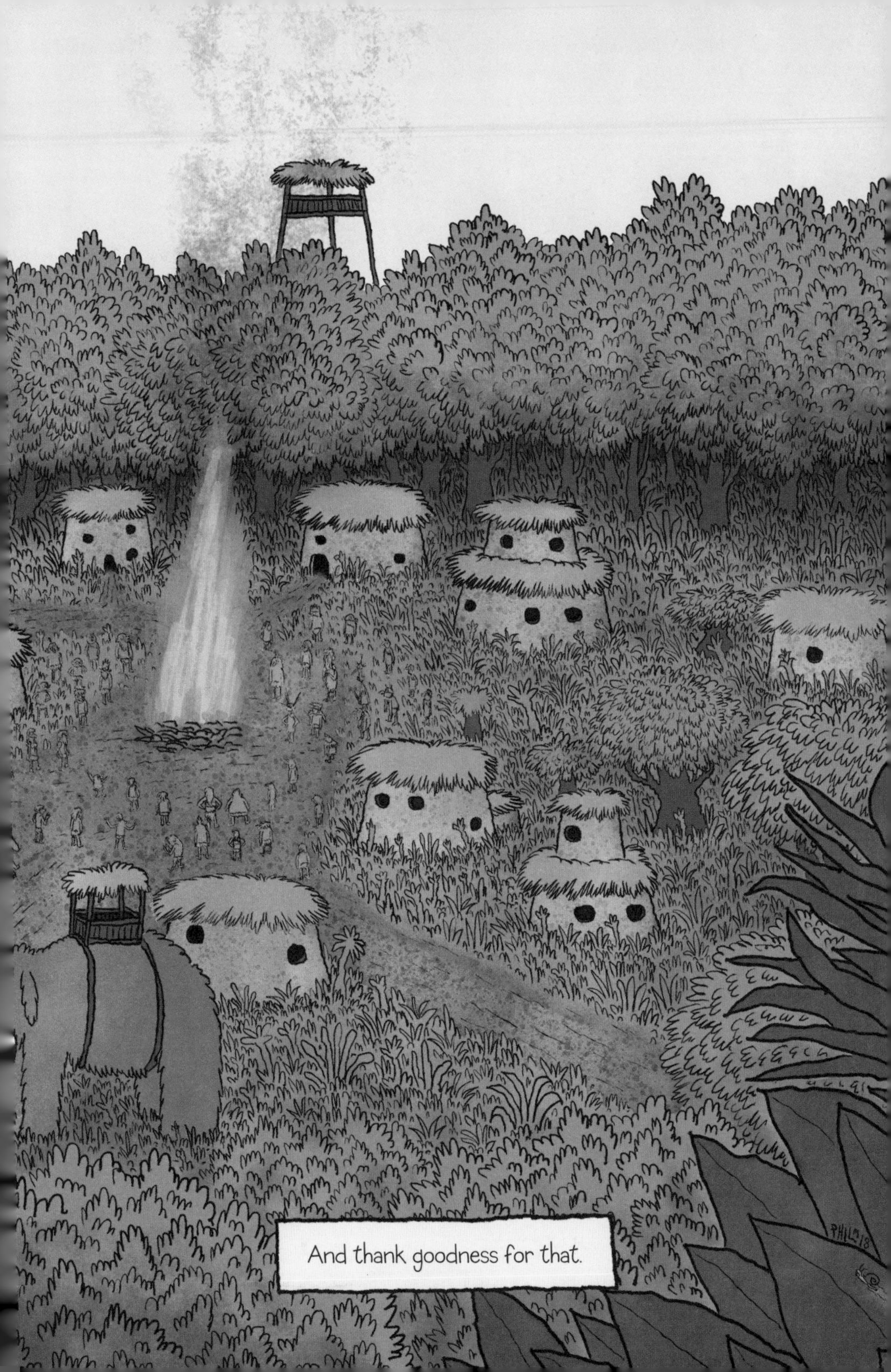
And thank goodness for that.

STARRING...

DAVE UNGA-BUNGA (Me!)

MR. UNGA-BUNGA
(My dad.)

BLA UNGA-BUNGA
(My sister.)

ROCKIE FIREGOOD
(She keeps me on my toes.)

UG SMITH
(He's 100% Ug....)